At Variance
Volume 2

7 novellas
adapted from screenplays

David R. Beshears

Greybeard Publishing
Washington State

Greybeard Publishing
P.O. Box 480
McCleary, WA 98557-0480

ISBN 978-1-947231-07-8

At Variance

Volume 2

Introduction

Movie Novella Series – Volume 2
Seven novellas adapted directly from screenplays.

The seven novellas included in At Variance Volume 2 are based on screenplays written over several years. Each has previously been published as an individual novella.

The narratives follow as closely as possible the original screenplays. The result of this very painstaking balancing act are seven films flickering before the eyes of the reader.

As with the first volume, these stories couldn't be more different from one another: science fiction, fantasy, ethereal, young adult scifi.

Welcome to the multiplex...

Choose your screen and enjoy the movie...

Table of Contents

The Britton Journals

Twenty years after the Second Truce between Shylmahn and humans, some fifty years after the great transport ships first reached Earth, a young Shylmahn historian visits one of the last surviving leaders of the human resistance, seeking the story of the migration as seen through the eyes of the aging Joseph Britton...

Shipwreck on ShadowWorld

Thirteen year old Jim survives a fiery crash landing in the desolate landscape of ShadowWorld, only to come face to face with bizarre aliens, mystifying cultures, and an unforgiving planet as he searches for rescue.

Planet of Stones

Chapter One

The gently sloping mountains were covered in a forest of tall trees, mostly fir and the occasional alder. The forest floor was a thick mulch of fir needles and twigs and a scattered sparse undergrowth of fern, was shadowed by the high canopy above.

A lone man followed a well-traveled trail, moving in and out of the shadows as he walked a casual, easy pace. He held a tall, wooden hiking staff in hand, wore a light backpack on his back. The figure was little more than a silhouette set against the shadows, with occasional rays of sunlight brushing across his frame as he passed through shimmering, mote-filled shafts of light. The world was quiet. Even the man's footfalls were muffled as he walked the mulch-covered path.

He followed the trail into a forest clearing. He walked past a rustic root cellar door that was set into the ground and continued on toward the outpost; a wall set into the side of a brush-covered mound.

Lieutenant Connelly was in his mid-thirties. He had a medium build, was clean shaven, and dressed in rugged, well-made clothes and boots. The brown hair pushing out from under his cap had grown longer than was standard for a military officer.

He leaned his staff against the wall beside the door, pressed the palm of one hand against the ident panel set next to the door. There was a hollow click sound. He lifted the latch and slid it aside, opened the door.

The station's main cabin was twelve feet wide by sixteen feet deep. The two long walls were lined with shelves, workbenches and cabinets. There was a narrow cot at the far end, a small table in the middle of the room.

Connelly slipped out of his gear, stowed the pack and his utility belt under a counter. He took A-I Box out of his pocket and set it on the workbench. The high-tech artificial intelligence device was a thin, palm-sized box of molded plastic.

He continued then across the room and stepped through a narrow door threshold.

The back room was small, with one counter and one chair. Connelly sat down and scooted forward. He picked up the headset mic and put it on, reached out to an equipment panel that was against the wall, pushed one of a row of buttons, tapped at the headset and began recording.

"Outpost Six, Connelly, log entry 433," he started. "I followed Alpha Tribe Three into the West Gorge for six days. Somewhat surprising, really. Of all the tribes, this group has been the least nomadic to now, the least likely to drift so far from home. From what I could tell, they weren't hunting, weren't foraging. They seemed to be... exploring." Connelly shook his head. "I don't know... they could have been hunting I suppose, but if they were, it wasn't for food. They were... searching."

Connelly thought on his next words for a few moments.

"Reaching the head of the gorge, they clambered up the hillside, over the ridge, and started back the other way. No reason that I could see. Anyway, I lost them for a time. When I found their trail again, followed it back; didn't see them again until I was nearly back to the Valley. At that point, I of course steered clear, many to avoid having the observer observed. ; worked my way back."

He hesitated then, managed a playful smirk.

"I'm afraid I hurt Box. Said it before, say it again. He's not as shockproof as we were led on."

Connelly shifted position, leaned forward and held his hand on the panel. "I'll try and fix him up tomorrow. Hope he isn't too pissed." He hesitated. "Report ends."

He deactivated the recorder, pulled the headset off, tossed it onto the counter.

Connelly was sitting at his small table, absently eating from a bowl. It was late, the room quiet. He stared ahead at nothing in particular as he ate in silence.

When he finished his meal, he slid back from the table, stood and took the several short steps over to the basin. He took his time washing the bowl and spoon. He set them into the tray to dry.

§

One overhead light was turned on, set very low. Connelly was asleep in his cot.

The sound of a soft alert delicately pushed at the quiet. The overhead light blinked half a dozen times, paused, then blinked again.

Connelly rolled sluggishly onto his side and sat up. He stood up and slowly stepped over to the communication station and dropped into the chair. He reached out and flipped a switch.

"Connelly here," he stated.

The sound of the Major's voice came through the small speaker. It was a steady, smooth voice.

"Lieutenant. Apologies for contacting you off schedule."

"Not a problem, Sir." He managed to sound sincere. "Good to hear your voice."

"That's what they all say, Lieutenant."

"Next time, I'll try to come up with something a little more original, Sir."

There was a moment's hesitation, long enough for Connelly to look up at the radio.

"I'm afraid there won't be a next time," said the Major. "We are returning all personnel to Point Zero. All six Monitors are recalled to Central."

"Sir? I have eight months on my—"

"Embarkation in four days, seven hours," Major stated firmly, cutting him off.

Connelly again stared at the radio.

"Yes Sir. May I ask why?"

"No, Lieutenant."

There was a long pause in the exchange, the Major seemingly waiting for Connelly to come to terms with the new orders, Connelly struggling to take it all in.

"Very well, Sir," Connelly stated at last.

"I'll see you in four days."

"Yes Sir. Connelly out." Connelly frowned as he reached out and flipped the switch, turning off the radio. He leaned back in his chair, looked uncertainly at the communication station.

He mumbled then to himself.

"That do be most curious."

§

Connelly sat at his workbench, working on the AI device in front of him. The back was off the case; he inserted a small tool and adjusted one of the connections.

He had been at it for about an hour, since finishing an early breakfast. He hadn't gotten much sleep after the Major's call and had finally risen early.

He took a drink from his coffee, absently set the cup back on the counter and returned to his work. After a few more adjustments, he closed the back panel and turned the device over. He used the tool to activate the device.

"Hey, Box. You in there?"

"Yes I am, Lieutenant Connelly," said Box. The voice was clear, the tone smooth and very human. "It is good to be back."

"Great." Connelly picked up his coffee cup, leaned back in his chair and took another drink.

"We are back at the outpost," stated Box.

"That's right," said Connelly. "Can you run a self-diagnostic?"

"Already done. I am fine."

"Glad to hear it." He took another sip of his coffee, managed a grin. "Sorry about the accident."

"Ah. I was wondering what happened." There was a moment's hesitation. "Nothing permanent, it would seem."

"Good." Connelly pushed back from the workbench, stood up and began putting away the tools. "It looks like we're taking another trip, Box. We're leaving for Central this morning."

"Lieutenant. We are not scheduled to return to Central for two hundred forty seven days."

"Yeah, well, change happens. Something's come up."

"Of course. I understand," said Box. "What might that something be?"

"We are returning to Point Zero. So I have been informed."

"Returning to Point Zero..."

"That's right." Connelly put the tool kit into the drawer. "And no... I haven't a clue."

Connelly climbed out of the root cellar, a canvas bag in hand. He closed the door and walked back to the outpost door. Streaks of sunlight speared through the forest of tree trunks and reached across the clearing. The world was eerily quiet, with only the faint sound of dewdrops falling from the vegetation.

Back inside, Connelly set the bag on the workbench beside the backpack and began transferring items from the bag to backpack, mostly bags of berries and assorted roots that he collected in his wanderings.

Box was on the workbench beside Connelly's gear.

"The journey to Central will need to be taken with caution," he said.

"I'll do what I can, Box. Can't do anymore than that."

"You will have only your walking staff for defense," said Box.

"As always, Box. Rules be rules." He continued packing. "What's the problem?"

"I am uncomfortable with this unexpected change in your calendar, and the unplanned, unscheduled journey to Central."

"Yeah, well, such is life." Connelly looked about the room, looking for something, for anything.

There was nothing else. He didn't have much.

"I guess that's it, then." He looked from his surroundings to the backpack. "Not much for two years of your life.

Box knew what was important...

"Have communications been secured?"

"Yes, Box."

Box hesitated, as if the A-I was lost in thought, spoke up then, almost warily.

"As I was offline when we returned to the outpost, and as you may not survive the next four days, I am obligated to ask... have your most recent observations been entered into the data crystal?"

"Have I ever not?"

"And yet I must ask."

"Yes, Box. Observations of our most recent outing have been entered. The time capsule is current."

There was yet another hesitation from Box.

"Thank you, Lieutenant Connelly."

"You're welcome, Box." Connelly closed his backpack and fastened the straps. He took a final look around the room. It had been his home for almost two years. He wondered if he would ever see it again.

Chapter Two

Connelly stepped out of the outpost. He wore his standard hiking gear of heavy shirt and pants, cap, hiking boots, utility belt and backpack. He latched the door, took his staff in hand and walked away from the station.

It was midmorning. The forest was still. Connelly worked his way up over the nearby ridge and followed the winding trail downslope on the other side. As he continued working his way down the mountain, the surrounding forest floor grew sparser. The day grew brighter as the sun rose higher and the canopy overhead thinned.

He came onto a wide path that followed the base of the next hill, this one lower and broader than the mountainside he had just descended. He followed the trail for another half hour before turning upslope and taking the hill. There were few trees now, much more brush and bramble.

Beyond this hill was another, and beyond that a third. Connelly moved out onto a rocky outcropping that looked out onto a flat plain beyond. He took it in for a few moments before stepping over to a rock that formed a natural bench. He leaned his staff against the bench and slid the backpack off his shoulder and set it on the bench. He brought out a pair of binoculars and walked again to the edge of the vista point.

He brought the binoculars up to his eyes.

The plain stretched away to the horizon. There were clusters of deciduous trees, shrubs, and spans of meadow. A river ran down the center of the plain. Green, tree-covered hills rose on either side.

Connelly lowered the binoculars, but continued to study the view with the naked eye for a long time.

Starting out again, it took him most of the afternoon to reach the plain below. He then continued north until evening, stopping for the night in a small clearing surrounded by thick brush. Far to the south, a low mountain range shadowed the horizon; his mountains.

He built a campfire in the center of the clearing, and when it was ready placed a small cooking pot above the forming coals. While his evening meal heated, he set about placing a series of small monitoring devices around the perimeter of the clearing. Kneeling then beside the last device, he pressed a small panel on side of the sensor box.

"That's it, Box," he said.

The Box device was resting atop the backpack near the center of the clearing.

"I'm reading all four sensors, Lieutenant," he said.

Connelly stood. He looked outward, over the low brush, out across the open plain to the distant mountain range.

"Two years in the mountains," he said. "Gotta tell ya' Box, I've never much liked it out here in the open."

"We have been here on a number of previous occasions, Lieutenant." Box's words were pointed then. "All were *scheduled* excursions."

"Yeah, I get that," Connelly said, a thin smile. The smile faded and he looked up at the sky. "I need trees."

Box said nothing to that. He had heard it before.

Connelly turned back to the campfire. Dinner was just about ready.

The night sky was black. Thick, dark clouds hid the stars. Connelly lay asleep beside the campfire, which was now only dully shimmering coals, the faint light pushing a bluish glow over Connelly's face.

A soft sequence of beeping sounds, barely audible, just enough to reach the outer edges of the clearing and no further.

Connelly's eyes opened. He spoke quietly, not yet moving.

"What do we have, Box?"

"There is movement several hundred yards to the north."

"Wildlife?"

"Likely not. Six life forms."

Connelly sat up slowly, then just as slowly got to his feet. He worked his way into the brush, a dozen paces from clearing. He knelt behind a bramble of branches and vines, reached forward and pushed aside the vegetation.

A hundred yards further beyond, there were six figures in silhouette. They were traveling in a line moving from his left to right, barely distinguishable in the night, little more than shadows. But he could see they were humanoid; the tallest stood about five foot tall, the others a bit shorter.

They move quietly, walking smoothly, steadily.

Connelly watches the tribe of Alphas until they are out of sight. He slid back then, stood and backed away, turned and started back.

Returning to the campsite, Connelly settled back into his bedding. He got comfortable and eventually closed his eyes.

"Alphas," he said matter-of-factly.

"You are certain..."

"Pretty much."

"That would place them well outside their traditional habitat," said Box. "And they are traveling at night."

"Mmm hmm."

The world returned to its late-night peace and quiet.

Connelly's eyes slowly opened. He listened to the night.

All was still.

Connelly squatted atop a grassy hilltop, binoculars in hand, looked down into the narrow valley below. A thread of a river ran the floor, deciduous trees growing along the banks. The valley walls on either side were blanketed in evergreen.

A tribe of several dozen Alphas was working its way along the river.

Humanoid, four to five feet tall, husky, with thick arms and legs; medium complexion, skin bare with mottles of dark hair. They walked fully upright, dressed in primitive clothing with no care as to aesthetics. Their feet were well protected in simple leather covering.

Connelly slid back and slipped below the ridge on the back side of the hilltop. He sat beside his backpack and his staff.

He pulled Box from his pocket and set it on his backpack. He spoke without looking at the device.

"Alpha Valley is no longer an option," he said.

"Alpha Valley is the route to Central," said Box.

"Yeah, well, it's full of Alphas."

"They most certainly should be avoided. We must not interfere with their natural course."

"I understand that," said Connelly. There was a hint of agitation. "That and the fact that the can tear my arm off and beat me with it."

"They have shown no such inclination, Lieutenant. They are in fact for the most part non-violent."

Connelly eyed Box, growing increasingly annoyed.

"Yeah, well, when they get annoyed, ya' never know. All right?"

Box decided it best to let that go.

"As Alpha Valley is home to all of the Alpha tribes, their presence was to be expected. You will proceed with caution, Mr. Connelly."

"I shall not, Box."

"Alpha Valley is the route to Central."

"Not the only route," said Connelly. He rested his elbows on his knees. "I can go through the Black Forest."

"No you cannot," said Box. "Black Forest is not an option."

"The Alphas don't look like they're going far, and I'm on a tight schedule here. So you give me another option."

Box was silent, the device sitting on the backpack.

"Right," said Connelly. He shifted about and readied to stand up. "Black Forest it is, then."

Chapter Three

Connelly started across a large, wide field of tall grass and wildflowers. The sun was warm. A slight breeze wafted pungent aromas as his feet and legs pushed through the meadow.

Ahead was a great wall of trees that stood two hundred feet high and loomed over the terrain. Connelly continued across the meadow and approached the wall. He entered the trees.

The Black Forest was a world of shadowy dark gray, with occasional streaks of fuzzy light. Massive trees were spaced widely apart; giant ferns; an open, mulchy floor. Connelly was dwarfed by his surroundings. The narrow beam of his flashlight pierced the permanent twilight.

An hour into the world of deep, heavy, ominous silence, Connelly came upon a small brook. He slipped out of his backpack, removed a water bottle from a side pocket. He knelt and filled the bottle from the brook. He dropped purification tablets into the bottle, swirled the bottle, and took a swig.

He returned the bottle to the side pocket, looked up and away from the brook. A growling animal sound reached Connelly from shadows.

Connelly stood still, only his eyes moving, scanning the dark beyond the nearest trees.

Only silence now...

Connelly slipped back into his gear. One more look at the shadows and then he stepped across the brook and continued on. He kept a casual steady pace. Following him... movement in the shadows behind the trees and brush. Glimpses of silhouettes moving parallel to Connelly. One at first, then three, then half a dozen, then more.

Barely three feet tall, they were nothing more than shadows within the shadows. They drew no nearer, seemed to be content to follow and observe.

Half an hour after leaving the brook, Connelly noticed a dozen or more faint lights ahead in the distance, some near ground level, some hanging high above the forest floor. As he approached, it was clear that they were artificial. Another minute then and he came into a large forest clearing. Lantern-like globes were hung in the surrounding treetops, giving the clearing a fuzzy glow.

There were a dozen wooden platforms scattered about the open space, each two to three feet high, surrounding a larger altar-like structure in the very center. The altar appeared to be a collection of several platforms that had been stacked precariously together. Each individual section was decorated with assorted living plants.

Eight small creatures moved from the perimeter shadows into the clearing. And then another four. And then another...

"Great," Connelly mumbled to himself. "Littles."

The Littles were three feet tall, fine featured. They had large dark eyes, clear and shining with intelligence, small nose and full mouth. Wispy hair fell past their shoulders and drifted as they moved.

Their garments were simple, well-crafted wraps that were tied at the waist, decorated with unique geometric patterns. They all wore soft foot coverings that reached above the ankles and were tied with leather straps.

Connelly stepped cautiously into the heart of the clearing. He stopped near the altar, turned slowly about as he warily watched the Little creatures close in, forming a circle that tightened about him.

He calmly shifted his staff into attack position, a warning more than a threat.

The circle of Littles stopped ten feet from Connelly. One tilted its head slightly as it studied the staff. He spoke side-glance to the others in the language of the Littles, his tone smooth and soft.

"Pen-tah, toh theh la mah the," it said.

One of the others tilted its head then, looked at Connelly as it responded to the first creature.

"Theh la mohn deh noh," it said.

The first speaker thought on that for a moment, turned its attention again to Connelly. It stared pointedly, mouth pursed. With that, several of the Little creatures started forward again, slowly closing in.

Connelly smoothly swung his staff in a level arc, which created a soft whoosh sound. The end of the staff brushed at several of the Littles and they all stopped, took a single step back. None looked to be particularly frightened; rather they appeared to be uncertain, maybe even a bit perplexed.

"Come on, fellas," said Connelly. "No reason for it to go this way. Just what seems to be the issue?"

One of the Littles calmly chattered a handful of unintelligible words and then fell silent.

"Really?" asked Connelly, albeit rather sarcastically. "Is that all?"

Two of the Littles moved incautiously. Connelly brought the staff about and jabbed it forward end first, popped one of the Littles in the chest. It stumbled back as Connelly attempted the same with the second Little. This one, however, was already stepping back and easily avoided Connelly's attack.

A moment later eight of the creatures rushed in together.

Connelly swung the staff about and jabbed it at the Littles again and again, knocking back several, forcing others to adjust tactics.

"Come on, guys."

Connelly was overwhelmed within moments, and was quickly brought to the ground. He struggled to push them off, managed to roll over onto his knees. The creatures grabbed at his arms, at his backpack, his shirt, his hair. He scrambled forward, struggled from his knees up to his feet, one of the Littles continuing to cling to Connelly's backpack. Connelly freed himself of the creature and stumbled out of the clearing at a run, somehow still hanging onto his staff.

Again in the permanent twilight of the forest floor, he moved at a quick, easy jog through the shadows. Glancing back over his shoulder, he could see the shadows within shadows... the small creatures pacing him.

Connelly sat on the trunk of a fallen tree, his open backpack beside him, along with his water bottle and a first aid kit. His shirt was open, bruises were visible, already forming on his torso amidst a number of cuts and scratches.

He spoke as he applied first aid to his wounds.

"I don't get it, Box. I've never gotten it. What do they want?"

"You, Lieutenant Connelly."

"Yeah, that's not telling me anything."

"The Littles have wanted to capture a Monitor. You have been a target since the day your presence was made known to them."

Connelly grimaced as he continued to treat the cuts and scratches.

"That doesn't give me the why."

"They clearly want you alive," Box stated. "Perhaps they seek information."

"All they gotta do is ask, my friend." Connelly picked up his water bottle and took a long drink. He lowered the bottle slowly then, stopped movement, looked coolly ahead of him.

There was a single Little standing just inside the clearing, directly ahead of Connelly.

They stared at one another, both silent for several seconds until Connelly finally spoke calmly to Box.

"Company," he said.

Box did not respond.

The Little continued to study Connelly from a distance.

Connelly slowly stood and began putting his gear together, glancing from the creature to his backpack, again to the creature. Closing his backpack, he looked across the clearing a final time.

The Little was gone. Connelly was alone.

"Okay," he said. "I wonder what that was about."

"Yes?" asked Box.

"One Little. Gone now."

"Perhaps it is time to move on, Lieutenant Connelly."

"A keen observation, Box." Connelly lifted his backpack. "We're done here."

Chapter Four

He was an insignificant figure crossing the forest floor, a drifting shadow amongst great trees and giant ferns, the beam of his flashlight stabbing at the dark out ahead of him. In the distance then, bits of gray and silver were sprinkled against the backdrop of many shades of black.

Connelly approached the edge of the forest, stepped out finally from the dark wall of trees and into a meadow of grass and wildflowers. Moving into the field, he had to shield his eyes against the bright sky, a startling contrast to the time spent in the permanent night of the Black Forest.

Reaching the far side of the meadow, he worked his way into and through high, thick brush and eventually found a wide, distinct trail leading up the valley.

"Here we go," he said, stumbling out onto the path. "Easy, here on out."

"I did advise against going into the Black Forest, Lieutenant," said Box. Connelly had buttoned the A-I device securely in his breast pocket.

"Yes you did. How very wise you are."

"And we are once again in Alpha Valley."

"Yes we are." Connelly was walking briskly up the trail. "But that was a given. I always intended to return to the valley. We have to. But now we are on the other side of the Alphas."

"We are past but the one tribe, Lieutenant."

"We came out of the forest well up the valley," Connelly said defensively. "We may be past five tribes; six tribes."

"There are only four Alpha tribes." A calm, matter-of-fact statement.

"I know that." Connelly continued up the well-traveled trail, glancing warily from side to side and into the brush. "Four tribes. So we're good."

He worked his way up the valley until evening, when he set up camp in a small open area. He decided against a campfire, even a small one, and ate cold rations. The proximity sensors were silent throughout the night, but he slept restlessly and started out again well before dawn the next morning.

He walked without a break for several hours, when he stopped briefly where the trail crossed a small brook. He refilled his water bottle and dropped in the purification tablet. He took a swig, refilled the bottle and slipped it back into the side pocket.

He had only just started out again, stepping across the brook and traveling a dozen yards, when he slowed his pace, hesitating, then stopping.

The brush on either side of the trail was thick with branches, leaves and vines, the vegetation towering three feet above him. The trail itself was six feet wide and looked to be well-traveled.

Connelly whispered to Box. "I don't think we're alone."

Looking about, he didn't see anything. But he was positive. He had heard something. Something or someone was near.

There...

He heard it again.

He pushed his way into the brush beside the trail, squatted down, pulled the brush back into place and hid from view. Moments later, the sound of movement up the trail was unmistakable.

An Alpha approached. It was following the trail and coming toward Connelly's position. Another was walking behind him, and another; a line of them.

The first passed Connelly's hiding place, followed by the second.

The third Alpha slowed, stopped near Connelly's position. It lifted his head and sniffed at the air.

The next Alpha in line shoved it from behind, grunting in irritation, urging it to continue forward.

The sniffing Alpha grunted angrily over its shoulder. It sniffed again, gave another low grunt. Its companion groused impatiently until the sniffing Alpha started forward again, the rest of the line following after.

The last of the Alphas passed Connelly and disappeared around the bend. The trail grew silent; empty and still. Another twenty seconds passed before Connelly came out of hiding, the vines and branches clinging to him. He worked his way free, looked back on the trail behind him, the way he had come, the way the Alphas had gone.

"And that do be one of those four tribes you mentioned."

"So it would seem," said Box.

"On our way then," said Connelly, turning ahead and starting forward again. "Not much further."

§

It was actually another four hours, not counting a brief break for lunch, before Connelly stepped from the trail and onto an open expanse several hundred yards in diameter. At the heart of the clearing stood a gray, four-sided concrete obelisk; ten feet high, eight feet wide on a side. A dozen paces to the left of the obelisk was a smooth, bench-like rock.

Connelly approached the obelisk. A steel door was set into the face. Beside the door was a small metal panel, eight inches square. Holding his staff in one hand, Connelly placed his free hand flat on the panel. The panel glowed for a moment, then faded again to gray.

A computer voice emanated from a tiny speaker set above the panel.

"Recognize Monitor Six. Connelly, Lieutenant." A moment's pause and then, "Access granted."

The door slid aside. Within the access shaft was a metal ladder leading down.

Connelly left his staff leaning on the wall beside the opening and stepped inside, onto the rungs of the ladder.

The door closed as he started down.

Chapter Five

The Central Control Room was dark. The only sound was a faint background hum.

Several ceiling light panels flickered to life.

The open room was twenty feet on a side, with an island counter in the center. The smooth, glossy floor shimmered with the reflection of the overhead lighting. One wall was lined with glass cabinets, two other walls had openings leading to wide hallways.

A door panel in the fourth wall slid open.

Connelly stepped through the opening and into the room. He looked about as he shifted out of his backpack and let it slide down his arm. He set it on the floor, absently leaning it against the wall beside the slowly closing access shaft door.

He called softly into the room. "Hello hello..."

There was no response. Apparently he was alone.

He moved to the counter island. He looked along the counter surface, took two steps to his left. He tapped at the surface, waited while a section of the glass surface came to life, the light reflecting up onto his face.

He brushed his fingertips across the surface, read what displayed on the screen, tapped again.

He frowned as he read.

"Hey, Box?"

"Yes, Lieutenant?"

"Are you getting anything from Central?"

"I am not."

Connelly mumbled *hmmm* under his breath and continued working the console.

"I can't access the logs," he stated. "And there's nothing from communications." He sighed loudly and deactivated the workstation. "It looks like nobody's home."

The Major's voice then came from a hidden speaker set in the ceiling. "Lieutenant Connelly. Welcome to Central."

Connelly glanced uncertainly up and to one side.

"Major? So, there you are." He looked to the other side. "Where is that, exactly?"

"I trust your journey from Outpost Six was uneventful."

"Not really, no." Connelly continued to speak into the air, one direction and then another. "But all's well that ends well, so I understand. I'm here."

"Very good," said the Major. "I am so glad."

Connelly took a step away from the counter, looked again about the room, then questioning toward the ceiling.

Something isn't right...

"And where might you be, Sir?" he asked warily.

"I am here, Lieutenant Connelly. In Central. With you."

"Is that so?" he asked. "And the other Monitors?"

"Not to worry, Lieutenant. All will be well."

"Right," hesitantly. "Next stop, Point Zero?"

"Soon enough, Lieutenant. A minor delay, at most."

"Right." Connelly took another hesitant step from the counter island. "Hey, Box?"

"Yes, Lieutenant?"

"Did you know about this?"

"Lieutenant?"

"The Major, Box. What happened to the Major?"

"I don't understand."

Major interrupted, speaking up again.

"Lieutenant Connelly. I can assure you. I am Major Broderick."

"Eh, I'm thinking not," said Connelly matter-of-factly. "You have the Major's voice. You may well have his knowledge. But I know the Major. He has two arms, two legs and an overly large nose."

"Lieutenant?" questioned Box.

"Box, you and I have spent the last twenty eight months together in rather close quarters. I know an A-I when I'm talking to one."

"I see," said Box after a long pause.

Connelly had the odd feeling that Box was taking the time to think what this might mean.

"Did you know about this?" he asked.

"I have had no interaction with Central," stated Box. "I have been with you."

Connelly gave a slight smirk as he moved over to his backpack. He picked it up, started casually toward one of the hallways.

"Right," he said as he crossed the room. "A definite non-answer if I've ever heard one. You my friend are more human every day."

"I can assure you—"

"Uh, huh. You too, eh?" Connelly walked unhurriedly down the wide hallway, bright with white walls and a glossy floor. Light panels were set into the ceiling. He peeked curiously into one room after another as he walked, never stopping for more than a few moments. He spoke in a calm, conversational tone. "So, Major... what happened to the Major?"

"I am the—"

"Yeah, yeah..." Connelly cut him off. "What happened to the Major I stood face-to-face with two years ago? The one I shook hands with the last time I was here?"

He stepped through a doorway and into a small sleep quarters. There was a bunk, small desk and chair, with a dresser set into one wall. He tossed his backpack onto the bunk. Taking hold of the back of the chair and casually turning it around, he straddled the seat and rested his arms on the chair back.

"All right, Major," he said. "Talk to me."

"Of course, Lieutenant." The voice of the Major came through a speaker set high in the wall beside the doorway. "What would you like to talk about?"

"To start... where are the other Monitors? When are we returning to Point Zero?"

There was a long moment of silence.

"Major?" Connelly prompted.

"Yes," said Major. "Those are questions that are difficult to answer with any precision, Lieutenant."

"Try."

When Major again delayed answering, Connelly took the conversation into a slightly different direction.

"Major? Major, why did you call me back?"

There were several more moments of silence. This time Connell waited patiently for Major to respond."

"Lieutenant Connelly," Major said at last. "I would ask that you do something for me."

"So? Ask."

"I... I need you to find me. I need you to find the Major."

"Excuse me?"

"I need you to find the Major with whom you... *shook hands.*"

Connelly frowned thoughtfully, hesitated. He stood slowly then, turned the chair about and straightened it, all while he continued to wear the studied expression on his face.

"Box?" he prompted.

"I knew nothing of this, Lieutenant."

"Sure," sighed Connelly. He spoke then again to Major. "And where might I find you? Him? Whatever?"

"I believe you should first seek out the circle of stones."

Connelly stood at the island counter in Central Control, worked quietly at one of the computer consoles set into the counter surface. He had been at it for ten minutes or more, moving through one file after another.

He stopped briefly then, hesitated. He curled his brow as he studied the latest text splashing across the screen.

"This... this can't be right," he grumbled softly.

"Lieutenant?" asked Box.

"If I'm reading this right..." the words trailed off, then back. "It can't be right."

"Sir?"

"Mission records."

"Yes?"

"The Monitors. The six Monitors." The words on the screen could mean only one thing. "I am alone."

"I don't understand," said Box. "Sir, there are six of you. As you have just noted."

"Six of us, yes."

The room went quiet. There was only the now familiar background white noise of Central's environmental systems.

"Lieutenant?" urged Box.

"Six of us," Connelly sighed. "But... we're in six different times. 1,000 years apart. We have all been observing this world, this same landscape, but in different eras." He put on a dark, thoughtful frown. He looked side-glance up at the ceiling.

"Major? Major, is this true?"

There is only silence from the A-I Major.

"Talk to me," ordered Connelly. "Is this true? Am I alone?"

A few more moments of silence, and then...

"You are the most contemporary of the Monitors, Lieutenant Connelly. You are stationed 95,000 years from Point Zero, with the other Monitors stationed 1,000 years apart going back to approximately 100,000 years from Point Zero."

"No. That's not right. We were all set down 100,000 years from Point Zero." Connelly looked back to the screen inset into the counter, shaking his head uncertainly. "Together. Together."

"You left Point Zero together, Lieutenant."

"But..." Realization slowed dawned. He placed his hands palm down on the counter.

Box spoke up again. "That wasn't the mission."

"The mission changed," said Connelly. He looked up from the counter. "The mission changed?"

"The mission changed," stated Major.

"Right. How could it have changed between the time we left Point Zero and Arrival?"

"I do not know, Lieutenant Connelly. I am sorry."

"How can you not—" Connelly was growing increasingly frustrated. None of this was making any sense. "And you? Where did you come from?"

"I am the Major."

"Yeah, yeah, I get that. How did you come to be?"

"I do not know."

Connelly leaned heavily on the counter, mumbled the Major's words back at him. "I do not know, I do not know." He began absently tapping his fingertips on the glass surface. "I am really, really not smiling here."

"I understand," said the Major.

"That's great," grumbled Connelly. "You understand. That's just, you know, great."

"Lieutenant," Box interrupted. "We have the location of the circle of stones. Perhaps we can—"

"Uh, huh," groused Connelly. "Not smiling here."

Central's small mess had three round tables evenly spaced in the middle of the room. There was a counter set along one wall with a food warmer and water dispenser. Several cabinets and another counter were set against another wall.

It was late. Connelly was sitting at one of the tables. There was a water glass and a bowl on the table in front of him. He ate his meal absently as he gazed outward, lost in thought. The world was still and quiet but for the faint background noise of running environmental systems and the humming of the lighting.

Connelly sat on the edge of the bed in his sleeping quarters. The lights were off, the only light coming from the hallway through the slightly open doorway. He was dressed for a hike. He rubbed his face with both hands.

He stood then, reached down and picked up his backpack.

He worked his way through the halls and then across the control room to the panel to the access shaft. He pressed his palm on the ident panel and the door slid aside with a soft whoosh.

The day was just dawning, the sunrise spreading light and color across the landscape and the clearing. Connelly took hold of his hiking staff and moved away from the access obelisk as the door closed behind him. He stepped over to the bench, set the backpack down and rested the staff against the bench.

He sat, watched the sunrise.

"Box... so what did you find out?" He closed his eyes to the warmth of the sun. "What the hell's going on?"

"I am afraid the information is rather unsettling," said Box. The device was tucked into Connelly's shirt pocket.

"You not telling me what's happening is what's unsettling."

"Of course. However, I do not believe this is going to clear things up for you."

"Box..."

"Yes, Sir," said Box. A moment's hesitation, and then, "Point Zero no longer exists."

Connelly opened his eyes, stared ahead at the horizon. "Excuse me, what?"

"Yes. It seems there was an incident. The Major was of the belief that it was something that occurred between 100K and 95K that resulted in the loss of Point Zero."

"What incident? What happened? Something we did? A Monitor?"

"The Major did not know," said Box. "But he believed that it occurred at some point in the timeline between 100K and now."

"What, so we're trapped here?"

"Until whatever was done can be undone."

"Bloody great." Connelly leaned forward, rested his elbows on his knees and clasped his hands. "And just how do we do that?"

"Such was the goal of the new mission as it was defined by the Major. He placed a Monitor every 1,000 years going back to the original 100,000 year mark. With the six of you in position, he was going to place himself into stasis with plans to come out at the time of Point Zero."

Connelly finished thinking through that line of reasoning. "And so then study the data crystals from all the Monitors, determine what happened that changed everything, and set things right again. And all is well."

"In so many words."

"Something went wrong?"

"I do not know," said Box. "I do not know that all the Monitors were successfully placed, I do not know that the Major successfully placed himself in stasis, and if he did, whether he in fact revived at Point Zero. Consider... if Point Zero does not exist, what exactly would he have awakened to?

Connell thought on that comment as he watched the sun complete its rise from the horizon.

"Right," he said. "Okay, so... and this version of the Major? The A-I that he created?"

"I found nothing specifically relating to the A-I. We can assume that it was created to oversee the Monitors while the Major was unavailable."

"And this A-I... he, uh, he hasn't gone like, evil A-I on us, has he? After all these millennia? Out now to destroy humanity as payback for all the bad we've done?"

"No. I don't think so."

"Right." Connelly straightened and looked about them. It was full daylight. He stood up, reached down and picked up his backpack. "We'll see, I suppose."

"Yes Sir," Box stated.

"A lot of questions still need answering. Most of 'em, as a matter of fact."

"Many of them may be answered once we reach the circle of stones."

"Such as what happened to the Major."

"Perhaps," said Box.

Connelly didn't respond to that. He reached down and picked up his hiking staff.

"We're not going directly there, are we?" asked Box. It was more of an observation than a question.

"No. We're not. First, I want to get a look at another of the outposts." He half turned and gave a nod, indicating direction. "The nearest one is that way, no more than half a day."

"What answers do you seek at an outpost abandoned thousands of years ago?"

Connelly started forward. "We shall see what we see, dear Box."

Chapter Six

Connelly turned off the main trail and followed this much narrower, meandering trail for almost an hour, followed it eventually into a side valley offshoot from the main Alpha Valley.

This smaller valley was thick with lush vegetation and crisscrossed with numerous narrow animal trails. Connelly frequently had to push through tall brush, his clothes quickly soaked from the heavy, broad damp leaves. On those occasions when he stepped out into open clearings, he often stopped to wring out his wet shirt and would spend a few minutes in the sun.

Several hours in, he entered another clearing, this one wide and open. He slipped out of his backpack, set his staff down and pulled out his canteen.

"Time, Box?"

"Two hours, twelve minutes since entering this valley."

Connelly took a second swallow, then a third. He closed the canteen.

"Good, good... we must be getting close." He looked up to the sky, spoke as he again started forward. "You know, Box, my life would be a lot easier if you had GPS."

"That would require satellites. What you ask for is—"

"I know that, Box," said Connelly, cutting him off. "You know I know that. I think you just like poking me with a stick; it gives your circuits a rush."

"Lieutenant..."

"I swear, you're more human every day."

Twenty minutes later he stepped out of the trailhead and into a long, narrow clearing. He slowed, looked about as he took a few more steps.

A thick bramble stood against a short, steep hillside. He moved toward it, used his staff to push aside the vines.

He saw only darkness within.

He lifted the staff and struck the end of it against a solid surface within the brush. The sound was dull, hollow.

He pushed his way forward, ignoring the thorny vines. Finding the smooth surface, Connelly reached out and pushed.

There was a moment of resistance and then the door collapsed inward and fell to the ground.

Stepping over the fallen door, Connelly found himself in the ruins of Outpost Four. The ceiling had collapsed, and daylight was coming through and into what remained of the interior. Studying the debris, he saw little that was recognizable. Wood was long gone. Metal and some plastic remained.

"The outpost, all right," he said.

"I doubt there is much remaining," Box stated.

"You're right about that."

The layout of the outpost was the same as Connelly's Outpost Six. He worked his way toward the far corner.

"Lieutenant Connelly, what do you expect to find?" asked Box.

"We shall see what we shall see."

"How could you—"

"It's an expression, Box. How long have we been together?" He reached the far corner. "Don't answer that."

"I had not intended to," Box stated, rather defensively.

Connelly pushed aside thick ivy. He found an opening and stepped through and into a tiny back room.

Here too the ceiling had collapsed. Connelly lifted aside rubble strewn across the floor. He found the remains of a small compartment set in the floor. Within, he found what should have been a sealed container. It appeared to be damaged.

"Yep," he sighed. He didn't sound all that pleased. He sat back on his heels. "There it is."

"Lieutenant?"

"The time capsule."

"And the data crystal?"

"The time capsule was broken into," said Connelly. "The data crystal is destroyed."

"How can that be?"

"Intentional. The question is, who did it?"

"I see."

Connelly stood up and worked his way back to the main room of the outpost.

"Someone didn't want the information reaching Point Zero," he said, picking his way carefully through the debris.

"That supposes the person who destroyed the data crystal understood its purpose," said Box.

"That it does."

"Lieutenant... you were expecting this?"

"I suspected it. It makes sense, considering." Connelly stepped out of the ruin and into the open clearing. "And so... we are alone here. There will be nothing from Point Zero."

"There is no Point Zero."

"Or if there is, either they never heard from us or what they did hear from us was bad."

"But your data crystal. From Outpost Six. It remains intact."

For the moment... thought Connelly.

"To the circle of stones, then," he said.

Chapter Seven

Connelly knelt beside his backpack and brought out a light jacket, slipped into it then as he stepped across the campsite and settled in before the small campfire. He picked up the stick that was on the ground beside him and absently poked at the flames. The open valley was visible beyond the campsite, the whole world graying with the dusk and the coming night.

The night passed quietly, and he managed to get a few hours' sleep. He started out again after a light breakfast just past dawn. He continued to follow the main trail up the center of the valley until he came to a well-defined junction where the main trail continued straight ahead and a slightly narrower path veered left.

He took the left fork, followed the trail as it wound through increasingly thick, tall brush. After an hour's travel he noticed the terrain starting to rise. The path took him into a wide, gently sloping bowl and then gradually upslope.

He rounded a bend in the trail, came face to face with three Alphas. He quickly noted more were half-hidden in the brush.

A very, very quiet bunch...

One of the Alphas stepped forward one step nearer Connelly. It grunted, jerked its head up and forward. It looked into the brush to either side.

A number of faces looked back at him. They grunted out encouragingly to their companion.

It looked back to Connelly. It wore a thin smile.

Well, that's new. And a bit unnerving...

Connelly nonetheless smiled in return. He held the smile as he spoke calmly to Box.

"Well, Box. It appears we are to be the guests of one of the Alpha tribes.

Box said nothing. The A-I knew when to keep silent.

Connelly held his staff out to the Alpha in a surrendering gesture.

The Alpha grinned openly as he reached out and took the staff. It grunted loudly to the others of the tribe, then lifted his free hand up in a half wave, signaling the group to move out.

They formed a line and started ahead, Connelly in the midst of the line.

"At least they're taking us in the right direction," he said.

The Alpha walking behind him gave Connelly a shove and growled crossly at him. Connelly stumbled forward, regained his footing and continued. He looked briefly back at the Alpha, gave a slight smile and quickly focused ahead.

"Quite the touchy bunch."

There was another shove from behind.

Connelly had noted throughout his earlier observations of the Alphas that were generally affable and quite social and seldom in any particular hurry. Such was case over the next several hours. They kept a steady pace, but were in no rush. They were often jovial with one another, joking and chuckling and occasionally rough with one another.

Connelly, however, was to keep his mouth shut and keep moving. The Alpha following directly behind him was quick to give him a shove and disapproving growl whenever Connelly spoke up or turned a glance one way or the other. So he quickly fell in line and fell silent.

After about two hours they arrived at a well-used clearing along the main river in the valley. Connelly was pushed to the ground in front of a thick bush. Several Alphas sat across the clearing from him as the others went to the riverbank.

It was midday, the sun was high overhead and warm.

Two of those at the riverbank rose up and returned to the clearing. They stood in front of Connelly, stared down at him. They each had a curious look, as if they knew something he didn't and...

The one with the staff poked at Connelly.

They both let out primitive guttural laughs.

The other then reached down and poked a finger at Connelly's side, grasped at Connelly's flesh. He straightened then and held onto his own belly as if testing for plumpness.

They both made light, cheerful yum-yum noises, laughed again, shoving playfully at each other before moving away to join the others on the other side of the clearing.

Connelly spoke matter-of-factly to Box.

"I can't say as I'm totally comfortable with that," he said.

"If I am interpreting correctly, then I would agree that should the situation play out unchecked, it would not be good for you."

"Hey... I go down, you're going down with me."

One of the Alphas gave him a threatening eye.

"Apparently food is supposed to be silent," Connelly mumbled, He attempted a pleasant smile in the Alpha's direction. "Hello," he said.

The Alpha let out a long, low rumbling growl.

Connelly tried to speak to Box then without moving his lips.

"Alphas... not quite the conversationalists as the Littles."

One of the other Alphas stood and took a step nearer Connelly, offered a menacing glare. Connelly smiled apologetically, tried to speak to Box without moving his lips.

"Though perhaps equally as short-tempered."

He fell silent, and a few minutes later they were on the move again.

Several hours later, Connelly was led into a well-defined campsite clearing, hard ground with patches of scrubby grass, large stones positioned to use as seats. At the far side stood an eight foot tall stake with rawhide ties hanging from near the top. Beyond the stake was an open field of grassland and low shrubs.

Connelly was led over to the stake. He struggled as he was tied by the wrists overhead. Those doing the securing appeared to be amused by the situation. They were grinning broadly and offering one another primitive chuckles.

Several were dancing lightly about the clearing.

"Okay, fellas, this really isn't funny anymore," he said. "Come on. Cut me loose, or I might just get angry. And I am not the best of party guests when I'm upset."

The members of the Alpha tribe ignored Connelly's jabbering. They finished their work, moved back, stood in a half-circle several yards from their prisoner.

They took a moment to admire their work.

At one word from one of the tribe, they all turned in tandem and quietly left the clearing.

"Was it something I said?" asked Connelly. "I did warn you, you know."

He was alone.

He looked about, sizing up his situation. He struggled at his ties, then relaxed as best he could.

He put on a dark frown.

"Oh, boy."

Connelly was half-asleep, which was the best he could do being tied to the stake, bound at the wrists above his head. His eyes were closed, his chin resting on his chest.

The faint sound of scuffling and rustling came from somewhere outside the clearing.

Connelly lifted his head and opened his eyes.

Eight of the Littles entered the clearing behind Connelly. Two were carrying overstuffed bags, a third carried a tall stool.

The bags were left on the ground in the center of the clearing. The Little creature with the stool positioned it behind the stake that Connelly was tied to.

"Hey, guys," said Connelly. "I wasn't expecting to see you folks again so soon."

The Little creatures said nothing. They freed Connelly from the stake, leaving his hands bound. Connelly spoke quietly to Box as he smiled at first to one Little, then another.

"Box, for now let's keep your presence between you and me," he said. "It would appear the Alphas have sold me to the Littles. I'm downright popular."

He spoke then directly to the Littles.

"I hope you don't take what happened at our previous get-together personally," he said.

The Littles continued to ignore Connelly's rambling. They directed him back the way they had come, leading him from the clearing and across the grassy field.

Chapter Eight

The Littles led Connelly across an open field and toward the two hundred foot tall wall of trees. Entering the Black Forest, he found himself once again travelling across the permanent dark twilight of the forest floor. Without the use of his flashlight, he couldn't really see where he was going, other than between and around the darker shapes that were the great trees and twenty-foot high ferns.

The Littles appeared able to see in the near darkness just fine. At least, they clearly knew where they were going. And other than an occasional hushed comment, they seldom spoke. Connelly was again struck by how quiet the Black Forest was. It was a silent world.

They followed a winding, twisting trail for what must have been two or three hours, then the group entered the village of the Littles. Connelly was led into the center of the small community. Around them were dozens of lightly-framed structures, if not actual buildings. Littles were moving in and out of the smaller surrounding trees, others scrambled up the trunks of the nearer giant trees, all with an eye to the human that was being brought into their midst.

Connelly was taken to a post and bound to a ring attached two feet above the ground. The Littles stepped away.

Standing beside the post, he looked down at the bindings; securely tied. He looked up then, just caught sight of the last of the Littles disappearing into the dark. He glanced casually again around the clearing; the structures, the lamps; another quick glance down at his bindings.

"I think we may have underestimated our friends, Box."

Box said nothing. Connelly again studied their surroundings.

"We appear to be alone, at least for the moment," he stated quietly.

"And your circumstances?" asked Box.

"They may be holding our earlier meeting against me." Another glance around the village. "Littles village. Full-on structures on the ground. Stairs leading into the canopy of trees along the perimeter. All in all, socially, culturally, they are way ahead of the Alphas."

"We suspected as much, Lieutenant."

"They're pretty good at knots, too." Connelly struggled at his bindings. "What is it with the locals and putting humans to the stake?"

Box assumed this was a rhetorical question and did not respond.

Connelly slid to the ground, his back to the post. He got as comfortable as he could, considering his position, and waited.

He didn't have to wait long, what he estimated as only a few minutes. There was movement across the plaza.

Three Littles entered the village. One was a head taller than the other two, walked with strong, sure confidence, as if he was certain of his role.

"Ah," Connelly said quietly to Box. "Their leader doth approacheth."

"Be wary, Lieutenant Connelly."

"Middle name, Box."

The Village Leader stood before Connelly, the assistants stepping up beside him.

Connelly looked up at Leader. "Good evening," he said.

There was no response from Leader, no reaction from any of the Littles.

"So, you be the big Kahuna around here?" asked Connelly, putting on a faux grin.

Village Leader turned his head slightly, studied Connelly as he contemplated the question.

"The leader," Connelly tried again. "Are you the boss?"

Village Leader studied Connelly some more. He lifted a hand then, indicated the surrounding village.

"Leader," he stated precisely. "Village."

Connelly was a little taken aback at hearing Village Leader speaking the two simple English words so clearly. He cleared his throat, shifted position.

"You, uh... you speak English?"

"English?"

"English. Language. The words you speak are in English."

"Yes. English." Village Leader thought on that for a moment. "We... watch."

"Watch," said Connelly. He grumbled then to himself, to Box, "I thought that was <u>my</u> job."

Village Leader's expression betrayed no emotion. Connelly tried to put on a smile, in spite of his current physical circumstances. His words, however, took on a bit of a snarky tone.

"You speak it very well. English. Great watching. Really." He indicated his bindings. "So what's the deal here?"

Village leader lifted his head while continuing to look down on Connelly. He firmly set his jaw.

"Stone," he stated flatly.

"Excuse me?"

Village Leader turned his gaze to somewhere beyond the village. He lifted hand, pointed outward.

"High Leader," he said. He continued to look outward. After a few moments he nodded, as if to some inner thought. He wore a slight smile.

Connelly frowned.

"Right," he said. "So, you're not the big Kahuna, then."

Connelly lay asleep, sitting on the ground with his back against the post. About him, several Littles milled about the village, the world eerily quiet.

He woke, shifted about and straightened as best he could with his hands bound to the post ring. He looked calmly about, noted where the Littles were. He spoke to Box under his breath.

"Box... was I out long?"

"One hour, forty minutes," Box said quietly.

"Did I miss anything?"

"I have been hearing comings and goings over the last few minutes."

"Quiet bunch, aren't they?" Connelly continued to study his surroundings, the Littles moving silently about the village. "No sign of Little Kahuna."

"I have not heard the Village Leader's voice."

One of the Littles approached then, stood a few feet in front of Connelly. He looked curiously at Connelly, cocked his head slightly to one side and studied the human.

Connelly forced a grin, nodded his head in greeting.

"Hey," he said. "How are ya?"

The Little said nothing. He straightened his head as another Little approached and stood beside him. Several more Littles came up behind Connelly; one began untying his bindings from the post ring. As he did, more Littles began gathering, encircling Connelly, cautiously looking on.

Village Leader moved through the group and stood directly in front of Connelly. He lifted his hand up, indicating Connelly should stand.

"Ah. Gotcha," said Connelly. He grumbled as he rolled onto his knees and stood. "You people need to make up your minds."

The group slowed as they approached a narrow creek. The Littles ahead of Connelly moved forward and spread out. They knelt at the bank and drank. Those behind Connelly moved to the left and right, stood watch. When the first group finished drinking, Village Leader stepped up beside Connelly, urged him forward to the creek. Connelly nodded without speaking, approached the bank and knelt down. The other Littles moved up to the creek as well, to Connelly's left and right, as the first group stepped across the narrow brook and waited on the opposite bank.

Connelly cupped his hands and drank. The water was a little warm, but it didn't taste bad at all. Still, he would have preferred his canteen and a purification tablet.

After a long march beyond the creek, Connelly began to notice a change in the dark up ahead. There was a flat blackness, a wall of darkness in the distance. It stood in the twilight thirty feet high.

The group approached a wall of woven sticks, canes and stalks. The line of Littles, with Connelly walking in the middle, marched single-file through a narrow opening in the wall. Connelly was led into the heart of a large, enclosed plaza. Lanterns were hung on the wall of woven sticks, putting the entire clearing into a golden glow.

A female Little sat on primitive throne positioned at the far end of the plaza. The High Leader was no larger than any other Little, but she had an air of authority about her manner. Her garment was more colorful than the clothing of the other Littles, and she wore a modest crown of wood and leaf and twig.

Three attendant Littles stood formally in a line to the High Leader's right.

She waved a hand for Connelly to be brought nearer. Village Leader took hold of Connelly's arm, and without a word guided him forward until they were standing two paces from the throne.

Village Leader stepped back and away. His work was apparently done.

High Leader looked unemotionally down upon the human. When she finally spoke, the words were in broken English.

"I see you, Monitor."

"Right," sighed Connelly. "I uh, see you too."

Another Little leader speaking in English...

He mumbled then to Box. "You heard that, right?"

"I heard."

High Leader straightened.

"I am High Leader." She waved a hand about her, indicating all the Littles. "We wait. Thousand cycles. I welcome Monitor." She lifted a hand from one arm of the throne, held it out and indicated Connelly. "Our Monitor."

"Um... thank you," said Connelly, a bit uncomfortably.

"Next stone."

Again with the stone...

"Stone? I, uh..." Connelly fumbled in his thoughts, mumbled to Box, "Does she mean...?"

"The circle of stones," said Box.

Connelly frowned. "It sounds way more ominous the way she says it." Connelly cleared his throat, smiled nervously at High Leader. "Stone? Next stone?"

High Leader stood. "Next stone waits. We go."

There was immediate movement all about the large throne clearing as the Littles all set about to prepare to leave.

Again? What is it with you people?

High Leader stepped down, took a step nearer to Connelly. She remained stoic, displayed no emotion.

The three attendant Littles stepped forward with their leader. She glanced briefly in their direction. As if on signal, they turned and started toward the trailhead at the perimeter of the clearing. High Leader followed. Other Littles moved in behind Connelly, two more to either side of him.

They waited expectantly.

Connelly gave a thin smile to one, then the other.

"Sure. I was, you know, headin' that way anyway."

They gave Connelly a stern look. Up ahead, the three attendant Littles and High Leader had already reached the trailhead.

"Right," sighed Connelly. "We go..."

Chapter Nine

Connelly and his companions traveled the forest floor in a long line, moving in and out of hazy streaks of light that reached down from the canopy. The edge of the forest was less than an hour from the throne clearing, and it was still midday when they left the forest and came out of the trees and into the outer edges of Alpha Valley.

They worked their way to the main trail and followed it up the valley. There was very little talk, and when Connelly on occasion looked back to the Little walking behind him and would offer a smile, the Little would return a stern gaze.

They left the main trail at a wide but rather obscure trailhead and within minutes were following a steep trail up the side of a hillside of dry grass and short, scrubby brush. At times Connelly found himself taking hold of exposed rock as he pulled himself up.

"Aren't we there yet?" Connelly grumbled.

"It would be difficult for me to extrapolate our current location in relation to the circle of stones," said Box.

"You stay out of this."

Connelly looked up at High Leader as she looked down at him. She said nothing.

Connelly gave another half-smile. "Coming, dear."

High Leader frowned as she turned about and continued up the hillside.

"The lady needs a sense of humor."

They continued the rest of the way in silence, reaching a trail that ran under the ridge. They followed this horizontal trail around the ridge and out onto a large landing. It was set just below the ridge, forming a jutting ledge that looked out across the great valley below. The ground was smooth, with tufts of grass and weed here and there.

About the perimeter of clearing were a number of granite rock formations towering ten to twelve feet high. Standing atop these rocks were a number of Littles.

In the center of the clearing was an array of seven closed rectangular stone boxes set in a circular pattern, as the spokes of a wheel, the head of each stone box facing inward to the heart of the circle.

Connelly was led onto the landing, the Littles coming in behind him and moving out along the perimeter of the clearing. Connelly followed High Leader into the heart of the circle of stones.

"Coffins," whispered Connelly.

"Lieutenant?" asked Box.

"The circle of stones. They look like coffins. You know what a sarcophagus is?"

"I do."

High Leader moved to one side with her entourage of three as Connelly moved to the very center of the clearing. He turned slowly about, studying the stone boxes.

"Seven of 'em," he said.

"One for each Monitor, and –"

"One for the Major," Connelly finished. He gave High Leader a nervous smile. "So, what's the plan, High Leader? Singing 'round the campfire? Marshmallows? Hot dogs?" A glance to the boxes. "Mummification?"

High Leader said nothing.

So, that would be no, then...

She rested the palm of one hand against her chest. There was a light chattering about the clearing, the Littles about the clearing moving slow, almost reverential. Those on the ground moved closer into the center of the clearing, closing in about the coffin-like stone boxes.

High Leader's entourage stepped back, leaving their leader and Connelly standing alone within the heart of the circle of stones.

High Leader was expressionless. She cocked her head slightly to one side. She calmly lifted one hand and raised a finger. As she did, the Littles about them fell silent. Those standing on the ground went to one knee, while those on the surrounding rocks stood unmoving.

High Leader waited, let the enveloping silence grow heavy.

She straightened then, spoke then to her people. Her voice was soft, her tone melodic.

Theh nemoh la deh. Mehloh nahm. Toh theh lohn noh.

The kneeling Littles rose and remained silent. The Littles standing atop the tall rock formations responded in unison to the High Leader.

Theh mehneh lohn noh.

The clearing again grew heavily quiet. Three of the Littles standing along the perimeter of the circle moved aside, allowing another Little to step into the circle. He approached Connelly and High Leader, walking slowly, carrying a metallic canister with all the deference due a ritualistic artifact.

Connelly whispered to Box. "Their ritual artifact is a sealed canister."

The approaching Little gave Connelly a brief, harsh glare as he passed, not appreciating the apparent disrespect for the ceremony in progress. Connelly responded with an apologetic grin.

The Little and High Leader stood facing one another for several moments.

High Leader held out her hands.

Tah meh shah toh. Ehm nah doh.

At that, the other Little lifted the canister, places it gently into High Leader's waiting hands. He took several steps back then until he was standing directly beside Connelly.

He dropped to one knee, looked expectantly up to Connelly.

Connelly looked from High Leader to the kneeling Little, back to High Leader.

High Leader appeared to also be waiting for something.

Connelly gradually realized what she was waiting for. He also then dropped to one knee, beside the kneeling Little.

High Leader gave silent acknowledgment, then stepped over to one of the stones. She placed the canister on the lid, slid aside a small panel set into the side of the canister, and pressed a hidden keypad.

"She knows how to open the canister," Connelly mumbled.

"Interesting," Box answered.

The Little kneeling beside Connelly turned another irritated gaze to the human.

Sorry...

High Leader opened the canister. All the Littles in the clearing intoned a brief, melodic chant.

Theh moh loh. Theh mohn lah.

The clearing again fell silent. High Leader lifted a small, square device from inside the canister: metal and plastic, about three inches square.

She lifted the device above her head. *Theh lohn Mehloh deh.*

The Littles in the clearing respond in chant: *Mehneh lohn noh deh. Mehol theh.*

High Leader lowered the device. She moved to the head of the stone box, carefully set the device into position on the stone lid.

She noheh deh noh.

Mehloh theh noh, responded the Littles.

There was a gritty sound as the lid began to slide open, back from the head of the container.

Opening the coffin...

"Uh, oh," mumbled Connelly.

"Lieutenant?" prompted Box.

"I'll, uh... tell you later." *Assuming I, uh...*

The lid slid back a third the length of the stone and stopped. High Leader moved to the side, reached in lifted another canister from within the stone box.

The Littles intoned another chant. *Mehloh noh. Mehloh theh noh.*

High Leader turned and stepped toward Connelly, who was still on one knee. She held the canister out to him. Connelly hesitated, finally reached out and took the canister.

High Leader spoke as if part of the ritual, the words clumsy yet clearly in English.

"We the people... future," she stated. "Major... lift the people. Major... make future so."

The circle of stones clearing again went quiet. Connelly had no idea what he was expected to do. He hesitated. He looked from the canister to High Leader, back to the canister. He gave a quick glance to the open stone box, then.

So, then I'm not going to, uh...

High Leader took a step back, looked about at the Littles standing in the enclosing circle, then to those on the tall rock formations along the clearing perimeter.

Loh theh noh shah toh. Ah Leh, she said.

And with that the Littles standing in the engulfing circle silently began to back away. They turned and filed away the way they came. The Littles standing atop the rock formations backed away, disappeared from view.

Within moments there was only High Leader and Connelly.

Connelly weighed the canister resting in his hands. "This is... this is from the Major?" he asked.

"It is."

"Ya' got any idea what's in here?" Connelly continued to study the sealed canister.

High Leader's expression was solemn. "My task... complete," she stated.

"Right. Right," said Connelly. "Long time coming, eh?"

High Leader considered the meaning of the question. She gave the hint of a nod, pursed her lips.

"My life," she said. "My ancestors before me. Many ancestors."

"Oh, I get that."

High Leader turned back to the open stone box. She pressed the device that was still sitting on the lid. The lid slid closed with a hollow grinding noise.

At the sight of the box closing, Connelly mumbled "So glad to see that. Smiling here."

"Lieutenant?" asked Box.

"Tell ya' later."

High Leader picked up the device, stepped back to Connelly.

"For you," she said.

Connelly tucked the canister that he was holding under his arm and took the device.

"And this is for...?"

"Answers come to you when answers you need."

Connelly stared down at the device in his hand as High Leader stepped past him and left the clearing of the circle of stones.

Alone...

"Right."

Chapter Ten

Connelly was sitting on the stone bench a dozen paces from the Central access obelisk. Sunset was a few minutes away, he watched as the sun slowly descended toward the horizon.

He wondered now about the bench. It hadn't been here when he first arrived from Point Zero, had assumed until recently that the Major had placed it here. It would have taken work, dragging it from wherever the stone had come.

Now, knowing that the other Monitors had lived out their lives in the five millennia before him, he realized it could have been any of them.

Good decision in any case. This was a favorite spot of Connelly's; and sunset was a favorite time.

Box interrupted his reverie.

"Lieutenant Connelly, in order to determine what is in the canister, you will need to look inside the canister."

The sealed canister was on the bench beside him. Box was resolute that they get on with it. They had returned from the circle of stones more than an hour earlier, and had yet to actually go into the center.

"Soon enough, Box. Soon enough. I'm just not in the mood to deal with A-I Major right now."

"Ah. And the electronic key needed to open the canister is in Central."

Both were silent for a few moments.

"I do love the sunsets here," said Connelly at last. He continued to watch the sun descend nearer and nearer the horizon. "Major set that ritual up, you know; created an elaborate ceremony for the Littles."

"Yes," stated Box.

Connelly reached over and picked up the canister. He studied it, weighed it in one hand.

"He intended that each Monitor receive one of these," he said, considering. "Can you imagine? Generation after generation, the Littles preparing for one brief moment every thousand years, just to hand off one of these?"

"By their very nature, the Littles were the perfect choice for such a task."

"I suppose that's so. They are... interesting." He returned his gaze to the setting sun, now only moments remaining. "And more than that. They worshiped the Major. I wonder how he managed that."

"I would think that he worked very hard at establishing such a relationship. Such would be vital if he wished for the ritual to continue across the millennia."

"So it was important." To himself, then, "Weird."

The sun finished its descent into the horizon. Streaks of orange and yellow and red reached out across the landscape, slowly faded to gray. The world grew steadily into dusk.

Connelly stood at the island counter in Central's main control room. The open canister was on the countertop in front of him, several wires running from the opening. Connelly was wearing a headset plugged into a jack in the counter, he was listening to the small, tinny sound of the Major's voice.

"Nothing we do will prevent Point Zero from vanishing," said the Major. "As it is the very future itself that is lost. By their actions. Not ours. Nothing we do here will change that. I have tried. What remains to us is to endeavor for a new future, a future that belongs to the Littles and the Alphas."

Connelly remained at the counter, listening to the message from the distant past, from the Major. The control room was quiet but for the environmental systems running in the background and the hint of the Major's voice leaking from the headset. It continued for another several minutes.

Finished then, Connelly pulled off the headset, set it on the counter.

The relative silence in the room was broken when the voice of A-I Major came softly over the speakers.

"Have you finished listening to the Major's message, Lieutenant?"

"I have."

Silence again. Box then spoke up.

"What did the Major have to say, Lieutenant Connelly?"

Connelly turned slowly about, leaned back against the counter and folded his arms across his chest. His expression was hesitant.

"The Major wasn't trying to make things right in order to get us all back to Point Zero," he said. "He's stopping us from getting to Point Zero in order to make things right."

"Lieutenant," said Box. "We suspected as much. Did we not?"

"Something like that. I suppose. Sort of."

A-I Major interrupted. "Can you explain, please?"

Connelly rose up out of his thoughts. "The future, it would seem, belongs to the Alphas and the Littles."

"But the Littles and Alphas are both dead ends," stated Box. "The valley and the Black Forest are—"

"Apparently our continued presence here can change that," said Connelly, cutting him off. "Can change everything. The Major believed it to be so. So much so that he has ensured that no one can return to Point Zero."

"I see," said Box.

"And not just the Monitors. He was also rather emphatic that none of our data reach Point Zero."

"That would explain the condition of the data crystal that we found at Outpost Four."

"I am directed to destroy my data crystal," said Connelly. "The same order was given to all the Monitors."

A-I Major interrupted again. "I hesitate to bring this up, due perhaps to the Major's role in my creation, but... was the Major insane?"

"He saw something," said Connelly, slowly shaking his head no. He began disconnecting the wiring and the headset from the canister. "Maybe when he returned to Point Zero, to what happened, he saw something. Something really bad. Something that eventually led him to believe that the world must be taken in a new direction."

"I understand," said Box. "Why couldn't this message be kept at Central and delivered to the Monitors through standard channels? Why this elaborate ritual with the Littles."

"Me," said A-I Major with some certainty. "It was me. Major was concerned how I might respond to this."

"That may have had something to do with it." Connelly sounded doubtful. "But I'm thinking it had more to do with the Littles. I think it may have been part of setting them on a path that he wanted them to follow."

"And perhaps you and the other Monitors onto paths of your own," said Box.

"Perhaps." Connelly started across the room toward the hallway. "At the moment, my path leads to the shower, the mess, and to bed. In that order."

Connelly was sitting on the hilltop ridge, binoculars in hand, looking out across the narrow valley below. His hiking staff and backpack were in the grass beside him, Box sitting on the backpack.

A group of Alphas were milling about a small encampment on the valley floor.

Connelly lowered the binoculars, continued to look down into the valley.

"The Alphas and the Littles were evolutionary dead ends." His tone was conversational. He glanced once at the device sitting on the backpack, turned his attention back to the encampment below.

"As I have stated," said Box.

"This valley and everything in it was an aberration."

"One of the primary reasons for the original mission in which you and the other Monitors were to participate."

"Yeah," sighed Connelly. "So you say."

"Such was the mission description."

"Right." Connelly lifted the binoculars and returned to studying the group of Alphas. "I was there."

"Of course."

Connelly frowned as he again lowered the binoculars. "The others. The other Monitors. What did they do when faced with... this?"

"They destroyed their data crystals."

"But how did they live out their lives? What did they do? How did their presence here impact our friends down there?"

"We see the Littles and the Alphas as they are now, Lieutenant. Without the other data crystals, we know nothing of what they were like previously beyond what little data we were given in the mission briefings."

"Did any of it really change things at Point Zero?" Connelly wondered aloud. "Does that world of 2058 now belong to the Littles? The Alphas?"

Box did not respond. He had no answer to those questions, and he knew that Connelly knew that.

"I am not smiling here, Box," said Connelly.

He let out a tired, frustrated sigh. He let the seconds pass, then got slowly to his feet. He took a step down the hill, glanced down into the valley again.

"We don't know that," he said.

"Lieutenant?"

Connelly looked back at the Box device set atop his backpack, spoke directly at it.

"We don't know that all the Monitors destroyed their data crystals. We know only that Monitor Four destroyed his."

"That is so," said Box. "And if they didn't?"

"Then, despite the Major's orders, Point Zero will have received info from the past." He stepped back toward his gear. He looked down at Box. "But if Point Zero no longer exists, it doesn't matter. Does it?"

"Unless the data crystals not being destroyed is the reason that Point Zero no longer exists. Such was Major's concern."

Connelly picked up Box and stuffed the A-I device into his jacket pocket.

"My brain hurts." He started walking along the ridge.

"We're going to visit all the outposts. Aren't we?" asked Box.

"Yup."

"And you were planning this all along, weren't you?"

"Yup."

Chapter Eleven

The night beyond the circle of light from the small campfire was near black, the flickering firelight reflecting on Connelly's face and the ruin of the outpost behind him.

This was his third outpost in a week. Each had been pretty much the same. He had dug through piles of metal and plastic covered in millennia of vegetation, getting to his hands and knees to reach in through the rubble, looking for the floor compartment and the canister containing the data capsule.

To be disappointed each time.

There was one outpost yet to go.

He reached down and picked up a stick, absently poked at the fire. Sparks rose up into the night.

Connelly scrambled down a steep, overgrown trail and stepped out into the middle of a wide clearing.

The ground was clear of debris, as if recently swept clean. There was a primitive sculpture of sticks and twine and bamboo in the heart of the clearing. It faintly resembled a humanoid figure.

"Things do be getting curiouser," said Connelly.

"Yes?" prompted Box.

Connelly was looking warily into the shadows and brush just beyond the clearing. There was an open trailhead to the left, and a gurgling creek was visible further downslope.

"The locals appear to have an emotional attachment to Outpost Five."

"In what way, Lieutenant?"

"Housekeeping, for one," said Connelly brushing at the swept and manicured ground with his feet. He approached the sculpture. "And primitive arts and crafts."

"I see," said Box, noncommittally. "And have you found the outpost?"

Connelly moved to the back of the clearing, where the level ground met the steep terrain that he had scrambled down moments earlier.

"I'm looking now." He pushed aside thick vines and bramble. Hidden in the vegetation was a metal door. "The door is still standing."

He reached in and pushed a palm against the metal. The door gave way and fell inward.

"Check that," he said. He leaned his staff against the wall of vegetation next to the opening and stepped into the darkness.

The roof of the outpost was still up, and the walls were still standing. Connelly brought out his flashlight. Much of the interior was in ruin. After a thousand years, only metal and plastic maintained any recognizable form.

Connelly worked his way across the room and toward the opening in the far corner.

The floor of the small back room was covered in layers of decomposed wood and twisted plastic and metal. Connelly stepped through the debris to get to the far wall. He went to his knees and pushed aside the rubble. He lifted an access in the floor and looked into the compartment beneath.

"The data container is still here," he said.

"And the data crystal?" asked Box.

"What say we find out?" Connelly reached into the compartment and brought out the container. "The container is sealed."

He stood and worked his way out of the back room, then across the main room. He stepped out of the outpost and into the clearing, the sealed container under his arm.

He stopped in mid-step.

"Uh, oh."

"Lieutenant?" asked Box.

"We have company."

There were three Alphas in the clearing. One was standing at the trailhead, the other two in the heart of the clearing near the handcrafted sculpture. Each had a wooden staff in hand. Their expressions betrayed no emotion, but none appeared aggressive at the moment.

They silently study Connelly.

Connelly struggled with a slight grin. "Good afternoon, gentlemen."

There was no response from the Alphas.

Connelly maintained his friendly expression as he spoke calmly to Box.

"I don't recognize them. I think they're from the North tribe."

"The North tribe seldom interacts with the others," said Box.

"Well, best I can figure, this is their territory."

Connelly looked from one to another of the Alphas, gave an acknowledging nod to the nearest of them.

"How are you today?" he asked. He gave the container that was tucked under his arm a pat. "I hope you don't mind." A frown and a mumble then, "I really, really hope you don't mind."

One of the Alphas frowned curiously slightly as he looked at the object that Connelly was holding. He focused again on Connelly's face. The frown faded.

Connelly indicated the trailhead, currently blocked by one of the Alphas.

"I um... I really should be going now." He put on a weak smile. "But it's been really great talking with you."

He took a step to his left, in the general direction of the trailhead. When none of the Alphas moved, neither to stand in his way nor get out of his way, he stopped, pointed again to the trailhead.

"I go now?" he asked.

One of the Alphas growled low, grunting.

"Um, is that a yes?"

Silence.

Box's voice then, soft and calming.

"Beware your level of smart-ass, Lieutenant Connelly," he said. "They may not understand the words, but the attitude comes across loud and clear."

The Alpha standing nearest Connelly let out a low *humph* sound. It scrunched its face, relaxed it then.

It spoke a word then in English, half in a growl.

"Jack-son." It looked to the sculpture of branch and twine and bamboo. It pointed to it as it looked sharply at Connelly. "Jack-son," it repeated.

"Holy crap," said Connelly, under his breath.

"I assume that was an Alpha who spoke," said Box.

"It wasn't me."

"Rather gruff perhaps, but it was quite understandable."

"That's impossible."

The Alpha standing beside the first now spoke up. "Jack-son."

Connelly looked to the one, then other, mumbled then to Box as he wore his least threatening facial expression.

"Setting aside for a moment the fact that these are Alphas, she's been gone a thousand years."

"Her name has been passed down through the generations."

"Again... *Alphas*," stated Connelly.

"Nonetheless."

"Right. And, it would seem that she made as much an impression on them as the Major made on the Littles."

"Yes," said Box. "So it would seem."

Connelly made eye contact with each of the Alphas in turn, then rested a hand on his chest.

"I am a friend of Jackson," he said, as friendly as he could manage. "Jackson, friend."

The Alphas warily study Connelly.

"I doubt they understand, Lieutenant," said Box.

At the very least, they had heard Connelly say Jackson. But then, for all he knew, an outsider speaking her name could be a bad thing. A very, very bad thing.

"Friend," said the first Alpha. "Jack-son."

He didn't look upset.

"Yes," said Connelly. "Jackson, friend."

In your face, Box...

"Jackson, friend," repeated the Alpha.

"Right. Exactly. You... friend?"

"Friend."

The Alpha had yet to change expression. All the Alphas had the same, unsettlingly emotionless expression.

So where were they going with this back and forth friend stuff?

"Friends. All friends here," he grumbled. To himself then, "This friend really needs to leave."

He gave a slightly uncomfortable nod and smile to the nearest Alpha, took a step toward the trailhead. He hesitated then, pointed back to his hiking staff, which he had left leaning against the vegetation beside the outpost opening.

"I, uh... my..." He pointed awkwardly, side-stepped back to the staff and took hold of it. "My... staff."

He slip-slid walked across the clearing and to the trailhead. He gave the Alpha standing there a final, awkward nod.

"I'll just be... going now."

Chapter Twelve

Connelly finished dressing in clean clothes after taking a long, hot shower. He picked the container up from where he had tossed it onto his bunk. He walked a narrow hall to the main hall, turned and followed the larger hallway, the container tucked under his arm.

A-I Major had pelted him with questions about his recent outing, and hadn't been satisfied with Connelly's answers. He continued questioning him as Connelly walked the hall.

"I am not certain that I fully understand what you are say, Lieutenant."

"What's to understand?" asked Connelly. "You know what I know. I've told you everything. You wanted me to find Major. I found him. He's in a stone box up on a mountain. Bunch of little people taking care of him."

He reached an archway on the left and stepped into the comm room. The room was small, a counter along one wall, with one chair. An equipment board was built into the wall above the counter.

A-I Major's voice followed him in.

"Your discovery in point of fact generates many more questions than it answers, Lieutenant Connelly."

Connelly settled into the chair, his response coming through in a heavy drone of a sigh.

"Man, do I hear that." He set the container on the counter. He opened it and removed the data crystal. "Why don't we see if this offers us any answers, shall we?"

He opened an access panel in the equipment board, inserted the data crystal. He flipped several switches, sat back in his chair and waited.

A female voice came through a pair of speakers set into the equipment board.

"Hey, Connelly... Jackson here. Long time, no see."

Connelly grinned. *Hey, Jackson...*

"Some weird crap going on, eh?" Jackson continued.

You got that right...

Box spoke up. "It would appear that Lieutenant Jackson has used the Outpost Five data crystal to leave a message. A message specifically intended for you."

"Ya' think?"

"Since you're listening to this," Jackson went on, "you already know that everything has gone wonkers. I can assume you've been given the line, and that you don't totally believe it."

Connelly settled back deeper into the chair...

The sun was just touching the western horizon. Sunset colors streaked across the landscape, reaching Connelly as he sat on the stone bench near the Central access obelisk.

The words of Jackson, the Monitor from Outpost Five, played back in his mind.

"So, if you're planning on trying to find a way around Major's work and get back to Point Zero, you can forget it. But not for the reason you're thinking. Ya' see, there never was a plan to return us home. Just the data. All they wanted were the data crystals."

Connelly leaned forward, elbows on his knees, clasped his hands. Jackson's words continued, not in any particular order, jumping back and forth from the message coming to him from a thousand years in the past.

"Major was part of it all, at least he knew about it. Maybe he just figured it out. I don't know what set him off, what set him against the Foundation."

"Lieutenant?" Box attempted to interrupt Connelly's thoughts. "Lieutenant?"

Connelly ignored him, perhaps didn't hear him. For the moment, there were only Jackson's words.

"I spent years in the Valley," she said. "With the Alphas. Spent more with the Littles. A most curious species, the Littles. The *First Ones*, as the Alphas call them."

Connelly stood slowly, took a step toward the setting sun.

"You take care of the Alphas," said Jackson. "The Littles call them *The Children*. They see them as the future. I didn't see it at first, but over time I..."

Connelly was still standing there, a few yards from the bench, after the sun had finished setting and the colors had begun fading to gray.

He and Box had exchanged a few words, for which Box was grateful, as grateful as an A-I could be.

He didn't want anything bad to happen to his only connection to the real world.

Connelly stuffed his hands into his jacket pockets.

"In the end, she decided not to let the data go to Point Zero," he said. "She never said why, not in so many words. It had to do with the Littles and the Alphas."

"She accepted the Major's reasoning," suggested Box.

"Maybe," said Connelly, not fully satisfied with that explanation. "Anyway, my being the only Monitor left in the timeline, I think she wanted to say hi."

"And so? What will you do, Lieutenant Connelly?"

Connelly pushed his hands deeper into his jacket pockets, took in the quickly graying dusk.

"I don't know, Box."

Connelly finished preparing his dinner at the counter and took his plate over to the middle table in the mess. He took Box from his pocket and set the device on the table beside his plate. He spoke then into the air as he stepped over to the water dispenser, his words and tone a bit hesitant.

"Hey, uh... Major. Ya' got a minute?"

"Of course, Lieutenant."

"You called all the Monitors back to Central just as you did me, right?" he asked. He finished filling the water glass and started back to the table. "I mean, when you recalled me, you said all the Monitors were being called home."

"That is correct."

Connelly sat down, set his glass on the table and pulled his plate nearer.

"So... did they hang around? Here at Central?"

There was a hesitation from A-I Major.

"Several did," he said at last. "For a time."

Connelly ate as he talked. "So, where'd they go, then?"

"I believe some returned to their outposts, at least at first. To the natives then, I would imagine. The Littles and the Alphas."

"You don't know?"

"To their outposts, initially," stated A-I Major. "Why do you ask, Lieutenant?"

Connelly looked thoughtfully up in the general direction of the disembodied voice of the A-I.

"It's just that... I gather that no one brought you news of the Major. I'm the first to do that."

"That is so."

"I take it they didn't take the news of our true situation quite as well as me, then," said Connelly. "And with you being the messenger and all..."

"I was not the messenger," A-I Major stated succinctly. In more of a conceding tone then, "However, as they realized the truth of their circumstances, I may have been the focus of their discontent."

"I can imagine." Connelly took another bite of food, glanced down to the Box device. "What about their Box devices?"

"Lieutenant?"

"Do you know what happened to the other Monitors' Boxes?"

"I do not."

There were several long moments of uncomfortable silence. Connelly inattentively poked at what was left of his meal with his fork.

"You've been alone... a really long time," he said. There was no response from A-I Major. "I mean, even if the other Monitors had stuck around, there were all those centuries in between."

"That is so."

Connelly quit pushing his food about with his fork at took another bite.

"That's gotta suck," he said.

"It has at times been unpleasant," A-I Major stated smoothly, only after a long pause. Both went silent then. Connelly continued to eat his meal, staring absently across the room.

Box did not speak at all. Connelly glanced once at the device, returned his absent gaze to the far side of the quiet room. There was only the sound of the environmental systems running in the background and the hum of the lights.

Chapter Thirteen

An early evening lay over the clearing. Horizontal shadows stretched across the circle of stones, pushed up against the tall stones along the perimeter. The last dim rays of the setting sun painted thin streaks of color across the cool, gray lids of the stone boxes.

Lieutenant Connelly entered the clearing from the only trailhead, walked into the heart of the circle of stones. He set his staff against one of the stone boxes, slipped out of his small backpack.

He glanced about the clearing as he took the access device of a side pocket of the pack. He moved over to one of the boxes, set the device on the lid. He pressed a key on the device, straightened and stepped back.

The lid slid open to the gritty, grinding sound of stone against stone. Connelly hesitated, warily approached the open stone box. Standing stiffly, he leaned in slightly and looked inside.

The clearing was fully shrouded in deepening gray, the sun having set, the darkness coming. Connelly was sitting on one of the stone boxes. All had been opened, all were now closed.

A movement drew Connelly from his reverie. He glanced up and to one side as the High Leader of the Littles came into the clearing. He noted movement in the shadows as other Littles hovered beyond the tall rock formations along the perimeter.

High Leader came into the center of the clearing and stood in front of Connelly.

Connelly indicated the stone boxes.

"All of 'em," he said. "They're all here, then. The Monitors."

"I have been told so," said High Leader.

Connelly nodded solemnly. He spoke then as if to himself.

"They all fell in line." He indicated the box opposite. "Behind the Major."

"Major lift the people."

"Right. So you said."

"We. First Ones," said High Leader. "We... watch. We help Monitors."

"So it would seem."

"We care for the Children."

"Right." Connelly looked thoughtfully at High Leader. "The Alphas. The Children."

"We, future. Children, future."

Connelly nodded at that, returned his gaze to the circle of stones, the stone boxes.

"And so it would seem," he said.

High Leader looked outward, looked away as if she was now lost in thought. It was several moments before she returned her focus to Connelly. She indicated the device sitting on the lid beside him, then pointed to the stone box from which she had taken the canister that she had then given to Connelly.

"When you ready, Monitor, we help."

"Yeah. So I figured." Connelly stared at the box that was one day to be his sarcophagus. He leaned forward and stood up. He gathered up his backpack and his staff. "That do be a long way off, my friend. Natural causes and all that."

He picked up the device, held it out briefly before unceremoniously stuffing it into his jacket pocket. "But let's keep in touch," he said. "That good by you?"

It took High Leader a moment to sort out the meaning of the question. She then gave a short, curt nod.

"We watch Monitor," she stated.

Connelly smiled cordially, spoke affably as he started across the clearing.

"I believe this may be the start of a long and most curious friendship, Your Highness."

Chapter Fourteen

The gently sloping hills were covered in a forest of tall trees. A thick, green canopy was spread high above a sparse undergrowth on the forest floor. The figure of Connelly, little more than a silhouette, moved into and out of the shadows of the trees as he followed the winding, narrow mountain trail, his ever-present hiking staff in hand, a light backpack on his back.

He stepped into the clearing, walked past the rustic root cellar door and on toward the outpost, the wall set into the side of a brush-covered mound.

Outpost Six. His outpost.

He leaned his staff against the wall beside the door. He pressed his palm against the ident panel. There was a hard click sound. He lifted the door latch and slid it aside, opened the door.

He stepped inside his outpost, set his backpack on the table and walked across the main cabin. In the back room, he knelt down beside the compartment set into the floor and opened it. Inside was the sealed time capsule, within which resided the data crystal.

Connelly hesitated, took a long breath. He reached into the compartment then and brought out the canister. Sitting back, he weighted the canister in hand. He stood, worked his way out of the outpost.

The day was warm, the sky clear, the sun high overhead. Connelly was sitting on the riverbank, a homemade fishing pole in hand, the line in the water. His hair was longer these days, his dress more casual. A canvas bag was sitting on the ground nearby. Next to the bag was a metal thermos.

Connelly appeared quite relaxed. He glanced briefly at Box. The device was resting against a stick that Connelly had pushed into the ground, making it appear Box was kicking back and relaxing alongside Connelly.

"Another utterly uneventful day, dear Box."

There was a moment of hesitation from Box.

"You can't put it off any longer, Lieutenant," he said at last.

"Oh, sure I can," said Connelly.

"You cannot. You must destroy the data crystal. You must do so now, before something happens."

"Why?"

"Lieutenant... you should have done it a year ago. It should never have left the outpost intact."

"Why?"

"Lieutenant..."

Connelly set his pole aside, pulled the canvas bag to him, brought out a bag of ration pellets. Leaning back on one elbow, he began munching on the food.

"I wasn't ready, my friend," he said. "I'm still not ready."

"What is the purpose in delaying what must be done?" asked Box.

"I haven't decided yet." He tossed another ration pellet into his mouth. "And... I may want to leave a message. Jackson did."

"Lieutenant Jackson's message was for you. There are no Monitors to follow."

"I know that."

"Lieutenant... You do intend to wipe the current data..."

"It is what the Major wanted, isn't it?"

"He ordered you to destroy the data crystal, not just the data in the crystal."

"Same difference."

"It is not."

"Too bad." Connelly closed the bag of rations, stuffed it back into the canvas bag. He picked up the thermos, opened it and took a drink. "Hey, Box... there is something we do need to make a decision on."

He closed the thermos, set it back on the ground beside the canvas bag.

"There is the matter of you, once I'm gone."

"I have considered the options, as well," said Box.

"No doubt." said Connelly. "Me, I really see only one."

"And that would be?"

"That you join the A-I Major."

There was along, uncomfortable pause before Box responded.

"Perhaps. When the time comes."

Connelly grinned as he reached over and picked up his fishing pole.

"Oh, so that we put off. I gotta destroy the data crystal like right now, but loading you back into Central, that can wait."

Another very long hesitation...

"I am... not ready," said Box.

Another grin from Connelly as he pulled lightly on his fishing pole.

"Uh, huh." A long pause then. "What a nice day. Eh, my friend?"

"Yes, Lieutenant," said Box. "A very nice day."

The sun was low on the horizon, sunset not far away. Connelly sat slowly and carefully on the stone bench near the Central access obelisk. His shoulder-length hair was gray, his skin pale and weathered. His eyes were clear and sharp.

The High Leader of the Littles came into the clearing. She approached Connelly, sat on the bench beside him.

"Good afternoon, Connelly."

The sun now just touched the horizon.

"Good evening, High Leader."

High Leader looked outward across the landscape. She smiled warmly.

"Yes," she said. "Evening."

The sun's rays streaked across the clearing, shone on the faces of both Connelly and High Leader. High Leader closed her eyes and wore a pleasant smile.

"Feel good."

"That it does," said Connelly.

They sat silent for several moments, took in the quiet evening.

Connelly spoke then while keeping his focus on the horizon.

"It's good to see you," he said. "Been a while."

"It has," said High Leader. "Good to see you."

They again grew silent. The sun sank below the horizon. A third of the sky was suddenly painted in dark red and deep orange.

"I do like the sunsets here." Connelly breathed out tiredly. He gave a quick glance to High Leader, returned his attention to the horizon. "Not today, my friend."

"I know," said High Leader.

Connelly managed an easy nod. He relaxed again, let out another sigh and repeated his comment of a few moments earlier.

"I do like the sunsets here."

Elderly Connelly and High Leader sat in silence then, side by side on the bench, and watched the sunset.

§

Two Littles stood at the edge of the central clearing, just within the brush. From here they could watch unobserved Elderly Connelly and High Leader sitting on the bench in the distance.

These Littles were dressed in future garb of slacks, shirt and flowing open robes.

They stood silent for a long time, observing the two in the distance, there expressions warm and yet somehow remote.

One then turned to the other. It gave a very slight nod. It looked back to those on the bench. As it did so, the two vanished.

High Leader felt something, sensed something. She turned slowly about and looked behind them.

She saw nothing. There was nothing.

They were alone.

She turned about again, continued to watch the sunset with her friend Connelly.

~ End

The Storekeeper

Chapter One

A wooden porch ran the width of the weathered storefront. The faded sign above the store read '*General Store*'.

On the porch was a wooden bench and an old, rickety rocking chair. A sign on the wall next to the screen door read '*Lunch Counter*', and at the corner of the building was a small sign with an arrow pointing behind the store that read '*To Trains*'.

To one side of the store was a very old gas pump with an equally old sign: '*No Gas*'.

Mrs. Mayfield, an elderly black woman, sat primly in the rocking chair, gently rocking. She wore a clean but well-worn dress and clutched at a plastic purse that rested in her lap. Her hair, more gray than black, was pulled back and bound in a bun.

The Storekeeper sat on the bench next to the rocking chair, relaxed, one arm draped along the back of the bench. He was middle-aged, friendly and outgoing. He dressed casually, wore a flannel shirt with the sleeves rolled up.

The screen door opened and Wayne Saunders stepped out onto the porch, a bottle of cola in hand. Hinges screeched noisily as the screen door closed behind him.

"I put a pair of quarters on the counter," he said. He didn't sound all that pleased about it.

Wayne was thirty years old, rather disgruntled with a world that just wouldn't give him a break.

"I thank you, Mr. Saunders," said the Storekeeper.

"Yeah. Whatever." Wayne took a long pull on his cola, sighed tiredly as he looked out at the highway. "Ya' get many cars come by here?"

"Not a one."

"Doesn't that make it tough to earn a living?" asked Wayne. "Ya gotta have customers to run a store, don't ya'?"

The Storekeeper gave a slow nod. He wore a knowing, confident smile.

"You are here, Mr. Saunders," he said, matter-of-factly. "And you have made a purchase. That would make you a customer."

Wayne thought on that a moment, finally held the bottle up in salute.

"Glad to help, Storekeeper." He took another swallow of his cola, then looked over at Mrs. Mayfield. "So what's your story, lady?"

"I beg your pardon?" She didn't much like this man's tone.

"What brings you here? You a customer, too?"

All of Mrs. Mayfield's defenses went up. She clutched all the more tightly at her black, plastic purse. "I'm sorry, sir. I don't believe—"

"Oh, dear," said the Storekeeper, jumping in. "Where are my manners. Mrs. Mayfield, allow me to introduce Mr. Wayne Saunders. Mr. Saunders, this wonderful lady is Mrs. Mayfield."

"Mrs. Mayfield," Wayne nodded politely.

Mrs. Mayfield regained her composure. "Mr. Saunders."

The Storekeeper patted the back of the bench as he spoke, smiling at the lady in the rocking chair.

"Mrs. Mayfield is on her way to visit her sister," he said. "Isn't that right, Mrs. Mayfield?"

Mrs. Mayfield nodded sharply, curtly.

"That's right. Cecilia asked if I might stay with her for a spell. She's all alone, now that her husband Walter passed away." She eyed Wayne. She continued to maintain distance, but certainly didn't want to appear rude. "And you, Mr. Saunders?"

"Leavin' one city, headin' for another."

"I see." She thought on that. Her rocking slowed to an easy stop. She paused, then began rocking again, slow and steady. "That sounds sad."

The Storekeeper brought his arm down and sat forward. "I'm sure Mr. Saunders is simply seeking out new and exciting opportunities. Isn't that right, Wayne?"

"Exactly." Wayne went to what he knew best. "I'm not one to sit still. Heck no. Ya' gotta reach out and take life by the scruff a' the neck."

"Of course," said the Storekeeper.

"The system works against folks like me. The breaks are never gonna go my way all on their own." Wayne gave a crisp nod. "So I gotta work that much harder' everybody else."

"Make your own breaks, so to speak."

"Exactly."

"Good for you, Mr. Saunders," said Mrs. Mayfield, attempting to sound genuine.

She was also now finished with this particular conversation, having met whatever etiquette requirements may have been due here.

She returned her focus to her rocking.

"Yeah, well," Wayne grumbled. He finished his cola, looked around for where to dispose of the bottle.

The Storekeeper motioned to the screen door.

"The recycle bin is inside, sir; next to the pop cooler."

Wayne looked behind him, a hint of annoyance at having to take the empty back into the store and return it to right near where he got it to begin with.

He nonetheless opened the screen door and went inside.

Mrs. Mayfield glanced past the Storekeeper and to the door, as quickly returned her attention forward.

"That young man does have issues," she stated.

"Yes, he does, Mrs. Mayfield. Yes he does." He saw then a pair of new arrivals out on the highway. He smiled. "Ah. I believe this is the Harris couple."

Peter and Helen Harris were just starting onto the dirt and gravel parking lot, walking toward the storefront. They were in their twenties. Peter was dressed in light slacks and a short-sleeved button shirt. Helen was wearing summer shorts and a pullover blouse.

They warily eyed the two on the porch as they continued walking slowly toward the store. They appeared disoriented and were clearly out of their element.

"Maybe they can tell us..." Helen mumbled, let the thought fade.

"Maybe," said Peter. "Doubt it. Don't expect it would hurt to ask..."

Back on the porch, Mrs. Mayfield stopped her rocking yet again. She leaned forward just a mite as she looked in the direction of the newcomers.

"You know them?" she asked the Storekeeper.

"Oh, but of course."

Peter and Helen stopped at the foot of the porch steps. The Storekeeper gave a pleasant, welcoming nod and smile from his seated position on the bench.

"Hello, dear friends," he said.

Helen wore a lost gaze. "Hello."

"Yes," said Peter. "I uh... I think our car broke down."

"Of course it did," said the Storekeeper. "Of course it did."

Peter looked back toward the highway. "Out on... out on the uh... highway."

"We've been walking," said Helen.

"You poor dear," said Mrs. Mayfield.

Helen looked at Peter, who turned now from the highway and looked again up on the porch.

"Our car," he said.

"Our car," said Helen. "It broke down."

"I'm so sorry to hear that," said the Storekeeper. "Why don't you go on inside and get freshened up? It's a warm morning. And it's going to get warmer."

"Yes..." said Peter. "Sounds good."

Peter and Helen took the steps up onto the porch. As they approached the screen door, Helen smiled meekly at the Storekeeper.

"Yes," she said. "Thank you."

"My pleasure, Helen."

Helen hesitated, almost stumbled. The Storekeeper had spoken her name. She didn't remember telling him her name.

But Peter had already opened the screen door, drew her inside after him.

The screen door clattered noisily closed behind them.

Mrs. Mayfield leaned back in the chair and returned to her slow, comfortable rocking.

"Such a nice couple. And you say you know them?"

"Helen and Peter. Yes. A nice couple. Very nice."

"They seem a bit turned around."

"The long walk, no doubt," Storekeeper said thoughtfully.

"Yes, I'm sure you're right. They did say they had been walking a long time, didn't they?" She leaned forward then and looked in the direction from which the Harris couple had arrived a few moments earlier. "My, my. More company, looks like."

"Ah! How nice!" said the Storekeeper.

Molly Chandler crossed the empty dirt and gravel lot and approached the store. She was sixteen years old, but her eyes showed that she had seen more than the years would suggest.

She wore faded jeans and a light jacket. She wore a knit cap, what hair was showing could have used a brushing.

She stepped to the foot of the steps, let a light backpack slide from her shoulder until she could set it at her feet.

The Storekeeper smiled broadly. "Good morning to you, Molly."

"Are you the Storekeeper here?"

"That would be me. And how are you this fine day?"

"I could use some water."

"You'll find the drinking fountain inside. Near the restrooms."

"Thanks." Molly picked up her backpack by a shoulder strap, climbed the steps up on onto the porch. She started toward the screen door. "I've been on the road for—"

She hesitated, as if she knew something, or thought she knew something; and then it was gone.

She stopped at the screen door, looked to the Storekeeper, over to Mrs. Mayfield.

"I've been walking..." she started again, hesitated again. "Been out... all morning..."

"The drinking fountain is inside," said the Storekeeper again.

"Right. By the restrooms."

"Exactly so."

"Yeah." Molly opened the screen door and went inside, hinges screeching, door clapping shut behind her.

Mrs. Mayfield returned to her easy rocking. "You recognized that poor girl. Molly, you said."

"Molly Chandler," said the Storekeeper. "Difficult time at home, I'm afraid. She's been on her own now for... well, for some time."

Mrs. Mayfield slowed her rocking, but didn't fully stop. "But... she didn't appear to know you."

"No, of course not," said the Storekeeper, quite matter-of-factly. "Why would she?"

"But..." Mrs. Mayfield was growing increasingly bewildered. "And the couple... they didn't—"

The screen door opened and Wayne came outside, cutting off Mrs. Mayfield's confusion. He looked curiously back inside as he let the screen ease closed.

"Hey, uh... Storekeeper. You may not get any cars passing by here, but you sure get a lot of foot traffic."

"It does look to be the day for it, doesn't it?"

"Kinda' odd, don't you think?" Wayne stepped to the edge of the porch, the top of the steps. "Way out here, middle a' nowhere, folks just walkin' up to your store?"

"Why would you think it odd, Wayne?"

Wayne looked a bit bewildered now himself. How could the Storekeeper not think...

"Cuz, you know... you're out here, in the middle of nowhere?"

"Nowhere, sir? Nowhere?"

"Well I—"

"I like to think of my little slice of paradise as the center of the universe."

Wayne looked back over his shoulder at the Storekeeper, still sitting on his bench.

"Really. You're kiddin', right?"

"I have an amazing sense of humor, Mr. Saunders, but when it comes to my world, I do not... *kid.*"

"All right, all right. No need to get all tetchy on me."

The Storekeeper let a brief, thin smile show through. "Not at all, sir. Not at all."

There was an uncomfortable silence, broken only by the creaking of Mrs. Mayfield's rocker. She clutched more tightly at the plastic purse in her lap, gave an amiable nod.

"I find it very peaceful here," she said.

"No argument there, lady," said Wayne. "Quiet as a grave."

Storekeeper slid back on his bench, again rested an arm on the back. He gave a slight smirk. "Except for all that foot traffic?"

"Okay. Yeah. 'cept for that."

Mrs. Mayfield let out a pleasant sigh. "It feels like it's gonna be a warm one, though. Don't you think?"

"Exactly so, Mrs. Mayfield," said the Storekeeper.

Will Dawson stood at the far edge of the dusty parking lot, just off the asphalt of the highway. He watched the activity on the general store porch across the lot.

Will was in his thirties. He looked to be quite comfortable on his own. He had a tall walking staff in hand, wore black jeans and a light windbreaker, the style rather less contemporary than the clothing of Wayne Saunders and the Harris couple.

He glanced once up the highway to the distant horizon, then looked back at the store and the group gathered in the shade of the porch. He started across the gravel lot.

Wayne kept his attention on the figure walking slowly across the lot towards them, grumbled in the general direction of the Storekeeper.

"More foot traffic, Storekeeper. Cancel that "quiet as a grave".

"That would be Will Dawson," said the Storekeeper.

Will approached the porch, planted a foot on the first step. "Hello, folks."

"Good morning to you, Will," said the Storekeeper.

"Morning," Will said warily. "Do I know you?"

"I wouldn't think so."

"Then—"

"Mrs. Mayfield, Mr. Saunders, may I present William Dawson. An anthropologist, if I'm not mistaken. Did I get that right?"

"You seem to be *not mistaken* about a number of things, Storekeeper."

"It comes with the job, my friend."

"Uh, huh. Which would be?"

Storekeeper smiled warmly and indicated their surroundings. "Minding the store, of course."

Mrs. Mayfield ceased her rocking, leaned forward, back straight, and entered the conversation.

"Good morning to you, Mr. Dawson," she said calmly.

Will gave a nod of the head. "Mornin', ma'am. Please, call me Will."

Mrs. Mayfield shifted back again, and again returned to her slow, steady rocking, clutching her purse.

Obligations met.

Will acknowledged Wayne. "Mr. Saunders."

"*Will...* ya' been walking long?"

Will thought on that. He looked curiously in the direction he had traveled from, then turned back to Wayne.

"Some," he said. "I suppose."

There was another moment of uncomfortable silence. The Storekeeper was about to say something when he stopped himself. He hesitated.

He waited... one more moment.

There came the haunting sound of a train whistle in the distance. It faded, drifted... the Storekeeper smiled contentedly.

"It must be eight o'clock," he said.

Will doubted that. He knew for a fact that it was later than that. He reached into his pocket, pulled out an old pocket watch and looked at the time.

"It's nine thirty," he stated flatly.

"I'm pretty sure it's eight," said the Storekeeper.

Will held up his watch for all to see. "Never more'n a minute off, Storekeeper." He returned his watch to his pocket.

Issue settled.

Storekeeper shook his head. "Nonetheless, Will. It is eight o'clock. Here."

Will had no idea how to respond to that.

Wayne, meanwhile, lifted his hands in exasperation, quickly dropped them back to his side. "Oh, geez. What is that supposed to mean?"

"Just what I said, Wayne. No more, no less."

Wayne sighed loudly and turned to Will.

"He always talks like that."

"Do I?" asked the Storekeeper.

"Yes. You do."

As their exchange faded, Will took several steps to the left, used the head of his staff to indicate the 'To Trains' sign that hung on wall near the corner of the building.

"You have a train station back there, Storekeeper?"

"Of a sort. Up to now, the train has never had cause to stop."

"And it does now?" asked Will.

Storekeeper appeared to get a warm feeling all over...

"Soon enough, my friend. It will soon enough."

The little world of the general store again grew quiet. There wasn't even a breeze. No one spoke. For the moment no one moved.

Mrs. Mayfield had stopped her rocking. She leaned forward now and slowly stood up. With that, Storekeeper stood and walked to the screen door. He held it open for her. She entered the store, still clutching at her purse.

Storekeeper looked to Wayne, who decided to follow Mrs. Mayfield inside.

Storekeeper let the screen door close and returned to his bench. He indicated the empty rocking chair. Will Dawson climbed the steps up onto the porch. He sat in the chair, held the staff casually in front of him.

The two silently enjoyed the quiet of the warming morning.

Chapter Two

The screen door opened with a screech and Storekeeper stepped outside. He had gone inside a few minutes earlier to see to his visitors, returned to his bench now and sat down.

"A dear, lovely lady, Mrs. Mayfield," he said.

Will Dawson was in the rocking chair. He shifted in the chair, leaned his staff against the wall and turned forward.

"Yessir." He leaned forward, rested his elbows on his knees.

"Storekeeper, I get the feeling that something just isn't right. And furthermore, I'm pretty sure that whatever it is that's going on, you are at the heart of it."

"All seems right enough to me, Will."

"See, now that's something right there," said Will, straightening again and looking over at Storekeeper. "You knew my name when I got here. You know me. How is that?"

"Why wouldn't I know you?"

"Because we've never met; because I've never seen you before."

"What does that have to do with it?"

"That." Will was increasingly frustrated. "What you just said. Ya' see, it makes sense. But it shouldn't make sense. None of this should make sense. None at all."

Will looked outward again, across the gravel parking lot, across the highway. It was all open fields and dry brush.

"There's stuff I should know," he said. "I know there's stuff I should know. There are... holes... in my mind. Empty places. I feel it. I'm not all here. I'm not... complete."

"Will Dawson, you are the most complete person here."

Will thought about that. He stood and stepped to edge of the porch. The world beyond the porch was still, was empty.

"Here," he sighed. "Yes sir, just where is that? Where is... here?"

"Here is the center of the universe, my friend."

Will turned his head and looked back at the Storekeeper.

"Your store. The center of the universe. Where it is always eight o'clock in the morning."

"Exactly so."

Will looked away again, frowned as he slowly shook his head in frustration.

"Sorry... I can't put my finger on it, but somehow that's wrong. Or, it should be wrong. That is wrong, where we are is wrong, and all of us... we are all so very wrong."

Storekeeper's cool, calm and collected sense of wellbeing remained strong. He stood up and stepped up beside Will.

"Do not be overly concerned, Mr. Dawson. All is well. Of all that you may doubt the world around you, I believe you know that you can trust me." He gave Will a gentle smile. "Is that not so?"

Will spoke without looking at his host. "What I believe is that you are smack-dab in the middle of what's going on. Trust you? Let us say that I have some concern when it comes to your motives. I should probably fear you. We all should fear you."

"And yet you do not fear me."

"No," Will mumbled softly. "I don't."

"That is good. As for my motives," Storekeeper's eyes grew just a little bit brighter. "They are brimming over with good intentions."

"Uh, huh. We'll see." Something in the distance caught Will's eye. He saw then a woman standing at the far edge of the lot. "More company. Why am I not surprised?"

"And so," said the Storekeeper, sounding quite satisfied. "We are all here."

Edie Paulsen started across the lot toward them. She was about thirty years old, but looked worn, as if life had beaten her down. Her clothes had been nice at one time, but now appeared as worn out as their owner.

"Excuse me," she said as she drew near. "I think I'm lost."

"Hello, Edie," said the Storekeeper comfortingly. "No need to worry. You are exactly where you need to be."

Edi looked at the store, then at Will, then back at the Storekeeper.

"I am?"

"You certainly are, my dear."

Edie again looked slowly over at Will. Will gave her a friendly nod.

"Will Dawson. And I am as confused as you are."

"I seriously doubt that."

"Will Dawson, this is Edie Paulsen," said Storekeeper. "Edie, meet Will Dawson."

"Hey," said Edie unenthusiastically.

"Nice to meet you," said Will.

"If you say so." Edie looked around her, behind her, back again to the two gentlemen on the porch. She took a step to one side, then another. She looked up at the sign that read 'To Trains'.

She looked pointedly then at the Storekeeper.

"Are we dead?"

This got Will's attention. He looked sharply at Storekeeper, quite interested to hear the Storekeeper's response.

The Storekeeper, for his part, was genuinely surprised at such a question.

"Oh, my no," he stated. "Absolutely not. What would make you think such a thing?"

"I don't know how I got here. I don't know where *here* is. And I don't know where I was before I was here."

"Yeah..." said Will. "Neither do I."

For the first time that morning, Storekeeper looked flustered. "Now you two stop all this foolishness. You are most definitely not dead. This isn't heaven. Or hell. Or anything of the sort."

"The center of the universe?" Will asked slyly.

"Exactly so. Yes. Exactly so." Storekeeper felt once again on familiar ground. "Welcome. Welcome to the center of the universe."

Edie pointed to the 'To Trains' sign.

"With train service."

"For you, my dear? Most certainly. Train service."

"For me," Edie said coolly. "Train service."

"Exactly so."

"To where?"

Will wanted the answer to that as well. "Yeah, Storekeeper. Just where does this eight o'clock train go?"

"Where does it go?" Storekeeper stumbled a moment in his thoughts. He grew introspective. When he spoke again, it was as if to himself. "It goes wherever we want it to go, wherever we need it to go. Wherever we take it, that is where it will take us. It goes to grand worlds, fantastical lands; to wondrous sights and sounds and dreams."

Will looked accusingly at Storekeeper.

"You don't know. Do you? It's the one thing –the only thing— that you don't know."

Storekeeper shrugged. "No one knows where the train goes. How can we? We haven't gone there before. So we can't know. Not until we get there."

"Am I going?" asked Edie. "On the train?"

"I would say that's a safe bet, Edie," the Storekeeper said confidently. "I can't say with absolute certainty, but it is a fairly safe bet." He looked to Will. "And I'm figuring you, as well. Most likely, most likely."

Storekeeper moved over to the screen door, opened it to the accompanying sound of screeching hinges.

"How about we go inside? Maybe have bite to eat? Sandwiches?"

"Sure. Why not," said Will. He held a hand down to Edie. "Miss Paulsen?"

Edie took the offered hand and took the steps up to the porch.

"Why not?" she asked. "I can't say as I remember when I ate last."

Will allowed Edie to go inside first. She passed by the Storekeeper, who gave her a welcoming nod.

Once alone on the porch, Storekeeper took a moment to look around. He smiled pleasantly, gave another slow, easy nod, then followed Will and Edie inside.

Chapter Three

Storekeeper stood behind a small lunch counter that ran along one wall, the sign behind him reading 'Sandwiches'. His arms rested on the counter-top, his focus on the others in his store.

There was a checkout counter with cash register near the screen door that led outside. Out on the floor were two small tables, each with three chairs. Beyond the tables was a single row of store shelves six-feet long containing boxed and canned goods.

On the wall beside a hallway leading to the back of the store was what appeared to be the very same 'To Trains' sign that had been posted outside.

Wayne Saunders sat on one of the stools at the lunch counter. He faced away from the Storekeeper, his elbows on the counter behind him.

Mrs. Mayfield sat at one of the two tables, her ever-present purse in her lap. Peter and Helen sat at the table with her.

Will Dawson, Molly Chandler and Edie Paulsen sat at the other table.

Everyone had either a soda pop or a cup of coffee near to hand. A few had what remained of their sandwiches.

Wayne looked keenly at Edie.

"Say, Edie... it is Edie, right? I know you. Don't I?"

Edie lifted her pop bottle to her lips and took a drink. She set the bottle back onto the table.

"I don't think so."

"Sure I do. Yeah, I'm just about positive. I have definitely seen you somewhere." He thought on that a moment, and then another moment. "Chicago. Yeah. You been to Chicago?"

Edie glanced up at Wayne for the first time, then looked casually over at Will and Molly, then down at her soda.

"Sorry. I don't think I've heard of the place."

"Yeah, right," chuckled Wayne.

Molly, sitting at the table beside Edie, furrowed her brow. "Chicago... it's back east, right?"

"What? No. You guys are messin' with me, right? Chicago... Windy City? Chi-Town? Heart of America?" Wayne looked from one face to another throughout the room. "The Big Onion?"

Blank stares looked back at him. He quoted from the song then, almost but not quite singing:

"My Kind of Town, Chicago Is?"

More blank stares.

"Of course, Wayne," said Storekeeper. "Chicago."

Mrs. Mayfield smiled sympathetically. "Yes, Mr. Saunders. Chicago. A wonderful city."

"Right," Wayne droned.

Will appeared to be mulling it over.

"Yes," he said hesitantly. "Al Capone. A gangster."

"Really?" asked Molly.

"I think so."

Wayne grew more flustered by the moment. "What is the matter with you people?"

"Well, it has been quite the long day, Mr. Saunders," said Mrs. Mayfield.

Will couldn't help himself. "Mrs. Mayfield, haven't you heard? It's only eight o'clock in the AM."

"Yes, of course." Mrs. Mayfield sounded uncertain. "That's right. I'm so sorry. My mistake."

"Now you're getting' it," said Storekeeper.

"Did I miss something?" asked Peter.

"Probably," Will said flatly. "I know I have."

Wayne shook his head doggedly as he turned about on the stool and leaned forward onto the lunch counter, facing the Storekeeper.

"I give up."

Storekeeper remained ever upbeat. "Don't be so downhearted, Wayne. It's not so bad. Trust me."

"Why?"

"Oh, Mr. Saunders, you are the Gloomy Gus, aren't you?" He looked past Wayne to those sitting at the two tables. "Did everyone get their fill?"

Mrs. Mayfield held up the last small piece of her sandwich.

"Why, yes. Thank you, sir," she said. "Thank you very much. I hadn't realized how famished I was."

"My pleasure, Mrs. Mayfield."

Mrs. Mayfield set the bit of sandwich down onto the open paper napkin that was spread on the table in front of her. She brushed her hands together to wipe away any remaining crumbs, looked across the table at Peter and Helen Harris.

"It was quite tasty. Don't you think?"

"Yes it was," said Helen. "It was very good."

"Yes, very good," Peter said absently. He looked curiously at the elderly woman. How had she ended up out here in the middle of nowhere? "Mrs. Mayfield, have you been on the road long? Traveling, I mean?"

Mrs. Mayfield put on a straight, slight smile, empty, with nothing behind it. Her words were mechanical, the tone oft-repeated, the statement verbatim what she had said earlier.

"Cecilia asked if I might stay with her for a spell. She's all alone, now that her husband Walter passed away."

"I see," said Peter. "That's where you're headed, then? To Cecilia's?"

"Yes. Cecilia. My sister. She asked if I might stay with her for a spell."

"Right..." said Peter. This was getting awkward. Still, he pushed on. "Where does your sister live?"

"Cecilia? My sister?" Mrs. Mayfield nervously straightened and re-straightened the napkin spread out in front of her. "I... um..."

She delicately pushed aside the napkin and the remaining bit of sandwich. She brought her black, plastic purse up from her lap, placed it meticulously on the table in front of her. She clutched at it protectively.

"Oh, dear. Isn't this something?" There was a hint of fear in her voice. "I'm afraid it's gone completely out of my head for the moment. Flew away. Just like that. I am so sorry."

"That's all right, Mrs. Mayfield," said Helen. "It's not important. Really."

"Oh dear, oh dear."

Helen's tone grew light, conversational. "So, where are you from, then?"

"The south," said Mrs. Mayfield, quick and certain. "I'm from the south."

"Is that right?" Helen's smile was slightly forced. "The south, you say?"

"That's right." She lifted her purse from the table and placed it back down onto her lap. "Yes. I'm from the south."

"That's nice. That's... that's really, really nice." Helen looked nervously to Peter. "Isn't that nice, Peter?"

"Yeah, sure," said Peter. "Nice."

Mrs. Mayfield nodded curtly and gave Peter and Helen a wry wink. A final sharp nod and then...

The conversation was concluded.

Mrs. Mayfield was done.

Peter rested a comforting hand on Helen's arm.

"How about we take a breath of air?"

"Yes. I think that would be... just splendid." Helen looked to Mrs. Mayfield. "Would you excuse us, Mrs. Mayfield?"

Mrs. Mayfield gave a dismissive nod. Peter and Helen took that as a yes. As they started toward the door, Wayne spun slowly around on his stool.

"I have a short journey of my own to take." He slipped off the stool and headed toward the back of the store, past the 'restrooms' sign and into the hallway.

Will Dawson stood up from the table then, picked up his cup and walked casually to the lunch counter. He set the cup down and slid it toward Storekeeper.

"Another again, barkeep, and don't be stingy with the caffeine."

"As you will, kind sir."

The Storekeeper reached below the counter, brought up a coffee carafe and refilled Will's cup.

There came then the haunting sound of a distant train whistle.

"Eight o'clock, then?" asked Will.

"Exactly so."

"And... it's always eight o'clock."

"Right."

Will reached down for his cup. "And, you don't find anything odd about that..."

"Not at all," said Storekeeper. "It's eight o'clock. Therefore, it is eight o'clock."

Will gave a slight salute with his coffee cup as he turned back to return to his table.

"An odd universe you have here, Storekeeper."

"I take that as a compliment, Mr. Dawson."

"That... is not a surprise."

Chapter Four

Will sipped at his coffee, leaned back in chair and studied the 'To Trains' sign that hung on the wall beside the hallway. It looked exactly the same as the sign outside.

He spoke to Storekeeper, still standing behind the lunch counter.

"You say there's a train station behind your store... it's through there?"

"It's not far. Quite a lovely place."

"I don't recall seeing it."

"No need to see it just yet. But soon. We'll head over there soon."

This was the first Molly had heard of this.

"We're taking a train?" she asked, not to anyone in particular.

Edie held her bottle of pop up before her.

"So the man says." She took a drink, set the bottle back on the table. Did you have plans to take a train ride today, Molly?"

"I, uh—"

"I didn't think so. I know I didn't. Not that I can remember. But then, I really don't remember much of anything."

"I, uh... train?" Molly looked anxious. "I don't have any money." She repeated to the Storekeeper. "I don't have any money."

"Not to worry, sweetheart," said the Storekeeper. "Train fare is on the house."

"Thank you. That's very nice of you." Apprehensively then, "Where are we going?"

Will snickered lightly at that, recalling the answer that he got when he had asked that same question earlier.

"Yes, Storekeeper," he said. "Please, do tell the young lady where we are going."

Storekeeper smiled warmly, not offended in the slightest at Will's light jab.

"We'll know when we get there, Molly." Storekeeper gave a sharp nod. "We will surely know when we get there."

Mrs. Mayfield perked up, clutching at her purse.

"I was on a train once. With my Herbert." She wore a nostalgic smile. "Oh, so many years ago. We took the train to... oh, dear. I'm not sure now just where. It was a pleasant trip. Yes. Though it was an awfully hot day. I do remember that. And the bologna sandwiches we brought with us? They were very warm. You know how bologna sandwiches can get."

She retreated back into her thoughts then, and the others grew politely silent. The quiet was broken only when Peter and Helen came back through the screen door. Peter had his cell phone in hand. He spoke to those in the room, to no one in particular, as he and Helen continued to their table with Mrs. Mayfield.

"No signal," said Peter. "I mean, nothing at all."

"Oh, no, no, no, Peter," said Storekeeper. "You won't be able to use that here. Oh, my no."

Molly looked curiously at the strange object in Peter's hand as Peter and Helen settled in at the other table.

"What is that?" she asked.

"My phone," Peter said absently.

"Your what?"

"Phone." Peter held it up. "You know... *phone*?"

"Really? Your own phone?"

"Uh, yeah..."

"Can I see it? Do ya' mind?"

"Yeah, sure." Peter leaned over and handed Molly his phone. "Just a lousy phone. Nothing fancy."

Molly admired the phone without fully comprehending it. Peter had turned back to his table.

"And apparently totally useless here, in the center of the universe." He looked over at the Storekeeper. "Do you have a landline I can use?"

"I'm sorry, Peter. There really isn't much use for one here."

"Don't know about that. I could use one 'bout now."

Storekeeper looked sympathetically over at Peter. "And just who would you call, my friend?"

"Well, I was going to call... uh—" Peter was suddenly uncertain, confused. "I, uh... well, I was..."

He looked pleading over at Helen. "Help me out here, Helen. Who was I going to call?"

"I don't know," said Helen. "I don't remember."

Peter looked lost. "A minute ago I was... now for the life of me, I can't remember."

Molly handed the phone back to Peter.

"How does it work?" she asked.

Peter stuffed the phone back into his pocket. "Didn't you hear? It doesn't."

"What doesn't?" Wayne came in from the hallway, walked across to the lunch counter.

"His own personal phone," said Molly.

At that, Wayne lost interest real fast. "Yeah. Ain't that just a real shocker."

"Probably cuz it's not connected up to anything."

Wayne chuckled lightly as he slid onto the stool.

"No doubt." He looked across the counter to the Storekeeper. "So, what's the plan, Stan?"

"The plan?" Storekeeper held his head back and thought on that. "Well, such as there is a plan, I suppose it would be simply that we will all soon walk over to the station in anticipation of the train's arrival."

"Good plan, good plan." Wayne parsed the Storekeeper's statement in his mind, curled his brow and frowned. "Somebody going on a trip?"

"We all are," said Molly.

"Is that so," said Wayne, looking over his shoulder at Molly.

"We can only hope," said the Storekeeper.

Edie shifted in her chair and folded her arms on the table. "What's that supposed to mean?" she asked. "Are we going to the train station or not?"

"Oh, my yes, Edie," said the Storekeeper. "We're all going to the station. That is why you are here. That is why you have all come to my store, to... the center of the universe."

"If that's so," said Edie, "Then what do you mean, we can only hope?"

"Excuse me?"

"You said a moment ago; we can only hope that we are all going."

Storekeeper continued his increasingly annoying knowing manner as he provided his easy yet thoughtful response.

"Ah. Yes. We draw nearer that moment in the great narrative when the determination will be made; the epochal decision that awaits each one of us. Each one of you." He paused, held a hand absently before him. "We shall all go the train station. We shall all be there when the train arrives at the gate. Of that, I am certain. I have no doubt. But as to who is to board that train? That I cannot with certainty say."

"Why not?" asked Molly.

"Because I don't know, dear girl. The decision has not yet been made."

Wayne looked sharply across the counter at their host. "What the heck are you talkin' about, Storekeeper?"

Storekeeper took a long, thoughtful pause, and when he spoke again, it was with considerable patience.

"In the story that has been your life, you have always known all that you needed to know in order to take each next step. Have you not?"

"Well, I—"

"Oh, you may have had doubts, concerns, questions, but in the end, you were able to take that step; at each and every critical moment."

"I suppose," Wayne said softly, rather uncertainly.

Storekeeper grew more somber. His tone was suddenly more serious than it had ever been.

"That is the way of it, Mr. Saunders. It always has been. For you..." He spoke then to the entire group gathered in his general store. "For all of you. You are truly unique. Truly. And so... the next step will come when it will come. For each of us. For each of you. It most certainly will."

He lifted his gaze upward. A few seconds later, there came again the haunting sound of the train whistle in the distance.

The Storekeeper waited for the train to pass, the sound to fade.

"Let us make our way to the station, my friends," he said.

Wayne turned about and slid off the lunch counter stool. "Heck, might as well. Curiouser and curiouser we go." He approached the tables, stopped behind Edie and held her chair as she slid back. "Miss Paulsen."

"Thank you," she said. She and Wayne continued to the hallway and were gone.

Storekeeper stepped around the lunch counter and approached the tables. "Folks?"

Will looked across the table.

"Molly? Shall we?" They stood and followed Wayne and Edie into the hallway.

Storekeeper stood before the other table. Mrs. Mayfield appeared quite calm, but Peter and Helen looked a bit anxious.

"How about you folks?" he asked.

"The train?" asked Helen. "Do you really think this is necessary?"

"Absolutely, Helen. It is, after all, the reason you are here."

"It is?" asked Peter. He sounded almost accusatory. "How can you know that? I mean, how can you know for sure that's why we're here?"

"There can be no other reason. You are here, you have come here, you will go now to the station, because you are... <u>you</u>. Each of you... you are... *you*."

Helen looked uneasily across at Peter. He reached out and took her hand.

"Helen," he stated, attempting calm. "We might as well."

Helen struggled to come to terms with it. She didn't even know why she was apprehensive, but she was. The train station meant something... important. Their lives would change there, and she didn't know that she was ready for what that change might be.

She finally took a long, shaky breath.

"All right." She stood, slowly. Peter stood with her and led her to the hallway.

"Good. Very good," said the Storekeeper. He focused his attention now on Mrs. Mayfield. He pulled one of the now-empty chairs to him and sat facing her.

"Mrs. Mayfield? How are you doing?"

"I'm doing just fine, sir," she said. "How about yourself?"

"I couldn't be better; not an ounce better. Are you ready to join the others?"

"Oh, I don't know. I was thinking I might just stay here. I mean, after all, I haven't even finished my coffee and sandwich."

"Dear Mrs. Mayfield." He gave his most compassionate smile. "I couldn't let you do that."

"Oh, you go on ahead, son. I'll be fine." She tried an amusing smile. "I promise not to steal anything."

"Mrs. Mayfield..."

Mrs. Mayfield looked away from Storekeeper. Her expression turned knowing, as did her tone.

"I don't imagine it will take long. When the time comes. Do you?"

"No," Storekeeper said softly. "No, I'm sure it won't."

"Well then, I'll just sit right here until it's over."

"No, ma'am. I can't let you do that." Storekeeper manner turned more determined. "Your presence is required at the train station."

Mrs. Mayfield looked directly at Storekeeper.

"Sir?"

"You will be on that train when it leaves."

"D'you really think so?"

"I most certainly do." He stood then, held out a hand for Mrs. Mayfield.

She looked up into Storekeeper's kind face. She smiled warmly and took the offered hand.

"Well, if we must."

"Yes, ma'am."

Chapter Five

The Storekeeper stood behind the ticket window. He now wore a black suit coat and a cap on his head. A sign beside the ticket window read 'Southbound 8:00 AM'.

A long, worn wooden passenger waiting bench near the center of the room faced the ticket window. Mrs. Mayfield sat at one end of the bench, her purse in her lap. Edie and Molly sat together at the other end.

A sign over an arched opening read 'Gate 1'. Hanging on the wall beside the gate was the familiar 'To Trains' sign.

Peter and Helen were standing on the platform beyond the gate, their backs to the gate. They appeared to be watching for the train.

Will came through the gate and into the station. He stepped up to the ticket window and rested an elbow on the counter. He looked from the group on the bench to the Storekeeper and back.

"Wayne is out there putting pennies on the track," he said.

Molly had never put pennies on tracks before, but she had heard of it. The train flattens the pennies as it rolls over them.

"How is he going to collect them if he's going with us?"

"That's what I asked him," said Will. He shrugged. "He said he'd have time."

Edie looked to the Storekeeper with the hint of a smirk.

"What do you say to that, Storekeeper? Will he have enough time? Maybe all the time in the world?"

"If you mean is he going to be on the train when it leaves, I really couldn't say, Edie. Not for certain. Not just yet."

"Not just yet? Well that's downright intriguing. You don't know yet, but you will? Are you saying that you _will_ know who is going and who isn't?"

Storekeeper responded with a tip of his hat.

"I wear the hat of ticket agent now, Miss Paulsen. The ticket agent usually knows who's getting on the train."

"But... shouldn't we all go?" asked Molly, increasingly anxious. "Shouldn't we all get on the train?"

Edie shifted about on the bench, continued to look at Storekeeper as she answered Molly's question for him.

"The decision is out of our hands," she said, then spoke directly to Storekeeper. "Isn't that right, Storekeeper?"

"Exactly so."

"But it's not in <u>your</u> hands, either. Is it?"

"No, ma'am. It certainly is not."

"And you don't know where the train is going," said Edie, an observation, not a question.

"I expect we won't know that until it gets there."

"Yes. So you said."

"Yes, ma'am. That I did."

Molly scooted forward, stood slowly. "I don't want to be left behind."

Edie reached out and placed a hand gently on Molly's arm.

"It's all right, sweetie. I'm sure you'll be going."

"You don't know that." Molly looked from Edie back to the Storekeeper. "You don't know that."

"No," stated Storekeeper. "I don't."

"Don't you worry, dear," said Mrs. Mayfield. "Comes to that, I'll stay here with you."

Storekeeper spoke tolerantly. "That's very thoughtful of you Mrs. Mayfield. But you know very well that's not how it works."

This comment by Storekeeper made just about everyone mighty curious. Will was the one who spoke up.

"Mrs. Mayfield?" he asked. "You know how this works?"

Mrs. Mayfield hesitated, thought on what the answer might be.

"Quite odd, really," she said at last. "I think so. Not that I could put any of it into words, mind you, but there's things spinnin' round in my head. Bits o' knowledge and curiosities; I've no idea how any of it got there. But it's all there just the same." She frowned and sighed. "I just can't seem to wrap my head 'round any of it. Seems, more I focus, the more it slips away."

"I'm really sorry to hear that," said Will. He turned sharply to Storekeeper. "I'll bet you could, though, couldn't you? Wrap your head around it? You got your head wrapped around it?"

"What I need to know comes to me when I need to know it, Will. I cannot reach out for it. It must come to me."

Mrs. Mayfield spoke as if from a daydream, soft and distant.

"It's like shadows in a mist." She glanced up to the others. "If you try to make out the shapes, they fade to gray."

Her words hung there in empty space for several long seconds. The Storekeeper finally broke the silence.

"Just so, Mrs. Mayfield. Exactly so."

Another several moments of silence. Molly took a stumbling step backward. "I'm gonna go outside." She turned and started toward the gate.

Edie stood and followed after her.

"I'll go with you Molly. I seem to recall that I enjoy standing at the tracks, watching for the train." She grumbled then as she went through the gate. "Not that I remember actually seeing tracks... or a train..."

Once beyond the gate, Edie turned left and continued after Molly. Peter and Helen, still standing near the tracks, turned at the movement and seeing them, followed them.

Will, still at the counter, turned to Storekeeper, standing on the other side of the counter.

"Well, Storekeeper... *Mr. Ticket Agent.* You appear to be frightening off the clientele."

"Not to worry, Will. All shall be right enough before the train gets here." He glanced to his right. He saw something on the counter that wasn't there before. "Ah! Here we go. So it begins in earnest."

He picked up the brochure-sized piece of paper. It was a train ticket. He took an envelope sleeve from a stack on the counter and slipped the ticket into the sleeve.

"Waddya have there, Storekeeper?" asked Will.

Storekeeper ignored the question. He stepped from behind the counter and approached Mrs. Mayfield. He took up position directly in front of the woman, gave a half-bow.

"Madam, I have your ticket."

"Oh, my. Do you really?"

"Yes, ma'am." He handed her the ticket. "And here you are."

"Oh, dear." She clutched at the ticket. "Oh dear, oh dear. Thank you."

"Not at all. You enjoy your journey."

Will waited impatiently as Storekeeper returned to his place behind the counter.

"Is that how this is going to go?" he asked. "We'll find out who's taking the train one at a time, whenever you feel like handing out a ticket?"

"I will distribute the tickets as they come to me."

"Come to you? You—"

"As they come to me," Storekeeper stated calmly.

"You tryin' to tell me you don't have the tickets back there waiting to be handed out?"

"As tickets are made available, I will present them to those named on the ticket."

Will gave the Storekeeper a long, thoughtful study.

"You are the odd one, Storekeeper."

"Yes, I suppose that is so." Storekeeper grinned. "But then, as you have already observed, I live in an odd universe."

At that moment, Wayne appeared in the gate portal and came into the station.

"You most certainly do," he said. He approached the counter, leaned an elbow on the countertop. "So, I've been talkin' with that kid. What's her name? Molly? Ya' know she's never seen a television? She's never even heard of 'em."

"That's kinda odd," said Will. "I know a lot a' motel rooms got 'em nowadays. You'd a thought she would a—"

"What?" Wayne cut him off. "That's not the..."

Wayne can't even finish the thought. *What the heck's going on here?*

Storekeeper smiled patiently. "It's not really all that surprising, Wayne. We each walk through our own individual worlds, live our lives through individual experiences."

"You can paint it with all the philosophizing you want, Storekeeper. She should know from televisions. And now I think on it, she looked at that couple's cell phone like it was magic."

This brought to the forefront Will's own questions, though for slightly different reasons. He started to say something, but in the end waved the thoughts away.

Wayne noticed the odd expression on Will's face.

"Yeah?" he urged.

"Nevermind."

"Sure," said Wayne. He looked carefully at Will. He thought about the group gathered here. Molly, Will, Edie... "Say... buddy. I'm getting an idea here."

"And?"

"Tell me, what year is it?"

"Year?"

"Simple. What year is it?"

"I, uh..."

"You tellin' me you don't know what year it is?" Wayne looked over at the Storekeeper. This went even deeper than he first thought. "Okay, so you tell me how he doesn't know what year it is."

"Will doesn't know what year it is because the year has never been an issue for him."

"What?" Wayne sounded incredulous.

The look in Will's eyes could have been fear.

"Storekeeper... I told you. I told you..." Will's words were soft, lost. "I have... empty places... in my mind. I should know what year it is. I told you. There's stuff I should know that I don't know."

"My friend," said the Storekeeper. "In all the story that has been your life, what importance the year? Has the subject ever come up? It has not. What matter does it have now?"

Will slowly shook his head. "No... don't start twisting this around like it doesn't matter. It should have come up. It should have." He leaned against the counter. "It should have come up. Shouldn't it? At some point, some time? Sometime in my life?"

"Of course it should have!" said Wayne. "What kinda' crazy talk is this?" He worked his way over to the long bench and plopped himself down. He rested his arms on the back of the bench.

"Okay. Let's think this through. We gotta be on drugs or something." He pointed at the Storekeeper. "That guy is messing with our minds. It's some kind of experiment."

"Mr. Saunders, I—"

"So, are you a scientist or a doctor or something?"

"No. No, I'm just a storekeeper." He indicated their current surroundings. "And, on occasion, a ticket agent, it would seem."

The Storekeeper glanced to his right a second time. There was another ticket on the counter. He reached out and picked it up.

"Here we go." He slipped the ticket into a sleeve, held it out to Will. "Mr. Dawson. Your ticket, sir."

Will took the ticket, looked at it, only half comprehending.

Mrs. Mayfield smiled openly. "Well, isn't that nice."

Will stared numbly at the ticket. "I'm going then."

"Yes, sir," said Storekeeper. "It looks that way."

"D'you ever doubt it?" smirked Wayne.

"Yes, actually."

"I didn't," said Wayne. "You always struck me as one of the surviving characters." He rested his elbows on his knees. "The way I'm seein' it, some of us are gonna survive this thing, some of aren't. You are one of the survivors. I saw that right from the start."

"I don't understand."

Storekeeper spoke evenly. "Mr. Saunders, a lot of protagonists fail to live through their own stories."

"That may be, but we're all protagonists here, aren't we?"

The Storekeeper was taken aback at Wayne's observation. This young man had seen something.

"That is very perceptive, Mr. Saunders. I believe you are... almost... correct."

"Almost, huh?"

"I believe so."

"Yeah, well, we may not all be the hero, but we each come from our own story."

"Isn't that always the case, Wayne?"

Wayne shook his head tiredly, again leaned back and placed his arms on the back of the bench.

"No, Storekeeper. You're not gonna get by using slippery words this time. I'm startin' to get a handle on this thing, and you know it."

Mrs. Mayfield shifted nervously. The conversation was making her uncomfortable.

"I believe I'll step outside for a bit."

"Of course, Mrs. Mayfield," said Storekeeper.

"Let me, ma'am." Will stepped forward and assisted Mrs. Mayfield to her feet.

"Very kind of you, Will." She slipped an arm through Will's offered elbow and the two stepped to the gate and out onto the platform just as Helen and Peter entered the station.

The Storekeeper placed two tickets into sleeves. "Excellent timing, you two," he said.

"Excuse me?" asked Peter.

Storekeeper stepped around the counter, and with some flair handed them their tickets. Peter and Helen sat down on the bench and Peter patted Helen's hand.

Wayne looked down the bench to them. They looked as bewildered as ever.

"Well, well. Congratulations."

They nodded uncertainly, Peter mumbling an awkward *thank you.*

Wayne returned his attention to the Storekeeper. "We're coming down to it, eh?"

Storekeeper appeared even more thoughtful than usual. He studied Wayne with a curious gaze, held it for an uncomfortable moment.

"It would seem so," he said quietly.

Wayne found Storekeeper's unexpected response really, really unsettling.

"Right," he finally managed.

Chapter Six

Edie came in from the platform. "Sweet kid, that Molly. If she isn't on that train..."

Storekeeper held up a hand and frowned.

"As I said, Miss Paulsen. I—"

"Yes, yes, I know what you said."

The Storekeeper's smile returned then. He began putting together another packet.

"Ah. Miss Paulsen, I have your ticket."

Edie moved awkwardly to the counter. She stared down at the ticket.

"If Molly isn't—"

"I am sorry," said Storekeeper. "I can't say."

Edie used a finger to push the ticket about on the counter.

"It is a relief, I suppose. Though for the life of me, I couldn't tell you why."

"I would think it obvious," said Wayne, still sitting on the bench. "Because it is for the life of you."

Edie took the ticket and turned about, gave Wayne a stern glare.

"What would make you say such a thing?"

"Just what do you think is going to happen to anyone left behind? Might this poor lost soul simply walk out of here? To where?"

"I couldn't say."

"It had to cross your mind. You're the one that mentioned the kid." He shifted his gaze from Edie to the Storekeeper, back again to Edie. "Let's make it a bit more personal yet. If you hadn't been given a ticket, where would you go once the train pulled out of the station, leaving you standing out there on the platform waving bye-bye?"

"I don't know," she managed.

"No, of course you don't."

"How can I? How can any of us?"

Wayne smiled. "My point."

Edie was done with this. She turned away from Wayne, moved around behind the bench.

"Excuse me," she said, speaking in the general direction of the Storekeeper as she looked about the station. "Where is the, uh..."

Storekeeper pointed to a narrow hallway. "Right through there, Miss Paulsen."

She left quickly then, leaving only Storekeeper and Wayne in the station.

"There was no need to upset Miss Paulsen," said Storekeeper. "She has her ticket, after all."

"Yes. And that leaves just me and the girl now, doesn't it? How many you figure are going to be stayin' on here after the train leaves the station, Storekeeper?"

"I have no way of knowing."

"Is that right?"

"Exactly so."

Wayne shifted around on the bench, looked back to the narrow hallway Edie had gone into, then the gate leading to the platform, finally back to the Storekeeper standing behind the counter.

His tone and expression lost all humor.

"I'm not going, am I?"

"I really don't know," said Storekeeper. "I had been fairly certain that you were. But now, now I just don't know."

What did he mean by that?

"What made you so sure? Before?"

"I couldn't say, really. I just thought you were... needed."

"And I'm not now," said Wayne. "I'm not... needed."

"I don't know," said Storekeeper. "Something has changed. Something is different. I can feel it."

"Right." Wayne leaned back, dropped his hands into his lap. "Me too."

Something caught Storekeeper's attention. Looking to his right, he saw that another train ticket was sitting on the counter. He picked it up, set about to place it into a sleeve.

"It's Molly's."

"I'm glad," said Wayne. "Good for her."

"I believe so," agreed Storekeeper.

"I wonder what role she will play, once the train arrives at its destination?"

"Odd you should ask, in just that way. I was wondering the very same thing."

Wayne looked curiously at the Storekeeper.

"What about you, Storekeeper?" he asked. "Will you be going? When the train leaves?"

"No, Mr. Saunders. My own role will play itself out here."
Storekeeper admired their surroundings. "My train station. My
general store... my world."

"The center of the universe."

"Its very heart." Another look around the station, then he
stepped from behind the counter and started toward the gate. "I
think I'll give this to Molly. She is no doubt anxious."

Wayne watched Storekeeper walk through the gate and
disappear from view. He stood up then, looked about absently
and then walked over to the counter, looked casually to where the
tickets usually showed up.

Nothing.

"Where'd everybody go?" asked Edie. She was standing near
the hallway.

Wayne wandered back toward the bench.

"Out to wait for the train, I expect." He tried to smile, but it
was difficult. "Growing impatient, I'll wager."

Edie stepped over to the gate, looked out as she folded her
arms. She turned back and looked around the near-empty
station.

"But not you?"

"I have yet to be blessed with a ticket."

Wayne climbed up on the passenger bench, sat on the back
with his feet on the seat. He clasped his hands together.

"Molly will be going," he said. "He's giving her ticket to her
now."

"That's nice," said Edie; *And a relief.* What would she have
done if Molly hadn't been going? "Yours will come, I'm sure."

Wayne didn't really think so, but he nodded in response. He
stared down at his clasped hands.

"You do remind me of someone, you know... but you're not
her."

"I know."

"You are her, but you're not."

Edie moved away from the gate portal, walked over to the
bench and sat down at the far end.

"She was a friend of yours?"

"More of an acquaintance," said Wayne.

"And I'm her, but I'm not her."

"The two of you were written different. You came later, I
think."

"Wow. That's deep." Edie ran Wayne's comment through her
mind a few times. "Very weird, but probably deep."

"That's me. Deep all over." A thin smile came and went. "Now, anyway."

Edie shifted on the bench, turning to look directly at Wayne.

"I do sense the change." A thoughtful pause, then. "The Storekeeper knew me, too."

"The Storekeeper knows everyone who comes to his store."

"But how? We've never met. I'm certain of that." Edie tapped at her temple. "There's a lot missing in here, but I would definitely remember him. He's quite an unforgettable sort."

"True." Wayne slid down from the back of the bench, sat properly. "The Storekeeper knows us because he knows the books we come from."

"Sorry? What?"

Wayne couldn't help but smile at the bewildered expression on Edie's face.

"The woman you reminded me of? She's a dancer. Pretty good one, I guess. She works a club I used to go to when I was living in Chicago."

"Okay... what does that have to do with me? Or with books?"

"She's a character from the book I'm from," said Wayne, quite matter-of-factly. "And you... I'm guessing you're a rework of that same character, only in another book."

"Yeah..." Edie said slowly. "Mr. Saunders, you have totally lost it."

Wayne chose to ignore that, continued unperturbed.

"And Molly... Molly is from a book with no televisions. Will Dawson, he's probably from fifty, sixty years ago; his character has spent a lot of time living in motels while doing whatever it is he does."

"Anthropology," said Edie.

"We're all from different stories, and from different worlds. We know as much as our characters need to know, as much as the writer thought we needed to know." Wayne slid a bit nearer to Edie, looked her in the eye. "The worlds we know are only as complete as our stories needed them to be."

Something about all this was creeping into Edie's thoughts, making her increasingly uncomfortable.

"All right, let's say this is all true. I'm not buying it, you're insane, and probably dangerous, but let's say that everything you're saying is true. So, what are we doing here? How did we miraculously jump out of these mysterious books of yours and show up... *here*?"

"I'm thinking that our writer, our creator I guess you'd call him, is trying to decide which of his characters from earlier books

are going to be in his next one." He leaned close to Edie,
continued in a faux conspiratorial whisper. "I don't think his
books have been all that successful, but he's not ready to give up
on his characters."

"So then... you're saying... whenever he decides on a
character, a train ticket shows up."

Wayne shifted back, leaned back against the bench. "That's
what I'm thinking."

"And the Storekeeper. Is he the writer?"

"I doubt it. No. No, I think..." Wayne thought long and deep.
"He's like... the librarian; a miniature librarian living inside the
writer's head, keeping track of all his stories and characters and
things like that."

"He doesn't know? Wouldn't he know?"

"He's starting to figure it out," said Wayne. "Same as me.
Heck, even ol' Mrs. Mayfield is starting to get it."

Could there be any truth to any of this? No...

"How did you?" asked Edie. "Figure it out, I mean? Where'd
you get all this?"

"Comin' to me in bits and pieces," shrugged Wayne. "More
and more as we get closer."

"Closer to what?"

"Ah. Well. For you? Getting on the train, taking it to the final
destination; taking on your *'role of a lifetime'*." Wayne looked
uneasily away from Edie, down to his tightly clasped hands. "Me?
Oh, I figure I'm done."

"No. No, that's not true." It was an automatic response,
spoken without really thinking what it all meant. The ensuing
silence was powerful. Edie turned away from Wayne, looked
across the station, looked at anything but this person sitting on
the bench beside her.

Was any of this true? Could any of it be true?

"I'm sorry," she said. "I really am."

"Hey, I was in the running for a while." Wayne shrugged one
shoulder. "Who knows? Maybe I can head back to Chicago.
Maybe hook up with that dancer."

Came then the haunting sound of a distant train whistle...

Wayne and Edie both looked upward, outward.

"That'd be for you," said Wayne. "You better go."

"This isn't right," said Edie. "He can't just..."

"Just what? Not write me into the story?"

"He has to. Now that we're..." She struggled with what all this
meant. She was only just beginning to come to terms with it.
"We're <u>here</u> now. We're not just characters in a book. We're not..."

She leaned forward and stood then, looked about the station. It was physical. It was here.

"We're *alive*," she said, almost pleading. "I just went to the bathroom, for Christ's sake."

"I'll be all right." A genuine smile from Wayne. "Really."

There was a final, single train whistle, quite near. Wayne looked to the gate. "It's here," he said. "Go on."

Edie looked anxiously from Wayne to the gate. She turned to the ticket counter, started towards it.

"Maybe your ticket is here. Maybe it came late."

She leaned over the counter. *Nothing there.*

Wayne stood.

"Don't worry about me." He moved across toward Edie, took her hand. He guided her toward the gate opening. "Who knows? Maybe I'll see you in the next book."

"Hey, that's right." A sudden sparkle in Edie's eyes. "You said you were in the running for this one. He must like you."

"Absolutely. I figure he just didn't have a part for me in this one." Wayne worked up a confident grin. "He probably has big plans for me in his next blockbuster."

"Yes. I'm certain." Edie felt Wayne let go of her hand. She stepped away. "I'll see you?"

"Absolutely."

Edie gave an uncertain nod, struggled to take another backward step. She turned quickly then, stepped through the gate opening, looked back. Wayne lifted a hand and held a wave. Edie smiled sadly, turned and was gone.

Wayne stared at the empty gate for several moments more, turned away. He hesitated, stepped finally back into the room. He stopped near the bench, rested a hand on the bench-back. He gazed into the emptiness.

The sound of the train whistle; it rose, then slowly faded, leaving behind silence.

The Storekeeper appeared in the gate opening. Seeing Wayne standing next to the bench, he came into the station and stepped up beside him.

"You should go collect your pennies."

"Pennies?" The word hung there in space, drifted, faded.

Wayne half-turned, spoke without looking at Storekeeper. "Ah. Yes. Pennies... tracks... yes. Maybe later."

Storekeeper looked with some concern at Wayne. "Wayne?"

Wayne breathed in, out, sighed, put on a warm smile. "Wayne..." He thought on that word a moment. Another moment... he shook his head... no...

"Wayne," he said. "Wayne is on his way to Chicago."

"I see," Storekeeper said softly. Realization slowly drifted across his face. "So you are... you are <u>him</u>..."

A slight, easy nod from Wayne. A slow survey of the room, and he indicated their surroundings.

"Quite a nice place you have here," he said. "And I really like your store as well. Very much."

"Thank you. It comes from your second book."

Wayne, now the Writer, smiled comfortably. "Yes. That's right." He indicated the station. "And this... this comes from my first."

"That's right," said Storekeeper.

A warm wave of nostalgia brushed across the face of the Writer. "Oh, I did love that book." He moved around the bench, continued to admire the station as he sat down. "I worked on it for almost three years."

Storekeeper sat down beside the Writer. "And how is the new book coming. I see you have all the characters."

Surrounding sounds began to fade. The world around them slowly grew more quiet, more ethereal.

"It's coming together very well, Storekeeper. Very nice. A good story; the characters are getting comfortable... real nice." The Writer slid back on the bench, leaned back. "It' going to be great. I can feel it. This one... this one is going to be my masterpiece."

"That's good. I'm glad," said the Storekeeper. "And I'm happy for them. They're good people. They are all good people."

The Writer relaxed, rested against the back of the bench. He continued to admire his train station.

"We should head over to the store later," he said. "Get a soda or something."

There was another long pause, then an easy nod from the Writer.

"Ah, Storekeeper... I do love this place."

~ end

Cemetery Shadows

The tiny cemetery was old and thick with shadows. There was a single, small mausoleum overlooking a dozen weathered tombstones. To the left stood a wrought-iron gate, to the right a slight rise with a single spreading oak tree on the ridge.

All the world beyond the cemetery was a black void. Beyond the gate, beyond the rise, there was nothing. There existed only this little graveyard.

Major stepped out of the small, one-room mausoleum. He clasped his hands behind his back and calmly took in the scene before him. Somewhere in his sixties, he stood prim and proper, dressed in his military uniform from some long-ago war.

Sunset was complete. Night now lay over the cemetery. A thin fog drifted through the graveyard before him. There were now three figures there amongst the tombstones.

Derrick Lassiter, about thirty years old, sat atop one tombstone. He was relaxed, dressed casually. His hair was wavy and curled around his ears. The look on his face suggested that he might break out into a smile at any moment.

John Saunders stood nearby. About ten years older than Derrick, John was a tall, thin black man. His hair was cropped short, his clothes were neat. He appeared more serious than Derrick.

Mrs. Margaret Weatherly, in her mid-fifties, walked slowly through the tombstones. Her hairstyle was out of the nineteen fifties, as was her faded pattern dress.

The Major, satisfied that all was as it should be, spoke in a calm, steady manner.

"Good evening, everyone," he said.

John Saunders nodded a silent greeting in response, and Mrs. Weatherly continued wandering slowly among the tombstones.

Derrick looked casually about before answering, nodded finally in the Major's direction.

"Major."

"Another pleasant evening, I would say," said the Major.

"Sure."

"Same as every evening, Major," said John.

"No less pleasant for that, Mr. Saunders."

"Ya got me there," said John, a slight smirk.

Derrick's attention drifted in the direction of the cemetery gate.

There... the silhouette of a young woman standing just inside the closed gate. The shadows made it difficult to see her features.

"You all seeing what I'm seeing?" he asked.

The others looked to the gate.

Isn't that something, thought John.

"After all these years," he said.

"Twenty? Thirty?" the Major wondered aloud.

"How would we know?" asked Mrs. Weatherly. She glided wraithlike around several tombstones and came to a gentle stop.

John looked side-glance at Derrick. "However long, you're not the new kid on the block anymore, Derrick."

Mrs. Weatherly looked across at the woman at the gate, shifted her head slightly to one side.

"Suppose we should welcome her..."

There was a moment of uncomfortable silence. It really had been a very long time. This person standing near the gate had just changed their world, such as it was.

"Sure," John said finally, tentatively. "I'll go say hello."

Sara Keyes stood inside the closed gate, watched warily as a strange man left the others near the tombstones and approached.

Sara was a bit younger than the others, somewhere in her twenties. She was slim, with dark hair and a medium complexion, dressed in pants and a long-sleeve shirt.

"Good evening, Miss. I'm John. John Saunders." The man indicated their surroundings. "Welcome to the neighborhood."

Sara looked behind John, at the Mausoleum, the tombstones, the three others gathered there. She looked back then to John.

"Sara," she said. "Sara Keyes."

"Hello, Sara, Sara Keyes."

"How did... How did I get here?" she looked at John with increased confusion. "Where are we? What is this place?"

John glanced briefly back at the others, turned again to Sara. He had a sympathetic look on his face.

"Plenty of time for that, Sara Keyes. Come. Let me introduce you to the others."

John turned and waited for Sara to come up beside him. She hesitated, joined him then and they started forward. They reached the others at the tombstones, Sara appearing all the more anxious, uncomfortable.

John did his best to look and sound comforting.

"Everyone, say hello to Miss Sara Keyes."

There were mumbled greetings and slow nods. Derrick held a hand to her and spoke up.

"Hello, Miss Sara Keyes. I'm Derrick Lassiter."

Sara smiled meekly as they shook hands.

John indicated Major. "This is the Major."

Major stood stiffly and gave a curt nod. "Welcome, Miss Keyes."

"Thank you."

John made his presence known again and then indicated Mrs. Weatherly.

"And this is Mrs. Weatherly," he said.

Mrs. Weatherly gave a thin smile and a slight turn of the head. "Hello, dear."

"Mrs. Weatherly," Sara said softly.

Derrick fumbled fretfully with his hands.

"Say, Miss Keyes... Sara." He pointed to the gate. What's the sign say?"

"Excuse me?"

"The sign." He again pointed to the gate. "Over the gate. What's it say? We can't read it from this side. Just wondering."

Sara gave a glance to the gate, turned back apprehensively.

"I'm sorry," she said. "I don't know."

"Ah. I see. Too bad." Derrick frowned, looking to Sara, the gate, and back to Sara. "Quite all right, I suppose."

"Yes, quite all right, Sara," said John. "Derrick has become obsessed with the sign. Got under his craw a few years ago, and it's driving him a bit batty."

Major harrumphed and grumbled. "And so therefore the rest of us."

"I really am sorry," said Sara. "I don't know what the sign says. I never saw it. I don't actually remember coming through the gate. I was just... here."

Major gave a steady, affirmative nod at the comment, and John placed a comforting hand on Sara's arm.

"The same for us all," said John. "None of us know how we got here. One by one, we were... here."

"Wherever *here* is," Derrick smirked.

"You don't know where we are?" asked Sara.

Derrick gave a nod to the gate. "There's the sign."

Major shook his head tiredly. "Which in all probability would tell us nothing as to our circumstances."

With that, Mrs. Weatherly began drifting again amongst the tombstones. John continued his explanation to Sara.

"The Major was first. He stepped out of the mausoleum one evening, found himself all alone."

"Yes," said the Major. "It was more than a few years before John showed up. I came out onto the step one evening, and there he stood."

"Just him and me then for a long time," said John. "Mrs. Weatherly didn't make an appearance for-"

Sara drifted away from the group in John's mid-sentence; a lost, haunted look, she wandered toward the rise and the lone oak tree.

"Well, I suppose that's that," sighed Derrick. "You always were a bit of a bore, John."

Give her time, Derrick. You remember what it was like."

"Not really, no."

A few minutes later, Major and stood at the step of the mausoleum. Derrick was looking in the direction of the rise, toward Sara and John near the tree.

"Waddya think, Major?" he asked Major, frowning.

"Miss Keyes?" The Major gives a stern look to Sara. "A broken bird, that one."

"There's something odd about her. Something... different."

"A bit of a shock, you know, this. We've each faced it, in our time."

The Major's attention drifted to where Mrs. Weatherly wandered amongst the tombstones. Her dress flowed about her as a drifting cloud.

He looked again to the rise, to Sara.

"Still... bit of a broken bird."

Derrick squatted, sat on the step. He looked about the shadowed cemetery.

"Yeah," he said absently. "Wonder how she ended up here."

Major gave another grumbling *hmm* but otherwise didn't answer.

Sara still appeared rather a deer in the headlights. Remembering his own arrival here, John wanted to do what he could to help her adjust to her circumstances, even if it was simply to be there for her. Standing beneath the one lone oak tree, they were looking outward, away from the cemetery. The world beyond was black and empty. A void.

Sara wrapped her arms about herself, turned away from black. She looked down into the graveyard. Mrs. Weatherly was walking slowly among the tombstones, almost gliding, the woman's pattern dress flowing.

John gave a hint of a smile.

"Mrs. Weatherly doesn't talk much," he said. "Spends most of her time on her own. As much as that's possible, here."

"Here," Sara stated. "We are dead, right? But I don't remember dying. This can't be heaven."

"We don't know, really." John sighed, looking about them. "General conjecture is we're somewhere in between. No way to know if that's so. Heck, we coulda' been kidnapped by aliens, all we know."

Below them, Mrs. Weatherly stopped before one of the tombstones. She appeared to look curiously, reading. She looked then to the tombstone to her left, then to her right.

She looked up to John and Sara.

Something was up...

"We should see what the lady wants," said John.

They worked their way down, walked through shadows until they stood beside Mrs. Weatherly. She glanced to John, then to the tombstones lined in front of them.

"She's not here," she said.

John looked to the nearer tombstone, then to those on either side. "Are you sure?"

"No new tombstone," stated Mrs. Weatherly. "She is not here."

Sara appeared afraid of what she didn't understand.

"What does that mean?"

John moved along the line of grave markers in front of them, but he knew that Mrs. Weatherly was right. He could only shake his head uncertainly.

"We all have one," said Mrs. Weatherly, matter-of-factly. She gave a nod to a tombstone. "Mine's there."

"Then how can I—"

"Except for the Major," said Mrs. Weatherly. "Major has the mausoleum."

Major was standing in front of the mausoleum, Derrick and John sitting on the step beside him.

Major lifted his gaze from the group at the tombstones up to the black above them.

"The night grows old," he said.

John looked up, then out across the cemetery. "They go by too quickly."

Derrick agreed. "This night in particular, what with our newest to stir things up. Eh?"

"Quite so, Mr. Lassiter." Major gazed outward. "Quickly or no, they each pass one after the other."

"Right," Derrick said absently, standing.

John stood then. He looked to Mrs. Weatherly and Sara amongst the tombstones. Mrs. Weatherly was standing to one side, looking about inquisitively, turning her head one way and the other.

"I should see to Sara," said John. "Her first sunrise and all."

Major gave an affirmative nod, his hands behind his back; he clapped the back of one hand into the palm of the other.

"Excellent idea, Mr. Saunders."

"No tombstone, eh..." Major wondered aloud, watching John approach Sara. "Most odd."

"I hear that, Major," said Derrick. "Downright peculiar."

Major gave his thoughtful *hmmph.*

Derrick gave a sigh in reply, then followed after John.

Major watched them both for a moment, then turned about and faced the mausoleum. He took a step toward the open door, stopped and looked back.

The others were gone. The cemetery was still but for the incoming fog drifting in.

"Peculiar, indeed." He turned about again, spoke smartly as he started inside. "To bed, then."

Shadows slithered and wound their way through the tombstones as night slowly fell upon the cemetery. Long moments passed in silence. Major stepped primly out of the mausoleum, stood on the steps and clasped his hands behind his back, looked out at the tiny graveyard.

There among the tombstones stood Derrick, John Saunders and Mrs. Weatherly.

The Major carefully studied the scene laid out before him.

"And what of our young Miss Keyes?"

The others looked about them. Derrick looked up then to the rise. Sara was standing near the oak tree, looking outward away from the cemetery.

"How'd she end up there?" he asked. "I mean, shouldn't she be, you know, here with us?"

"No tombstone," John stated flatly.

"Ah. Yes." Derrick looked to the line of tombstones. "Quite right."

John stepped around the grave markers and worked his way up to the rise. Reaching Sara, he looked from the horizon, said nothing for a few moments, waiting. When she didn't she didn't acknowledge him, he quietly cleared his throat.

"Sara?" he asked. "Are you all right?"

"I don't know. I don't think so."

"Are you concerned that you don't have a tombstone? Don't be. It could mean anything. It could mean nothing at all."

"No. No, it's not that." She continued looking outward, into the black beyond the cemetery. She hesitated, frowned. "Where do you go? With the sunrise?"

"Excuse me?"

Sara turned to him, then. "Where do you go during the day?"

"Um... to sleep."

"But to where?" she asked.

"Ah." John looked from Sara to the void. He thought on the question. "To nothing," he said, almost a whisper. "First, it all goes black. And then... and there is nothing. No thoughts, no passage of time, nothing. Until we wake."

He turned and indicated the graveyard below them.

"And then we are there," he said. "It is the same, every day, every night."

Sara acknowledged John's answer with a slow nod. She turned about, looked down upon the graveyard and those gathered.

"Not so for me."

John felt a strange numbness drift through his body. It wasn't just her words, those four simple words. There was something in the way she spoke them; and something in her eyes.

"Sara?" he managed to ask. "Where did you go?"

"It was bright, but a soothing bright," she said softly. "And warm, comforting. I belonged. I was one with all that was around me." She looked directly at John. "I did not want to leave. I did not want to come back."

"Did you ask her about the sign?" asked Derrick.

"Mr. Lassiter, please," said Major. He grew thoughtful. "Her appearance here is unique. There is a reason she has been brought to us."

"Brought to us from where?" asked Mrs. Weatherly.

"That you ask the question suggests that you know the answer, Mrs. Weatherly."

"I think it's obvious," said John.

"I agree," said Derrick.

"As do I," Major stated matter-of-factly.

"All right," Derrick said in a low sigh. "What now?"

"What do you mean?" asked Mrs. Weatherly.

"I mean, what are we supposed to do?"

The four of them went into their own thoughts. Mrs. Weatherly drifted around behind the row of stones. She looked up to the rise, to Sara, now a silhouette beneath the oak tree.

"What *can* we do?" she asked.

"We can but wait, my friends," said Major.

"We have that down solid by now," said Derrick.

"Yes," said Major. "That we do."

Major watched Mrs. Weatherly continue to move away. John then wandered off, and finally Derrick.

Major looked up at the still figure of Sara on the rise beneath the oak tree. He appeared troubled.

Another sunset.

Major stepped out of his mausoleum. He noted the others gathered at the tombstones. He silently acknowledged Derrick's wave, watched Mrs. Weatherly begin her drifting among the grave markers, resting a hand on one, then another.

John started up to the oak tree. Sara was there, a silhouette against the darker black of the void beyond.

John reached Sara, said nothing as he stood beside her.

"I don't have any answers for you," she stated.

"That's all right," he said.

Sara looked back behind them, to the others below.

"I do know that this is wrong," she said. "Something about this place... is wrong."

"No doubt," said John. Nothing new there. "Were you sent to fix it?"

Sara hesitated a long time before answering. "I am being drawn to this place, just as you were."

"Not like me, Sara. Not like the rest of us. You're different."

Way, way different... he thought.

"I may not go where you go during the day, and I may not have a tombstone..." she looked down at the graveyard. "But I am drawn here, to this place. Just as you.

"From heaven?"

Sara looked thoughtfully to John, but didn't answer. Her expression suggested the answer was yes, but it was as though she was afraid to say so.

"So then," John urged. "What of us? Where do the rest of us come from?"

"Maybe you just haven't made it there quite yet."

Even as she said that, she felt there was something more. There was something deeper.

She looked again down at the graveyard... at the tombstones, the single mausoleum, the wrought iron gate.

"This is wrong," she said, the words hushed. "This place... something is wrong."

Major stepped out of the mausoleum to another sunset. Fuzzy rays streaked across the scene before quickly fading.

He silently let the last light fade from his face and drift to dusk, to night.

He looked down at those gathered around the tombstones. He said nothing. He looked up then at the rise, at the silhouette of Sara standing beside the oak tree.

His expression was solemn.

Major stepped from the mausoleum. Those gathered among the tombstones watched as he took the rise, approached the oak tree and the young woman standing beside it.

He stood beside her, looked outward as she did. It was several long moments before he spoke, still not looking directly at her.

"I know why you are here, Miss Keyes," he stated. "I saw it."

Major took a long, hard breath, continued before she could respond.

"You cannot do this."

Sara had turned to look to Major.

"I can't do—" she began, unsettled. "Why am I here? You know why I'm here?"

"I won't let you take them. You can't take them." A shuddering breath, then. "I won't be left here alone."

"I'm sorry, but I don't understand. I don't know what you're talking about."

"I saw it," Major said sharply. He turned his gaze outward again, to the darkness. "I saw it just as the sun set. It came to me... it came with the last rays..."

Realization spread across Sara's face, a golden light across her cheeks, her eyes.

"You..." she said calmly. "Each night, you bring them back. It's you, isn't it? Every night. You draw them back. Before they reach the light. Before they..."

Major appears almost tormented. Sorrowful, he was afraid to look away from the darkness, afraid to look to Sara. He did then. He turned to her, confessed to her.

"I think so... I think so... But I didn't know. I swear I didn't know. I really did not know." He looked away again. "I don't want to be alone. Miss Keyes. Sara. Why do I have to be alone?"

It was a long time before Sara could answer.

"I'm so sorry."

The path that led to the cemetery was seldom-used these days, hadn't been used for decades. Old, decaying brush encroached upon the trail from both sides, threatening to overwhelm it altogether. Not that anyone would have noticed.

No one came to the cemetery anymore.

Above the wrought-iron gate was an old, weathered sign, the words now hardly legible: "Pet Cemetery".

Within the tiny cemetery, Major stood on the step in front of a small mausoleum. His hands were clasped behind his back. He looked out across the cemetery, empty now but for himself and a couple of deteriorating tombstones.

He stood stoic, silent. Behind him, within the mausoleum, a single, small sarcophagus stood in the center of a sparse room. The sarcophagus was barely four feet long.

At eye level on the back wall of the room was a plaque.

The plaque read: "Major, beloved pet and dear friend".

Major stood on the step outside his mausoleum. Sad, melancholy, but ever watchful.

He turned his head slightly at the whisper of a breeze, as if he heard something.

There was nothing.

~ end

Last Day at Sharp Park

Chapter One

The small, rundown motel had long ago been converted to four tiny, drab apartments. It sat at the end of a narrow road, the road ending at a small gravel lot in front of the motel. A man-made embankment separated the beach from the motel and the lot.

A grandmotherly woman in her late sixties stepped out of one of the apartments. She had a kind face encircled by short, wavy gray hair, wore a faded pattern dress. She walked across to a bench at the edge of the lot, the world about her enveloped in a slowly drifting fog.

The sound of a bus reached out from the fog. Just visible in the gray mist, the late-fifties school bus stopped at the intersection a hundred yards up the road where the road met the street. Half a minute later the bus departed and moments later the silhouette of a small boy formed in the fog as he walked down the road.

Anna stood and waited. Seeing his grandma, six year old Jack grinned and hurried to her.

He was a small boy and painfully thin. He had wild, blonde hair, was dressed in faded blue jeans, a button shirt and a light jacket.

They hugged briefly and then pulled apart.

"Hello, Jack," said Grandma. "And how was school today?"

Jack grinned. "You ask me that every day, Grandma. Every, every day."

"And I'll be standing right here tomorrow, and I'll ask you again."

They hugged again and then Anna took the boy by the hand.

"How about a walk on the beach before we go inside?"

§

Will Bennett started back up the long driveway from the wrought-iron double-gate toward the house. He had a bundle of mail in hand and was absently looking through it as he walked.

Will was in his mid-twenties, was slim without being thin. His thick hair curled around his ears. He pants and shirt were contemporary, casual, comfortable.

The grounds surrounding the large, two-storey house consisted of a sprawling lawn that could use a mowing, and a scattering of shrubs and trees. The house was a large, square structure with a covered front deck that spanned the width of the house from one corner to the other.

Will took his attention from the mail long enough to climb the steps up onto the covered porch and approach the large front door.

The foyer was a large, open room. There were open doors to the left and right, and a staircase directly across from the front door.

Will closed the door behind him and started to the open door on the right. His sister Ellinor came in through the opposite door and followed Will toward the west wing hallway.

Ellinor Bennett was a year younger than her brother. She had wavy, shoulder-length brown hair, and was wearing comfortable slacks and blouse that showed her attractive figure without really calling attention to it.

Will acknowledged her as they entered the hallway. It was wide, carpeted; several lamps were set high on the walls, spreading a golden glow.

"Sister."

"Brother," said Ellinor.

"How was your trip?" Will was again sorting through the mail. "You came in pretty late last night."

"Oh, Will... you'd have just loved it."

Will gave an absent grin to the sarcasm. "Sounds exciting."

"Thrilling."

Will gave one of the letters another look, handed it to Ellinor.

"Another one from Jason Anders," he said.

Ellinor glanced at the envelope without really looking at it. She handed it back.

"Grandfather's business."

"Second one in a week." Will's expression grew thoughtful. "I know I've heard that name before. Don't know where. *Anders.* Have you heard that name before?"

They reached an open double-door on their right and turned into the dining room. A large table occupied the center of the room. The wall behind the head of the table had a large window, and there was a fireplace in the center of the wall opposite the door.

Miles Bennett, the patriarch of the Bennett family, sat at the head of the table reading a newspaper. A glass of orange juice sat on the table in front of him.

Miles was well-dressed and well-groomed. He was in his sixties, had salt-and-pepper hair, and an air of calm, confident sophistication about him.

Will set the mail onto a side table and he followed Ellinor to a buffet that ran the length of the wall beside the doorway. On the buffet was a tray of breakfast rolls, a pitcher of orange juice and juice glasses, a covered dish of bacon, another of scrambled eggs.

"Good morning, Grandfather," said Ellinor, speaking over her shoulder. She began filling her plate.

"Good morning, Ellinor." Miles glanced up briefly, returned to his newspaper. "I trust your trip went well?"

"Well enough." She filled a glass with orange juice and started to the table. "The final paperwork from the attorney should arrive this afternoon. Work on the wind farm should start the beginning of the month."

Mrs. Bailey came into the room carrying a bowl of assorted cubed fruit. She stood beside Will and made room on the buffet for the bowl.

"Good morning, Mrs. Bailey," said Will. He eyed the fruit. "Don't ever leave me, Mrs. Bailey."

Mrs. Bailey was in her sixties, was a bit shorter than average, a bit heavier than average. She spoke with calm self-assuredness.

"Good morning, Master William. You really should see about getting a life." She turned about to lock to Miles. "I'll be away this afternoon, Mr. Bennett. I'll set out sandwich fixings for lunch before I go."

"Thank you, Mrs. Bailey," said Miles. "You are very kind."

Mrs. Bailey nodded and left the room as Will carried his breakfast over to the table and sat down beside his sister.

"I do love that woman," he said.

"Of course you do," said Ellinor. "She's spoiled you rotten your whole life."

"Not so." Will considered as he took a bite of fruit. "She helped me with my homework now and then."

"You spent your entire childhood in her kitchen."

"Where she helped me with my homework."

Mr. Gray entered the dining room then, pausing briefly to take in the scene. He was sixty years old, tall, dressed in a dark suit. He had a calm, steady demeanor about him.

"Ah, Mr. Gray." Miles folded his newspaper and set it aside. "Have you seen Alice yet this morning?"

"I believe she is in the study, Mr. Bennett," said Mr. Gray, taking a single step nearer Miles.

"Aunt Alice has been really moody lately," said Will, taking another bite of fruit. "I mean, from her normal level seven moody up to a ten."

"Yes, I have noticed the shift in her disposition as well." Miles took a drink of his juice. "We will give her time, and space, for now."

"Something's up," said Will.

"As I said," Miles sighed dismissively. He turned to Mr. Gray. "Apologies, Mr. Gray. You wished to speak with me?"

Mr. Gray gave a slight nod. "The confirmation request arrived regarding your attendance at the High Council meeting scheduled for this morning."

"I replied?" asked Miles. "Am I looking forward to the meeting?"

"You did. And of course you are."

"Of course I am. Thank you so much, Mr. Gray."

"Of course, sir." Mr. Gray stepped back, gave a nod of acknowledgement to the others at the table. "Master William, Mistress Ellinor." He started back to the door, noted the bundle of mail and stepped to the side table.

"William," he stated. "If you insist on collecting the mail, then I must insist that once you have finished sorting through it that you complete the delivery by bringing it to my office."

"Sure, Mr. Gray. Anything to help." Will took another bite of breakfast, looked then across to Miles. "Grandfather... you got another letter from Jason whoever. Second one this week."

Miles looked from Will over to Mr. Gray. "Mr. Gray?"

"I'll take care of it, sir." Mr. Gray left the dining room.

Miles looked to Will. "Mr. Gray will take care of it." He took another swallow of juice.

"Right. Sure..." Will grew introspective. "I know that name. *Anders*. Where have I heard that name? Is something up?"

"Nothing is up," stated Miles. "A personal matter. That's all."

"Right..." Will glanced over at the door through which Mr. Gray had departed. "Right... And Mr. Gray will take care of it."

§

The study was a room of warm woods, warmly glowing lamps, thick pile carpet, built-in book shelves and a fireplace inset into the long wall. Alice stood at the one window at the far end of the room. The drape was pulled aside enough for her to see outside, sunlight on her face.

Alice looked to be in her late forties, tall and thin. She was dressed in a long-sleeve blouse and full-length skirt. Her long brown hair was pulled back into a thick ponytail.

She didn't acknowledge Miles coming into the room, continuing to look out the window.

"Good morning, Alice," said Miles. He moved to his desk and settled into his leather chair. "We missed you at breakfast."

"Good morning, Father." Alice spoke without turning. "I'll get something later."

Miles pulled a stack of folders to him and opened one. He lifted out an open envelope with a letter stapled to it. He read it silently.

Alice held her arms across her chest, cupping her elbows in her palms. She gave a side-glance to Miles as he put the letter back into the folder

"From Jason?" she asked absently.

"Nothing of any importance." He set the folder aside and opened the next one in the stack.

Alice grew thoughtful, continued to look out the window, to let the sunlight wash over her face.

"How is your project coming?"

"Quite well. Thank you."

"Wind farm. Interesting."

"I think so." Miles picked up a pen and began making notes in the margins of an official looking document.

"And most philanthropic," said Alice.

"I suppose that's so. It should provide enough electricity to support the entire town."

The town, a mile and a half down the road, had a population of just over 30,000.

"Which you will provide at cost." Alice now did turn to look at her father. "And you intend to offer the land on which the wind farm will sit to local the farmers at no cost."

"Our contribution to the cause, my dear."

Alice turned back to the window. "The Society isn't going to like it."

"Not their concern."

"Of course it is. And you know it."

"I don't answer to them."

"You are them."

Miles leaned back in his chair, rolled his pen through his fingers. He said nothing.

"Your philanthropy is generating publicity," said Alice. "That makes you visible. And that makes the Society nervous."

Miles turned slowly about in his chair and gave Alice a studied look.

"That is not what is bothering you. Is it?"

Alice hesitated, finally acknowledged the question. "No, Father. We can deal with the Society."

"You more than I, I should think," said Miles. "And so?"

Alice continued to stare thoughtfully out the window. She took in a long breath, let it out slow. She held a hand up before her, her palm to the sunlight.

"A shadow passed before my eyes," she said. "Three days ago. I reached out to it, but I hesitated... I'm sorry."

"The shadow. Light or dark?"

"I don't know." Alice let her hand drift nearer the window, held it up near the pane of glass without quite touching it. "It remains near, just beyond my sight. It is drawn here. It is... searching; that, and something more. There is sadness."

"Can you tell—"

"If I knew more..." said Alice, cutting him off. She turned her head slowly from the window, looked to her father. "The boy is nearby?"

Miles didn't answer at first. He looked up at his daughter, then away.

"Not far," he said softly. "Is it related, then?"

"You can reach him." It was a statement more than a question.

"If need be."

Alice turned again to the window, her face to the sun. "Perhaps you should do that."

"Meeting," grumbled Miles. "Later, perhaps."

The windowless room was lined with bookshelves. A round table sat in the center of the room, with three chairs evenly spaced around the table. An opening in one wall revealed the study beyond.

Miles brought a wooden box down from a shelf and set it on the table. The box was nine inches square, made of fine wood and set with small brass latches and hinges.

He lifted a latch on the box, lifted the lid, and lowered the lid and one attached side onto the tabletop. This revealed a crystal cube within the box. The cube was eight inches square.

He lowered the remaining sides of the box. He reached out, rested a hand on the top of the cube. It began to pulsate.

He sat back in his chair, continuing to focus on the cube. The pulsating stopped, the glow brightened, and in moments filled the room.

Miles was sitting at the same table, only now he was in the Council Chamber. The room beyond the table was hidden in darkness.

The other two chairs were occupied.

One council member was a gray haired woman in her sixties, dressed in a heavy, multi-colored robe with a high collar.

The other council member, also in his sixties, was a tall man with salt-and-pepper hair and a well-trimmed beard. He wore a tan, collarless jacket.

"Good morning, Miles," said the councilwoman.

Miles nodded to her, then to the councilman.

"Good morning," he said.

"Shall we get the meeting started?" asked the councilwoman. She brought her hands together, steepled her fingers. "Miles. I understand we may have issue with Jason Anders."

Chapter Two

Ellinor turned into a narrow hallway, followed it to an open door on the right and entered Mr. Gray's office. It was a mirror image to her grandfather's study. Bookshelves lined the wall opposite the door, and to Ellinor's left a single window in the wall behind Mr. Gray's desk let in natural light.

"Mr. Gray," said Ellinor. "Have you seen Grandfather?"

"Council meeting, Miss Ellinor," said Mr. Gray. He looked up from his work and indicated the shelves along the wall.

Ellinor acknowledged that with a short nod, then looked restlessly about Mr. Gray's office. She glanced to the bookshelves, back finally to Mr. Gray.

"Has he been in there long?"

"I don't imagine he'll be much longer."

Ellinor hesitated, finally approached the wall. "Maybe I'll wait inside," she said at last.

Mr. Gray was again focused on his work. "As you wish, Miss Ellinor."

"I'll see you at lunch."

"Sandwiches," stated Mr. Gray, with very little enthusiasm.

Ellinor reached into the shelves and released a hidden catch. There was a solid clicking sound and a section of the shelf wall opened a few inches.

"I like sandwiches." She took a step back, pulled the shelf wall fully open, and entered the Closet.

The glow of the cube in the center of the table was just beginning to fade. Miles was sitting before it, his expression distant. The back wall behind him was slightly open, revealing his study beyond.

Ellinor watched and waited as the last of the glow of the cube began to dissipate. It was another fifteen or twenty seconds before Miles' focus returned fully to his surroundings.

He looked up at his granddaughter.

"Good morning, Ellinor." He began closing the box, lifting the sides and latching them into place. "What can I do for you?"

"How is the council taking the project?"

"The matter never came up." Miles finished closing box, slid it across to Ellinor. She took it and carried it over to the shelf.

"Something more important than the bright light of unwelcome publicity shining on the Society?" She slid the box into position on the shelf. "Is there something we should know?"

The thought crossed her mind that she sounded way too much like her brother.

Miles slid his chair back and stood up. "Nothing of interest, Granddaughter."

He started toward the opening to his study, Ellinor followed. Behind them, Mr. Gray closed the opening to his own office.

Entering the study, Miles walked over to his desk as Ellinor closed the access to the Closet.

She wasn't ready to let Grandfather's last comment go.

"You are being rather less than forthright, Grandfather," she stated coolly and took the two steps to stand before his desk.

"Sorry, my dear. Way of the world." Miles settled into his chair. "Is there something else I can help you with?"

Ellinor gave her grandfather as sharp look. She folded her arms across her chest.

"Jason Anders."

"What about him?"

"I did a little digging."

"Did you?"

"He's Society," she said. "It seems there was a big fuss-up about fifty years ago, which the Society managed to keep quiet."

Miles leaned back in his chair, looked up at Ellinor, seeming to consider a response.

"For the most part," he said at last. "Why the interest?"

"Will asked if the name sounded familiar. It did."

"I see... and so?"

"And so apparently his son went missing; disappeared with Grandma. Word at the time was that it had something to do with Jason."

"Such was the rumor," Miles said guardedly.

"And I could find nothing after that. Not a word. No one ever saw Grandma or the boy again."

"That's right."

"Now Jason Anders begins sending you letters; fresh one every couple of days. After all these years?"

Miles straightened in his chair, leaned over his desk, appeared ready to end the conversation.

"We were friends once. He's reaching out. Nothing more."

"Grandfather."

"There is nothing there that concerns you."

"Grandfather..." increasingly frustrated.

"I want you to let it go."

Ellinor held her silence. Her expression grew stern, her folded arms squeezed a little tighter. She stared intently at her grandfather.

The conversation was definitely at an end.

The old-style kitchen was high-ceilinged, airy, with lots of tall cabinets and plenty of counter space. It had been around for a long time, and yet was both efficient and comfortable.

Will sat at the large island counter, a glass of iced tea in hand as he watched Mrs. Bailey go about preparing trays of sandwich fixings.

"I'm telling you, Mrs. B, there's something going on in this house. Folks are acting real peculiar."

"I've been with your grandfather twice as long as you've been alive. I watched your father take his first steps, right there in your grandfather's study." Mrs. Bailey spoke as she continued about her work. "I don't recall a day gone by that there wasn't something peculiar going on in this house."

"I get that, but this is different. And it's not just Alice." Will considered that a moment. "Though I suppose her weirding way could have the others spooked."

"Your aunt's *weirding way* is a great gift," said Mrs. Bailey, managing a patient grin. "It has helped your grandfather more times than I can remember. Got your father out of a fix a time or two as well."

Will thought about that, looking down at his glass of iced tea. He took a drink, gently set the glass down on the table.

"I've always thought it strange that my father wasn't born with the same gift as Alice."

"Being twins doesn't make 'em the same. Your father has made do just fine with what he was given."

Will prepared to take another drink and then didn't. "Suppose so. And that would be more than me."

"Oh, poor William," said Mrs. Bailey. "Ya' got your wits, boy. And I expect there's a little of your family in you. You'll find it."

Will held his hand before him, rubbed his fingertips together. There was a faint sparking, each the size of a sand granule. He sighed, then looked fondly at Mrs. Bailey.

"Hey, I got you, Mrs. B. I'll make do with that."

"Uh, huh..." She pushed one of the trays across the counter. "Here. Take this into the dining room."

Ellinor came into the dining room, looked curiously about and then stepped over to the buffet. She spoke over her shoulder to Will as she began putting together a sandwich.

"Where is everyone?" she asked.

Will was sitting at the table munching on half a sandwich. The other half was on a plate in front of him beside a glass of milk.

"Here and gone." Will took another bite of his lunch. "Where you been?"

"Following up on a few things." She brought her lunch over to the table and sat down. "I think you were right about that Jason Anders."

She took a bite of her sandwich.

Miles entered the Closet, closed the opening leading from the study. He lifted the wooden box from its place on the shelf and set it on the table. He lifted a latch on the box, lifted the lid, lowered the top and one side onto the tabletop, revealing the crystal cube within the box.

Miles sat down then and lowered the remaining sides of the box. With the cube fully exposed, he rested two fingers on the cube. It began to pulsate.

Anna was standing on the beach watching the surf, the hint of melancholy on her face. Fog drifted across the beach. Miles approached through the mist. Anna didn't look at the approaching figure, neither did she appear to be surprised at the arrival.

Miles reached Anna and stood beside her. They stood together, looking out across the ocean.

"Anna," said Miles at last.

Will came into the study, Ellinor entering behind him.

There was no one there.

"Well, this is where he was headed," said Will. "He seemed a bit anxious about it, actually."

"That doesn't sound like Grandfather," said Ellinor. She nodded to the Closet access panel in the book shelf wall. "The Closet?"

Will gave a shrug and they stepped up to the shelves. Ellinor reached in and released the catch. There was the familiar solid click sound, and she pulled the access open.

The Closet was empty but for the cube on the table.

Will looked down at the cube. "He's in there?"

"Where else?" Ellinor stepped around to the side of the table.

"But they already had their Council meeting. I'm telling ya. Something is going on..."

"I brought up that very question."

"And?"

"You know Grandfather."

Will frowned at the cube. "Miles does have his secrets."

Alice came into the Closet then. Will and Ellinor watched her approach the table, watched as she looked thoughtfully down at the cube.

"Your grandfather has not gone to the Council Chamber," she said.

"I don't understand," said Will. "Where else would he be?"

"The Nexus Cube is addressing somewhere else." Alice lifted a hand, held it palm out midway to the glowing cube.

"I knew it," Ellinor whispered heavily.

"I didn't know it could do that," said Will. "I thought it was just the door to the Chamber."

"Of course it can do that," said Ellinor. She looked to Alice. "Where is he? Where did he go? To Jason?"

"Not to Jason," said Alice. "Sharp Park. The boy."

Ellinor took a moment to catch her breath. "Can we go there?" she asked then.

Will looked uncertain. "Ell?"

Alice looked to Will, then to Ellinor. She indicated the chairs. "Sit."

She waited for them to sit down, then reached out, lightly rested two fingers on the cube.

An elderly woman's bedroom, gray and dull; a small bed, an old, four-drawer dresser upon which sat a cheap jewelry box with a miniature plastic ballerina on the lid.

Will and Ellinor entered the room from the small closet, pushing their way through half a dozen old, faded dresses. Ellinor moved cautiously into the middle of the room, looking about for signs of danger. Will stood just outside the closet.

"That was rather stale," he mumbled, brushing dust off his shirt.

"I don't think we're in Kansas, Toto."

"I don't think we're in the twenty first century, Dorothy." Will studied the room. "Nineteen sixties, I'd say."

They left the bedroom and went into the living room. There was a couch and an easy chair, a black and white console television; a dinette set in the kitchen area; all a snapshot out of the early 60s.

No one home.

"Curiouser and curiouser," said Will. "Definitely early sixties."

Ellinor poked her head into the other bedroom. It was just large enough for a twin bed and a dresser; plain, no decorations. Atop the dresser was a small collection of plastic toys; toy soldiers, cars.

She stepped back into the middle of the living room.

"I don't think Grandfather was expecting to deal with this today. This surprised him."

"That may be. Either way, Miles knows a lot more than he's telling."

"That's my point," said Ellinor. "He's not telling anything."

That is so Miles... thought Will.

"Well, according to Alice, he's here. Somewhere."

"Wherever here is," said Ellinor.

"*Whenever* here is."

Ellinor gave a nod to the front door. Will gave a short nod in answer.

They came out of the apartment and onto the front stoop. They hesitated a moment at the sheer bleakness of it all, then stepped out into the narrow road.

There was a gravel parking to their right, where road ended. A short embankment ran beside the motel and parking lot. The sound of gentle surf reached them from the other side of the embankment. To their left, the road disappeared into the fog.

The entire world was ugly and run down.

"Do you suppose it's always this miserable?" asked Will. "Or are we here on a particularly bad day?"

They both turned about and looked behind them at the building they had come out of.

"Roach motel?" Ellinor wondered aloud.

"Converted to apartments." Will looked carefully at the handful of small windows and narrow doors. "Most of 'em look empty."

They turned about again. Ellinor made a face.

"Do you smell that?"

"Rotting seaweed." Will indicated a set of grayed wooden steps that ran up the short embankment. "Shall we?"

"If we have to." Ellinor started toward the steps. "Not your typical tourist destination."

Chapter Three

Miles and Anna were walking casually along the beach. The tide had retreated some and the sand beneath their feet was damp but firm. The fog had thinned a little, though the sky overhead remained gray.

"How's the boy?" asked Miles.

"He's doing well. You know Jack." They walked in silence for a few moments, each lost in their own thoughts. "And so, your visit... has Jason found us?"

"Possibly. I don't know. Not yet."

They stopped walking. Anna looked side-glance at Miles.

"You don't know?" she asked.

"It was Alice." Miles shrugged. "Very cryptic."

Anna looked curiously, piercingly at Miles. He shook his head dismissively.

"Yes," he said. "Typically Alice."

A movement caught his attention. He turned his head and looked up the beach. Ellinor and Will were standing atop the embankment at the parking lot.

Miles grimaced, obviously not pleased at seeing them.

"Anna, I do apologize."

"Quite all right. They belong to you?"

"The grandchildren."

"Oh my," said Anna. "The last I recall, they were just babies. Now look at them."

Miles smirked. "They really haven't changed that much."

The statement drifted into silence. Miles looked tiredly at his grandchildren in the distance. Anna watched him, waited. She finally raised a brow, silently urging Miles forward.

"Very well," he stated. They started up the beach. Reaching the embankment, they climbed up to stand with Ellinor and Will.

"Hello, Grandfather," said Ellinor. "Would you mind explaining this?"

"I would mind. Very much. You need to leave."

"I don't think we can do that, sir," said Will.

Miles sighed heavily and turned to Anna. "Again, I am so sorry."

"Not at all, Clive," said Anna.

At hearing the name Clive, Will and Ellinor looked curiously at Miles, but said nothing for the moment.

Anna reached out to shake hands with the young people.

"Gregory and Donna's children, I understand."

"That's right," said Ellinor, warily. She looked side-glance at Miles.

"So nice to meet you," said Anna. She turned to Miles. "You must excuse me, Clive. I have to see to Jack. He'll be coming home soon."

"Of course." Miles watched Anna take the steps down to the parking lot.

"*Clive*, Miles?" asked Will.

"At one time."

The words were cool, distant. Will and Ellinor waited for something more. Nothing more came. Below, Anna crossed the gravel lot and stood beside the bench.

"You know her," stated Will.

"This is none of your concern."

"Of course it is."

"We're family, Grandfather," said Ellinor. "Don't push us away."

The school bus arrived then, stopping at the end of the road. The little boy Jack walked out of the fog and approached his grandma.

"What's going on, Grandfather?" asked Ellinor.

"I should think that was obvious. Jack is coming home from school."

"You know what I mean," Ellinor said, a forced calm. "The woman, the boy... They haven't aged a day in fifty years. Have they?"

Miles ignored her, ignored the question. He quietly watched Jack and his grandma go through their daily ritual.

Ellinor pushed on. "It's more than just magic. Isn't it? It's this place."

Miles continued to ignore her, to ignore them both, his attention focused on the scene below them, the far side of the parking lot.

"That boy does adore his grandma," Will said absently.

Miles started down the steps.

"We're leaving."

§

A shadowed room with book-lined walls, a large desk in the center. The view beyond the window revealed a dark night.

The heavy door opened and Carlson, a tall, thin, very proper gentleman in his mid-sixties, entered Jason Anders' library. The butler stood to one side and Jason followed Carlson into the room.

Jason was in his seventies, appeared withered and as faded as the house coat he wore. His gray hair was wispy and near white.

He walked toward the desk as Carlson went to a cabinet set against the far wall. The butler brought back a small, ornate chest, set it carefully on the desk. Jason waved him dismissively aside with one hand and stepped up before the desk.

"Will there be anything else, Mr. Anders?" asked Carlson.

"Nothing, nothing," grumbled Jason. "Go away."

Carlson gave a barely perceptible nod as he took a step back. He turned and started toward the door. Jason peered up through his bushy eyebrows at the closing door. Only then did he reach into the pocket of his house coat and take out a key. He inserted it into the chest's lock, turned it. It gave a satisfying click. Jason lifted the lid.

He reached into the chest and brought out a cloth-covered package, set it on the desktop beside the chest. He carefully unfolded the cloth, exposing a hundred year old book. He brushed a wrinkled hand over the cover.

The book visibly trembled.

Jason carefully opened the book, slid a hand delicately across the pages. The book trembled again, the pages fluttered. The sound was dry and crisp.

Jason slowly sat down, gave a thin smile. He laid his hand again on the book.

Now... my dear boy...

Miles was alone in his study. It was late, the house was quiet. He was sitting in one of the easy chairs, reading by the light of the pole lamp standing beside the chair.

A muffled shuffling sound disturbed the quiet. Miles glanced up, looked curiously about.

There was no movement. The silence returned.

Miles returned to his book.

The shuffling sound again...

Miles looked up again. He glanced then to the bookshelves. He leaned forward.

An old book, leather spine, sat alone on the shelf just at eye level.

Miles stood, eyes not leaving the book.

The book appeared to shudder, if only slightly; a hollow, shuffling sound.

Miles walked over to the shelf. He reached out haltingly, grasped the book. He carried it over to the desk, set it on the desktop. He held his hand out over the book, delicately brushed two fingers across the leather cover. It vibrated at his touch.

He brushed his fingers across the book again.

The book opened on its own. A moment passed and all was still, quiet. A page rose then, turned. The turn of another page, and then another.

The book grew still. A thin wisp of fog rose up, lingered just above the book. There were silhouettes in the fog; movement... people.

Miles stared uneasily at the book, the fog, the silhouettes... a woman and a small boy.

Jason... what are you up to?

Jason lifted is hand from the pages of the leather-bound book, his fingers raised and slightly apart. A thin wisp of misty fog followed the hand's movement. Within the fog, the ethereal image of Jack, of Anna; of the beach.

Jason gave a gentle, sympathetic smile.

Warm morning light streamed into the dining room. Miles sat at the head of the table, his newspaper folded and sitting on the table beside his cup of coffee and a small dish with an untouched breakfast roll.

Alice stood at the window, the warmth of the early sun on her face. Will was at the buffet preparing a plate of scrambled eggs, bacon, and fruit. Ellinor was sitting at the table, holding a cup of coffee in both hands.

Miles moved his cup and dish aside, looked to Will at the buffet, then to Ellinor.

"I believe Jason has found them," he stated flatly.

"Excuse me?" asked Ellinor.

"Jason Anders. He has found them."

"I see."

Will moved from the buffet to the table.

"Actually, I could use a bit more info."

Miles gave an absent nod, gathering his thoughts as he watched Will take the chair next to his sister.

"As you have no doubt surmised, Jason was a wizard; is a wizard; a wizard with... passable talents. Nothing extraordinary, but passable. He has long been dissatisfied with his less than extraordinary abilities and so has continually strived to improve upon them."

"I would call that a positive personality trait," said Will, munching on a piece of fruit.

"Yes, well... that depends very much on the personality involved." Miles rested his elbows on the table, clasped his hands. "And he was also burdened with being a sorcerer out of his time. Specifically, the mid-twentieth century. A particularly awkward era in which to be a wizard of mediocre abilities. One was plagued with being looked upon as a sideshow magician of top hats and bunny rabbits."

"No one believed in wizards anymore," Alice said matter-of-factly. She spoke softly, her face aglow in the sunlight. "All to the good so far as the Society was concerned. It allowed us to once again retreat into the shadows."

Miles acknowledged the comment with a nod, then continued.

"And then there was Jack. His son. The boy was showing signs of exceptional conjurer power even before he could walk. This drove Jason nearly mad. Not that he had far to go. Obsessed with his desire to grow beyond his limited talents, nothing he did helped. He managed to acquire a few artifacts, became moderately successful in business, but nothing made him a better wizard."

"Or a better person," suggested Ellinor.

"Yes. Exactly," said Miles. "Meanwhile, Jack's abilities grew stronger. Untrained in the budding mind of a six year old boy, it became impossible to hide his talents from the real world. Anna grew fearful of what Jason might do to Jack to acquire the boy's abilities."

"So Grandma took the boy," said Will. He stabbed a piece of fruit with his fork.

"And they went into hiding," said Miles, nodding.

"For half a century?" asked Ellinor.

"And why there?" asked Will.

Alice continued her focus to the morning sun beyond the window. She closed her eyes, let the sun's rays feed her.

"The beach is here," she stated. The room grew quiet. Miles stared ahead, to some empty spot across the table.

Will looked up from his plate over to Alice.

"Here? Alice?"

"It's here," she said, hardly above the whisper. "They are here. At the estate."

Alice looked from the window to Miles, who continued to look across the table, his hands clasped in front of him.

"That place," she continued. "It is hidden by very powerful magic."

"You're hiding them?" Will asked Miles.

"No. I am not hiding them." Miles pulled his hands back, turned and looked at Alice. She looked directly at him, her gaze betraying no emotion. She said nothing.

Miles looked again to Will and Ellinor.

"The boy. Soon after they arrived, he removed it from the physical realm." He frowned, pursed his lips. "It is real. It does exist. It just isn't... physical."

"It's not physical..." Will sounded dubious. "It's not physical, but it's here."

Ellinor curled her brow, staring down at her coffee cup. Her expression suggested that she was starting to get it.

"Not just the passage, but that world. Is here."

"Exactly. Well, sort of." Miles looked pointedly at those in the room. "The important thing now is that I believe Jason has found them."

Miles stepped off the front stoop of Anna's apartment and walked toward the bench that sat at the edge of gravel lot. He reached it just as Anna and Jack came over the top of the embankment from the beach and started down the wooden steps.

Miles gave them a warm smile as they walked across the lot and approached.

"Good evening, Clive," said Anna.

"Anna." Miles looked to the boy. "Hello, Jack."

Jack gave only a slight smile, the barest hint of a nod. Miles looked again to Anna and indicated the bench.

"Do you have a minute?" he asked. "We need to talk."

"Of course." Anna moved around the bench, an arm around Jack's shoulders.

Miles waited for them to sit down, then sat down beside them.

§

Alice came out of the study and started down the hall, on her way upstairs. She was half lost in thought when Mr. Gray came up behind her, walked beside her. They spoke as they walked.

"Miss Bennett."

"Yes, Mr. Gray."

"Your brother called earlier. He wishes to speak with you. At your convenience."

"Thank you, Mr. Gray," she said. "I'll be in my room."

"Yes, Ma'am." Mr. Gray slowed, turned back as Alice continued.

Entering the foyer, Alice took the main stairs up to the second floor hall and on to her rooms.

The front sitting room of her suite was informal and open. There were assorted comfortable chairs, floor lamps and side tables. Her bedroom and bath were through a set of sliding double doors.

She walked around behind her desk, the wall behind her covered with full drapes. The drapes were open and revealed a large window, allowing sunlight to stream through.

As she moved between desk and window, the computer monitor turned on. Looking out the window, she casually lifted her hand and raised two fingers. The monitor flickered with images, the screen filled with a nature scene. She folded her arms and waited.

An image of a man's face appeared on the screen.

Gregory Bennett looked very much like Alice, his twin sister, though at the moment his hair was a bit wild and he could use a shave.

"Hello, sister," he said.

"Hello, Gregory." Alice looked briefly back at the screen, turned again to the window. "I understand you need to speak with me."

"I'm doing fine, Alice. Thanks for asking. Yourself?"

"Sorry," she said softly. "You are worried about me, yes?"

"As a matter of fact... you have been troubled these past few days."

"And you reach out halfway around the world because you sense my moodiness..."

"You know it's more than that, Alice. You are concerned. I too sense the shadow near you."

"Yes," she said. "It is near."

Gregory grew reflective, thoughtful. "I do not feel it as deeply as you, but it is strong."

Alice now turned away from the window, looked directly at the monitor. She continued to clasp her arms about her.

"I believe it has something to do with the boy."

"The boy?" asked Gregory. He thought a moment. "Jack? After all this time? All these years?"

"I am almost certain."

Gregory grew quiet for several moments. Alice waited.

"Perhaps," he said at last. "Perhaps, yes. And yet, there is... something else."

"Perhaps that is what is troubling me. It is as yet so unclear." Alice looked away from the image of her brother. "So, brother. How are things with you? The Andes treating you well?"

"The Andes are beautiful, if somewhat lacking in oxygen."

"And Donna?"

Gregory looked briefly off camera, back to Alice.

"Beautiful, if somewhat lacking in oxygen."

There was a long pause, then. Gregory's expression grew solemn.

"Go to the boy," he said.

Alice again looked briefly at the monitor, again out the window.

"See you soon, brother."

"The Gathering. Three weeks. Don't be late."

"I'll be there."

Alice raised two fingers, her arms still folded across her chest. The monitor grew dark.

She fully faced the window then. She closed her eyes, her headed drifted back, relaxed. The light and the warmth of the sun washed over her face, warmed her, fed her.

Chapter Four

Will was sitting on the bench at the edge of the parking lot, looking patiently up the road, into the fog. Ellinor came of the apartment, started across to her brother.

"No one here," he said.

Ellinor sat down beside her brother, followed his gaze up the road.

"This place is always the same," she said.

"Dreary."

"No. I mean the same. Literally the same. It never changes."

The sound of the school bus then, approaching and coming to a stop at the end of the road, half-hidden in the fog. It left a few moments later, leaving behind only silence.

Will and Ellinor waited... but there was no little boy.

"Well, that's interesting," said Ellinor. She looked questioning at Will.

"Curiouser and curiouser," said Will. "What was that about change?"

Ellinor leaned forward, slowly stood up. She turned about and looked across the parking lot to the embankment.

"What say we look around?"

Will agreed silently. They walked across the small lot and took the steps up to the top of the embankment. The fog had begun to thin somewhat and they were able to see a short distance up the beach. Alice was standing near the surf's edge.

"Now that's really curious," said Will. "Alice outside the estate?"

"This is the estate. Remember?"

"Right. No," droned Will doubtfully. He looked up into the gray sky, again toward Alice half-hidden in drifting fog. "Not the best locale for the Sun Princess."

Ellinor frowned at her brother, started down the embankment to the beach.

"Come on."

They scrambled down the embankment and walked over to their aunt.

"Alice?" asked Ellinor. "What are you doing here?"

Alice did not respond at first. She looked out across the waves for a long time.

"Something's not right," she finally said, continuing to look out at the ocean.

"So we've noticed," said Will. He looked up and down the beach. The fog had begun to close in again, to thicken and darken. "Have you seen anyone else around?"

Alice looked away from the ocean, to Ellinor and to Will. She indicated then a set of footprints in the sand. The gentle, foamy surf reached the prints and was threatening to wash them away.

Ellinor looked down at the footprints, then up the beach in the direction the prints led.

"They look like Anna's," she said.

"Right," said Will. "Grandma."

"Made sometime after the last high tide." Ellinor started up the beach then without saying another word, following the tracks into the fog.

Will looked from Ellinor to Alice.

"Alice? You coming?"

The three of them worked their way up the beach, the fog drifting about them in a slight breeze.

"She walked alone," Will noted after half a minute or so.

"She went looking for the boy," said Ellinor.

"On the beach?"

"He wasn't on the bus."

"True." Will glanced curiously at Alice, who had again grown silent, then again to his sister. "The kid doesn't strike me as the kind to play hooky. So where do you think Grandma is headed?"

Ellinor indicated the top of the cliff that began to show itself, a wall of dark shadow materializing in the fog. It rose from the sands of the beach, eighty feet high, sloping back just slightly. A narrow, steep trail wound its way up to the top.

Will didn't like where this was going.

"You expect us to climb that? There's gotta be a way around."

"Anna did it."

Fine time for Alice to speak up.

"Yet to be determined, Aunt Alice."

"Come on, Will," said Ellinor. "Do you really want to wait down here while we're up there discovering the secrets of the universe?"

"Sure."

"Don't be a wuss." Ellinor stepped up to the foot of the cliff and started up the steep trail. Alice started forward then, glancing back to Will.

"William?"

"All right, all right." Will frowned darkly as he followed. "Why not? Let's find the hardest way to do everything, shall we?"

Jason stood at the front door of the Bennett house, glanced up and down the large deck as he waited. The door opened, revealing Miles.

Neither spoke at first, and Miles stepped outside.

"Jason." Miles eased the closed the door behind him. "While I'm not surprised to see you, I must admit that I am rather surprised to see you *here.*"

"Hello, Clive. You left me little choice."

"Did I?"

"It is important that I speak with you."

"Apparently." Miles hesitated, then indicated that they should walk. "Very well."

They moved to the steps and took them down to the concrete walk. Miles then led Jason off the walk and they started across the lawn.

Miles gave Jason a *talk to me* look...

"I need you to allow me in," said Jason.

They walked in silence for a few moments.

"I'm not the one preventing it," said Miles. They stopped, turned to face one another.

"Clive..."

"Miles. It's Miles, now."

"Really?" Jason frowned. "I assumed that was just for the public."

"No."

"Too bad."

"What do you want, Jason?"

"You did read my letters?"

"Mr. Gray responded, did he not?"

Jason studied Miles a moment. They started walking again.

"I have accepted my limitations, Miles. It didn't come easy, mind you, but I have." Jason thought carefully about his next words. "And my mortality, as well."

"Good," Miles stated flatly.

Jason looked almost deferentially at Miles. "Not an easy thing for we mortals to come to terms with."

"Jason..."

"No, I'm all right with it, now. Really. It's all right. It really is."

"I'm glad to hear it, Jason. I truly am. But I—"

"I have been looking for Mother and the boy. I want to tell them..." Jason's tone grew soft and melancholy. "I want to apologize; to the boy, to Mother. I want to tell them how sorry I am. Before I... well..."

They reached the corner of the house, started around to the side yard.

"I don't know if that will be possible, Jason."

Jason had no response to that. They continued to walk about the grounds, across the side yard.

"I'll see what I can do," said Miles.

The small, west-coast elementary school was right out of the early nineteen sixties. One wing of the building contained the classrooms, another the administration offices and library; the third wing was the cafeteria/gymnasium. The building sat in the center of a large, flat lot of asphalt, tufts of weed growing through the cracks. To one side was a playground of four-square, tetherball and dodge ball courts. There was an empty parking lot in front of the administration wing.

There was no one about.

Ellinor, Will and Aunt Alice started across the playground. They approached the apex of the building complex. A colorful poster on the wall of the building pictured a cartoon of the stop-drop-cover scenario, with a bright mushroom cloud rising in the background.

"*This do be* a school from the middle of the last century," said Will. "Back then, it was all about earthquakes and atom bombs."

"Scaring the hell out of little kids?" asked Ellinor.

"*Thems was the times*, Sister. Early sixties on the west coast."

They continued to a door and entered the building.

The central hallway of the classroom wing was wide, with glossy linoleum floors. Doors with inset narrow windows lined both sides of the empty hallway. The school was eerily quiet.

Ellinor and Will looked into several empty classrooms. Alice stopped at a drinking fountain that was set low for elementary school children. The fountain worked. She took a drink, wiped her mouth dry as she moved to a bulletin board on the wall beside the fountain. She silently read several of the posted notices.

"There's an assembly this Friday," she said dolefully.

Will turned from a classroom door to Alice.

"Attendance mandatory? That could be a problem."

Further down the hall, Ellinor stood at another door.

"Here," she called out softly.

She opened the door and went in as the others approached. Rows of first-grade desks faced the front of the class. A blackboard behind the teacher's desk spanned the front of the room. The wall opposite the door was filled with windows looking out onto the asphalt playground.

Jack was sitting at a desk in the middle of the otherwise empty classroom. He was looking forward, saying nothing, doing nothing.

"What's he doing?" whispered Will.

"What does it look like?" Ellinor shrugged a shoulder. "He's sitting in class."

Will studied the boy for a few moments more, then stepped around his sister and walked slowly over to stand beside the boy. The boy ignored him.

Will looked down at the desk in the next row directly beside the boy. He struggled then, managed with some difficulty to wiggle into it. He placed his hands on the desktop, clasped his fingers... and stared ahead, as the boy was doing.

Over by the door, Alice moved around to stand beside Ellinor. Her gaze was curious, almost penetrating. She tilted her head slightly to one side, studied the boy.

Nothing happened for a long time. Then Jack looked side-glance at Will, quickly forward again; a second time then, as quickly, covertly.

"Makes sense," said Ellinor. "Will is bound to connect with a six year old who's been around for half a century."

Ellinor and Alice were out in the hall, just outside the classroom. They had left Will with Jack a few minutes earlier, hoping the private time would give him more opportunity to connect with the boy.

"He does this every day..." Ellinor wondered aloud, looked over at Alice. "Jack."

"He comes here every day. As for what he does once he's here..." Alice shook her head. "Today is different."

"Today he didn't come home," agreed Ellinor. She looked through the narrow window in the door, into the classroom. "Will is talking to him... he's talking back." She looked away, contemplative. "The boy sits alone in an empty classroom. Is that—"

"We don't know that," said Alice, cutting her off. She responded then to Ellinor's curious look. "We don't know that it's empty."

"Um…"

"It's empty to us. Who knows what the boy sees? It may not be empty at all. To him."

"Wow," said Ellinor. "That's heavy."

There was a sound then from down the hall. Footsteps… Miles and Anna, approaching.

"I see you found her," Ellinor said to Miles, while looking at Anna.

"She was never lost."

"So, where have you been?"

"Teacher's lounge," Miles said, matter-of-factly. "Where else?"

The sound of the school bell rang throughout the halls and classrooms, faded then, leaving a hollow silence behind.

"Ah," said Miles. "There we go."

"Where we go?" asked Ellinor.

Alice's gaze drifted down the hall. She spoke in a distant whisper.

"Do you hear that?"

The hallway was quiet.

"Alice?" asked Ellinor.

The classroom door beside them opened, Will and Jack came out. Seeing Grandma, Jack appeared puzzled at first, but quickly broke into a broad smile.

"Grandma?" He hurried to her and they hugged. "Grandma!"

"Hello, dear." Anna brushed at the boy's hair with one hand. "Are you ready to go home?"

"Yep," said Jack. "Home?"

"Home, sweetie."

They turned and started down the hall, Miles walking beside them. Will gave a shrug and they all followed after them.

Alice stopped at the drinking fountain and bulletin board. She stared at the board. She lifted a hand, rested it on the board.

Will stopped then and looked back to Alice. He rested a hand on Ellinor's arm.

"Uh, oh," said Will. "I think Auntie is weirding out on us, Sis."

Further down the hall, Miles slowed and turned about, appearing to sense something. Anna and Jack stopped beside him. They watched Will and Ellinor move up beside Alice.

"Alice?" asked Ellinor. "What is it?"

Alice lightly brushed her hand across the bulletin board. There was a thin glow beneath her fingertips. She spoke as if from somewhere very far away.

"Chalk…" a slight tilt her head. "Bubble gum."

Will's expression and tone was now cool and serious.

"Alice? Alice, where are you?"

"One plus two is three. Three plus four is seven." She tilts her head sharply now while keeping her focus on the bulletin board. "Red ball... red ball..."

"Right..."

"Atomic weight..." Alice furrowed her brow. "My mother told me to choose the very best one and you are it." Her expression turned dark, her tone somber. "Stop... drop... cover."

"Alice?"

Alice's expression changed again... surprised.

"Oh! Bologna sandwich..."

She grows quiet. Again. Will and Ellinor waited. Miles stepped toward them, leaving Anna and Jack watching.

Alice turned to the group; her expression transitions slowly from somewhere far away to now numbly overcome.

"Not empty. Real. Real. Alive."

"Excuse me?" asked Ellinor.

"Teachers. Students. Classrooms, hallways... Laughing, learning... noise." Alice appeared dazed. "But... the same... every day; The same. Always... every day... the same. The same day."

She delicately brushed her cheek with her fingertips. "Over and over and over."

"Uh, yeah..." said Will. "How do you—"

Alice's thoughts continued to drift. "All the lines. All the lines come together. Here. Intersection. Crossroads... It's all... here."

Ellinor reached out and took Alice's hand. "Alice?"

"Today," said Alice.

"What happened today?" asked Ellinor. "What about today? Why is today different?"

Miles took another step nearer the others. His words were calm and matter-of-fact.

"It's ending," he stated.

Alice slowly turned her head, looked to Miles, through Miles.

"It is... ending." She brushed at her cheek again. "It is time to go home."

Chapter Five

Miles was sitting at his desk, hovering over paperwork. A philanthropic wind farm project involved lots and lots of paperwork.

Alice was at her place before the window, looking out at the bright, clear day. She closed her eyes to the sunshine that was streaming in, warming her face. She lifted a hand, slowly, palm out to the sun. Her breasts rose and fell, slow, regular.

Young Jack was sitting on the floor in the middle of the room. He was building a castle with children's blocks. The structure was very well done. There also appeared to be some magic involved. There was a tiny gray cloud hovering above the structure, and a moat encircled the castle. In the moat, live miniature alligators.

Will and Ellinor came into the study. Miles looked up briefly, returned to his paperwork. Alice turned briefly from the window, returned to the view outside. Her raised hand turned slightly. There was the hint of tiny sparks dancing from fingertip to fingertip. She closed her eyes again. A faint glow enveloped her hand, lay across her face.

"Mrs. Bailey has lunch about ready," said Ellinor.

"Be there in a minute," said Miles, without looking up from his work.

Will moved over to Jack. He took a moment to look at the castle of children's blocks, then squatted down beside the boy.

"Cool castle."

"Thank you." Jack positioned another block on the structure.

"Looks like you've done this before." Will shifted position as he tried to get comfortable on the floor.

"Some." Jack shrugged.

"At school?"

"Some."

"Right," said Will. "You liked it there? At school?"

Jack shrugged again, said nothing. He continued building his castle. The tiny clouds above the castle darkened. There was a flash of light within the clouds.

"I'm going to miss my friends," said Jack then, unexpectedly.

"Right," Will said again. "Sure."

One of the alligators in the moat surfaced, glided forward and slid again beneath the surface.

"What are your plans now, Jack?" asked Will. "What would you like to do?"

Jack stopped with a block in hand, thinking about the question. Ellinor listened, watched from several steps behind Will.

"I have to take care of Grandma." Jack placed the block into position.

"Right," said Jack. "That's important. Your grandma is a great lady."

"Yes. She is."

"You and your grandma, you've been together a long time."

Jack hesitated again. He looked now directly at Will, for the first time.

"Tomorrow's my birthday," he said. "I'm going to be seven."

This took Will a bit by surprise. The statement brought home the reality of the boy's situation. Jack had been six years old for half a century. And it was only now that they were out of Sharp Park that time had begun to move forward again for Jack and his grandmother.

"Umm, right," said Will. "Well... we should do something about that."

The front door opened and Will came into the foyer. He absently closed the door behind him, sorted through the mail as he started across the room.

Sensing something, he looked up, stopped.

Mr. Gray was standing in the middle of the room, looking coolly at Will. Will hesitated, smiled, and held the mail out to Mr. Gray.

"Good morning, Mr. Gray."

"Good morning, William." Mr. Gray took the mail. "Thank you."

"My pleasure." He gave Mr. Gray a thoughtful curl of the brow. "Say... Mr. Gray. Your thoughts on birthday cake. Chocolate or white?"

Mr. Gray had been dealing with unexpected questions from Will for the young man's entire life.

"White cake, chocolate frosting," he answered with hardly a moment's hesitation.

"Sounds good. I like it," said Will. He started away in the direction of the kitchen. "Thank you, Mr. Gray."

Anna stood at the water's edge. The ever-present fog drifted slowly past. The only sound was that of the light surf.

Miles walked up the beach toward her. As he neared, he spoke nostalgically.

"Do you remember the first time we came here?"

"The six of us." Anna kept her gaze to the horizon. "The motel had been open only a few weeks."

"The fog was the same." Miles stood beside Anna, looked out toward the same horizon in the distance. "I don't remember the smell being this bad."

"It was. You were too busy to notice."

"Ah, youth," said Miles nostalgically.

"Absolutely," said Anna. She looked from the ocean to Miles. Her attention drifted then to the embankment up the beach, the unseen motel on the other side. "Jack was three when Jason and Sarah came here one summer. The boy loved it. He talked of nothing else for weeks afterward."

"And so when..."

"Yes. We came here. Jack brought *here* to us."

They stood silent then, listening to the surf. After a few moments, Miles turned his head and looked up the beach. A lone figure waited in the distance.

Jason stood patiently waiting. He looked old and withered.

Miles turned to Anna. He raised a questioning brow.

Anna gave a kind smile and gentle nod in reply. Miles placed a soft hand on Anna's arm before starting away. He walked up the beach toward Jason.

Jason started forward and they met a dozen paces from Anna.

"Thank you, Clive," he said.

"We have only a few minutes," said Miles. "Try to make the best of them."

"Thank you." Jason continued up the beach toward Anna, stopped two paces from her. He waited, watched for some sign.

Anna turned her attention back to the sea, to the horizon beyond.

"Mother," said Jason.

"Hello, Jason," said Anna, not yet looking at him.

Further up the beach, Miles reached the base of the embankment. He turned about, stuffed his hands into his jacket pockets and watched Anna and Jason for several moments.

He started then up the side of the embankment.

Alice stood before the window in her room, the sunlight warming her, feeding her. The world was quiet, calm, peaceful. Her eyes were closed, and she drifted, drifted...

A dark place, an empty place. A void. There, in the distance, a shifting shadow in the black. It reached out to her, reached for her...

She opened her eyes, wide, afraid. She quickly sucked in a breath and leaned forward, placed both hands flat on the glass of the window. She spoke in a desperate, fearful, harsh whisper.

"It wasn't him. Not, not him. Dark, dark, so dark... it wasn't Jason."

She pulled back from the window, stepped back, stumbled back. She turned about, looked into the room, ready to call out, to warn them, to warn everyone.

But she was alone.

"It's coming," she said. "It's coming."

~ End

Willow City

Chapter One

The train passenger car was old, well-worn, well-used. Narrow, wooden bench seats faced one another, most of them occupied. The passengers wore simple clothes; some were in quiet conversation, but most were silent. There was a gentle rocking to the train car, the hollow clack-clack sound of train wheels on tracks.

Alan Thornton was sitting near a window, staring into the darkness beyond the glass. He was one of but a few passengers with a bench seat to himself. He was in his late thirties, clean-shaven, his hair military cut without being tight and high. He had the look of military without the uniform. He wore a plain, inexpensive sport jacket, a white shirt with no tie.

He turned from the window and glanced about at the passengers.

A young woman and a four year old boy were sitting on the bench directly across from him. The boy was looking at him. Alan looked casually back without comment.

The boy's mother looked from the boy to Alan, back to the boy. She leaned near her son and whispered something. The boy ignored her and continued to look blankly at Alan.

Across the aisle, a man was reading a newspaper. He looked up from his paper to Alan. His expression didn't change. He turned the page of his newspaper, refolded it and returned to his reading.

Alan looked again to the woman and the boy. Both were watching him now. He tried to ignore them, turned again to the darkness beyond the window; the sound of wheels on the tracks, the gentle rocking of the passenger car.

The door at the front of the car opened, the conductor came in. He closed the door behind him and started down the aisle. "Three minutes. Three minutes to Willow City." He continued past Alan. "Three minutes."

Passengers began moving about, preparing for their arrival in Willow City. There were no raised voices, no happy comments. The conductor reached the rear of the car and exited.

Alan looked away from the passengers and again to the darkness beyond the window.

He was in no rush.

Alan stepped down from the passenger car and onto the station platform, an olive-drab duffle in hand. He was the last one out of the train. He took a moment to look about the platform.

A drab-colored wall ran the length of the platform, narrow gate openings every forty feet with turnstiles through which passengers were passing. There were old posters on the wall, their edges torn, corners curled with age. One pictured a proud soldier welcoming fellow solders home, another encouraged joining in the defense of the Federation. All the posters were either in support of the city-state or of the national government. All had a strong authoritarian air.

There was very little conversation on the platform considering the number of people moving about. Alan walked to the nearer gate and waited in line. A heavily-harmed transportation security officer stood near the turnstile, to one side of the transportation official. He studied each passenger as they inserted their ID cards into the reader before passing through.

Alan's turn came. He brought his ID card from his shirt pocket as he approached, slipped it into the card reader. When the indicator turned green, he pulled out the card.

The transportation official watched a monitor. Alan's picture and personal data displayed:

Thornton, Alan, Master Sergeant, Retired.

When a second indicator light turned green Alan continued on through the turnstile and took a set of stairs up into the station. A row of ticket cages ran along one wall, two rows of wooden benches lined the wall opposite. Tall windows and several double doors were set into the front wall directly ahead.

Two security officers watched travelers coming and going. The station was relatively quiet, voices muffled.

Alan started across the floor toward the exit. As he neared the doors, a middle-aged man came through from outside wearing a long, gray coat and shaking a wet umbrella as he readied to close it. He stepped to one side and let Alan pass.

The world outside was dark, still, quiet. The street, sidewalks and buildings all had a wet sheen from the recent rain. The air felt damp.

There were three taxis parked at the curb, the vehicles older, nondescript, high-profile sedans. Alan walked to the first taxi in line, opened the back door and tossed his duffle. He climbed in after it. A video display was set into the back of the driver's seat, an ID reader directly beside the display. Alan slipped his ID card into the slot, pulled it out when the indicator showed green.

Only then did the driver say anything, speaking to the rear view mirror.

"Where to?" he asked, no emotion.

Alan settled into the seat. "Veterans Center."

"Which one?"

"The one with the fewest fleas."

"That'd be Vet Cen 6." The driver started the vehicle. "On Broadway."

"That's fine." Alan turned his attention to the view beyond the side window.

The taxi pulled away from the curb. Alan absently watched the scene passing by as they traveled the city; dark streets with glowing globes on tall, evenly spaced lamp poles, wet brick buildings with lighted windows. There were only a handful of vehicles on the streets, most of them other taxis. There were a few pedestrians about, most wearing dark or gray coats.

The taxi slowed only slightly as it maneuvered past a police van, the rear doors open. Several bound prisoners were being roughly pushed into the back of the van. Another prisoner, at the direction of another armed police officer, was removing posters from the side of a building.

The driver turned the taxi onto Broadway, worked his way up the empty street before pulling up to the curb in front of Veterans Center 6. Alan climbed out of the back, reached back in and pulled out his duffle. He closed the door without a word to the driver, turned his attention to the building in front of him as the taxi pulled away.

The veterans center was a wide, squat three-storey building. There were several large windows along the first floor, rows of smaller, evenly spaced windows on the second and third floors.

Alan crossed the walk and entered the lobby. There was an open-space lounge to the left with a mismatched assortment of old couches, chairs, side tables and coffee tables. A television monitor was mounted on the wall.

Alan continued ahead to the front desk on the right and set his duffle at his feet. The desk clerk looked like a retired military man, though a few years of civilian life appeared to have softened him up some. He had put on a few extra pounds, but had kept his hair cropped short and his clothes neat and trim.

"Yes sir?" he asked.

"I need a room," said Alan.

The desk clerk slid a card reader across the counter. Alan took his ID card from his pocket and slipped it into the slot. When the indicator light showed green, he pulled the card out and slipped it back into his pocket.

The desk clerk looked at the display that was set behind the counter.

"Master Sergeant Thornton," he stated. "Welcome to Willow City. How long will you be staying?"

"Retired," said Alan. "A couple of weeks, at least."

The clerk moved to one side, began working at a keyboard as he looked at another monitor.

"I'll put you down for a month, with an option for more, just in case."

"That'll be fine. Thanks."

The clerk finished entering data, hit a key. He brought a plastic key card out, slid it across the counter to Alan.

"Room 304," he said. "Two flights up, but its real quiet."

Alan took the key card. He nodded acknowledgment to the desk clerk as he picked up his duffle and looked in the direction of the staircase at the far end of the lobby.

"Much appreciated," he said, starting to the staircase.

Three older veterans watched from the lounge. The television monitor on the wall was displaying a news story of a small group of unruly disruptives being collected and hauled away so that school children could continue their outing to the Willow City museum.

Alan reached the third floor and started down a wide, dimly lit hallway. The carpet was old, faded and well-worn from years of foot traffic. He reached the door with "304" displayed on it. Sliding the key card into the slot, he heard a hard click sound and pushed the door open.

The room was simple, sparse; a twin bed and bedside table, a desk and chair. A narrow door led to the bathroom. There was a small flat-screen television monitor mounted on one wall.

He tossed the duffle onto the bed and walked to the window. Pulling the curtain aside, the view was of the street in front of the center. There were evenly spaced globe lamps on tall poles. Across the street was a dark, two-storey building of brick, a handful of windows on the second floor, all dark.

Chapter Two

Come morning, Alan worked his way downstairs to the main floor. A young soldier in uniform stood at the front desk, his duffle at his feet. He was talking with the desk clerk behind the counter.

Alan turned right at the foot of the stairs, went through an open doorway and entered the phone center. The room was square, two walls lined with old phone booths of wood and glass; a handful of the booths were occupied.

A well-armed security officer was standing to one side, quietly observing all activity while appearing slightly bored.

Alan went to the nearest available booth, closed the door and sat on the small bench. He slid his ID card into the slot. The indicator light turned green, and he returned the card to his shirt pocket. He reached down and brought a small notebook from his jacket pocket. Opening it, he turned several pages until he found the page with a phone number written on it and nothing else.

He returned the notebook to his pocket, lifted the phone receiver and keyed in the number. There were two muffled rings, then a hollow click.

He heard a voice then. "Chavez."

"Alan Thornton," said Alan.

"Hello, Alan," said Chavez. "When'd you get in?"

"Last night." Alan glanced out into the phone center. Several people were walking across the room. The security officer quietly watched it all. "Are you free today?" he asked.

"I can be," said Chavez. "Six o'clock?"

"That's fine. Gray Swan."

"Six, then. See ya', Alan."

"Chavez." Alan placed the receiver back in the cradle. He took a moment, then opened the door and slid out of the booth.

The security officer eyed Alan, his focus drifted then to another of the phone center customers.

Alan left the phone center, took the short side hall to the Vet Center's cafeteria. It was small for a cafeteria, with eight tables scattered about the room, half of them occupied, veterans eating their breakfast in silence.

A self-serve buffet counter was set along the back wall. A drink dispenser was set against the right wall next to a counter with silverware, glasses and napkins.

Alan worked his way across the room to the buffet. He took a tray from the stack, grabbed a plate. Working his way along the buffet, he spooned up a serving of scrambled eggs and grabbed two pieces of toast. He placed a fork and napkin on his tray and walked to an empty table.

He ate in silence, glanced now and then at those at the other tables, but other than that he kept to himself.

He looked up again, briefly, when someone new came into the cafeteria. He ignored the man as he approached his table and rested a hand on the back of the chair across from him.

Cavanaugh appeared calm, confident. He was in his thirties, dressed casual but not inexpensive. His hair was well-groomed, combed back from a high forehead.

"Master Sergeant," he said calmly. "Mind if I sit down?"

Alan kept eating, but indicated the chair.

"Retired," he stated.

"If you say so." Cavanaugh pulled out the chair and sat down. "The name's Cavanaugh. I wanted to drop by and welcome you home."

"Thanks." Alan scooped up another forkful of scrambled eggs. "How's Cain holding up these days?"

Cavanaugh smiled at Alan's observation.

"Mr. Cain is doing quite well. He sends his best."

"Uh, huh," Alan managed. "Tell him I said hi."

"I'll certainly do that." Cavanaugh leaned forward then, rested his arms on the table. He clasped his hands. "Mr. Cain would also like you to know that if there is anything he can do to help you with your endeavor, you have but to ask."

"Is that so?" Alan took another bite of scrambled eggs. "Cain could save me a lot of trouble. A few answers, maybe point me to where I need to go."

"Mr. Cain doesn't have your answers, Sergeant Thornton." Cavanaugh slid his arms from the table, leaned back in his chair. "But I can assure you that if he can open a door, perhaps clear a path—"

"I have but to ask," finished Alan.

"Exactly." Cavanaugh took a sharp breath, gave a half-smile. He slid his chair back and got to his feet. "Again, welcome home."

Alan used his fork to draw the last of his scrambled eggs into a pile, scooped up the forkful.

"Thanks." He shoveled scrambled egg into his mouth. "I might just take Cain up on his offer."

Cavanaugh nodded acknowledgment and good-bye. Alan picked up a piece of toast and took as bite as he watched him leave the cafeteria.

The desk clerk stepped up to the counter when Alan stepped from the staircase and approached the front desk.

"Good afternoon, Sergeant Thornton. How is your room?"

"Very quiet, as you said," said Alan. "How can I get a cab?"

The desk clerk reached for the phone behind the counter, picked up the heavy receiver.

"One quick call," he stated.

"Thanks." Alan moved away from the counter and started toward the front door.

Outside, evening gray would soon be giving way to dark. Alan waited at curb, stood patiently, looking patiently up and down the street. A police vehicle passed slowly by, the officer in the passenger seat eyeing Alan with indifference.

It was several minutes more before a taxi appeared, approached the veterans center and pulled up before Alan. He opened the back door of the cab and climbed into the back seat. He slipped his ID card into the reader, pulled it out when the indicator turned green.

He spoke to the cabbie as he slid back in the seat. "The Gray Swan."

The outside of the nightclub was little more than a plain wall with a simple door. Above the door was a simple sign that read "The Gray Swan".

The taxi came slowly around a corner and pulled up to the curb in front of the nightclub. Alan climbed out, closed the door. The taxi pulled away as Alan walked toward the nightclub door.

Entering the nightclub, the Gray Swan was narrow and deep. Booths lined one wall, a bar lined the other. There were several dozen tables on the floor, with a stage at the far end, raised about a foot and a half above the club floor.

Carl Underwood was sitting at a piano to one side of the stage, tickling the ivories without really playing.

Carl was forty five years old, African American with close-cropped hair that was graying at the temples. Hard-rimmed glasses sat on his large nose. He held a cigarette between his lips; the ashtray atop the piano was half-filled with ash and butts.

Other than Carl there was only Eddie, standing behind the bar, and two men sitting at one of the tables nursing their drinks. The place was open for business but things wouldn't begin to pick up for another hour.

Carl looked out across the room, watched Alan cross the club floor to the bar. He gave Alan a nod when Alan looked in his direction, continued working the piano keys, watched absently as Alan placed an order with the bartender.

Carl's sister Bonnie Harper walked across the stage and leaned against the piano. She was in her forties but a hard life was reflected as wear-and-tear on her face. She was wearing a dressing gown, as if she were partially dressed for the evening's show.

Carl glanced briefly up at his sister, noted that she saw Alan standing at the bar waiting for his order.

"He just came in," he said, returning to his piano keys.

"So I see," said Bonnie. "He shouldn't have come back."

"Come on, sis. What choice did he have?"

Bonnie watched Alan turn from the bar, tall glass in hand, and walk across the floor toward the row of booths. "Five'll get you ten that Cain already knows he's here," she said.

"Ten'll get you twenty Alan knows that." More tickling of the keys; he stopped then and looked over at Alan, who was just sliding into a booth. "He's here to find his brother. Arthur Cain may be able to help."

"Oh, I expect Arthur Cain knows exactly where Richard is buried." Bonnie pushed away from the piano, on her way backstage to finish getting ready for the evening's shows.

In the booth, Alan took a long drink from his glass, watched Bonnie Harper leave the stage. He looked over then to Carl. Carl gave Alan a slow nod, returned his focus to tickling the ivories.

As the late afternoon drew nearer to early evening, activity in the club slowly picked up, though it remained fairly quiet. The pair of men at the table in middle of the floor continued talking back and forth. Now and then someone new entered the club; a woman went to the bar, a couple settled at a table near the stage. Carl continued working at the piano.

Chavez slid into the booth opposite Alan.

"Alan... long time, my friend. You look good." Chavez was Hispanic, in his late thirties. He had a dark complexion and dark hair, was husky but not overweight. He was dressed in khaki pants, a button shirt and light jacket.

"Good to see you, Chavez." Alan took another drink from his glass. "How's the wife and kid?"

"Keepin' outta trouble," said Chavez with a shrug.

"That's as good as it gets, these days."

"Can't expect more, my friend." Chavez looked across to the bartender. He caught his attention, and that was all it took. Eddie nodded, took a mug and began pulling a draft.

Chavez indicated Alan's glass. "Still with the iced tea, eh?"

"Never ran across a reason to change," said Alan.

"The war," Chavez stated flatly.

"I'm done with that," said Alan.

"Yeah... so I hear," said Chavez. He leaned back to allow the bartender to set the beer mug on the table. "Thank you, Eddie."

Eddie winked conspiratorially to Alan as he responded to Chavez.

"Booth service costs you extra, Chavez."

"Ah... and so explains the gross miscalculation on my tab."

Eddie gave another look to Alan before turning from the booth.

"Don't let this guy lead you astray, Thornton," he said.

"That's gonna be tough, Eddie," said Alan. "The man just oozes trust."

"I see that... the aura is blinding."

Chavez half-grinned at the departing Eddie and took a swallow from his beer.

"Done your twenty and out, eh?" he asked Alan, setting the mug back on the table.

"I'm done with that," repeated Alan.

"I get ya'," said Chavez, a bit darkly. "It never was what they said it was."

There was an uncomfortable pause, then. Alan's attention drifted out across the nightclub. Another group was settling in at a table near the stage.

Chavez took another drink from his beer.

"You home for good, then?" he asked.

"Depends."

"Right," sighed Chavez. "That."

"That."

"It could be difficult, my friend. What you're doing, what you're looking to do, is most inconvenient for those who thought the matter closed."

"They thought wrong." Alan looked down at his iced tea, turned the glass about, took a drink. "So what happened to my brother?" he asked.

"Sorry, man. I don't know." Chavez indicated the nightclub. "He was here that night. Disappeared sometime after that."

"Who do you think *disappeared* him?"

Chavez shrugged. "He'd been pissing in the mayor's cereal for two years. "Could be the city-state."

Alan watched several newly arrived customers move past the booth on their way to another.

"What about Arthur Cain?"

"Possible, I suppose," said Chavez. "Richard didn't make many friends there, either."

"I've already had a visit," said Alan. "Offering to help."

"No doubt. You take him up on it?"

"It's an option."

Chavez frowned, shook his head. "Cain, the Mayor, Chief Archer... interesting bedfellows. A complicated relationship."

"I might be able to use that."

"Tread carefully there. That relationship has been strained of late."

Alan only nodded at that. He didn't really know how he might use that situation to accomplish his goals in any event. It was something, though, to put on the shelf to bring down later.

Chavez watched Alan a moment, took another drink from his beer.

"It's really great to see you again, Alan, but I'm not sure what I can do to help. The city has only gotten darker since your last visit. I've mostly been laying low. What connections I had, what feeds I had, long gone or outright dead."

A waitress made an appearance out on the floor, stood at a table ready to take an order. Several more customers entered the nightclub.

"I gotta think of the family," Chavez finished.

"I get it. It's cool." Alan lifted his glass. "I'll dust off a few of my own old connections, see if any of 'em are still breathing."

"Other than me?" Chavez smirked. "You got connections other than me?"

Alan ignored the comment. He took a cautious look about them.

"I could use a weapon," he stated. "Couldn't bring anything into the city."

"That won't be easy."

"I don't want you to put yourself in Archer's headlights."

"No." Chavez hesitated. "I may know someone. Give me a couple of days."

Alan considered. "A couple of days should be about right."

"You plannin' on walkin' into something where you need a gun?"

"Not at all," said Alan in a flat tone.

Chavez studied Alan's blank expression for a long moment.

"Yeah," he said at last, rather cautiously. "I can't promise anything, but I might be about to come up with something."

Bonnie Harper appeared on the stage then, fully dressed for her show. She walked over to Carl at the piano; they fell into conversation.

Chavez finished off his beer, slid out of the booth.

"Gotta run," he said. "Vet Center 6, right?"

"Room 304."

Chavez rested a hand on Alan's should as he passed him on his way out. "Watch yourself, my friend."

Alone again, Alan settled back, watched as Carl and Bonnie made preparations to start their first set.

He took a final swallow of his tea then, looked across at the waitress standing beside a nearby table. When she looked his way, his lifted the empty glass. She nodded acknowledgment.

Up on the stage, Bonnie moved to the microphone, looked out across the nightclub floor.

"Good evening, everyone," she said. "What say we get this started?"

There was a light clapping from the audience, which was still somewhat sparse.

"All right, then." Bonnie looked in Carl's direction, and he began working the keys. Bonnie turned again to the audience, repositioned the microphone, and began a classic, smoky, 40s song in the film noir style...

Several hours later, the overhead lights were dimmed, most of the tables and booths were occupied. Alan was alone in his booth, leaning back, one arm resting on the table, the other on the back of the booth seat.

On the stage, Bonnie stood at the microphone, a soft-lit spotlight on her. She was in the midst of another song as Carl backed her at the piano. When they finished, the audience clapped appreciatively and the house lights came up.

"Thank you, ladies and gentlemen," she said. "My brother Carl and I will be taking a short break, but we'll be back for the second set before you know it. Don't you be going anywhere."

She nodded another thank you, took a step back and turned to walk over to the piano to a second round of light clapping. She took the cigarette from Carl, drew on it, then handed it back and breathed out a cloud of smoke.

Alan shifted position as she stepped off the stage and walked in his direction. He leaned forward and placed his forearms on the table as she slid into the booth opposite him.

"Bonnie," he said. "You sound great."

"Thanks." She pulled Alan's glass of tea across the table, took a swallow, and slid it back. "What the hell are you doing here, Alan?"

"Listenin' to bluesy jazz."

"You don't do cute very well."

"Good to see you, too."

Bonnie frowned then, took a slow breath and studied Alan.

"I've missed you," she said at last. "Now get your ass out of town."

"I can't do that," Alan stated calmly.

"You won't find your brother. You'll just end up dead. Hell, ya' got the mayor and police chief on one side, Arthur Cain on the other, and you're not exactly on the best of terms with either."

"So long as neither's the cause of whatever happened to Richard, I got no quarrel with either."

Bonnie slid forward, leaned over the table.

"The last time you were in town," she said, "you called the mayor a tyrant and Cain his flunky."

"Okay, I was wrong on that," Alan said, smirking. "The mayor's the flunky."

"Damn it, Alan. You stirred up a lot of crap. And you're only gonna make things worse coming back looking for Richard."

"And you really think I can let this go..." Alan's words were a cool statement.

"What's to let go? I'm sorry. He's gone."

Alan grasped his glass as he leaned in close. "Whatever happened to Richard, I will know who is responsible."

Bonnie reached out and placed a hand on Alan's arm. Carl approached the booth and Bonnie looked to him for support as he slid in beside Alan.

"Yeah, we kinda' figured that," she said.

Carl nodded curtly. "About time for the next set, Sis."

Bonnie gave a slow nod in response, looked warmly across at Alan, still holding his arm.

"It really is good to see you." She leaned back and slid out of the booth.

Carl spoke to Alan as he watched his sister walk back to the stage.

"Times are bad right now, Alan. The mayor's really clamping down. Laws changing, policies; and he's got the chief black-booting all over town."

From all that Alan had heard, and in some cases had witnessed, it was the same with the other city-states.

"What about Cain?" he asked.

"Arthur Cain's a whole other story," said Carl. "The syndicate is as strong as it ever was, but he's still gotta dance the tune with city hall."

"I understand there's a bit of strain there."

"You could say that. Something'll give soon, and when it does... it's gonna get ugly 'round here." He slid out of the booth then, held a hand out to shake hands. "Gotta get back. Good to see you, Alan."

"Thanks, man."

They shook hands, and Carl leaned in close.

"I got someone who might be able to help. She'll be at Sally's at ten." He pulled back, gave Alan a pat on the shoulder. "Enjoy the show, my man."

The night was dark, damp and a bit muggy. The asphalt streets and brick walls shone with damp. A car passed, a few moments later another. Alan approached the intersection; Sally's Café was on the corner across the street, large windows facing the cross streets.

What appeared to be an unmarked police car was parked across from the café. Two people were sitting in the front seat.

Alan crossed the intersection, looked in through the windows and noted the few customers in the café before entering.

Booths lined the exterior windowed walls, a lunch counter ran the length of the café. Two of the stools at the counter were occupied, and a group of men were sitting in a booth at the far end of the café.

A woman in her thirties was sitting alone in a booth near the door. Her thick, blonde hair fell in waves to her shoulders. Her dark eyes always seemed to be in shadow, creating an air of the femme fatale.

Alan slid into the booth opposite the woman. She hardly looked at him, pointedly ignoring him. She took a long sip from her coffee, set the cup onto the saucer with a soft clink sound.

Alan waited for some acknowledgment from her. She looked at him briefly, but said nothing.

"Valerie Baker?" he asked.

"Who's asking?" she asked.

"Alan Thornton."

Valerie studied Alan a moment.

"I see the resemblance," she said at last.

"You know Richard?"

Valerie slowly lifted her cup and took another sip of her coffee.

"I knew him," she said.

The waitress came to the table. She held a pad and pencil and looked expectantly at Alan. He glanced up at her, then past her at a glass display case behind the counter.

"Coffee and apple pie." He took his ID card and handed it to her.

"You got it."

Valerie looked side-glance at the receding waitress.

"That a valid ID?" she asked Alan.

"Yes."

"Then they're tracking you."

The barest hint of a grin. "I expect that's so."

Valerie thought that comment over for a moment, realized what he was saying.

"I see. You watch yourself, Mr. Thornton."

"I'm hearing that a lot lately." Alan straightened, leaned a bit closer to the table. "What happened to my brother?"

Valerie took another sip of her coffee, set the cup back onto the saucer. She looked dispassionately across to Alan.

"I don't know."

Alan stared back. "I was told you could help," he stated flatly.

"And just what is it that you need help with, Mr. Thornton?"

"I want to know what happened to my brother."

"And?"

"And hold those responsible to account."

"Good luck with that." There was a moment's hesitation. "You're certain something bad happened..."

"Are you saying different?"

"Not at all. I know something bad happened. But what makes you think so?"

"Because he's disappeared and nobody can tell me where he's gone. Can you?"

The waitress returned then with a slice of pie, a coffee cup and a carafe of coffee. She filled Alan's cup, then refilled Valerie's. She set Alan's ID card beside his plate of pie.

Valerie nodded a thank you to the waitress and when the woman left she slid her cup aside and looked again to Alan.

"Richard and I spent time together off and on," she said. "Our circles didn't exactly overlap, but I think we had something. We weren't going to walk down the aisle anytime soon, but we sometimes held hands."

"You don't seem his type."

"As I said, different circles. I think he liked that." Glancing out the window, she could see the unmarked vehicle parked across the street. She looked back to Alan, indicated his pie. "Eat your pie. You don't want to draw attention."

Alan pulled the plate toward him, then ignored it.

"All right. So you hold hands."

Valerie took a drink from her coffee, lifted a brow at Alan and his untouched slice of pie.

She waited.

Alan picked up his fork, took a bite of the pie.

Only then did she continue.

"Richard and I were at the Gray Swan the night he disappeared," she said. "We left about eleven, went to my place, held hands. That was the last I saw of him; the last anyone saw him, best I can tell."

"His friends?"

"I was the last to see him."

"You went to the police?"

Valerie gave a half-smirk, took another drink of her coffee. She placed the cup carefully back onto the saucer.

"Sure."

She glanced down at the pie. He took another bite, took a swallow of his coffee. She glanced over at the two people seated at the counter, then at the men in the booth at the far end of the café. No one appeared to be paying any mind to her and Alan.

"Listen, if I can help, I'll help. But I've gone down this path. I'm not sure what more we'll find."

"Thanks," Alan said evenly. "So, what's in it for you?"

"Simple justice." That came all too quickly, all too matter-of-factly.

Alan eyed her as if waiting for Valerie to change her answer. She took a thoughtful breath, stared down at her now empty cup.

"Maybe a little revenge," she said.

Alan continued to study her, holding his silence. She gave a shrug then.

"A little money wouldn't hurt."

"Just how do you plan on accomplishing that?"

"No idea. Till you showed up, this whole thing was stuffed in a box."

"Right." He looked away, looked down at the partially eaten pie. He looked up at Valerie. "So what do you think happened?"

"No shortage of ideas on that. Like I said, I've gone down this path. Ideas, not many answers." Valerie wondered aloud then. "William might have something."

"William?"

"A friend," said Valerie. "William kept digging when everyone else gave it up. I can see if he's willing to talk about it."

"I'd appreciate it. You can reach me at Vet Cen 6."

"I know."

At that, Alan looked questioningly at Valerie, and she responded by indicating the ID card on the table. She slid out of the booth.

"Finish your pie," she stated. She left the café.

Alan looked down at the last of his pie as he absently drank the last of his coffee.

Chapter Three

Alan lay asleep in his darkened room, lit only by the dull glow of a neon light coming from outside. A banging on the door brought him awake, though he didn't appear particularly startled. Nor was he surprised or concerned.

He sat up, looked over at the clock on the bedside table. It showed 1:30.

Another bang, bang, bang at the door.

He stood and walked casually to the door, dressed only in undershirt and boxer shorts.

He unlocked and opened the door, again not surprised at what he saw.

Two Willow City police officers stood in the hall. Sgt. Burke was forty years old, tall, strong featured and barrel-chested. His partner was shorter, thinner, younger. Both were wearing well-fitting police uniforms, weapons in holsters.

Burke stepped smoothly through the open doorway, forcing Alan to take a step back into the room. The police sergeant showed a thin, menacing smile, had a sparkle in his eye.

"Good evening, Thornton," he said, looking about the room. "It's been a while."

"Hello, Burke... a few years," said Alan. "I could have gone a few more without seeing your pretty face." He watched Burke's partner come into the room behind Burke, move off to one side and look methodically about.

"Not my call," said Burke. He waved a hand to his partner for him to search the room. He spoke calmly to Alan as he casually watched his partner toss aside blankets and look through drawers. "What brings you back to our fair city, Thornton?"

"Visiting family."

"I heard about Richard," said Burke. "Tough, that."

His partner turned to Burke and shook his head. Alan raised a brow.

"Were you looking for anything in particular?"

"Not really." Burke gave a final look about the room. "Get dressed. Detective Sullivan would like a word."

At that, Partner reached down and grabbed a pair of pants that were folded on the chair, tossed them to Alan. Alan grabbed them out of the air.

"Sullivan keeps strange hours these days," he said, putting on his pants.

Partner spoke for the first time. "We're none of us happy about it," he said. "We got you to thank for it."

"You know how Sullivan works, Thornton." Burke tapped at his temple. "Always thinking, working the angles." He indicated the door. "Grab your shoes. Let's go."

Alan sat on the edge of the bed and slipped on his shoes, then grabbed his jacket and followed Burke out the door, Partner following.

There was a black sedan parked at the curb in front of the building. Burke guided Alan from the front door across the sidewalk and deposited him into the back seat of the sedan as Partner moved around the vehicle to climb into the driver's seat.

A nondescript man watched from the nearby shadows.

Alan was escorted through the heavy double doors and into the police station lobby. Benches lined the front wall behind them as they entered, currently occupied by several glum-looking customers. Ahead of them was a tall counter with a desk sergeant at his station talking with someone standing before the counter. Beyond the counter, several officers worked at cluttered desks.

Partner moved off as Burke took Alan's arm and guided him across the room toward a wide hallway. He was taken to a small interrogation room and left alone to sit at a metal table to wait for Detective Sullivan. Short curtains were drawn closed in the center of one wall, the familiar interrogation room two-way mirror behind it.

A minute passed. And then another.

The indicator light on the camera that was mounted on the wall turned off as Alan watched.

A minute later, Detective Sullivan entered the room, two folders in hand. He was dressed in a simple suit, his dark hair neatly combed. His expression was calm, unbothered. He looked placidly at Alan as he walked to the table, pulled out the chair opposite Alan and sat down. He set the folders on the table in front of him.

"Hello, Alan," he said. "It's been what, two years?"

Alan slid his arms off the table, sat back and dropped his hands into his lap.

"Detective Sullivan. How's the wife?"

"Which one?" Sullivan spoke as he opened the top folder and began looking through the paperwork.

"Things all right between you and Karen?"

"They are now," said Sullivan. "It's surprising what a divorce can smooth over."

"I'm sorry to hear that."

"Yeah." Sullivan looked over one of the documents in the folder. "Are you enjoying your visit?" He put on a slight smile. "How's Sally's apple pie?"

"Great."

"It is, isn't it? I need to drop in again one of these days. I just never seem to be able to find the time."

"With the hours you keep, I'm not surprised."

"Such is the life of a police officer." Sullivan closed the folder. "You should have come to us, Alan. We'd have been more than happy to provide you with what information we have regarding Richard's disappearance."

"That so?" Alan asked casually.

"All part of the job. We serve the people of Willow City."

"Hey, I'm all ears."

"Yes, well..." Sullivan set aside the top folder, opened the second. He began reading through the documents. "Honestly, there's not much to it. He was brought in for questioning on the evening of June 12, some three months back. He was released several hours later."

"And?"

Sullivan turned the page, glanced over the next sheet. He closed the folder then and set it atop the first.

"He was to be kept under surveillance, but he managed to lose his monitors almost immediately."

"Really..." Alan sounded dubious.

"His whereabouts have been unknown since that evening." He glanced briefly up at Alan, then to the pair of folders. "It is believed that he went into hiding."

Alan studied Sullivan for a long moment. What the detective had said hadn't given him much, but it was information that he could build on. Also, knowing what they were willing to give, and not give, could be valuable.

"Thanks for the info," he said. "Why am I here, Detective?"

Sullivan slowly leaned away from the table, held his hands out in a friendly gesture.

"Just chatting, Alan. Catching up."

"All right. In the spirit of chatting… mind if I ask a question?"

Sullivan said nothing, smiled in answer. Alan took that as a yes.

"Why was Richard brought in for questioning to begin with?" he asked. "He's no criminal. And he has no strong political beliefs one way or the other. He was certainly no threat to Willow City."

Sullivan leaned nearer the table again, indicated the folders that he had set to one side.

"The reason for his interrogation was not specified."

"Really?"

"Curious, I know," said Sullivan. "However, from what I recall of that time, your brother's business interests had grown questionable."

"Richard ran Intercity Trade. Import export. He wasn't even one of the big players. His business was small potatoes; literally."

Sullivan drew a tight smile. "His professional engagements had been broadening."

"Waddya mean, *broadening*?"

"Just what I said."

Alan let that statement lay in the heavy silence for a few moments. What Sullivan was saying may have been true, probably was. It was information Alan would file away for later. But the statement itself… was Sullivan trying to lead Alan toward something, or away from something?

For now, he continued along the line Sullivan was traveling.

"And these *broadened engagements* conflicted with city hall," he stated.

"His discord with others perhaps even more than with us," said Sullivan. He grew thoughtful, silently considered whether to expand on the city-state aspect of that comment. "The bureaucratic dynamics of our city-state haven't changed much since your last visit. Political evolution is a slow process."

"Slow? With one party in permanent control, I'd say it's a dead crawl."

"So you understand. T'wasn't always so, but we work with what we have. Yes?"

Alan said nothing.

Sullivan gave a reflective expression. "I don't believe your brother ever fully got that." He gave an easy nod then. "But you do."

"I do?"

"I can see that. I believe Chief Archer sees it, as well."

Alan pulled on his jacket as he stepped down from the police station front doors and onto the sidewalk. The air had turned cool, the night was dark but for cones of golden light shining down from street-lamp globes.

A vehicle was parked at the curb a hundred yards down the otherwise empty street. Its engine started. It moved slowly forward, stopped in front of Alan. The passenger window opened and Valerie Baker leaned across from the driver's side and looked up at Alan.

"Need a ride?"

Alan opened the passenger door and climbed in. Valerie pulled away from the curb and started up the street.

"So, how ya' doin'?" she asked, a bit heavy on the snarky.

Alan ignored the question. "Doesn't anyone ever sleep in this town? I seem to remember people sleeping."

Valerie, meanwhile, continued along her own thoughts. She glanced briefly at Alan before focusing again on her driving. "One on one with Sullivan?"

"He offered the full support of the Willow City Police Department," he stated flatly.

"Yeah. Quite a guy, that Detective Sullivan."

Alan accepted the sarcasm with a nod, stared out the passenger window, watched the buildings and side streets that passed by.

"Everyone is eager to help," he said. "All this assist, I should have everything wrapped up lickety-split."

"Lickety-split?"

"Sorry. Probably works better if you snap your fingers when you're saying it." He gave an embarrassed shrug. "Kid in my unit used to say it, drove me nuts, but I guess it stuck with me."

They traveled the streets in silence for a time, Alan watching the city passing by. He looked on dispassionately at the sight of several people quickly finishing putting posters up on the side of a building and then hurrying into the shadows.

They turned onto another street. Valerie's expression changed subtly then, the look a bit uncomfortable.

"Sullivan may run his own little fiefdom, but never forget that he works in Archer's shadow, and Police Chief Archer is the mayor's hellhound. They're each on their own power trip, but that power runs uphill, right to city hall."

She looked side-glance at Alan again, noted his blank expression.

"And you, of course, already know all this."

Alan said nothing.

"And you're poking the bear," she realized. "Why are you poking the bear? I'm sure you have a perfectly good reason for doing that."

Alan turned again to the view beyond the passenger window.

"Sometimes the best way to get answers is to listen to their questions," he said.

They reached an intersection and Valerie turned right. She eased the car to the curb in front of the Veterans Center.

Alan looked to Valerie as he opened the door.

"Thanks for the lift." He climbed out of the car, started to close the door, hesitated. He leaned back in, one hand on the roof of the car. "What can you tell me about Richard's business?" he asked.

"He ran Intercity Trade."

"Other than that."

"He kept busy," she said with a shrug. "Beyond that... I couldn't tell you."

"Okay." Alan frowned thoughtfully, finally patted the roof of the car. "Thanks."

"Sure."

He closed the door, watched the car pull away. He looked up and down the street, stuffed his hands into his jacket pockets, turned to the Veterans Center entrance.

The alley was clean. There were several trash cans and a garbage bin lined up neatly along one wall. Doors were set into the brick walls on both sides.

It was pre-dawn, the sun yet to rise above the city. The light that reached into the alley came from a street lamp on the street at the access to the alley.

William Valentine entered the alley, passing under the street lamp. William was middle-aged, middle-height, middle-weight, and a bit disheveled in his clothes and his attention to detail.

He slowed his walk midway down the alley, glanced back once behind him as he continued to a simple door. He pressed a set of numbers on the keypad beside the wall, opened and stepped through the door.

He walked a narrow hallway that was lit by several light fixtures set high on the left wall. There were two security cameras at work. He rounded a corner and started up a steep stairwell. Another camera was set high in one corner at the top of the stairs.

Reaching a tiny landing, he entered another set of numbers on another keypad beside the only door on the landing.

The loft he entered was divided into several areas. To the right was the living area, with couch, chairs and kitchen space; beyond a curtain was a bed and dresser.

To the left was the work area. Computers and monitors were on a long counter beneath a wall of barred windows. Most of the displays were flickering images, video and data. One monitor was displaying the video feeds from the security cameras.

A commercial printer and several smaller printers were lined up along one wall. Stacks of newspapers were piled on tables and chairs, some bundled and bound with twine, some stacked loose.

The loft had the air of constant clutter.

Valerie Baker was sitting on the couch reading a newspaper.

William was of course not surprised at seeing her there.

"Valerie," he said. "Have you been waiting long?"

Valerie set aside the newspaper, indicated a security camera mounted in one corner. "I believe you know exactly how long I've been waiting."

William grinned sheepishly as he moved to the kitchen area. He set about making a pot of coffee.

"I do enjoy the print, William, but it's dangerous. You should stick to your blogs and online news feeds."

William continued making the coffee. "It's all dangerous, Valerie. And I reach a whole different audience with the print."

"Don't give me that," she said. "You print because it bugs the crap out of City Hall."

"There is that." He grew more serious then. "Besides, with the stranglehold they have on tech these days, about the only folks that can read my online feeds are sitting in City Hall."

"Yeah... and they're going to get you one of these days."

"They'll get me in any case; one of these days." He moved to the table and sat facing Valerie. Behind him, the coffee pot was already beginning to burble. "Are you here about Thornton?" he asked.

Chapter Four

Chief Archer entered the Gray Swan and walked toward a booth. At sixty years old, he had a strong, athletic frame, sharp features, and an intense expression. His police uniform was tailored and crisp.

A young police officer followed two paces behind, stood silent nearby as Archer slid into the booth.

The nightclub was empty for Archer, his security man, and the bartender. Eddie drew a mug of beer and brought it over. He set it on the table in front of Archer.

"Good afternoon, Chief. Haven't seen you in here in a while."

Archer picked up the beer and took a swallow. "And yet you remember exactly what I need."

"The secret of a successful bartender, sir," said Eddie. "Never forget a man's favorite poison."

"The stratagem for life, Eddie." Archer took another swallow of his beer. He looked about the empty nightclub. "How's business these days?"

"Good enough to keep the doors open; occasionally a bit more."

"And the show?"

"You know Bonnie and Carl. Never a bad night in the Gray Swan."

"Good to hear," Archer said absently, watched Carl step onto the stage from backstage.

He took another deep draw from his beer.

"Another of these, Eddie. And one of Carl's poison."

"You got it, Chief."

Eddie started back to the bar as Carl came down from the stage and worked his way to Archer's booth. He didn't look particularly pleased to see the police chief, but managed cordiality nonetheless.

"Chief Archer. What brings you to the Gray Swan?"

Archer indicated that Carl should sit; Carl slid in opposite.

"Recent events seemed to warrant an appearance," said Archer.

"Alan Thornton," Carl said matter-of-factly.

Archer's slight grin said yes. "And it offers an opportunity to say hello," he added.

They grew silent when Eddie returned with another beer for Archer and water with lemon for Carl. Archer ignored Eddie, but Carl gave a nod in thank you. Eddie headed back to the bar with the empty mug.

Archer offered Carl a silent salute with his fresh beer, took a swallow.

Carl lifted his water glass but waited to take a drink. "And why would Alan's return home from the war warrant the police chief's visit to our quaint little establishment?"

Archer set his mug carefully down in front him. He watched Carl take a drink of his water and set his glass onto the table.

"I understand Thornton has been dropping in," he said.

"We're a friendly place," said Carl. "He has friends here. And he is living out of the vet center, after all. Where else 'he got to go?"

"Of course." Archer downs the last of his beer, sets the mug down less delicately than before. "And who might these friends be, Carl?"

"Friends. Me. Eddie. Folks."

"Of course. You run a nice club. I've always said so." He glanced casually about the club, back to Carl. "How's your sister these days? Her voice holding up?"

"Bonnie is fine, thanks. Quite well, actually."

"Good to hear. Maybe I'll drop in later, catch a set."

"Any time. We'll be here."

"Good, good." Archer slid out of the booth. He looked down at Carl. "And Carl... next time you see Alan, you be sure tell him I said hello."

"I'll do that," Carl said coolly.

The security officer stepped to one side as Archer started to the door, then followed after him two paces behind.

Carl took a drink from his water, stared thoughtfully at the glass. Eddie came over to the booth while looking questioningly in the direction of the closing front door.

"Carl? What the hell was that all about?"

"I can't say for sure, Eddie. But if I had to guess, I'd have to say it was a warning." He lifted his glass. "*Watch your step... they be watching.*"

§

The "Truth in Reporting" news broadcast was displaying on the television monitor in the Veterans Center lounge, the newscaster sitting at her anchor desk. The screen behind her was displaying an image of the broad avenue in front of the Federal Capital building.

Alan and an elderly veteran were sitting in a pair of easy chairs in the lounge, watching the broadcast.

"Welcome back to the afternoon edition of Truth in Reporting, a service of the National Education Office." read the news anchor. "We take you now to the Federal Capital, where excitement is building for this year's Founding Day and Ball."

The monitor display expanded to focus on the image behind the newscaster, filling the screen, changing then from a static image to a video showing workers putting together bleachers, barriers, canopies. The elderly veteran sitting next to Alan grumbled and shook his head sorrowfully, his attention focused on the story.

"Veterans find work," said the old vet, somber sarcasm.

"Excuse me?" asked Alan.

The old vet nodded at the monitor displaying the workers in action.

"Two weeks work. A week putting it all together, a week taking it all down." He gave a side-glance to Alan. "Oh, joy."

Cavanaugh came into the lounge then, dropped into a chair near Alan. He glanced once at the monitor, quickly dismissed the story and looked at Alan.

"Thornton. Do you know you already have this town abuzz?" he asked.

"I haven't done anything yet," said Alan, while pointedly continuing to watch the monitor.

"You're too modest. Your very presence is shining a light on what most around here would prefer remain in the shadows."

"Oh, you're just saying that."

The exchange was bringing a curious gaze from the elderly veteran. The news story on the television monitor continued, now little more than background noise.

Cavanaugh shifted nearer Alan. "Mr. Cain would like to meet with you," he said.

"To offer his help?" Alan's kept his eyes on the monitor.

Cavanaugh grinned. "In person."

The Truth in Reporting broadcast returned to the studio and the woman at the anchor desk.

The large, black sedan pulled up to the curb in front of Cain's Club. The front passenger door opened and Cavanaugh stepped out. A moment later the rear passenger door opened and Alan stepped out onto the wide, clean sidewalk.

The building before them was two-storey, with small windows spanning the second floor on either side of a colorful sign reading "Cain's Club" above the glass front door.

Cavanaugh walked to the front door and opened it, moved aside and gestured for Alan to enter.

A security guard in the foyer stood silent in Alan's path. Alan lifted his arms and held them out. The guard patted him down and then moved aside, nodded crisply to Cavanaugh as Cavanaugh escorted Alan the rest of the way into the club.

Arthur Cain was sitting at a table near the back of the club, was focused now on two ledgers that were on the table in front of him. An associate dressed in suit and tie stood nearby.

Cain was in his sixties, had a large frame, was neat and well-groomed. He glanced briefly up at the approaching Alan and Cavanaugh, closed one ledger, returned his attention to the open pages of the second.

Alan and Cavanaugh stopped several short paces from table and waited. Cain closed the second ledger, gathered the two books together and handed them the waiting associate. He nodded dismissal and the associate departed with the ledgers.

Cain focused his attention then on Alan.

"Mr. Thornton. Good of you to come."

"Happy to oblige, Mr. Cain." Alan's tone was flat.

Cain gave Cavanaugh a dismissive nod. Cavanaugh nodded in answer, took a step back, turned about and left. Cain indicated that Alan take the chair opposite, then waited for him to sit down.

"I understand you are home for good, Mr. Thornton."

"Can't say that's definite," said Alan. "Not yet."

"You're retired, I hear."

"That's right."

"Messy thing, the war." Cain appeared to grow thoughtful. "I never fully understood it, myself."

"Yeah, well... done with it, now."

"Home safe, then."

Alan gave a knowing half-smile at that comment, held his silence. Seeing Alan's smirk, Cain chuckled lightly in understanding.

"Yes, I suppose safety is a relative concept, isn't it?"

Alan held his slight smile, held his silence. After a few moments, Cain continued.

"You are looking into your brother's disappearance," he stated.

"I am," said Alan. This time it was Cain who held his silence, and so Alan went on. "Is this something you might be able to help me with?"

"I could make a few inquiries," said Cain.

"Nothing you can pass along right now, then..."

"Nothing beyond what you no doubt already know. Our city-state's uniformed finest picked him up; that was that."

"Any idea what my brother might have gotten himself into that would have attracted the wrong sort of attention?"

Cain considered, wore a shrewd smile. "Richard ran a trade business, so I understand."

"That doesn't quite answer my question though, does it?"

Cain looked to one side, raised a hand. His associate appeared as if out of nowhere. Cain looked back to Alan.

"Thirsty?" he asked.

"I'm fine," said Alan. "Thanks."

Cain spoke to his associate. "A water, please."

The associate left to get his water and Cain looked back to Alan.

"Richard had been pursuing certain gray market activities for several months prior to his disappearance," he said. "I believe the mayor suggested that he find another hobby."

"Gray market... outside his trade business."

"So I understand," said Cain.

"Like what? The man was trading vegetables, textiles."

Cain's associate returned with his glass of water. Cain waited while he set the glass on the table and again stepped back into the shadows.

"I have been told that his interests had expanded beyond acceptable boundaries," he stated then. "Who's to say why? Who's to say where such a path might lead?"

"Expanded to what?"

Cain only shrugged in answer, calmly took a drink of his water.

Alan frowned. "I would think such a path undertaken by my brother would be something you would be interested in; one way or another."

"When his activities drew the attention of City Hall, I began monitoring the situation. His subsequent disappearance precluded pursuing it further."

"I can't imagine you would let something like that go so easily," said Alan.

"Let it go?" Cain slowly shook his head. "Why do you think you are here?"

"You are monitoring the situation." Alan's statement was a flat comment.

Cain gave a placid, considered smile in response. They were silent for several long moments.

"What's going on, Cain?" Alan asked at last. "Where's my brother?"

"I honestly don't know," said Cain. "If I did, I wouldn't need you."

Alan said nothing to that. Cain continued.

"As you noted, the path Richard chose was of some interest to me."

"And I am here because...?"

"I am touching base with an old friend."

Cavanaugh reappeared, apparently in response to some unseen signal from Cain. He stood several paces from the table and waited. Cain ignored him for the moment, continued his conversation with Alan.

"I have enjoyed our visit, Mr. Thornton. It really takes me back." He took another drink of his water, set the glass down in front of him. "We shall do this again."

Alan slowly slid his chair back and stood up. "I look forward to hearing the results of your enquiries."

"Of course, Mr. Thornton." Cain gave a curt nod in Cavanaugh's direction. "Mr. Cavanaugh will see you home."

Alan was dismissed. He followed Cavanaugh toward the front of the club. Cain didn't give him a glance. He looked across to the bar, subtly raised a hand and lowered it.

The bartender began preparing a drink.

Alan sat at the small desk in his room, was looking over an old-style revolver. Turning the spindle, he could see there were three cartridges.

Chavez leaned against the wall beside the desk. He folded his arms across his chest.

"I put out a few feelers, asked a few questions," he said, watching Alan. "Not much new, I'm afraid. The connections just aren't there anymore."

"I understand," said Alan, reseating the spindle. He turned the spindle to an empty cylinder against the hammer.

"Word is, though... you're making some folks nervous," said Chavez. "Folks who were happy to see the Richard Thornton disappearance fade away."

"I've been hearing the same thing." Alan indicated the weapon. "This is in no way traceable back to you?"

"Clean as they come, my friend." He watched Alan opened a desk drawer and placed the weapon in the drawer. "What do you plan on doing with it?"

Alan closed the drawer, leaned back in his chair. "Nothing. I hope."

William walked across the room and opened the front door. He welcomed Valerie and Alan into his loft with a gesture.

"Good afternoon, Valerie." He gave a nod then to Alan. "Mr. Thornton. Welcome." He closed the door behind them and followed them back into the room.

"Nice place," said Alan.

"I like it." William started toward the table, urged them to sit and then went to the kitchenette counter. "Coffee?" he asked.

"Water, thanks," said Alan.

"Nothing for me, William," said Valerie, sitting opposite Alan. "Thank you."

William brought a glass down from the cupboard and filled it at the sink, spoke then as he brought it to Alan. "Thornton, Alan. Master Sergeant." He quickly raised a finger. "Retired."

Alan indicated the empty chair, waited for William to sit down.

"William Valentine," he said then. "Newspaper man, investigative reporter. Trouble-stirrer extraordinaire."

"I do nothing more than take information that I find and put it into words."

Alan looked side-glance to Valerie, then pointedly to William.

"The talent is to know where to find that information, and then to understand what it is you are seeing."

William accepted the complement, leaned back in his chair.

"You're looking for information on your brother's disappearance."

"That's right," said Alan. "What can you tell me?"

"A bit, though probably no more than what you already know."

"I know that he was pulled in for questioning, that he disappeared sometime after that."

"Your brother had been butting heads with City Hall for some time leading up to that night," said William. "It was inevitable."

"He had been involved in the gray market," stated Alan.

"So I understand."

"What specifically, in this gray market?"

"To get him disappeared? More than your everyday contraband. Everyday smuggling shouldn't get you gone." He gave a slow shake of the head. "You're brother wasn't political. His activities may have been criminal, but not political. So... I figure there's something else."

Valerie entered the conversation with an observation.

"He seldom talked politics," she said. To William then, dubious, "William?"

"He wasn't trying to bring down City Hall, but he always seemed to be at odds with 'em; them, and with Cain."

Alan shook his head and frowned. "Cain doesn't know where he is. I'm fairly sure of that."

"You are probably correct. I do think, however, that he knows something of how he disappeared."

"You do..."

William set his hand with his thumb out as if readying to count points. Beginning with point one... "Richard Thornton was released from custody following interrogation. That we know."

"And they had him followed," agreed Alan.

One of William's fingers joined his raised thumb in counting points. Point two... "And they lost him. I don't think he accomplished that on his own."

"You think Cain snatched him," said Alan, a statement more than a question.

Another finger up. Point three... "Or tried to."

"Like I said, I'm pretty sure Cain doesn't know where Richard is."

"And I agree."

"So?"

William slowly closed his hand, brought it down. He shrugged.

"That was as far as I my investigation took me. He gave them the slip when they first tried to snatch him up, or he got away from them later, or they let him walk and he ditched 'em..." he looked hesitantly to Valerie. "I don't know."

The three were silent then.

William indicated Alan's glass of water, as yet untouched.

"I have lemon," he said. "Would you like lemon with that?"

Several hours later, William stood at the sink washing a dinner plate as classic jazz played quietly in the background. Evening gray showed through the wall of windows.

The music stopped.

An alert beeped softly and then stopped.

William turned about and looked across the loft in the direction of the security monitor. He stepped around the table and moved nearer the monitor.

The display showed three police officers walking up the alley. They stopped at William's alley door. One of the officers pulled the cover plate from the keypad beside the door and another attached two wires from a small electronic device he was holding to the internals of the keypad.

William moved away from the security monitor and over to the bookshelf. He reached into the shelf, released a catch to a hollow click sound. He pulled the shelf wall open, revealing a hidden closet behind. He stepped into the closet and pulled the shelf closed to the sound of the hollow click.

The security monitor displayed the police officers working their way up the narrow stairwell to the landing.

From inside the closet, William heard the front door opening. He heard the rustling of the officers moving about in the loft. There came the sound of furniture being tossed aside, computer equipment being tossed to the floor.

It grew quiet then...

Out in the loft, one office stood stoically at the wall of windows, was looking out at the evening. A second officer stood amidst computers, monitors and printers that were now scattered about the floor. He was holding one of William's recent newspapers, was casually reading to himself.

The third officer was in the kitchen area, was holding the dinner plate in hand. It was still warm from recently having been washed. He looked back into the center of the room. He casually tossed the plate aside. It crashed to the floor.

In the hidden closet, William nervously closed his eyes to the sound of the officers again shuffling about in the loft. After another minute, there came the sound of the front door closing.

He waited a few moments more, then lifted a hand and pushed a button in the wall beside him. A small monitor inset in the wall came to life, the light of the monitor shining on his face.

The display showed the three officers descending the stairs.

In the loft, another half-minute passed. There was a hollow click sound, and the shelf wall opened. William stepped cautiously out of hiding.

He moved into the middle of the room and took in the midst of the destruction all about the loft.

Chapter Five

The Gray Swan was two-thirds full. Carl and Bonnie were up on the stage, Carl at the piano, Bonnie at the microphone. They were nearing the end of a song heavy on nightclub blues. Chief Archer was sitting in one of the booths, Alan and Valerie in the next booth over.

Valerie looked past Alan in the direction of the police chief. She leaned across the table and said something to Alan. When Alan turned and looked back over his shoulder, Archer lifted his beer in a silent hello, his expression giving away nothing. Alan gave an acknowledging nod in return, turned about again and faced forward.

Up on the stage, Bonnie finished her song. Alan and the others in the audience clapped politely.

"Thank you, everyone," said Bonnie. "We're going to take a short break, but we'll be back with another set in a few minutes. So don't you go anywhere."

She looked briefly to Alan; her smile faded when she saw Archer in the booth beyond. She took the few steps over to Carl and leaned on her brother's piano. She took a drink from a glass tumbler, took a lit cigarette from Carl and drew on it, handed it back. She turned again to look out across crowd.

Below in the audience, Alan and Valerie were in quiet conversation.

"Just what is it you do, Miss Baker?" asked Alan.

"It's *Miss Baker*, now?"

"Valerie," conceded Alan.

Valerie accepted that, sighed thoughtfully. "Oh, a little of this, some of that. You know."

"Interesting line of work, that. Does it pay well?"

"It keeps me off the street," she said.

"Good to hear." Alan took a drink from his iced tea, set the glass down with more care than was necessary. "This work... is that how you met William?"

"William and I have been friends a long time. You might say his work and mine occasionally coincide."

"Is that so? That's revealing in a shadowy sort of way," said Alan. "And Carl?"

"What about Carl?"

"How does his work and yours coincide?"

"Why do you ask?"

"Just curious. He works a nightclub, and yet he sends me to you. Have you been friends a long time as well?"

"Our paths cross now and again," she said, keeping her slight smile.

Alan studied Valerie for a few moments, absently took another drink.

"I've known Carl and Bonnie a while, myself," he said. "Strange that your path and mine have never crossed."

"Is it?"

"It is."

They grew silent then. Alan looked again over his shoulder to Archer. He turned back to Valerie, pushed his glass aside.

"On the subject of crossed paths... back in a sec," he said. He slid out of the booth and worked his way to Archer. He gave a quick glance to security, a friendly smile to Archer.

"Evening, Chief. Mind if I sit down?"

Archer indicated the bench opposite and Alan slid into the booth.

"Dropped in for the show?" he asked.

Archer clasped his beer with both hands, indicated the stage.

"I just had to catch a song," he said. "She's quite the lady."

"You dropped in to catch a song?"

"What other reason could there be?"

"I can't imagine," said Alan.

"And you?" asked Archer, though more of a statement than a question. "Are you just here for the show?"

"I like the company."

"Of course. I believe I heard as much."

"Is that so..."

"It is." Archer took another long swallow of his beer. He set the mug down and looked absently at it as he spoke. "Will you be in town long?"

"I haven't decided. It could go either way."

Archer smiled knowingly at that. "I can appreciate that. A lot of factors come into play, do they not?"

"Two or three."

"You let me know if we can help with any of them; glad to help, you being an awarded veteran and all." Archer looked past Alan to the stage then, where Bonnie appeared to be preparing for the next set.

"Ah. Here we go," he said. "The lady sings."

The conversation appeared to be at an end. Alan studied Archer a second more, then slid out of the booth. He made brief eye contact with Bonnie, up on the stage, as stepped back to his own booth. There was a hint of concern in her expression.

He slid in opposite Valerie.

"And?" she asked.

"Apparently City Hall is eager to help returning veterans."

Valerie looked over Alan's shoulder to Archer. He was focused on Bonnie.

Bonnie began another bluesy jazz song.

City Hall was a solid, imposing structure. Steep steps rose from the wide sidewalk street-side up to four concrete pillars fronting the building through which a set of double doors was visible. A security officer stood at either end of the pillar landing.

A long black sedan pulled up to the curb. The front passenger door opened and Archer's personal security man got out. He moved smoothly to the back door and opened it.

Chief Archer climbed out of the sedan. He took a moment to let the morning sun warm his face, gave an absent nod to his security before walking across the sidewalk and climbing the steps, his security several paces behind.

Another pair of well-armed security guards stood beside the doors. They said nothing as Archer passed through.

A security officer stood beside the check-in station in the center of the main foyer, a large, hollow main hall. Archer ignored the station and the guard, walked past and on to the wide staircase beyond, leaving his personal security to move to one side of foyer, stand with his back to the wall and wait.

Archer took the stairs to the second floor. He entered the mayor's office reception area; the mayor's personal secretary sat at her desk, prim and proper and dedicated to her duties. The chief passed a small waiting area on the left and continued ahead and around the reception desk on his way toward the large, heavy wooden door beyond. A brass plate on door read "Mayor".

The receptionist looked up from her work.

"Chief Archer. The Mayor is expecting you."

"Thank you, Betty."

The Mayor glanced across his desk as Archer entered the office, but he otherwise ignored his police chief. He was leaning back in his leather chair, in casual conversation on the phone.

The Mayor was in his sixties, was graying at the temples, his straight hair combed neatly back. His attire was professional but casual. He appeared strong and healthy. His voice was clear and confident.

The office consisted of fine wood, curtain-trimmed windows, leather furniture. Fine paintings hung on the walls. A television monitor was mounted on one wall, at the moment turned off.

The Mayor sat behind a large, heavy desk. On the desk was a flat-screen computer monitor and keyboard, a stack of several folders, and a small figurine of a dragon.

Archer took another step nearer the desk, then to one side. He stood silent, waited patiently.

The Mayor was talking on the phone to the president.

"No sir. No sir. I understand," he said, then listened for several moments. "Absolutely, Mr. President. You're absolutely right, sir."

The Mayor shifted about and faced forward, leaned forward and placed one forearm on the desk.

"Of course, Mr. President," he went on. "Count on it. Absolutely. No, no, I certainly will."

There was a long pause as the Mayor listened. There appeared to be a shift in the one-sided conversation. The Mayor smiled then.

"Yes sir. Yes sir. Jenny is looking forward to it. We both are. I'll see you then, Mr. President." There was another moment's pause. The Mayor gave another smile. "Yes sir. I will, sir."

The Mayor let out a long sigh as he hung up the phone. His smile vanished as he looked darkly across at Chief Archer.

"Federation Founding Ball next week," he said.

"Yes, Mr. Mayor," said Archer.

"I hate the Founding Ball."

"I understand, sir."

"The music is annoying. And I don't dance. I don't like dancing."

Archer let the comment go, waited for what he expected to be coming.

The Mayor breathed noisily, frowned and shifted his shoulders.

"The president has concerns. The president has no problem expressing those concerns."

"Sir?"

"It is imperative that whatever issues we have in own little city-state stay within the borders of our own little city-state."

Archer said nothing, waited for the Mayor to continue. The Mayor stared down at his hands, leaned back then in his chair. He spoke without looking up at Archer.

"Eight autonomous city-states in the Federation, and Willow City dominates the President's daily brief more often than not; one thing and another." He hesitated, frowned darkly, looked up at Archer. "I'll not have Federation boots on our streets, Archer."

There was a long moment of uncomfortable silence between the two men. Varied thoughts appeared then to cross the Mayor's face as shadows.

"What's all this nonsense about Richard Thornton's brother?" he asked.

"Alan Thornton is not a problem, Mr. Mayor."

"Why is he still breathing?"

"Sir..." said Archer. "I'd like to keep our options open. We might be able to use him. He might be able to open doors that we cannot."

The Mayor looked piercingly across the desk to Archer.

"To find his brother?" he asked. "Do you really think Thornton is still alive?"

"I've never thought otherwise."

The mayor thought through his next words very carefully, spoke his next words very precisely.

"If he is alive, then get him. I want this done once and for all. I want that network. Then throw him in the river, his brother after him."

Alan stepped out the front door of the Veterans Center, paused to take in the early evening. He frowned when he saw Sgt. Burke's partner leaning against a car parked at the curb, his arms folded, watching him.

Alan walked toward the car, noting Sgt. Burke sitting in the front passenger seat, the window rolled down.

"Burke," said Alan. "Out for an evening drive?"

Burke looked sidelong up at Alan.

"Detective Sullivan asked that I pass along a message." Burke's words were dry. "He managed to squeeze that visit to Sally's into his busy schedule."

"Good to hear. Those little moments are important."

"Right," said Burke. He rubbed the bridge of his nose. "There is an invitation attached."

"Ah..." Alan straightened, looked up and down the street. "I'm finding myself in a number of these chats lately."

Burke wasn't thrilled at playing Sullivan's messenger boy. "Uh, huh. I expect you're downright popular."

Partner opened the rear passenger door and waited. His expression was cool, his eyes cold.

"Thank you, my man," said Alan, climbing in.

Burke looked absently outward as Partner climbed in behind the wheel and started the car.

Alan came into the café, calmly took in the scene. A few people sat at the counter, several of the booths were occupied. Detective Sullivan was sitting alone in one of the middle booths and looked to be working on a slice of apple pie.

Sgt. Burke gave Alan a light shove from behind, pushing him away from the door so that he and his partner could get around him and head to the counter. Alan walked down the row of booths, slid in opposite Sullivan.

The detective set his fork next to the plate, picked up his coffee cup and took a sip. He set the cup down onto the saucer. He picked up his fork and took another bite.

"Second slice," he said. "Best pie in town."

"I'm surprised you were able to make the time."

"Simple matter of priorities, Mr. Thornton." Sullivan took another forkful of pie. "Speaking of which, how's your investigation going?"

"Only just starting," said Alan.

The waitress made an appearance with a coffee mug and carafe. She filled the cup and set it front of Alan, then refilled Sullivan's.

Sullivan pointed to his pie and then to Alan, gave a wink to the waitress.

"A slice for my friend here," he said.

"Coming up." The waitress left to get Alan's pie.

Sullivan took a sip of from his refilled cup. "I understand you dropped in to see Cain."

"I accepted his invitation."

"Right. I've had a few of those myself over the years. Turning it down could prove awkward."

"The man offered his help."

Sullivan took the last bite of his pie. His set his fork onto the empty plate.

"Did he?"

"I've gotten a few such offers."

Sullivan grinned at that. "I'll bet."

The waitress returned with a slice of pie for Alan.

"Thank you, my dear," said Sullivan.

"Yes, thank you," said Alan.

"You're welcome." The waitress looked from Alan to Sullivan, then left.

Another grin from Sullivan.

"I get a discount," he said.

Alan took a forkful of pie. Sullivan watched.

"Good, huh?" he asked.

Alan poked and prodded at his serving of pie.

"Listen, Detective," he said. "The pie's great, the coffee's great, and I don't want to sound unappreciative... but why am I here?"

Sullivan glanced casually about the café... in the direction of the waitress behind the counter, at Burke and Partner at the end of the counter. He took another swallow of his coffee, looked again at Alan.

"We've known each other a long time, Alan. Now and again, we've even been friends. Of a sort."

"All right," said Alan. "I'll give you that."

"Good. So, given that, we may not be double dating these days, but you need to know we're not on opposite sides."

Alan considered, finally lifted a fork of apple pie. "Hey, we're sharing Sally's finest."

"A positive sign, at that," said Sullivan. "With that in mind, I want you to think hard on what I say."

Alan gave a slow nod.

"All right," he said. "You have my attention."

Sullivan pushed aside his empty pie plate and leaned nearer Alan while trying not to appear conspiratorial.

"I'm not asking you to stop searching—"

"Good call."

"Yeah, well, no one expects you to just walk away from this. It is for that very reason that interested parties have decided to wait and watch."

"Oh, I got that," said Alan.

"Good. And when you start getting answers?"

Sullivan watched Alan for a sign that he understood. Meanwhile, Alan waited for more, but nothing came.

"Right," said Alan. "I get it."

Sullivan accepted that. He leaned back, bringing his cup with him. He took a deep swallow of coffee, stared at the cup, looked then about the café.

"Alan..." he said quietly. "I'm not Archer."

"I'd hate to think there'd be two of him."

Sullivan didn't appear amused. He stared wearily at Alan. Alan shrugged, wore a slightly apologetic look.

"Now and again, you're not so bad."

"Right," Sullivan sighed tiredly. He slid out of the booth, looked down at Alan. "Step carefully, Master Sergeant."

He looked over at Sgt. Burke and Partner, sitting at the counter. When Burke looked his way, Sullivan gave a nod and started toward the door.

Burke and Partner slide off their stools and followed as Sullivan left the café.

Chapter Six

The cab pulled away from the curb and continued down the street, leaving Alan standing before the warehouse. There was one door set into the otherwise featureless wall; a small sign above the door read "Intercity Trade Co.".

The Intercity Trade warehouse was one of a number of nondescript one- and two-storey warehouse structures set along the wide, low-traffic street that ran down the heart of the east district. Alan walked past the door and on to the corner of the building, then to an open gate that was set into a tall cyclone-mesh fence. There were several loading bay doors along this side of the building, two box trailers parked in a far corner of the enclosed lot.

Alan took a set of wooden steps up to an unmarked door and went inside. He walked across the small lobby and stepped around the counter. There was no one at the only desk. Windows set into the wall on Alan's right revealed the open warehouse floor. He could see half a dozen collections of assorted boxes and crates, but the floor was otherwise empty.

He continued into a narrow back hallway. He looked through the first open door into an office that appeared to have recently been in use. Lights were turned on, the computer monitor was active. The small plaque on the open door read "John Benton".

No one was in the office.

Alan continued to the next office door. This one was closed. The door plaque read "Richard Thornton." He opened the door and went into the office; it was simple, sparse. Bookshelves covered the wall on the left. A plain desk and chair was in the middle of the room, a guest chair to Alan's right.

He didn't know what he was looking for, didn't know if he would recognize it if he saw it. He wandered over to the shelves, glanced at the titles of several books. He picked up and looked through a stack of folders.

He sensed something then, looked in the direction of the door.

John Benton stood in the open doorway, his shoulder resting against the jamb, arms folded.

Benton was thirty years old, clean-cut, dressed in casual button shirt and slacks.

"I expected you long before now, Alan," he said.

"Hey, John." Alan set the folders back on the shelf, started over to the desk. "Distractions. You know..."

"So I hear."

Alan sat at Richard's desk, leaned back in the chair. He looked about the office, then to Benton, who was still standing in the doorway.

"Business in a slump?" he asked.

"City hall pulled our license," said Benton. "They confiscated what they wanted, left me to sell off what's left in inventory."

"How'd they do that? Pull your license?"

"Tagged Richard with illegal activities."

"Right. Sorry, man," said Alan. He began looking through the desk drawers. "What was he up to?"

"I don't know. Honest." Benton pushed off the door jamb and took a step into the room. He nodded in the direction of his own office next door. "My office was mostly for show. I didn't really do much around here. Assistant's assistant at best. Our secretary had more status, and she was part time."

Alan didn't respond, continued looking through the desk.

"Honest," said Benton.

"Oh, I believe you. Richard is a one man show from way back." Alan lifted a box from the large bottom drawer and set it on the desk. "So, what are your plans now, Mr. Benton?"

"I'm taking my time shuttering up the place." A weak smile then. "You never know."

"Sure," Alan said absently. He looked through assorted items in the metal box, brought out a key card. "Is Richard's apartment still over on Ashland?"

The apartment complex consisted of six single-storey fourplex buildings nestled into garden-like grounds. Alan walked the grounds to the building with Richard's apartment, heard a voice call out to him as he approached the door.

"Hey, sweetie. Long time, no see."

He turned to see Wanda coming towards him, following the winding walkway across the grounds. She was about forty years old, tall, slim, her hair in a beehive hairdo, wrinkles at the corners of her eyes behind frame glasses. She wore casual slacks and blouse.

"Hello, Wanda."

Wanda stopped a short pace from Alan. She folded her arms across her chest and gave a smile.

"I heard you were back in town," she said.

"Must've been a flyer put out," said Alan.

Her smile broadened, and there was something behind it. "You always were one to keep things interesting, sweetie." Her smile faded. "You holdin' up okay? Ya' know, your brother and all?"

"I'll be fine."

"Of course you will." She gave a nod to the apartment. "He's gone, ya' know. Tough to say, tougher to hear, but..."

"Might be so."

"City won't let me put the apartment on the market. And no compensation, to boot."

"I'm sure they'll let it go before too long, Wanda. The facts will come out, soon enough."

"Hope that's so," said Wanda. She considered for a moment, studied Alan. "I heard you were retiring, Alan. Ya' home for good?"

"Might be. A few things to sort out before I can say for sure."

Wanda gave another nod to the apartment. "Ya' interested?" she asked. "You'll be needin' a place."

"Might be. Let's see how things play out." He raised the key card and indicated that he was going into the apartment.

"Yes, Sure. Of course." she started away, stopped and looked back. She gave a smile and a wink. "Love to have you as a neighbor, sweetie. Just say the word."

She turned away again, disappeared around the corner of the building. Alan turned back to the front door of the apartment.

The main room of the apartment was divided into living and kitchen areas, separated by an island counter. The living area had a couch and chair, coffee and side tables, a television monitor on the wall. The kitchen area beyond the counter was dully lit, sunlight streaming hazily through a pair of windows in the far wall.

Much of the apartment was in disarray; furniture pushed askew, drawers open and items strewn on the floor. It appeared the apartment had been searched.

Alan conducted a quick cursory search of his own, looking into several open drawers and the front closet. He squatted down beside assorted mail that had been strewn on the floor, reading the envelopes and tossing them back to the floor.

He moved into the kitchen, opened and looked in the cupboards. Opening the refrigerator, he found a number of jars, a few sealed plastic containers, and two plates with leftovers long ago gone bad.

He stepped back into the living area and on into the hallway. He looked briefly into the one bedroom, then the bathroom. He returned then to the living room.

He stood unmoving for several moments, then went to the front door. He reached out and turned the lock as he looked back into the living room. Safe then, he went into the kitchen and found a butter knife in the utensils drawer. In the living room, he pulled the couch away from the wall. Kneeling down at the wall, he used the knife to free a section of the baseboard. This exposed an opening in the wall two inches tall, twelve inches wide.

He pulled a small box from the hidden compartment.

Whatcha got here, Richard?

Opening the box, he found small ink cartridges lined up side by side. He lifted one out, looked curiously at it. It was a cartridge for an inkjet printer.

What the... Alan wrinkled his brow.

Why had Richard hidden half a dozen ink cartridges in his secret wall compartment?

He turned the cartridge about in his hand several times, frowned, put it back with the others. He closed the box and returned it to its hiding place.

Valerie was sitting alone in her usual booth in Sally's Café, both hands absently wrapped about a cup of coffee. It was evening, and the city beyond the wall of windows was gray, the evenly spaced street lamps creating misty globes of light in the thin fog.

Several of the other booths were occupied, as were a handful of the stools at the counter. The waitress stood behind the counter, her arms crossed, looking a bit bored.

Carl came into the café. He looked about, took in the scene, and then walked over to Valerie's booth.

"Good evening, Valerie," he said, sliding into the booth opposite.

"Carl." Valerie took a sip from her coffee, set the cup carefully onto the saucer. "How are things at the Gray Swan?"

"Same as always. Getting by."

The waitress came over to the booth, stood silent. Carl glanced up at her.

"Nothing, thanks," he said.

The waitress looked coolly down at Carl, made no sign to leave. Carl sighed, pulled out his ID card and held it out for her.

"Coffee," he stated.

"On me," said Valerie.

Carl smoothly withdrew his card before the waitress had a chance to take it.

"Thanks," he said.

They waited then until the waitress left and they were again alone.

"The loft was trashed," said Valerie. Her voice was low but not an obvious whisper. "No sign of William."

"They get him?"

"I don't think so. We'd have heard something."

Carl took a moment to think that through. "He's gone dark then," he said at last.

The waitress returned with a coffee carafe and cup. She filled the cup and set it before Carl, then refilled Valerie's. Valerie held her ID card up by two fingers. The waitress took the card and stepped away from the booth.

"D'you hear anything from the Alliance?" asked Carl.

"They're not talking."

"But you think they know something."

"They're Alliance," said Valerie. "Of course they know something."

"Are they hiding him?"

"Maybe. At the very least, protecting him."

Carl frowned, hesitated, finally took a drink from his coffee. "William is one of theirs," he said.

"Some rather close ties," said Valerie, shrugging. She leaned nearer. "He's my friend."

"They know that." Carl leaned back. He and Valerie looked thoughtfully at one another for several moments. Muted voices came from other booths.

"They've pulled back," he said. "Not likely to open up to anyone not fully Alliance."

"Oh, you've noticed that, eh?" Valerie stared down at her cup. "No one wants to talk. No one wants to be seen with folks like us. And business... gone to ground."

"I don't see that changing until Alan finds Richard."

Valerie gave a half nod, considered.

"Everybody has something to hide. Everybody has something to protect."

"Everybody wants something," said Carl.

"Including me." Valerie lifted her cup, looked over the rim at Carl. "Including you."

Alan's face was faintly aglow from the neon light shining in through the window into his room. He was relaxing on his bed atop the covers, his feet up, legs crossed at his ankles; his shoes were off but was still otherwise dressed. He was watching a news broadcast that was displaying on his television monitor.

The broadcast image was of the mayor and his wife walking to a limousine, his security ever present. The newscaster noted that the mayor and his wife would soon be departing for the Federation Capitol, where they would be attending the Founding Ball.

The Mayor was looking forward to it.

Alan appeared bored, stared dully at the flickering monitor.

Chapter Seven

Midmorning in the Gray Swan; the lights were on. Eddie was sweeping the floor; a teenager was bussing a booth.

Carl and Alan were sitting at the bar facing one another, water glasses on the counter beside them. The nightclub was otherwise empty.

"So, how do you know Valerie?" asked Alan. "What's the connection with Richard?"

"Valerie and Richard had a thing," said Carl, almost matter-of-factly.

"I get that. They held hands. It's more than that."

Carl sighed softly, lifted his glass of water, set it back on the counter.

"Valerie and I..." he started, "had a shared concern that Richard was getting involved in something that was going to get him into trouble."

"You were concerned for Richard's wellbeing, Valerie was concerned for his wellbeing, and that brought the two of you together?"

"Something like that."

"I see." Alan took a drink of his water. He looked about the room, ensured that the kid cleaning the tables was out of earshot. "And how did this involve ink cartridges?"

"Ink cartridges?"

"Ink cartridges. For printers."

Carl shook his head, looked away from Alan.

"Richard had been getting deeper into the gray market," he said. "I suppose that could include ink cartridges."

"Ink? Really?"

"Ink is controlled. So is paper."

Carl was looking across at the wall behind the bar, making it hard for Alan to read his expression.

The man was hiding something...

"Ink cartridges, worth a disappear?" he asked.

"I guess that would depend on the market," shrugged Carl.

"And what would that market be?"

"I couldn't tell ya." Carl turned about on the stool and stood up. "Sorry, man. Things to do. See ya' later?"

"Yeah. Sure. Later." Alan faced forward, took a drink from his water as Carl walked toward the back of the club.

Eddie worked his way along the bar until he was standing opposite Alan.

"Refill?"

Alan stared down at his glass, swallowed the last of his water. He set the glass on the bar.

"One's my limit," he said, slid off the stool. "Later, Eddie."

Leaving the club, he walked out to the curb. The street was quiet; no people, no cars, this despite it being the middle of the day.

He stuffed his hands into his jacket and started up the street.

An unmarked police car appeared then, coming up the street from behind Alan. It traveled slowly. There was a simple flashing light magnetically attached to the roof just above the front passenger window.

A prisoner van was following directly behind the sedan.

The two vehicles passed Alan and continued up the street. They crossed the intersection ahead, continued on and turned at the next intersection.

The street was again silent and still but for Alan.

Alan came in through the front door and started across the lobby of the Veterans Center. Several veterans were relaxing in the lounge for the evening, the monitor displaying the mayor and wife arriving in the Federation Capitol.

The desk clerk stepped up to the counter as Alan neared the front desk on his way to the stairs.

"Master Sergeant Thornton," he called out, holding a small envelope. "A message for you."

"Thank you." Alan took the envelope, opened at it as he moved from the counter. He slowed his steps then, stopped. He looked thoughtfully as he turned about and started back to the front door.

He gave an absent, acknowledging nod to the desk clerk as he passed.

The desk clerk nodded in response. "Good evening, Sergeant," he said.

§

Alan hesitated, looked curiously back at the unlocked door of William's loft as he slowly closed it. He looked into the room again. Soft evening light was glowing a dull yellow through the wall of windows and into room.

The damage that had been done was still evident, though much of the previous disarray and destruction had been straightened up. Security cameras were working, the monitors creating a brighter glow in that part of the loft. They were displaying the stairwell, hall and alley.

Valerie was sitting on the couch.

Alan walked a wide circle around the loft, Valerie watching.

"What happened here?" he asked.

"William may have gone too far," she stated flatly.

"They took him away?"

"I expect he's gone into hiding."

Alan reached the table, sat on the corner and looked across at Valerie.

"All right," he said. "I doubt his disappearance is why I'm here."

"Might be related."

There was an awkward silence in the loft that lasted for several long moments.

Alan folded his arms across his chest. "He's in deeper than even you knew..."

"It would be just like William," Valerie said, the hint of a smile.

"Right," said Alan. There was another long pause. Alan let his gaze drift from Valerie to the wall of windows, slowly back to Valerie. "I had a chance to chat again with Sullivan."

"Yes? And what did our friendly neighborhood detective have to say?"

"This and that." Alan lost his smile then. "So, Valerie... is there someone interested in our activities that I don't yet know about."

"Ah..." Valerie fumbled with her thoughts. She sat forward on the couch.

"And so," Alan stated. "This is why I'm here."

"I may have an idea who Detective Sullivan might be referring to."

She stood then, folded her arms as she stepped away from the couch. Alan watched her move to the wall of windows. She stared out into the early evening.

Alan pushed away from the table. "Uh, huh."

Valerie continued looking out the window, silent. To Alan it was as if she was anxious about something.

"So?" he urged.

Valerie sighed.

"They call themselves the Alliance," she said at last.

"And they are?"

"Company bosses, rich folks, heads of families." She shrugged. "I don't know names. Secret organization, after all."

"And just what is this secret organization about?"

"They're all about surviving in the system, whatever that takes."

Alan thought on that...

"And the city knows about them," he stated. Not a question.

"And they want to bring them down," said Valerie. She turned from the window and looked directly at Alan. "Your friend Cain knows of 'em. He wants a piece of the action; that or remove the competition."

"Action?"

"Smuggling."

"I see. And that's where Richard comes into the picture."

"Maybe," said Valerie. "Where in the picture, I don't know."

Alan struggled to take all this in. This changed things, and created more questions than it answered.

"You're a member of this Alliance?" he asked.

"No... not a member," said Valerie. "I occasionally, rarely, act as an independent contractor."

"Really." This also created more questions, but he decided to let this one go for the moment. Another question, though... "And why haven't I heard of this Alliance before?"

"They tend not to advertise."

"The Mayor and Cain know about them."

"And neither wants the general population to know there's a secret organization working in the shadows of Willow City."

Alan moved up beside Valerie, leaned against the counter.

"All right," he said. "And you chose not to tell me about them until now because...?"

"Come now, Alan," said Valerie. "First you were a high-ranking NCO in the military, their military. Now you're a retired NCO with a very bright spotlight shining on you."

"You don't trust me."

"Nothing to do with me. Recent events have made them nervous. They're an antsy bunch to start."

"I'm just trying to find out what happened to my brother."

Valerie gave a sympathetic smile and a shrug. Alan turned away, looked again about the loft. They must've really trashed the place. He hoped the guy was all right. He looked back again at Valerie. She was watching him.

"Do they know where Richard is?" he asked.

"No one knows where Richard is."

"You know that for sure?"

"From what I see, they want to find him as much as you do."

"Is Richard part of this Alliance?"

"Uh... no. No, I can assure you, Richard is not a member."

The evening was cool and gray, the city quiet. A dark sedan was parked half a block from the alley entrance leading to William's loft. Burke and his partner were sitting in the car, absently observing.

Carl appeared from around the corner and walked up the street toward the alley. He saw the sedan parked inconspicuously nearby and quickly took it for what it was. He lifted the hood of his jacket up over his head and continued up the street, passing the alley entrance.

Back in the loft, Valerie stood near the window, appearing somewhat uneasy. Alan walked from the kitchen sink, glass of water in hand, and stood near the kitchen table. He looked curiously across the loft to Valerie.

"Are you all right?" he asked.

"Yeah. Yeah, I'm fine." She didn't sound all that convincing.

"You don't look fine."

Valerie looked briefly in Alan's direction, back out the window.

"I was expecting someone."

"Oh?" An unsettled tone.

"Don't go jumping out the window," said Valerie. "Nothing to freak on."

"I get enough surprises."

"Yeah, well... he should have been here by now, so... not happening in any case." She moved away from the window. "He must have been held up. No matter. We can meet up with him another time."

"And whom might that be?" asked Alan; still not happy. "Part of the Alliance revelation?"

Valerie looked across to Alan. "I should talk with him first."

§

Sgt. Burke and his partner watched from their sedan as Valerie left the alley and turned up the street. She reached her car a block further up.

They watched then as Alan came out of the alley and started in the opposite direction. He continued on foot until he reached the corner and turned up the next street.

As Burke watched, he absently brushed at the stubble on his cheek with two fingers.

"Didn't take long for Thornton to move in on his brother's lady," he said.

Partner started the car, sneered. "Didn't expect different."

Chapter Eight

John Benton was at his desk, hovering over paperwork and folders, occasionally put pen to paper. He finished then, closed the last folder. He tossed the pen aside and leaned back in his chair. Glancing across at the computer monitor, the desktop screen clock showed 3:40 PM.

Good enough...

He reached over, set his hands to the computer keyboard and struck several keys. He turned off the monitor then, stood up and took the folders to the four-drawer file cabinet. He opened the top drawer and inserted the folders.

He left his office, flipping off the light switch on his way out. He took the narrow back office hallway to the front office of Intercity Trade. He opened the door to the supply closet. He glanced once back behind him before reaching into the closet.

He pulled at a hidden release and the back wall of the closet opened, revealing a staircase beyond. He descended the stairs to an underground room.

Two of the walls were lined with shelves stocked with office supplies. There was a cot set against one bare wall, a narrow horizontal window set high in the wall above the cot. A work counter was set against another wall, cluttered with small boxes and a small backpack.

There was a pallet of boxes near one corner; the labels on the larger boxes identified the contents as paper. Several smaller boxes sitting on the boxes of paper were labeled "ink cartridges, laser printer" and "ink cartridges, inkjet printer".

There was a folding table and one chair in the middle of the room. On the table were the remains of a meal. Next to the plate and glass was a stack of folders, one open and exposing papers.

William Valentine came into the room through a narrow door, the only other access to the room. He looked over at Benton as he returned to the table.

"John," he sat down, grabbed a half-eaten roll and took a bite as he pulled the open folder nearer. He spoke without looking at Benton. "Where's the computer I asked for? I need to get online."

"We've been through this," said Benton. "You stay in the dark."

William closed the folder, tossed the last of the roll into his mouth and turned in the chair to face Benton.

"That's not your call," he said.

"Nor yours." Benton moved into the middle of the room. "I just came down to see if you need anything. I'm heading home."

"I'm not a prisoner." William pushed aside his plate and looked up at Benton. "I didn't agree to this."

"Sure you did. You had a choice. I on the other hand did not."

William leaned back in his chair. He looked over at the pallet of paper and ink cartridges, then to Benton.

"They can be very persuasive, at that."

"Yes," Benton sighed. He looked in the direction of William's focus, moved over to the pallet. "Alternatives were non-existent."

He lifted one of the smaller boxes and looked at it... ink cartridges.

"I knew Richard was mixed up in something, of course," he said. He set the box back on the pallet.

"But not the Alliance," said William.

"I never heard of 'em," said Benton. "Oh, I knew there were shady groups out there. This is Willow City after all, but not..."

"Not anything so much a part of the system."

"I don't know what I thought. I just kept my head down and did my job." Benton put on a sad grin as he pushed the box of ink aside. "Guess I should have looked up once in a while."

"Why?"

"Maybe I'd have seen this coming."

"And?"

Benton thought about that, tried to come up with something, but had no answer; not if he was honest with himself.

He moved away from the pallet and returned to the staircase.

"Do you need anything?"

"Computer access."

"Not happening. Your handlers said no."

"I don't work for the Alliance," William insisted.

"So you said. You don't like it, leave." With that, Benton climbed the stairs.

Once alone, William looked down at his plate. He picked up a piece of food and tossed it into his mouth.

A nondescript sedan entered an underground parking garage, traveled down a row to an interior wall. It turned and followed the wall, stopped before an elevator door.

A man in a dark suit stepped out of the front passenger door as a woman stepped out of the rear driver's side door. Neither showed any emotion.

The man went to the elevator as the woman opened the passenger side back door.

Valerie climbed out of the back of the sedan. The woman escort indicated the elevator door. Valerie approached as the man escort slid a key card into a slot on the wall beside the elevator. The indicator light turned green. Moments later, the door slid open.

The three entered the elevator car. The man pressed a button and the door slid closed.

Valerie entered an understated office, the woman escort entering behind her and moving silently to one side.

A tall, slender man dressed in tailored slacks and button shirt was standing behind a large, simple desk, his back to the desk. He was facing a wall of windows, his hands clasped behind his back.

He turned slowly about to face Valerie. The Alliance leader was in his fifties, had the look and air of calm confidence.

"Miss Baker," he said with a slight nod. "It has been a while."

"Yes sir," said Valerie. "Thank you for agreeing to see me."

"Of course." The Alliance leader indicated the guest chair as he moved around his desk. He sits on the front corner of the desk, waited for her to sit down. "I understand you are seeking information."

"I'm looking for someone," said Valerie.

The Alliance leader raised a questioning brow, waited for Valerie to continue.

"William Valentine," said Valerie.

"And what makes you think I can help you in locating this William Valentine?"

"I believe you know where he is."

"Is that so?"

"Only the Alliance would be hiding him," said Valerie. "Process of elimination."

"I see," said the Alliance leader. "William Valentine, you say?"

"I admit, I don't know why you would hide him," said Valerie. "In the grand scheme of things, William isn't all that important."

"It would appear that he is important to you."

"I just want to know that he's all right."

The Alliance leader stood, moved around to the leather chair behind his desk. He sat and scooted forward.

"A friend of yours," he said calmly.

Valerie didn't answer. The answer was obvious.

The Alliance leader managed a smile.

"A friend of mine, as well," he said.

"Is he?" Valerie hadn't expected that.

"Yes, ma'am." He set his elbows on the desk, looked at his hands, intertwined his fingers. "What do you think of our friend's journalistic skills, Miss Baker?"

"They will get him disappeared one day," she answered quickly, confidently. "If they haven't already."

"I too believe he has talent." The Alliance leader's tone grew more somber. "His endeavors have drawn the ire of one; how William acquires his information however, is both the desire and the threat of many."

"Is he a threat to the Alliance?"

The Alliance leader slid his arms off the desk as he leaned back in his chair. He gave a subtle signal to the woman escort standing to one side. She took a step forward as the Alliance leader looked again to Valerie.

"William is under our protection," he said matter-of-factly.

The escort took another step forward. The Alliance leader nodded sharply; a sign that the meeting was at an end.

Valerie rose from the guest chair. She followed the escort to the door, stopped then and looked back to the Alliance leader.

"Richard Thornton?" she asked.

The Alliance leader put on a thin smile.

"Not the doing of the Alliance, Miss Baker."

The sun was just setting, dusk was on the way. The limo driver stepped quickly around the black limousine that had stopped at the sidewalk in front of Cain's Club. He looked vigilantly about. Seeing no threats, he opened the passenger side back door of the vehicle.

Arthur Cain stepped out. He spoke dismissively to the driver.

"That'll be all this evening."

The driver closed the back door as Cain walked to the front door of the club.

Inside, the sound of bluesy jazz was playing quietly in the background, coming from hidden speakers placed strategically throughout the club.

The security man was in the lobby. He stepped back and out of the way. Cain ignored him as he passed through the lobby and entered the club proper. Less than half the tables and booths were occupied. The sound of muffled voices mixed with the blues music.

Cain walked across the floor, greeted several guests with a quick hello or a pat on the shoulder as he worked his way across the room. Rather than going to his private table, he approached a booth where Alan was sitting alone, a glass of iced tea in hand.

Cain slid into the booth opposite Alan.

"Good evening, Alan," he said. "Good of you to drop by."

Alan lifted his glass in response, set the tea back on the table without taking a drink.

"I appreciate the invitation," he said. "I understand you have news."

"Information," said Cain, after a long pause. "It is for you to determine whether or not it is news."

A waitress approached the table with a glass of water. Cain leaned back as she placed the glass on the table and departed.

Cain shifted on the padded booth bench, rested his arms on the table and held the water glass in both hands.

"Richard... your brother... well, let's just say that he pretty much stumbled his way into the gray market."

"Okay," said Alan. "No news there."

Cain looked up from his water. There was no humor on that face.

"You understand... he is of little value on his own. It is rather his connections to the network."

"These connections, is that what you're after?"

"For a start," said Cain. "Such would potentially offer inroads into a market that I have long sought access to."

"Smuggling," said Alan. "Ink?"

Cain smiled briefly, took a long breath.

"That particular product was why the city-state was interested in your brother," said Cain. "They already control the Internet. Take out the network that is bringing in paper and ink, and they control the majority of the underground information market."

"They had Richard," said Alan. "And lost him."

"Embarrassing, to say the least," said Cain. He took a drink from his glass of water. "Which presents a suitable segue... since the city-state is actively seeking your brother, then they don't know where he is. And, as I also do not know where he is... who does that leave?"

"The Alliance?"

"Very good, Mr. Thornton. That was my thought as well." Cain took a long breath. "Alas, no."

"No? Then who?"

"Ah. Therein the information that I provide." Cain leaned forward. "I offer the question. If not the city and not the Alliance, is there someone new in the picture?"

Chapter Nine

Carl was at his piano, casually working at the keys; light piano jazz. A cigarette was burning in the ashtray on the piano near him. Next to the ashtray was a glass of water with a slice of lemon.

The evening had yet to get started; less than half the tables were occupied. Bonnie was moving about the floor, stopping at one and then another table to give a friendly hello to the customers.

She returned to the stage, leaned against the piano. She took a drag from his cigarette, returned it to the ashtray.

Carl stopped his playing. There were a few quiet hand claps from the audience as he took a drink from his water.

"Slow start," he said. "Quiet crowd."

"Don't sweat it." Bonnie was looking out across the audience floor. "First set isn't for half an hour."

Carl took another drag from his cigarette and put it back in the ashtray.

"Recurring nightmare," he said, again tickling the keys. "I come out one night and no one shows up."

"Oh, never fear, brother. I'll always be here. And I know Eddie would never miss the show."

"I feel reassured." Carl let his gaze drift then across the audience as he continued to absently work the keys. "Nothing from Valerie," he said then.

"Did you expect Miss Harper to come rushing back to give you the good news?"

"I did. I absolutely did." Carl ran the keys, stopped and reached for his cigarette. He took a last drag, put out the butt. He returned to the keys. "I expect she's chasing down whatever news they gave her."

Bonnie smirked. "How rude of her."

Carl gave a knowing smile, refocused on the keys. Bonnie turned about, looked out across the club.

"Or they disappeared her," she said with a sigh. "But at least then she'll know where William is."

§

Alan was sitting on one of the couches in the Veterans Center lounge. It was late, he was alone. He was only half paying attention to the display on the monitor. It was showing the mayor returning to Willow City. He was walking across a tarmac from his personal jet to a limousine, his spouse several paces behind. The mayor waved to a small crowd standing behind a barrier as a security man opened the rear door of the limo.

Valerie entered the lounge and sat on the couch next to Alan. The two watched the monitor in silence for a few moments. Alan looked side-glance once at Valerie, continued watching the monitor and waited for her to initiate the conversation.

Valerie spoke then, eyes on the display.

"I have news. And I have... what's the opposite of news?"

On the monitor, the display showed the limo leaving the tarmac.

Alan ignored Valerie's question.

"The mayor didn't look happy," he said.

The mayor entered his office foyer. One dim light faintly illuminated the room. Being evening, the receptionist desk was unoccupied.

The mayor walked to his office door.

The overhead light of his office was on. Walking across to his desk, he glanced over at Chief Archer, who was waiting in one of the chairs set against the wall.

Archer stood and walked across the room as the mayor moved in behind his desk. The mayor sat down, indicating the guest chair.

Archer sat.

"I trust your trip went well," he said.

"Such trust is misplaced, Archer."

"I'm sorry to hear that, Mayor."

The mayor grumbled and looked aside.

"If the ball wasn't bad enough, and it was ghastly, it was the pull-aside with our president that truly made the trip dreadful." The mayor turned his focus on his police chief. "The Federation knows far too much of Willow City's day to day, Archer. I don't like it. I don't like it one damn bit."

"What did the president have to say, sir?"

"Enough to tell me that he knows what's working and what isn't, and he enjoys letting me know as much." The mayor wore a darker frown then. "We look less than sparkling in Federation eyes."

"Yes sir," Archer said hesitantly. "Sir, we've known all along the Federation has eyes and ears in the city."

"I fear something much more organized than just a few moles." The mayor stared coolly across the desk. "And more than that, I fear where this might be leading."

Archer suspected where the mayor was going with that thought.

"The city-states are fully autonomous, Mr. Mayor," he said. "Any Federation interference in the internals of one would risk reprisals from all."

"The president is a sly one, Archer. What interference he might take would be subtle, yet effective."

"Yes sir," said Archer.

The mayor leaned back in his chair, grew thoughtful. He brought his hands together, steepled his fingers.

"Question one..." he began. "What would be the purpose of this interference? The action must serve to benefit the Federation directly, perhaps the president indirectly."

He paused then, let that first question settle in the mind.

"Question two..." he continued. "What form would such interference take? This would depend on the purpose."

"Did your pull-aside with the president provide any clues as to the purpose?" asked Archer.

The mayor pulled his hands apart, leaned forward and slid his forearms onto his desk.

"What news of Richard Thornton, Chief Archer?" he asked.

Archer hesitated, considered the sudden redirection...

No, not a redirection. The Thornton matter must have come up in the pull-aside with the president.

"Mr. Mayor... while we have yet to locate Thornton, our investigation suggests that neither Cain nor the Alliance is responsible for his disappearance."

"He could not have eluded us on his own," said the mayor. "He had to have had help."

"I agree."

The mayor looked critically at Archer. "And has his brother been of benefit to your investigation?"

"Not as of yet, Mr. Mayor."

"Then I want him gone," the mayor said darkly. "I want Master Sergeant Thornton erased, and then I want him gone."

The taxi pulled up to the curb just as Alan came out of the veterans center, the sun just beginning to burn off an early morning mist. He climbed into the back seat and slipped his ID card into the reader.

He waited then, ready to pull out the card.

After too many seconds, the indicator light turned red instead of green.

Alan looked to the driver. The driver looked back at Alan through the rearview mirror. He said nothing. He took no action whatsoever. He waited.

Alan pulled his card from the reader and climbed out of the taxi. He stood on the sidewalk then, watched the cab pull away from the curb and drive down the street. He noticed then a black sedan parked nearby... almost as if it was waiting for him.

He approached the sedan. Detective Sullivan was sitting in the rear passenger seat, the window rolled down.

"Good morning, Alan," said Sullivan. "Problem?"

Alan gave a thin smirk as he looked up and down the street. The gray mist was continuing to burn away, the day growing brighter.

He walked around the car and climbed into the back seat beside Sullivan. The driver started the vehicle and started up the street.

Sullivan looked over at Alan, grinned then and focused on the street ahead.

"I'll see what I can do about clearing your ID," he said.

"Archer's doing?" asked Alan.

"Probably," said Sullivan. The initiator field had listed "city-state", which was the default value when a new record was added to the database.

He looked directly at Alan, then.

"It was going to happen, sooner or later," he said. "The timing suggests they're looking to push you down a path of their choosing."

"I'll choose my own path, all the same to you," said Alan.

"Sure." Sullivan looked out his side window, watched the passing scene for a few moments. "Whatever the reason for bringing your brother in that night, however they lost him, most thought him dead soon after."

"But no longer?"

"They've been following your every move since you came into town, hoping you'll lead them to him," said Sullivan. "So someone thought he might still be alive."

"Are you saying that's changed?"

"Your brother being alive? Don't know. Not what I'm suggesting." Sullivan turned from the side window to look at Alan. "Maybe the mayor has run out of patience; maybe he's feeling pressured. But they're no longer looking for you to lead them to Richard."

Sullivan waited then, watched for some sign that Alan understood what that meant. Alan in turn looked away from Sullivan, turned to the view beyond his own side window.

"Right," he said.

"Not so good for you," said Sullivan.

"Right," Alan said again.

The vehicle came to a stop in from of Sally's.

Sullivan nodded in the direction of the café.

"Join me for breakfast?" he asked. "I'm buying."

"I appreciate the offer, but no thanks."

"Other plans?"

"I've eaten."

Sullivan gave a slow nod, laid a hand on the handle and opened his door. "You watch yourself, Alan."

"I'll do that."

Sullivan looked to the driver. "Take Sergeant Thornton wherever he wants to go."

The driver looked at those in the back through the rearview mirror. He nodded once.

Sullivan slid out of the car. He leaned back in, one hand on the door, the other on the roof of the car.

"Alan... this is Willow City. There are always interests working in the shadows. There are sides hidden in sides, hidden in sides."

"And what side might you be on, Sullivan?" asked Alan.

Sullivan lifted his gaze, looked up and down the street, looked back to Alan with a slight, sad, knowing expression.

"I walk a path to a better Willow City, my friend." He leaned down, looked in to the driver. "Back for me in an hour."

Sullivan straightened and closed the door. He gave the roof of the vehicle two pats with the palm of his hand, then watched the sedan pull away from the curb.

He turned and looked into the café. A few of the booths were occupied, and most of the stools at the counter.

He smiled in anticipation and started to the front door.

Chapter Ten

Alan used the remote to turn off the monitor, walked across his vet cen room to the accompanying sound of knocking on the door. Opening the door, Sgt. Burke and his partner stood out in the hall.

"Good evening, Sergeant Thornton." Burke moved into the room, his partner following, forcing Alan to step aside.

"Doesn't Sullivan ever take time off?" asked Alan. He had just seen Sullivan that morning; early that morning.

Sgt. Burke put on a menacing grin, said nothing.

"Sullivan?" Partner snickered.

Alan looked curiously from one to the other of the officers. "Oh. I see."

He took the two steps over to the desk chair, took his jacket from the back of the chair. Holding his jacket in one hand, he casually opened the desk drawer.

The revolver wasn't there.

Doing his best to maintain calm, he slowly closed the drawer, turned from the desk.

"Shall we?" He put on his jacket as he led the way to the open door.

Sgt. Burke wore the hint of a grin as he glanced briefly at the desk, then followed the others out of the room.

Reaching the first floor, Sgt. Burke and his partner escorted Alan across the lobby, passing the front counter on their way to the front door. The desk clerk came in from a back room and stood at the counter.

"Good evening, Sergeant Thornton," he said.

Alan gave a friendly nod, said nothing.

Sgt. Burke ignored the desk clerk; his partner coldly eyed the man as they passed the front desk.

The desk clerk waited for them to leave the center, then reached down and pick up the heavy receiver of the phone that was hidden behind the counter. He dialed a number from memory.

§

Sgt. Burke assisted Alan into the back seat of the sedan parked at the curb, followed him in. Partner slid in behind the wheel and started the vehicle.

It was early evening, the quiet streets near-empty. Burke eyed Alan, looked ahead, again looked to the Alan.

"Just curious, Thornton," he said. "Just what did you hope to accomplish, bumbling about in the dark?"

Alan said nothing, watched the passing scene, the empty streets, the shimmering walls of the buildings, damp from an increasing fog.

"I mean, did you really think you'd find anything?" asked Burke. "You some great detective?"

Alan continued to hold his silence, to watch the scene beyond the window.

Sgt. Burke reached into a pocket and brought out an old revolver... Alan's revolver, the revolver that had disappeared from the desk drawer in Alan's room.

"And just what did you expect to do with this?" Burke held the revolver in his lap. He grinned. "Yeah, we dropped by your room earlier."

Alan looked down at the revolver, quickly looked away, again out his window.

"You understand..." Burke said in a heavy sigh, "these are so, so not allowed in a peaceful society such as ours."

Alan kept his focus outside the sedan. "So what happens now?"

Sgt. Burke didn't answer.

Partner turned the vehicle off the street and down into the police station parking garage. He steered the vehicle down one row, down a ramp to the next level, parked then in an isolated area of the parking garage.

Sgt. Burke urged Alan out with a sharp nod of the head. The partner took his arm and escorted him around to stand beside Burke.

Alan looked about at their isolation. Several parked vehicles, no one around. A dull-colored wall twenty feet away, an elevator door, a card reader on the wall beside the door.

"Is this where I get disappeared?" he asked.

Sgt. Burke appeared slightly amused by the question.

"Oh, that will happen, and we have begun taking the necessary steps to get us to that result..."

"I'm sensing a but."

"You see," said Burke. "We realized early on that in your case a simple disappearance would create static that we would have to deal with. Most annoying. Therefore..."

Sgt. Burke paused very briefly as he brought out the revolver and calmly shot his partner in the man's shoulder. The sound of the gunshot echoed throughout the garage.

Burke continued then.

"... we first need to establish the circumstances necessary to take us where we need to go."

Partner fell back, stumbled as he grabbed his shoulder, dropped to his knees.

"What the—" Partner fumbled, burbled, "Burke..."

"Stop whining. You'll live." Burke looked then to Alan as he put the revolver back into his pocket, pulled his own pistol from its holster. He put on a mock frown. "Damn. He sure did a lousy job of frisking you. How the hell did he miss a big, bad gun on your person, Thornton?"

"Now you just shoot me?"

"Oh, God no. There would be way too many questions. First we take you upstairs. Then we disappear you in plain sight. <u>Then</u> we shoot you."

Burke looked unceremoniously at his partner.

"Get up," he said. To Alan, then, indicating the elevator door with a wave of his weapon. "Let's go. Archer is waitin' on us."

They stepped past Partner as he struggled to get to his feet. Partner stumbled to follow them, blood oozing through his fingers pressed to his shoulder.

Sgt. Burke brought out a key card and inserted it into the reader next to the elevator. The indicator turned green.

At that moment came the loud, echoing sound of screeching tires. Another moment and two vehicles appeared: a dark sedan followed by a black shiny van.

The side door of the van slid open and four figures wearing black body armor and black masks jumped out and rushed Alan, Burke and his partner.

The elevator door hadn't yet opened.

Sgt. Burke fired his weapon at the nearest masked man, the bullet striking him square in the chest. It barely slowed him down. The two went hand-to-hand, the attacker with a stunner in hand.

A second attacker reached Burke's partner, who was unable to fight back, pressed his own stunner against Partner's chest and pulled the trigger.

The elevator door slid open. Partner was shoved into the car, collapsed to the floor.

Another attacker reached Alan, grabbed him by the arm and rushed him to the waiting sedan.

Sgt. Burke and his attacker continued to struggle. Burke was finally stunned; the attacker took one arm as the fourth attacker took his other. They half dragged Burke to the elevator and shoved him in. They backed away then as the elevator door closed.

Alan was pushed unceremoniously into the sedan; his face planted into the back seat. The door was slammed shut and the vehicle started away as Alan struggled about and sat up.

Detective Sullivan was in the back seat next to Alan. He looked forward.

"Good evening, Mr. Thornton."

The vehicle left the garage, turned onto the street. Behind them, the black van turned in the opposite direction.

"Sullivan." Alan rubbed at a sore arm. "So, where are we going?"

"Safe house."

Alan stood in the middle of a small living room. Sullivan looked into the bedroom, then poked his head into the open door of the bathroom. All clear. He moved then to a window, stood beside it and looked out onto the street below.

Alan watched, looked disinterestedly about the simply furnished apartment.

"Are you Alliance?" he asked.

"Alliance?" Sullivan turned from the window, shook his head no. "Consider this a rare apex where we and the Alliance have a common objective."

"And what might that objective be? Me *not dead*?"

Sullivan managed a light chuckle at that.

"You are a nuisance to both, my friend," he said. "And to just about everyone else. Then, I'm thinking that was what you were going for."

Alan said nothing, looked for Sullivan to give him more.

Sullivan continued. "You dead or disappeared, most would breathe a lot easier."

"Then why the timely rescue? And who the hell are you?"

Sullivan considered his answer, handed Alan the apartment key card as he started toward the door.

"If forced to take a side... Federation." He opened the door. "I'll pick you up in the morning. Important meeting, first thing."

Late evening, the old veteran was alone in the Veterans Center lounge, sitting in one of the easy chairs, watching the television broadcast on the monitor.

Displayed on the screen, the woman newscaster was sitting at the news desk.

"Welcome to the Late Night edition of Truth in Reporting, a service of the National Education Office," she said.

The Veterans Center desk clerk came into the lounge, coffee cup in hand. He sat on the arm of one of the couches. He took a sip of his coffee and watched the program with the old veteran.

The screen behind the newscaster displayed the image of a city street, a number of uniformed men and women forcibly gathering a smaller group of dissidents and shoving them toward the back of a police wagon. Several other dissidents were being forced to remove posters from a brick wall.

The woman newscaster was speaking: "The city-state completed another sweep last evening, removing a number of unsavories from our streets."

The old veteran grumbled.

"Thereby making the city safe for all," he said sarcastically.

"More volunteers for military service," said the desk clerk. Another sip of his coffee.

On the screen, the image behind the newscaster displayed a battlefield, smoke drifting across the landscape. Soldiers were marching across the field.

"It won't always be so, Sergeant," said the old veteran.

The desk clerk continued watching the monitor.

"We shall be the change, Major," he said.

Chapter Eleven

A quiet side street lined with townhouses. Early morning, the sun just coming up.

Alan closed the door of one of these townhouses, took the steps down to the sidewalk and to the open back door of the dark sedan. He climbed in beside Detective Sullivan and closed the door.

Sullivan waited for the vehicle to pull away from the curb before saying anything.

"You slept well?" he asked. Alan.

"Fine, thanks," said Alan. "My first safe house."

"Stayed there myself, once."

Alan looked curiously at Sullivan, quickly decided not to ask... he looked at the passing scene as they turned onto a main thoroughfare.

"Where are we headed?" he asked.

Sullivan looked to the driver, who looked back through the rearview mirror.

"I told you last night," he said then. "We're meeting with someone who may be able to help."

"Yeah, I got that," said Alan. "You were rather light on specifics."

Sullivan looked briefly again to the driver, then out a side window.

"I hear ya," he sighed.

"Uh, huh." Alan looked curiously from Sullivan to the driver, back to Sullivan. "Right."

They turned down another street, drove past brick-walled buildings. Posters haphazardly pasted on the walls reflected resistance to the city-state, highlighted the oppression of the administration and policies, encouraged taking a stand, fighting back, resisting authoritarianism.

The car turned into an open-air parking area next to a small warehouse complex. They pulled into a space near the warehouse side door. A plain sign above the door read "Marshall Distributing".

Inside, the driver led Sullivan and Alan along a hallway, passing several closed doors. He stopped at one, knocked twice, hesitated, then opened the door.

Mrs. Marshall entered her office through a side door as the driver escorted Alan and Sullivan in from the hallway. At sixty years old, she was a strong woman, which shown in her manner and stand. She was well-dressed in professional slacks and blouse. Her well-combed hair held streaks of gray.

She waved her guests fully into the office.

"Come, come," she said. To the driver then, "Thank you, Steven."

Steven the driver/escort nodded and backed out, closing the door as he left. Mrs. Marshall moved into the middle of the room, held her hand out to Sullivan. They shook hands.

"Detective Sullivan," she said. "I've heard many good things about you. So wonderful to finally meet you."

"Thank you, Mrs. Marshall."

She looked then to Alan, shook his hand as well.

"Mr. Thornton. I'm Amanda Marshall."

"Ma'am," Alan said curtly.

Mrs. Marshall moved around behind her desk, indicated the guest chairs as she sat down. She watched them take the chairs.

"To business, then." She looked to Alan, leaned over the desk and clasped her hands. "I hope you appreciate the risk we're taking, Mr. Thornton; revealing our presence in this way."

"And you are?"

Mrs. Marshall wore a slight smile, a thoughtful smile.

"We represent Federation interests here in Willow City."

"And you would prefer that these interests, and your presence, remain private."

"Our activities are best served by remaining undisclosed to certain parties."

She caught then Alan looking thoughtfully over at Sullivan, back to Mrs. Marshall.

"Yes," she said. "The Federation footprint in Willow City is small, and our presence highly compartmentalized." Another smile in Sullivan's direction. "As for Detective Sullivan, his has no doubt been a lonely existence, his focus as per Federation interests somewhat isolating."

"I appreciate the importance of our charge here, Mrs. Marshall," said Sullivan.

"Of course. And yet the lack of timely communication has no doubt on occasion been frustrating."

"On occasion."

Mrs. Marshall slid her arms off the desk as she leaned back in her chair. She studied Alan for a long moment.

"What to do with you, Mr. Thornton?"

"Should I be concerned?"

"You misunderstand. Yes, your queries have drawn attention to matters that are incidentally related to Federation interests, but nothing that we can't deal with." She looked thoughtfully at Alan, considered. "No, the issue before us is whether and how to afford you the protection that Detective Sullivan here has advocated."

"And what form might this protection take? I won't be disappeared."

"Mr. Thornton, again you misunderstand." Mrs. Marshall's tone grew firm. "The Federation has no interest in whether you live, die or disappear. What action we choose to take will serve Federation interests, no matter Detective Sullivan's sponsorship... or what wishes you might entertain."

"As you did with my brother?"

"It became necessary to step in when it was clear the city-state intended to use your brother to ascertain the gray market network. Exposure of that network would have threatened discovery of our own."

"The city-state doesn't know of your network?"

"They don't know of our presence at all, beyond the occasional mole or spy that we allow to be known or suspected."

Sullivan reentered the conversation then.

"Mrs. Marshall? The Federation has Thornton?"

"Detective Sullivan," she acknowledged. To both of them then, "Richard Thornton was with us until just under a month ago."

"Is he all right?" asked Alan. "Where is he now?"

"He left our protection of his own accord, and without our knowledge."

"So where is he?"

"I'm sorry, Mr. Thornton."

"You don't know?"

"We believe he has left Willow City, but he has yet to make an appearance in any of the other city-states."

"I see. And once he does?"

"We will ensure that he is not a threat." Mrs. Marshall stated firmly.

"You're not... you won't—"

"No," she stated. "I do not believe that will be necessary."

Well, at least there was that.

Alan sat back in his chair. He looked to Sullivan, back to Mrs. Marshall across the desk.

"And what about me?"

"Yours is a complex circumstance, Mr. Thornton."

"I get that," said Alan. "A lot."

"I do not doubt that," said Mrs. Marshall. "As for the Federation, the light created by your presence in the city-state pushes back the shadows and threatens to expose our own."

"And Federation interests must be protected, which means hush-hush," said Alan. "Got it."

"A quiet word spoken here, a covert action take there, we may be able to dim that light." Mrs. Marshall leaned nearer. "And you will do your part."

"Which is?" Alan asked warily.

"You must cease looking for your brother."

"Mrs. Marshall—" Sullivan started.

"I won't do that," Alan stated firmly.

Mrs. Marshall calmly lifted a hand, two fingers raised. The call for silence. She was clearly used to giving direction and having that direction taken.

She straightened, looked at Alan with purpose.

"It must be clear to all that you no longer have reason to search for your brother."

"Mrs. Marshall, I—"

"Mr. Thornton. Once we have located your brother, we will let you know."

Sullivan looked from Mrs. Marshall to Alan.

"Alan, let them find your brother," he said. "What can you do on your own? He's not even in the city."

"If that is true."

"Your brother is alive, Alan. Take that." Sullivan stood then, looked across the desk to Mrs. Marshall. "I will see that Mr. Thornton does his part."

"Thank you, Detective Sullivan."

Alan looked dubious, but held his silence.

The Alliance leader stood with John Benton and William Valentine in the front office of Intercity Trade. He was looking out the window onto the warehouse floor, where the pallet of paper and ink was being loaded into the back of a box truck.

He turned from the window.

"Thank you for your assistance, Mr. Benton," he said. "We'll be out of your hair in a few minutes."

"Not a problem," said Benton.

The Alliance leader put on a knowing smile.

"Kind of you to say so," he said. He looked to William. "Mr. Valentine. Chief Archer is still interested in speaking with you. He will be until city hall no longer considers you of value."

"And the Alliance?"

"Your threat to the Alliance is being minimized as we speak."

"You mean, as soon as connections that I have to the Alliance are removed, you'll be cutting me loose."

The Alliance leader appeared consoling. "We'll try and do you better, Mr. Valentine."

A young man came into the office from the warehouse, came up beside the Alliance leader.

"We're about ready, sir," he said. "The roads are clear."

"Thank you."

The young man looked to both John Benton and William.

"We're short six ink cartridges," he said, more than a hint of accusation. "Any idea what happened to them?"

"Me?" Benton almost smirked. "This is all new to me. And after today, it's history. I am gone and gone."

The young man looked then to William.

"I expect Richard held onto them," said William.

"The merchandize does not belong to Thornton," said the young man.

William shrugged. "Handlers fee?"

Benton couldn't help but grin.

"Sounds like Richard," he said.

The Alliance leader gave a dismissive nod to the young man, a sign that he should let it go. The man gave a final disapproving frown to Benton and William, turned about and left.

The Alliance leader then looked to the others.

"Mr. Benton, we should be able to help you *be gone*, as you wish." To William then, "Mr. Valentine?"

William shook his head no.

"I have unfinished business here in Willow City.

The Alliance leader gave William an approving smile.

"Very good, Mr. Valentine."

The mayor was at his desk, hovered over paperwork, signing one document and then another. His receptionist stood waiting patiently beside him. Chief Archer was sitting in a nearby guest chair.

The mayor signed a final document. He gathered the papers together and handed them to his receptionist.

"Thank you, Betty," he said. He looked to her then with an afterthought. "Call my wife. I'll be available for lunch, 1:00 PM."

"Yes, Mr. Mayor." The receptionist stepped away from the mayor and left the office.

The mayor leaned back in his chair, swiveled about and looked across his desk to Archer.

"Richard Thornton," he said, prompting his police chief.

"Yes sir. Numerous sources conclude that Thornton is no longer in the city."

"Excuse me. He left the city? Without our knowledge? That is not possible."

"Nonetheless, sir. It appears to be the case."

The mayor grew contemplative, pursed his lips, tapped at his chin.

"Federation fingerprints."

"Perhaps, Mr. Mayor."

The mayor sat up and leaned forward in his chair.

"What of his brother?" he asked.

"His only value, to anyone, was the possibility that he might lead us to Richard. With his brother gone, Alan Thornton is irrelevant."

"And he's still breathing?"

"Sir—"

"I am certain that I asked this issue be dealt with."

"Yes sir," said Archer. "I'll see to it, Mr. Mayor."

The two grew silent. The mayor raised a brow then, a silent suggestion that the meeting was over. Archer got the message. He stood.

"Right away, sir." He turned to leave.

Mayor watched after him, spoke out before Archer reached the door.

"Archer."

Archer stopped and turned. "Sir."

"Archer." The mayor considered for several painfully long moments. "On reflection... let us monitor only. For now."

"Sir?"

"Brother Alan may yet be of value. He may not have found his brother, but his search may have engendered a few network connections of his own. Let us see where they lead."

"Of course, sir," Archer said with an abbreviated nod.

"And keep an eye out," the mayor continued. "I have no doubt the Federation is scurrying about in the shadows."

Archer gave another, affirmative nod of the head. The mayor spun his chair slowly about, his focus to the window.

He didn't look happy.

"I'll not have Federation boots in my city."

Archer gave a final nod, uncertain, looking at the back of the mayor sitting his chair.

He turned and left the office.

Chapter Twelve

Sgt. Burke sat in the front passenger seat of the unmarked police sedan, the vehicle parked across the street from Sally's Café. His new partner was sitting behind the steering wheel.

Burke took a swallow of coffee from a thermos cup, looked across the street to the café, his expression cool and detached. In the café, visible through the window, Detective Sullivan was sitting in a booth, taking a forkful of what was most likely a piece of pie.

What is it with Sullivan and apple pie?

Burke's new partner opened a small paper bag and took out a plastic bag of apple slices. He pulled out a slice, held it out to Burke.

"Sergeant? Apple slice?"

Burke's expression didn't change. His focus on the window of the café didn't change.

He took another swallow of coffee.

"No."

The new partner pulled back the apple slice.

"All right." He bit into the slice of apple. "Honeycrisp."

Sgt. Burke closed his eyes briefly and set his jaw as if pushing back pain. He took a long sigh, continued watching the café.

Morning in the Gray Swan. Carl and Bonnie were sitting at the bar, Carl with a glass of water with lemon, Bonnie with a cup of coffee.

Eddie was standing behind the bar opposite the couple. He looked briefly across at Carl, then focused on the cup he was holding in both hands.

"I wouldn't sweat it, Carl," he said. "We'll get through this."

"Evidence to the contrary," grumbled Carl.

"The city's quieting down. Our friends are seeing to that."

"They can't undo the attention that we've gotten over this."

"They're doing nothing to protect us," said Bonnie, her frown darkening. "City finding us out wouldn't be a threat to the Alliance, so what do they care?"

"The Gray Swan will be fine, Bonnie," said Eddie. "We lay low, provide entertainment and a few hours escape to the citizens of Willow City. Just like always."

Valerie came into the club. She walked over to the bar, stood at the counter beside Carl and Bonnie. She said nothing. Eddie poured a cup of coffee and set it in front of her.

"Thanks, Eddie." She held onto the cup, spoke then without looking at the others. "How's things?"

"You tell us," said Bonnie.

"Don't know much." Valerie took a sip of her coffee, set the cup on the counter. "I'm hearing Richard left town."

"He's all right?" asked Bonnie.

"Guess so. Word is, he left town on his own."

"And he didn't tell anyone?" Bonnie struggled to hide a grin. "He didn't tell you?"

"So it would seem." Valerie looked past Bonnie to Carl. "And I hear they're cleaning up the mess his brother's been making."

"I heard that, too," said Carl. "It looks like Alan is safe. For now."

Bonnie shook her head.

"He should take a cue from Richard, leave town while he can," she said.

"Yeah," said Carl. "I don't see that happening."

Valerie moved her cup aside.

"I don't know Alan very well, but he doesn't seem the kind to just walk away, job not done."

"What's left for him to do?" asked Bonnie.

Valerie looked across at Eddie and pointed to her near-empty cup as she answered.

"Don't know," she said. "But it doesn't feel done to me."

Alan stood in the lobby of Cain's Club, arms held out. Cavanaugh watched the security man pat Alan down. Once cleared, Alan followed Cavanaugh into the club.

A woman was behind the bar organizing inventory. Cain was sitting at his table at the back of club, his associate standing discretely to one side. Cain was eating a piece of toast, a juice glass and a small plate on the table in front of him.

He set the toast on the plate and lifted the glass as he looked side-glance at Alan's approach, Cavanaugh moving to one side.

"Good morning, Mr. Thornton." Cain drank from his juice. "Don't you spread sunshine and buttercups wherever you go? I have to say, I'm thoroughly enjoying your visit to our otherwise gloomy city."

"Yours be a smiling face in a crowd of frowns," said Alan.

Cain indicated a chair, spoke again as Alan sat down.

"And is that what brings you here this morning? Longing for a friendly face?"

"I thought I'd check in, see if you've heard anything."

Cain studied Alan's face for a few moments as he toyed with his juice glass.

"You've no doubt heard the same scuttlebutt as I." He took a swallow of juice, studied Alan a moment. "Ah. I see. You come seeking verification."

"Yes sir."

"I am afraid that I cannot. Not yet."

Alan took a moment to process the '*not yet*'.

"I would appreciate any future updates that may come your way," he said then.

"But of course, my friend." Cain said smugly. He gulped down the last of his juice, set the glass gently aside. "I can assume then that you will be honoring us with your presence for a while longer."

"A reasonable assumption."

Alan walked across the garden-like apartment grounds, carrying his duffle, the duffle he had with him when he had first stepped off the train.

Approaching Richard's old apartment, he saw Wanda near the door, leaning against the porch post, her arms folded across her chest.

"Good morning, neighbor," she said, smiling. She unfolded her arms, held out one hand, showing a key card.

"Thank you, Wanda."

Alan took the card, Wanda pushed off the post and stepped to one side.

"True about Richard, then?" she asked. "He left the city?"

"That's the word."

Wanda waited for more. Nothing more came. She took another step away.

"News could have been worse. Right?"

"Absolutely," said Alan. He gave an awkward smile, held up the key card. "Hey, I got an apartment out of it."

Wanda appeared thankful of Alan's weak attempt at humor.

"I'm so pleased," she said. She started away, stopped after a few steps and looked back at Alan. "Lovely having you as a neighbor, Alan."

Alan gave another awkward smile, watched as Wanda turned again and walked away. He looked up at the blue sky then, back to Wanda's receding figure. He looked down at the key card in his hand.

He weighed his duffle, gave a confident half-grin and turned to the front door of his apartment.

~ *End*

The Britton Journals

Preface

A short story from the universe of "The Shylmahn Trilogy"...

Twenty years after the Second Truce between Shylmahn and humans, some fifty years after the great transport ships first reached Earth, a young Shylmahn historian visits one of the last surviving leaders of the human resistance, seeking the story of the migration as seen through the eyes of the aging Joseph Britton...

The Britton Journals

EsJen was settled comfortably in one of the half-dozen seats of her small shuttle. She looked over at the only other passenger in the main compartment. The young Shylmahn historian was leaning near one of the portholes, looking down at the thick forest they were passing over.

LaTehl was a bit shorter than EsJen, at just under five feet tall. She was thin, with thin, delicate bones. Her skin was a pale gold, soft and smooth to the touch. Her hair, as with all the Shylmahn, was a shimmering golden brown. Her face was petite, her nose, mouth and chin fine featured; her neck narrow and slight. She was dressed as EsJen in the standard brown shirt and pants that most Shylmahn wore.

EsJen felt the shuttle lean slightly, shift slightly. She leaned to her left and glanced out.

The sky was blue and clear. The mountainous terrain beneath them was blanketed in green. They were several hundred feet above the forest canopy and appeared to be slowly descending.

A Shylmahn stepped into the main cabin from forward. He was dressed in the same shirt and pant uniform that EsJen and LaTehl were wearing. He approached EsJen, stopping when he was near enough to speak without having to raise his voice.

"We'll be arriving in three minutes, EsJen."

"Thank you, NaMehn."

NaMehn had been with EsJen for almost twenty years, was in charge of the escort team assigned to protect the leader of the Shylmahn.

He nodded a silent response, turned about and returned forward.

They were on their way to site 43369553w, a monitored Chehnon community the humans called John's Park. It had been a small town of several thousand humans prior to the arrival of the Shylmahn, when it had been all but abandoned until repurposed following the completion of the migration. It now had a population of 140 natives, humans that had been deemed too disruptive to society to remain amongst the general population, but as part of the truce agreement had been brought to John's Park to live out their days rather than simply eliminated.

One of the community's residents was Joseph Britton. He and others in the Britton family had been key leaders in the resistance that had fought the Shylmahn's migration to this world, a resistance that had been doomed to fail from the start.

EsJen had befriended Joseph early in the migration, and had done what she could to protect him and the others in the Britton family even as their disruptive activities grew increasingly troublesome. In the end, that friendship hadn't been strong enough to stand against the opposing forces of the Shylmahn and the resistance.

She visited Joseph now several times a year, had been doing so since his placement in John's Park some twenty years past. Their relationship had strained to near the breaking point leading up to the Second Truce, but they had managed to rebuild the relationship to where they could at least carry on civil conversations. And EsJen felt, as she had from the very beginning, that a working relationship with Joseph was constructive to the success of Shylmahn society here on Chehno, what had once been called Earth by the natives.

EsJen glanced over again at LaTehl. The young historian was putting together the complete history of the Shylmahn migration to this, their new home. It was interesting that the person chosen to prepare the history hadn't been born when the first ships arrived here on Chehno. She would have to rely completely on the memories of others.

That included the perspective of one of the last surviving members of the human resistance.

EsJen had agreed to allow the interview, though the decision as to whether to allow the inclusion of what came of the interview had yet to be made.

§

NaMehn and another of the escort team stepped down the ramp first, accompanied by a sleek spheroid probe about eighteen inches in diameter. The probe moved out ahead, hovering six feet above the ground, using all of its sensors to monitor for signs of danger. Meanwhile the escort moved to either side of the ramp, allowing EsJen and LaTehl to step down from the shuttle and onto the landing field.

The landing field had once been a parking lot for an office building at the edge of town. The perimeter had been cleared for security and it was maintained now for the use of the weekly supply shuttles and occasional administrative visits.

The last two of the security team followed EsJen and LaTehl out of the shuttle and they all started up the town's main street, the probe taking the lead. They passed a number of storefronts, most long ago converted for the personal use of the few habitants of the town. The street and walks were kept clean, though the asphalt suffered from ever-widening cracks through which weeds continually grew.

A middle-aged human female stood at the door of one of the building fronts, her shoulder against the frame, her arms folded across her chest. She said nothing, showed no emotion, as the group of Shylmahn passed.

To all appearances the escort ignored her, but EsJen knew better. They were ready. LaTehl, however, betrayed a mix of curiosity and concern. Shylmahn seldom interacted with the humans; some had never seen one. Yet here was one right up close, just a few yards away.

You could almost reach out and touch it.

And then they were past. Another half dozen steps and EsJen nodded in the direction of a large building on the left.

"There," she said.

"Joseph Britton?"

"It's where he spends his days."

NaMehn knew where they were going, slowed as he reached the two storey structure. The building had once been what the humans called a theatre; some form of entertainment had been performed there.

The probe slowed and stopped, moved to within a few yards of the theatre door and waited. One of the security escort stood watch beside the door as NaMehn went inside.

EsJen didn't wait. She followed him in, leaving LaTehl to hurry in after them. The remaining escort took up positions across the street.

The theatre lobby had been rebuilt and remodeled, having been near collapse years after the town had been abandoned. Most of the building had been gutted and repaired, the work taking several years. The lobby now had clean carpet; pictures hung on painted walls, there were a number of chairs and lamps about the large room. A long counter ran before one wall.

A human female stood at the top of a wide staircase set against another wall. She looked down at the arrivals.

"EsJen," she said. The woman sounded neither surprised nor concerned.

"Hello, Jenny," said EsJen. "How are you?"

"I am well." Jenny was Joseph Britton's daughter. She was closing in on fifty years old, was slim and fit. She had been deeply involved in her father's resistance prior to the truce, as had been her brother Michael, though his role had been much more complicated.

"And how is your father?" EsJen walked to the stairs and waited.

"He is expecting you," said Jenny. She took a step back. "This way."

EsJen looked over at NaMehn and with hardly a gesture signaled that he should wait downstairs. She started up the stairs then, and LaTehl followed.

There was a balcony at the end of the upstairs hall, beyond which the darkened theatre could be seen. Jenny reached a door on the left well before the balcony, opened it and stepped to one side. She held a beckoning arm out for the two Shylmahn to go in.

The room was lit by several pole lamps and a single overhead light. A set of French doors at one end opened to a private balcony that looked out across the theatre. There were several comfortable chairs and side tables about the room. Two walls were lined with shelves filled with books from a human history that was quickly fading away.

Joseph Britton was sitting in one of a pair of chairs near the French doors. He had a notebook in his lap, a pencil in hand. There was a large coffee mug on the table between the two chairs.

EsJen silently noted that Joseph had changed considerably since her last visit. To now he had been aging well for a human, but at eighty his years were beginning to catch up to him. His hair was gray and beginning to thin. His skin appeared dry and drawn. The knuckles on his hands looked swollen.

His eyes, however, looked clear and sharp. He focused on his guests and watched them, studied them, as they approached. He set his notebook and pencil aside.

"Good morning, EsJen. Long time, no see."

"Hello, Joseph. You look well."

"Ah." Joseph managed a smirk. "The quality of your lying continues to improve. You must be spending a lot of time with BehLahk."

"BehLahk sends his best," said EsJen. "He intends to visit soon."

"Of course." Joseph looked over at the other Shylmahn. "This is your historian?"

"This is LaTehl," said EsJen. "LaTehl, I introduce Joseph Britton."

LaTehl took a step forward and bowed her head slightly. "Hello, Joseph Britton."

"LaTehl," said Joseph. "Excuse my not standing. I'm having a bit of trouble with my hip this morning."

"Not at all," said LaTehl. She understood that humans were short-lived creatures, but Joseph Britton's appearance was nonetheless unsettling.

"So." Joseph studied the young Shylmahn for a moment. "You want to hear about the invasion from my side, eh?"

LaTehl appeared startled. She looked quickly from EsJen, back to Joseph. "The... migration, yes. I have just a few questions... about you, and your family..."

"Right. The legendary Britton family."

"Yes," said LaTehl, a bit clumsily. "Exactly. A few questions."

Joseph looked down at his hands, rubbed at his knuckles. "Legendary," he mumbled.

Jenny had been standing to one side, letting the conversation play out. She took a step forward now, stepping between her father and the Shylmahn. "I'll go put together some refreshments," she said. "If you will excuse me."

"Thank you, Jenny," said EsJen.

Joseph watched her leave, then indicated the nearby chair. "Please. Sit."

LaTehl gave another nod and settled into the chair. She took out a recorder and set it on the table between them. "Do you mind?"

Joseph shook his head. She activated the device and slid back in the chair. She looked small; but then, all Shylmahn looked small.

EsJen moved quietly across the room, glanced at the titles of row upon row of books. Joseph knew that she had learned to read English, was almost as good at the written word as the spoken. He also knew that she read the titles of every book in this room at each visit, though seldom brought down a book and opened it.

While he wasn't allowed to leave John's Park, Jenny could. She was here of her own accord, had been granted permission several years after his internment. She took trips out at least every other month; often to Seattle, sometimes south to Portland, on occasion further south. With each trip, she made an effort to find books to bring back to her father.

With her memory, EsJen probably new which books had been added since her last visit; every visit. But the books in this room were only a small part of the collection. The larger library was downstairs. Voices from a past that Joseph feared would soon be lost.

He turned his attention from EsJen to the historian.

She had been quietly watching him. She smiled then, and it was a most human smile. On LaTehl it looked somehow all the more alien.

The Shylmahn scientist BehLahk had known from very early on that for this to truly be home to the Shylmahn, they would have to adapt to this world as much as this world adapt to them. And yet this had been one of their greatest fears. It would mean becoming less *Shylmahn*, a concept that went against everything their culture told them what it meant to be Shylmahn.

"What shall we talk about, LaTehl?" asked Joseph.

LaTehl began by asking about Joseph's thoughts regarding their arrival. She commented that when interviewing Shylmahn who had been around at the time, they spoke of the great adventure that was the migration; their first steps on a new world, the beginning of a new life.

Joseph had to point out that for humans it had been something quite different. It had been an invasion, and a bloodthirsty one at that. He mentioned that his own home had been destroyed during the first moments of the invasion. His best friend had died on the first day.

LaTehl looked uncomfortable, but managed to move quickly onward.

"Was that when you joined the resistance?" she asked.

"No," he said, growing thoughtful. "No, that came much later."

Jenny entered the room with a tray of cookies, a small water pitcher and three glasses. She set the tray on the table beside the door and quietly backed out of the room, taking only a moment to listen to her father and the historian. They were discussing the human internment reservations and clearly had very different views on the subject.

Stepping back into the hallway, she found EsJen on the main balcony overlooking the theatre. Standing beside the leader of the Shylmahn, she looked silently down into the shadows of the large, open space below them. There were only a handful of low energy light fixtures turned on, barely enough to reveal that the seating had long ago been removed and the floor space had been tiered, providing six level floor sections, with steps down from one to the next. Each section contained rows of book shelves.

"It sounds like they have a ways to go," she said at last, her gaze continuing on the floor below.

"I expect you are right," said EsJen.

"So..." Jenny hesitated. "Just how much of what my father is telling her will actually appear in her history of the, uh... *migration?*"

"Some, I would think," said EsJen. "It is why I brought her here."

"Is it?"

EsJen didn't respond to that, but when it came to the Shylmahn, silence could mean anything.

"How is Michael ?" Jenny asked then. She hadn't seen her brother for several years. Their relationship had suffered much in those final months leading up to the Second Truce, and on those occasions when they did see one another, the meetings were usually uncomfortable. "Is he well?"

"I have not seen him since he stepped down from the council," said EsJen.

Michael had served as head of the council for many years, effectively the representative of the humans to the Shylmahn. He had chosen to leave the council a year earlier, returning to private life. Michael and his wife Victoria were living in Portland, the second largest human free district in the northwest, second only to Seattle.

"I see," said Jenny.

"I believe he is doing well," said EsJen after a few moments. "So I understand."

They fell silent once more. Jenny remained on the balcony with EsJen out of courtesy. The Shylmahn were the captors of those here in John's Park, and yet EsJen's visits always had the feel of company dropping in and Jenny felt strangely responsible to her guest.

It was bizarre...

"You developed a relationship with EsJen very early on in the migration, did you not?" asked LaTehl.

"It was an association of mutual benefit," said Joseph. "We each sought to gain information that would help our people."

"Did it not grow to something more? You became friends, Shylmahn and human?"

"Of a sort, perhaps. As much as was possible, her being an invader and all," said Joseph. "And it was short-lived, as it turned out."

"Due to your becoming part of the resistance?"

"That was inevitable."

"How so?"

"You invaded us and took over our world."

"But..." LaTehl started awkwardly. "Not all humans joined the resistance."

"Not all were in a position to do so."

"Of course," said LaTehl, nodding. Again, a human gesture. "Those in your family, your brothers and sisters. They were in a position to do so."

"Most of 'em."

"And you were their leader," said LaTehl.

"Oh, hell no," said Joseph. "I never knew a Britton who took well to leaders."

"Is that why—"

"We each had our strengths, our weaknesses. We each had to discover the role that we each would play, though that was certainly not anything conscious on our part." Joseph smiled thoughtfully. "And I don't think team concept ever came into it."

"Are you saying that you didn't work together? I have heard that—"

"Our paths hardly crossed," said Joseph, cutting her off.

"But in the end, did they not all follow your strategy?"

Joseph had spent most of the years following the initial invasion in isolation, slowly laying the groundwork for a multi-pronged plan to drive the Shylmahn out, and once in place moved those efforts forward. Only then was he able to bring his brothers and sisters on board.

"As my efforts took form, they agreed to support what I was doing," he stated coolly.

LaTehl shifted position in her chair, looked across at the human.

"The island," she said, tentatively. "Your brother's island. Much earlier, I believe. Were you not together then?"

"That was strictly family," said Joseph. "It had nothing to do with the resistance."

"From what I have been able to determine, strictly from our own perspective to be sure, but it would seem that the event was a major milestone in the timeline of the resistance."

"As I said, it was family. We all knew... the island, Bril's efforts... it served no purpose but for Bril. We couldn't leave Bril. Even if it meant going down in some foolish last stand."

"I think I understand," said LaTehl after a considered pause. *The strength of family, human family, most evident in the Britton clan. I have seen evidence of it again and again...*

"Do you?" asked Joseph, doubtfully. "That would be something."

"EsJen put her position at risk in trying to bring everyone safely out," stated LaTehl.

"Yeah, that didn't work out so well, did it?"

Jenny returned to her father's small library, stepped aside and allowed EsJen to follow her in. Closing the door behind them, she could hear Joseph and the historian talking quietly back and forth. Hearing the word "Veltahk", she looked uneasily at EsJen.

Veltahk... one of the three nightmarish components of Joseph's multi-pronged plan to drive the Shylmahn from Earth. It was a human-designed variation of the planet-wide foliage that had driven the Shylmahn from their home, though this Earth variety had been genetically designed to die out after several years; in spite of that, isolated pockets remained even twenty years later.

It had been obvious at the time that the Earth variation of the Veltahk had been Joseph's brainchild, that he had used EsJen's story of the Shylmahn plant during their conversations against them.

For EsJen, it had been the final betrayal.

She moved now across the room, stood near the bookshelves along the far wall. As uncomfortable as she was with this subject, she was ready to let LaTehl hear it from Joseph.

The story of what Joseph had done was well known to the Shylmahn.

"I am sorry, Joseph," said LaTehl. "I struggle to comprehend. For all Shylmahn, your creation of this form of the nightmare plant is beyond understanding."

"Kind of the plan," grumbled Joseph.

"But... Joseph..." LaTehl continued to struggle with the concept. "You cover your world, our world, our shared world..."

"Shared? Really?" Joseph's tone sharpened and he pushed himself forward. He gave himself a moment to return a sense of calm; calm, firm, resolute. "On the day you arrived, hundreds of millions of us died; without a word from you as to why. In the days and weeks that followed, hundreds of millions more. Never a word as to why you were doing this to us. Shared? The Veltahk may not have gotten rid of you, but it helped put the word on your tongues."

There was a long, uncomfortable moment of silence. EsJen stepped away from the bookshelves, moved into the middle of the room.

"Have you completed your interview, LaTehl?" she asked. It was not a question.

LaTehl slid forward in her chair and stood up. She gave a half nod to Joseph.

"I thank you for your time, Joseph Britton. My work is improved by today's discussion."

"Glad to help," said Joseph. He didn't sound as though he cared much one way or the other. He managed an impish grin then. "I don't imagine there'll be an English translation anytime soon?"

LaTehl gave an awkward glance to EsJen, looked back to Joseph. "I am sorry. I do not know."

EsJen took a step nearer. "I'll see what we can do," she said.

"Thanks."

EsJen took another step nearer to Joseph.

"It was good to see you, Joseph," she said. "I look forward to my next visit, and the opportunity to simply... visit."

"As do I, EsJen."

LaTehl picked up her recorder and turned it off.

"This way, please," said Jenny. She escorted EsJen and the young historian to the door. LaTehl turned back to Joseph as Jenny opened the door and stepped aside.

"Joseph... might I ask a final question?"

"Of course," said Joseph.

"I have heard, on several occasions, that you experienced a vision ahead of our arrival, portending our arrival."

"That's right," he answered flatly.

"Might I ask... what did you see?"

He hesitated, and a shadow spread across his face. "I saw the end of us," he said at last.

LaTehl was visibly shaken, despite having heard something similar from others who knew of Joseph's visions.

"Thank you," she said quietly. "Joseph... do you know how you came by these visions?"

"Yes," Joseph stated.

"Yes?"

"You should take your question to TohPeht," said Joseph. "To TohPeht-ShahnTahr."

LaTehl looked briefly to EsJen, as if for some confirmation.

ShahnTahr had been the AI responsible for guiding the Shylmahn people on Shylmah for hundreds of years, for bringing the migration to Earth, for supporting the migration through the early years. ShahnTahr had been EsJen's closest advisor during her first years as the Shylmahn leader.

TohPeht-ShahnTahr was the hybrid of the A-I and Shylmahn.

When EsJen gave no response to LaTehl's silent plea, the historian turned again to the human.

"Thank you, Joseph. I shall do that."

Jenny guided her out of the room. EsJen stopped briefly in the doorway, turned back and looked to her one-time human friend.

"I shall see you soon, Joseph."

"I look forward to it, EsJen."

LaTehl followed EsJen and her escort across the lobby floor as the human Jenny Britton watched from the top of the stairs.

Once they were outside, the guardian probe started up the street and NaMehn and another of the security team moved in a few yards behind it. EsJen and LaTehl followed, and the remaining escort moved in from across the street and brought up the rear.

They were some distance yet from the landing field when EsJen broke the long silence.

"All that you heard today... will die with the Chehnon Joseph Britton."

"Excuse me?"

"It ends with Joseph."

"But... I don't understand, EsJen. Did we not come here to gain Joseph Britton's perspective?"

"I wished for you to hear Joseph's perspective regarding our migration. However, what happened is what we say happened. How those events happened are how we say they happened."

"I did not intend to take all that he said on faith, EsJen, but if they can be verified—"

"The migration is as it was seen from our eyes."

"Then why did we—"

EsJen held up a hand and silenced LaTehl.

They were nearing the landing field. EsJen slowly brought her hand to her side. "If any of Joseph's words can fill in gaps of our own, without altering what we know happened, or how we know it happened, then you may bring it to me for consideration."

They started across the landing field and toward the shuttle, the security team moving to either side of the craft's ramp.

"Yes, EsJen," said LaTehl. "Thank you, EsJen."

They reached the foot of the ramp and stopped. EsJen gave the historian a sympathetic expression.

"What you are doing is important for future generations, LaTehl. They will look back to our time and will know how we came to be here, the sacrifices that many made. They will understand our place in this world. Our world. Chehno."

"Yes, EsJen."

EsJen looked back in the direction of the heart of John's Park.

"And they will know the humans' place in this world." *It must be so...*

EsJen turned about and took the ramp up into her shuttle.

Jenny found the French doors to the private balcony standing open. She stepped through and stood beside her father. The lights of the converted theatre were turned up now.

"Dinner is ready," she said.

"Thank you," said Joseph. "I've built up an appetite."

"I could bring it up."

"Don't be silly. I'll be right down." While Joseph's age was indeed beginning to catch up with him, he wasn't nearly as infirmed as he had let on to the visiting Shylmahn.

Let the guards believe him incapable of moving across the room.

Jenny looked behind them to the doors, forward again. She rested her forearms on the baluster.

"Everything is set," she said. "I'm leaving in the morning. You'll be all right while I'm gone?"

"Jenny..."

"Of course you will," she said. "Deanna will check in now and then, see if you need anything."

"Deanna's a good girl."

"I should be back in ten days."

Joseph looked side-glance at her, gave a half-grin and said softly, "I know that."

"Right," she said. "Right."

"This trip is no different than any other, Jenny."

"Yes, it is." Jenny took a long, deep breath. "She should come here, Dad."

"She can't. You know she can't."

"Not so. She's not supposed to. Not the same thing."

Carolyn was living in Seattle, one of the free districts established as part of the Second Truce. While she had been as heavily involved in the resistance as anyone, negotiations had managed to place Joseph's sister in Seattle rather than John's Park. One of the requisites was that she was not allowed to leave the district.

No one who knew Carolyn Britton believed that she had actually spent the last twenty years within the Seattle District boundaries without the occasional excursion.

"You're right about that," said Joseph, a hint of humor. His sister was fiercely independent. And certainly not one to have boundaries forced upon her.

"She knows the importance of what we're doing, Dad."

"She does. And she understands that her story is critical to the history," said Joseph.

"And here is where she should tell that story."

Joseph reached out and took his daughter's hand. This was her project, had been hers from the beginning. The idea had been hers; she was the driving force behind it. They had been working together on the manuscript for almost five years. The story of the invasion, of the resistance.

The Britton Journals.

"Jenny," he said. "We will finish the journals. They will be published."

"They have to be," said Jenny. "And we have to get it right. The truth, not what the Shillies say it is. The future must know what happened."

"You go to Carolyn, bring back her story."

Jenny looked at her father, held tightly to his hand and nodded. She stepped back to the French doors then, gave her father a smile.

"Come to dinner."

"On my way."

He watched her leave, then turned back to the view beyond the balcony. He looked down at the row upon row of shelves, at the thousands of books.

Voices from the past.

~ end

Final words regarding **The Britton Journals**...

If you've already read the trilogy, we hope you enjoyed this brief revisit to the world of the Shylmahn, a snapshot view of what that world looks like twenty years after the time of "Genesis".

If this is your first visit, welcome! If this short story has piqued your interest, the three novels of the Shylmahn Trilogy are available on Amazon in print, large print, ebook and audiobook formats. Bundle specials and signed editions are available at Greybeard Publishing.

Shipwreck on ShadowWorld

Chapter One

The ground beneath Jim was hard as stone and there was a small rock digging into his back. The dull red sky of the alien world hung heavy above him. The air felt thick in his lungs.

He rolled to one side and sat up slowly, an inch at a time. The pain in his head pounded at his skull, and the throbbing caused his vision to go fuzzy. It took a few moments to clear. When it did, he looked around him. The small landing craft was a few hundred yards away, fuselage twisted and broken, other unidentifiable debris scattered about the landscape, some of it still burning.

He saw no one moving. It took a few moments more for him to realize that he also saw that there was no one who was *not* moving.

From where he was, he could see no bodies.

There had been two other passengers, a man and a woman. They had escaped into the shuttle with him.

They were nowhere to be seen.

Jim guessed that he had been unconscious for a long time; hours at least, maybe longer. He had been thrown a considerable distance from the ship. Maybe they hadn't seen him; but why hadn't they looked for him?

I'm alone...

Jim was thirteen years old. He was slim, strong and healthy. He had been traveling alone, having left Earth three weeks earlier, and was scheduled to arrive at Port Kimara in two weeks. His family would be waiting for him; but he would not be coming. Not now.

He managed to stand, though his legs were shaky. The ground beneath his feet was bare and hot and dry. The heat of the two suns beat down in waves and made it hard to breath.

Turning about in a slow circle, he could see the rolling terrain spread out and away from him in all directions. He could see for miles... but there was nothing, absolutely nothing, to see.

I'm out in the middle of nowhere...

He turned to face the wreckage, took a step and started towards it. Small whorls of smoke rolled across the crash site as the slight breeze pushed the hot alien air over the smoldering ground.

The passenger compartment was split in two and one side of the forward section, the section that Jim had been sitting in, was torn away. He climbed in and looked around, not sure what he was looking for. Water, certainly. He would also be needing food and clothing.

He found nothing in the forward section. The rear section was in even worse condition, but he managed to come out with two water bottles. He stuffed them into his jacket pockets.

What was left of the pilot's cabin was thirty yards from the two sections of the passenger compartment. Jim had to step around torn and twisted metal, broken seats, and viewing ports from the fuselage to reach it. Coming up along the left side, he could see that the forward section of the shuttle hadn't fared any better than the rest of the craft.

Its occupants had fared worse.

Jim looked only very briefly at the two men still strapped in their seats before turning away and walking quickly back to the passenger section of the wreckage.

So there had been at least two casualties.

The pilot and copilot had not survived the crash.

When he returned to the passenger compartments, Jim straightened one of the seats that had been thrown from the cabin and sat down. He brought out one of the water bottles and took a deep drink.

Realization about what had happened began to sink in.

They had crashed. People had died. He still had no idea where the other two had gone.

Had the pirates followed the shuttle down?

Jim doubted that. It was more likely they would have stayed with the cruise ship.

Pirates...

The pirates had attacked the space liner several days before, coming at them in three smaller ships. With no weapons, the cruise ship had no chance.

Only one small landing craft, this shuttle, had managed to slip away. There had been two people in the forward passenger section with Jim; a man and a woman. Jim hadn't known them, but he had seen them around on the liner a few times during the voyage.

They had been lucky to find this planet, but then their luck had run out. Something had gone wrong, and now the small craft was strewn all around him in hundreds of shredded pieces.

Jim laid his head back against the seat and let out a tired sigh.

I can't stay here, he thought.

No one knew that he was there. No one knew where the shuttle had gone down, or even that it had crashed. In all likelihood, no one knew they had come to this planet.

If there had been any survivors, they had left. They wouldn't have left him behind if they had known that he had been there.

Since no one knew that he was there, no one was going to come looking for him. With no food and very little water, he wouldn't last long.

He downed the last of the water from the first bottle and tossed the empty container aside.

He laid his head back and closed his eyes.

The world around him was so quiet. The only sound was the occasional whispering brush of wind across the dry terrain, the empty rustling of torn metal shifting in the breeze.

I have to find help.

He opened his eyes and sat up.

Where... which way?

There was a slight rise to his left, two small to be called a hill. He stood and walked over to it, stood atop and looked around him in all directions.

There... far to the west, set against the horizon, was a small silhouette of something unmoving. It took a moment for the image to come into focus in heavy, hot, shimmering atmosphere.

It was a small peak, just barely visible.

There was nothing else, absolutely nothing else in any direction.

He took one last look back at the wrecked shuttle, turned uncertainly toward the shadowy silhouette on the horizon. A hundred steps out, he had a strong urge to turn and look back at the crash site. He fought it at first, but finally, after taking another dozen steps, he stopped and turned around.

The broken shuttle was already lost from view. They had crashed in a low-lying shallow hollow.

Jim turned and started walking again.

The ground was firm beneath his feet, the vegetation sparse. Clumps of dry grass and short, spindly brush struggled to survive in the harsh soil, beneath two unforgiving suns.

The smudge of shadow that was the peak on the horizon faded into and out of view. With no other landmarks, Jim used the larger sun as a guide, following it as it dropped slowly toward the horizon near the silhouette. Not until it had set, several hours later, did he take a break. There was nothing to sit on, so he dropped down to the ground. It was warm beneath him, but with the setting of the first sun, the air was already beginning to cool.

He took out the second bottle and took a small drink, carefully put the cap back on put the bottle back in his pocket. He had no idea how long his meager water supply would have to last.

The dull red color of the sky paled. He could feel a slight breeze brush across his face, but there was no sound. The world was absolutely quiet. In spite of the breeze, there was no movement. The grass was still. There were no birds in the sky. There were no insects or small animals scurrying across the ground.

There was nothing.

The smaller sun moved quickly towards the horizon. Reluctantly, he rolled over onto his side and climbed to his feet. He realized then just how tired he was. He considered sitting back down again, but the thought was as unappealing as plodding onward.

He followed the second sun until, not more than an hour later, it too set below the horizon. The color of the sky shifted from its pale red to a dark violet, grew steadily darker until, within minutes, the sky was an empty black canvas.

Jim walked several more minutes before stopping, afraid that if he continued without a landmark of some kind that he would end up walking in circles. Besides, he was too tired to go any further.

He eased himself down to the ground. A few hours rest would do him good. He sat, his weight on one arm, and stared up at the black night sky.

Stars began to appear, more with each passing minute; strange, alien patterns. Before long, the black tapestry above him was filled with thousands upon thousands of stars. The surface of the planet glowed eerily in alien starlight.

The slight, cool breeze grew a little colder, and began to blow just a little harder. The exposed, bare skin of Jim's face began to tingle chillingly. Looking around him, he thought he could see a depression in the ground twenty paces away. He went over to it, stood before it.

It wasn't much of a hole, but it was a bit lower than the surrounding terrain and was protected from the wind on one side by a little rise, several feet high, that formed a tiny hill.

He slid down into the hollow and curled up, covered his face against the increasing cold. Despite his exhaustion, sleep was a long time in coming.

There was a strange glow coming from somewhere...

Somewhere...

Daylight. A curious, red daylight...

The glow was the new day shining through his closed eyelids. He felt the warmth of one of the suns washing its warm rays over his face.

Somehow, perhaps subconsciously, he managed to bring his face up to the sunshine. It felt good. He brought his arm up and shaded his still-closed eyes with a cold, icy hand. Slowly then, he opened his eyes.

All was in a bright glare and it took time for his eyes to adjust.

After a few moments more, he sat up straight and began massaging his arms and legs. Looking around, he saw the shadow on the horizon far to the west.

It was still a long ways off, but it was nearer.

He stood up. It hurt. The muscles in his legs were cold, near frozen. He had barely survived the night. He knew that. He knew that he wouldn't be able to survive another, particularly if he was weak from lack of food.

Best to start now and keep moving, he thought. He moistened his cracked lips and started walking. He realized immediately that the cool air was gone, replaced by warm air that was already growing hot. The red, cloudless sky hung heavy over him. His lungs, which had struggled against the cold air of the previous night, now fought against the hot, thick day of this harsh planet.

It was as though there wasn't any oxygen in the air.

He brought out the water bottle as he trudged forward, lifted it to his mouth, let the last of it trickle onto his tongue and soothe the back of his throat.

That's it, then...

He had to find water; he had to find food.

The hours passed and his pace slowed. The morning crept into afternoon. Beyond the peak, the larger sun was very large indeed, painted against the distant sky, still several hours from slipping below the horizon.

The base of the peak was cluttered with hundreds of rocks of all sizes. It towered hundreds of feet over Jim, rising up out of the flat plain, blotting out both suns, the first of which was setting, the smaller following several hours behind the first.

He had to find water soon, and he had to find shelter before nightfall. Backing away from the peak thirty or forty steps, he began walking the perimeter, looking into crevices and shadows for signs of a cave or plant life. Vegetation would mean moisture.

As he came around to the far side of the peak, he saw that the larger of the suns had set. It was still warm on this side, but the air was already growing cooler. He looked at the position of the smaller sun. It would be down in another hour.

The angle of the small sun's rays created strange shadows on the wall of the peak. Jim had to step nearer again and again to make sure that he wasn't missing something.

Then... *was that a sound?*

He stepped close, rested a hand on the rock face. He felt a dull rumbling coming from somewhere deep within the mountain.

There was definitely something in there.

What is that?

Finally, just as the second sun began to disappear below the distant horizon, Jim found the mouth of a cave.

The entrance was ten feet above ground level, but easy to reach. Standing in front of it, the roof of the entrance was just above his head. There was a cool breeze emanating from within, and he could feel moisture in the air.

It was pitch black inside. Going in, Jim had to hold his hands out in front of him so that he wouldn't walk headlong into a wall. Almost immediately, he noticed that the tunnel sloped downward. It gave him the odd sensation that he was being swallowed up by some gigantic alien monster. Only hunger and thirst kept him going. He went slowly, inching his way ahead.

The seconds, and then the minutes, ticked away. Time began weighing heavily on him, down in the darkness, deep within the hollows of this alien place; the tons of stone above him, the pressure of eternity pressing down on him. The fear of spending forever there in that black gut of the peak...

But the air was still fresh. And it continued to grow cooler and smelled of moisture, as after a morning rain. He could feel a dampness, like a mist, against his face. It soothed his dried, cracked lips.

He reached another winding, downward curve in the tunnel, and following it, he began to hear a sound. It was a rumbling, the same rumbling that he had felt beneath his feet since first entering this maze of tunnels; the same rumbling that he had felt when he had pressed his hand against the cliff wall outside.

The further he traveled, still blind in the darkness, the louder the sound became. At first, he dared not hope, but with each passing minute, with each bend in the tunnel, he became more anxious and grew more excited.

Jim stepped into a high-ceilinged cavern. Bands of rock along the walls and ceiling shimmered in their own light. He had heard of phosphorus, a mineral giving off its own peculiar illumination, and guessed that this was something similar, some alien version.

Coursing through the middle of the cavern, an underground river shimmered in the strange darkness, white foam glowing as the water rushed along its underground path.

Jim rushed to the river and stopped short. The surface was a good six feet below the edge of the bank, and it was a sheer drop. Looking up and downriver, he could see no spot where the bank was low enough to make for easy access to the water, but despite the light from the glowing bands of rock in the walls, the cavern was still too dark to see very far.

Turning right, Jim followed the river's edge until it disappeared beneath the wall of the cavern. Finding no access to the water in that direction, he hurried back to the left. He finally found, not far from the opposite wall, a spot where the bank sloped down all the way to the water's edge.

Kneeling, he took a cautious sip. The water was cool and delicious. He took a deeper drink, and then another.

Already feeling a little better, he dipped his head into the water, came up sputtering and smiling. He sat down then and took off his jacket and shirt. He cleaned himself up as best he could, lastly dipping his head into the water again and rinsing his hair.

Refreshed, if still hungry, he climbed up and away from the river, carrying his jacket and shirt. Yes, he needed food, but he needed to rest. He walked over to one wall and dropped his jacket onto the floor, pulled on his wet shirt. He sat then, leaning his back against the wall. He surveyed the cavern, what he could see of it, as he absently rolled his jacket into a makeshift pillow.

Chapter Two

Jim sat bolt upright.

He had been startled by something... awakened by something...

He didn't know what.

He looked carefully around him. The strangely glowing bands of rock within the walls and ceiling continued to illuminate the large chasm. Everything looked as it had when he had fallen asleep. To his left, the river ran from an opening in the wall behind him and disappeared into the darkness at the far end of the cavern. The sound of the river was the only sound.

From where he sat, Jim could see two tunnels, both to his right. The tunnel that he had entered by was further away, hidden in the darkness.

Click, click, click...

Jim stiffened, slid backward and pressed his back against the wall.

The sound had come from one of the tunnels.

Click, click, click...

The sound was louder. Someone, or some *thing*, was coming closer.

Click, click, click...

Jim slid further from the two tunnel entrances and stood, keeping his back against the wall. He couldn't tell from which tunnel the sound came.

Click, click, click...

But it was coming nearer.

He looked quickly around him. His options were limited: He could rush into the darkness, or in the direction of the tunnel that he had come through, or he could jump into the river and take his chances on where it would take him.

Or lastly, he could wait for whatever was in the tunnel to come into the cavern.

He moved quickly away from the wall, toward the middle of the cavern. He turned and faced the two tunnels, the entrances almost side by side, like black, empty eye sockets.

Click, click, click...

Jim took several more steps back, moving further back into the center of the cavern.

The walls deep within one of the tunnels began to glow with artificial light.

Whatever it was, it was bringing its own light with it.

Click, click, click...

A shadow formed within the glow. As it drew nearer the mouth of the tunnel, it started to take shape. The silhouette looked... human-like.

It appeared in the tunnel entrance, took a step into the cavern.

The alien was a small, graying gnome-like creature. Standing a head shorter than Jim, it was dressed in brown robe and cloak, held a lamp in one hand and a wooden staff in the other.

The glowing sphere of yellow light formed by the lamp reached out as far as Jim. The creature stared at him. After several seconds, it tapped its staff on floor of the cavern: *click, click, click*. It waited for some reaction from Jim.

Jim watched all of this uneasily. He had no idea what to make of it.

Click, click, click...

The little man watched and waited.

"Hello," Jim finally stammered.

The little man studied Jim carefully. He took a short step and stopped. "You speak Earth," he said at last. "You are human." These were statements, not questions.

"That's right."

"I am Nebo."

Jim wasn't sure if Nebo was the alien's name or the name of his race.

"My name. I am Nebo."

"I'm Jim."

"What are you doing here? Jim."

"We were attacked." Jim pointed up, as if this would explain that he meant they had been in space. "Pirates. We escaped. We crashed."

"We?" Nebo asked. He looked quickly about the cavern, but could see only Jim.

"I'm alone now. I... I don't know what happened to the others."

"Ah," Nebo nodded thoughtfully.

"I was looking for food and water."

Nebo considered this statement. He finally pointed his staff in the direction of the underground river. "You have found water."

"Yes."

Nebo studied Jim a moment more, finally reached into a fold of his robe. There must have been a pocket, because he pulled out what looked like a large, dry biscuit. He tossed it to the young human. Jim grabbed it out of the air, gave it only a brief sniff before taking a bite.

It didn't have much flavor, either good or bad, but he began salivating with hunger as he chewed. After two bites, and two swallows, Jim slowed.

"Do you live in here?" he asked, chewing and swallowing his third bite.

"From time to time," said Nebo, watching Jim eat. He cocked his head to one side, then, warily eyed the human. "Have you seen another... like me?"

"I haven't seen anyone."

Nebo looked about the cavern, this time more studiously. He frowned.

"I seek Hishta," he said. He sounded faintly anxious.

"Is that your wife?"

Nebo suddenly rolled his head back and laughed. Jim's question apparently struck Nebo as very funny.

"No, human, no! Hishta *sister*!"

Jim recovered from Nebo's outburst and swallowed the last of the large biscuit. He felt awkward talking at such a distance, as they were still four steps apart, but as yet he wasn't too keen on getting any closer to the little alien. He finally took one small step.

"Is she lost?" he asked.

Nebo's expression grew very serious. He leaned forward on his staff. "Perhaps. Perhaps not. In here, it can be very bad. Outside, it can be worse. There are many dangers. In here. Out there."

Nebo pulled back, brought his staff to his side. He tilted his head back, to one side, to the other. Jim couldn't tell if the alien was listening, looking or smelling. Maybe all three...

"Would you like me to help you find her?" Jim asked. "Your sister?"

Nebo brought his gaze forward, looked curiously at the human.

"Are you not also lost?"

"I don't know," said Jim. He hadn't thought about that. He had crashed on a hostile planet. He had traveled across a desert plain and was wandering in the tunnel maze of a rocky peak. "I mean, I don't really know where I am, but does that mean I'm lost?"

"Interesting."

"I can still help you look."

Nebo suddenly turned about and spoke sharply. "Very well. You can come with me. We can look together."

With that, Nebo started down the next tunnel. He immediately began tapping his staff against the tunnel wall. Jim hurried after him. He didn't think that he would lose Nebo, not with that incessant tapping, but the tunnel was pitch black beyond the circle of light formed by Nebo's lantern.

Jim was much taller than Nebo, and able to see over the little man's head and into the tunnel beyond. For the first time, he was able to see the sandpaper-smooth surface of the tunnel walls and floor, the shimmering of particles within the rock.

They passed a number of side tunnels, some so small that only Nebo would have been able to enter into without bending over. Each time, after only a few moments and a few taps of the staff on stone, Nebo chose to continue down the main tunnel.

"Why do you do that?" Jim finally asked. Nebo continued tapping the wooden staff against the wall of the tunnel.

"Do what?"

"That. Why do you tap your staff against the wall?"

"It lets those whom I do not wish to see know that I am coming."

"Like wild animals? Does that scare them off?"

"No," Nebo stated flatly. "Not wild animals. I do not scare anyone. They do not wish to see me any more than I wish to see them. I give them time to remove themselves from my path."

"I see," said Jim. He wasn't sure that he saw at all.

"Hishta... Hishta will know it is Nebo," said Nebo. "It is easier than calling to her."

Now that, Jim understood. But as for the other, what was out there in the dark that Nebo didn't want to meet up with, if not wild animals?

What dangers might exist in these tunnels?

Nebo stopped suddenly.

Ahead of them, the tunnel forked into two passageways. Nebo was looking cautiously down the left tunnel and listening intently.

"What's wrong?" Jim whispered.

Nebo did not answer. After a few moments, he looked down the right tunnel. There was a faint glow coming from somewhere beyond the bend.

"That is the way out of the peak," said Nebo. "That is the way you should go."

Jim looked to the dull glow emanating from the right tunnel. He then looked into the darkness of the left tunnel. Despite Nebo's ominous tone when he spoke of those whom he did not wish to meet, Jim nonetheless would rather continue with Nebo than step back out onto the hot terrain outside.

He indicated the left tunnel. "Hishta went that way?"

"I am not certain," Nebo stated.

"But you think so."

"Perhaps."

"Then I will go with you," said Jim.

"You should leave the peak."

"Why?"

"There are dangers here."

Jim indicated the right tunnel. "There are dangers out there."

"That is true," said Nebo. "Very well."

He started down the left tunnel, again leaving Jim to hurry after him.

The two traveled in silence but for the sharp clicking of Nebo's staff against the walls of the dark, cool passageway. Time seemed not to exist within the peak, as if the universe had stopped and Jim and Nebo were traveling in the space between one second and the next, and all the rest of the world was waiting for them to reach some unseen point in space and time.

The coolness of the air within the tunnels began to take on humid warmth, growing steadily heavier. Jim felt himself pushing against the thick atmosphere as he went forward, step by step.

And then Nebo's steady tapping of wooden staff against stone wall began to slow.

Nebo stopped.

The air was still. Without the *click, click, click*, the tunnel was oppressively quiet. The only sounds were those of Jim and Nebo's breathing.

And then there came another sound...

Jim wasn't sure at first that he had really heard it, but it grew steadily louder, from barely perceptible to clear and distinct.

It was a gritty, abrasive sound; as of something rubbing coarsely against stone.

"What is that?" Jim whispered.

Nebo said nothing.

"Is that what you were talking about? Is that what you were tapping at, to warn away?"

"Yes."

"Then why isn't it going away?"

"I could not say with certainty, but if I had to guess... perhaps it wishes to speak with us."

Jim felt a sudden chill. He shouldn't feel a chill. The air here was warm.

"What is it?" he asked.

"It is Tunnel Maker."

Chapter Three

The tunnel ahead lost its light as something filled up the space. Nebo held up his lantern and stood immobile, his staff held to one side.

Directly before them appeared a long, snake-like mole creature, short rear legs barely visible at the back of a smooth body, its front legs more like arms, its hands with long, narrow fingers.

Most striking though, was its massive head, which was almost as wide as the tunnel itself, that rested on a slowly twisting neck.

"Wow," Jim whispered.

"Tunnel Maker," Nebo mumbled softly.

Tunnel Maker stopped about six feet in front of Nebo. The air between them was warm and damp. The breath of the creature was hot.

It looked beyond Nebo at Jim with small, dark eyes, and leaned forward as if to get a better look. The thought struck Jim that the creature probably had poor vision. Living down in the dark, it probably didn't use its eyes much, instead relying on its other senses.

It looked decisively at Nebo, sniffed at the air. When it spoke, it was with a smooth voice, and yet the tone was direct. The language was very alien to Jim. The only sound he recognized was when the creature spoke Nebo's name.

Nebo responded in the same language. Without the smoothness of Tunnel Maker's speech, the words came out as little more than grunts and squeaks and gurgling sounds.

Tunnel Maker responded quickly to whatever Nebo said. The words seemed harsher this time. It was not happy.

Nebo spoke then over his shoulder.

"He does not recognize your smell, human. What he does not know, he does not like."

"What's wrong with my smell?"

"What he does not like, he does not trust. He feels threatened by you."

Nebo turned his attention back to Tunnel Maker and spoke again in the creature's language. They appeared to argue back and forth. Jim took a step back, hoping to appear less threatening.

The discussion between Nebo and Tunnel Maker stopped and started several times, and during each silence Nebo would stand unmoving, and Tunnel Maker would slowly ease its massive head forward and back.

And then Nebo sharply spoke half a dozen words and nodded curtly. A moment later Tunnel Maker squirmed and writhed and began to slither backward. Its face faded into the darkness until it was finally completely lost from view.

After a few long moments, it must have started down a side tunnel, because Jim again heard the strange gritty noise coming out of the black, the rasping sound of the creature's body rubbing against the walls of the tunnel.

"Is everything all right?" asked Jim.

"Well enough," said Nebo. He turned sharply and there was a hint of concern in his expression and stance. "We must go."

There was a sudden urgency in the tone, and Jim again began to feel uneasy.

"Is he coming back?"

"Of course not," said Nebo, and he started forward at a quick pace. He was no longer tapping his staff.

Jim followed right behind him, easily keeping up with the little man. "He had news of Hishta?"

"We must travel up to the sky."

Nebo's pace was steady, his step sure and focused. He seemed to know exactly where he was going and he obviously wanted to get there quickly. Without the constant *click, click, click* of the staff, the tunnels were strangely empty and silent.

They traveled up, always up, climbing higher and higher within the peak. The yellow sphere of light from Nebo's lantern pushed ahead of them in one tunnel after another, exposing one side tunnel after another. Again and again Nebo would turn suddenly down one of the side tunnels, somehow knowing, or somehow sensing, that this was the correct route.

And time after time, without warning, the glowing sphere of light from Nebo's lantern would suddenly burst out in all directions as the tunnel emptied into some cavern, walls spreading out away from them, ceiling rising up into the dark beyond the reach of the light.

Jim felt his thirst returning, as well as the pang of hunger. It had been hours since he had eaten the biscuit.

He felt a cool breeze brushing against his face. Several more minutes passed, and the breeze grew more steady.

Then Nebo and Jim stepped out under a night sky.

They came out onto a ledge very near the top of the peak. It looked out over the vast alien plain. The shelf was some twelve feet deep and twenty feet wide, large enough that Jim didn't feel uncomfortable.

Nebo walked to the very edge and stared out across the vast expanse. Moving up beside him, Jim could see what Nebo was looking at.

Far in the distance, the plain was aglow with a cluster of campfires.

"What is that?" asked Jim.

"That is the All."

"All?"

"That is what they call themselves, so that is what we call them."

Jim nodded uncertainly. "You knew they were there?"

"No."

"Oh," Jim mumbled. "You came up here to look for them?"

"That is correct."

"Hishta is with them?"

Nebo let out a low, fluttering breath. He had a very worried look on his face. "The All are a peculiar race. They think very logically, but they use that logic to twist events and situations to suit their needs."

"Sounds pretty normal to me."

Nebo's worried expression darkened. "Hishta and I have crossed paths with them many times. They have no doubt used these confrontations to justify taking her."

"What do they want with her?"

Nebo turned away from the edge and walked to the far side of the ledge. He stepped around a recently used campsite. Stones encircled a small fire pit. Near the pit were two piles of dried vegetation that looked like they had been used as bedding. To one side was a bundle of wood bound together with twine.

It had to have taken some effort to bring firewood all the way up here.

Nebo gathered some of the smaller kindling and began to prepare a fire.

"They will sell her," he stated.

"They can do that?"

"There are circumstances in which being sold into bondage serves as payment for crimes or debts."

"But that's not right."

"It is not."

Nebo rose from the small fire that he had started and settled onto one of the beds. He pulled a ball of cloth from one of his many hidden pockets and carefully unfolded it, revealing a round of bread. He tore a piece from the round and handed it to Jim.

"Eat. Then sleep," he said.

When Jim woke in the morning, the air was very cold, the sky was slate gray before the rise of the first sun. Nebo was stirring the fire to life.

Jim slid nearer the rising flames, looked out across the plain in the direction of the camp of the All. He could just make out the silhouette of a very large, boxlike vehicle.

"What is that thing?"

Nebo handed Jim a thick wedge of cheese and a biscuit. He spoke without looking up. "An All transport." He stood then, picked up his staff and pointed it toward a different horizon, where Jim could make out a smear of a shadow. "Beyond the forest is the City of Shannyn. It is many days travel from here. That is where you must go."

"I'm going with you."

"You must not."

"Why not?"

"Shannyn is the largest city on ShadowWorld. The space port is there. Your rescue is there."

"But what about you? What about Hishta?"

Nebo indicated the All encampment.

"My path lay there."

"Then so does mine," Jim said flatly.

Nebo smiled sadly. "Young human, the thought is a kind one, and it warms me. But you would risk your only hope for rescue in a cause that is almost certain to fail. A cause that is not yours."

"I want to help," said Jim. "I can go to Shannyn anytime."

"If you come with me, you may indeed see the city, but it would be as a captive. If your survived the encounter."

Jim tore at the biscuit, put a piece into his mouth.

"I'll take my chances."

Nebo stood and handed Jim a water flask. Jim took a big swallow and handed it back. Nebo continued to stare silently at the human until Jim finally had to turn away from the calm gaze. He frowned, finally turned again to face the alien.

"Maybe I just don't want to be alone," said Jim.

Nebo studied Jim a moment more before giving a knowing nod.

"Come then," he said. "I leave now."

With both suns high in the sky, the desert plain grew increasingly hot. This didn't seem to bother Nebo very much, and the small being continued a steady pace across the landscape. Jim said nothing, not wanting to admit that maybe Nebo would have been better off without him.

After several hours march, Nebo handed Jim the water flask without saying a word, and Jim had to drink as they walked.

They didn't stop until midday, when they reached a small cluster of tiny hills covered in small trees and shrubs. Nebo led Jim into a gulley running between several of the hills. There they sat in the relative cool of the shadow of one of the trees and in the protection of the surrounding shrubs and rise of the hillsides.

Jim saw then that the morning's journey had indeed taken its toll on Nebo. He was nearly spent. He had pushed them both in order to get them here before the day grew truly hot.

"There," said Nebo. He pointed to a spot in the ground, a depression set into the small hillock beside Jim. Jim held out his hand and set his palm on the cool earth.

"Here?"

"Dig."

Jim gave him a curious side-glance but did as he was asked. He scooped out handfuls of earth with one hand at first, before shifting position and using both hands.

He uncovered a buried cache of supplies, pulling out a cloth bundle. Unfolding it, he found several small metal boxes and two ceramic water flasks.

"It is food and water," said Nebo. He moved over to Jim and took one of the boxes. Inside were two rounds of cheese wrapped in cloth. He handed one to Jim and began eating the other.

They waited until the first sun was low on the horizon before moving out again, away from the protection of the natural shelter. The air was heavy and hot, but slowly began to cool as the larger sun fell nearer the horizon.

They reached the All encampment an hour before the second sun had set. A long shadow stretched out from a low ridge along the perimeter of the camp. Jim and Nebo scrambled within the shadow and crawled on hands and feet up to the top of the ridge.

The camp was spread out across a wide area, several hundred feet from left to right and just as far across. The massive, boxlike transport vehicle was parked along one side. Beside it were two smaller personal vehicles.

There were a number of individual campsites scattered about the encampment. At each, there were water barrels, benches, tables and chairs.

The All were everywhere. They were short, squat, hairy creatures. Their thin, bony arms seemed to come directly out of the sides of their bodies. They moved quickly from place to place. When they stopped to talk with one another, they would rise up and down in sudden jerks. Jim thought maybe the movement was part of their language.

He saw Hishta sitting alone at one of the campsites on the far side of the encampment. She looked as though she could have been Nebo's twin. Perhaps she was.

"There she is," he said to Nebo.

Nebo nodded curtly. He had seen her. He pointed to a campsite near the transport vehicle. A human man and a human woman sat glumly beside the camp fire.

"Do you know them?" he asked.

"No. Yes," said Jim. "Well, sort of. They were in the shuttle with me when we crashed. I didn't know what happened to them. How'd they get here?"

"There are only two possibilities that come to mind, Jim. They were taken captive at the crash site, or they were taken captive once they left the crash site."

Oh, that's real helpful, thought Jim, but he said nothing. Instead he studied the perimeter of the large encampment. There was a low ridge in front of the All transport that might offer Jim cover enough to get him close to the human couple. But there would still be a good thirty feet from the top of the rise down to the campsite.

Reaching Hishta looked even more daunting. They would have to walk in a wide circle and come back through a small grove of scrubby trees, and from there to Hishta was at least fifty feet.

Neither looked possible without detection.

Nebo had been conducting a similar examination of the camp.

"I would say difficult, but not completely impossible," he said. "You should work your way around behind their transport vehicle, come in behind the ridge. While you go to your human companions, I will go around and approach Hishta from the grove."

That was about how Jim figured it. "Nebo... what do we do once we reach them?"

Nebo's face scrunched up as he brought his lips together into a tight, uncomfortable expression.

"Ah," he grunted.

When he didn't say anything further, Jim prompted him. "Nebo?"

"They are not bound," Nebo said at last.

The two humans were sitting on their own, hands and feet free. Looking to Hishta, she was also unbound and on her own.

Jim thought this was a good thing.

Nebo did not. "This concerns me," he stated.

"But why?"

"They do not consider escape to be possible. Neither are the All much concerned that the captives will attempt an escape."

Jim scooted around and into a position where he could again study the camp.

There were a lot of All. At any one moment, the two humans and Hishta were always within sight of dozens of them. And, while the captives were indeed not too far from the perimeter of the camp, there was still some distance to any cover.

Jim looked beyond the camp, at the desert plain that surrounded them.

"I see," he said. What would do once they did make it away from the camp. They were a long way from anywhere. Where would they go? The All could recapture them any time they wanted. "So, what do we do now?"

"You are free to do as you wish, Jim," said Nebo. "As for me, I go to Hishta."

Jim crawled the last few feet up and peered over the top of the low ridge. The man and woman were sitting beside the campfire thirty feet away, at the foot of the hill. The man was leaning close to the woman, speaking low, always with an eye to the All that were moving about the encampment.

Eight feet from the couple was a heavy bench on which sat two water barrels. As Jim watched, an All came up the barrels, filled a metal cup at a spigot and drank. It returned the cup to its hook, looked disinterestedly at the human couple, and went on about its business.

Jim was pretty sure that he could reach the water barrels, and once behind the barrels, he would be out of sight of most of the camp. From there, he could get the attention of the humans.

And get a drink of water...

That thought was enough to urge Jim on. He lifted himself up and slid over the top of the ridge, slid down the other side and pushed himself forward, before finally rising up onto his knees and scrambling downhill towards the bench and the water barrels.

Using the shadow of the barrels for cover, Jim scooted around and looked out across the camp for any indication that he had been seen.

Satisfied that for the moment he was safe, or at least relatively so, he pulled back and leaned against one of the barrels.

It felt cool to the touch. He could smell the water inside the wooden cask.

The metal cup was hanging on a hook beside the spout, on the other side of the barrel... the side facing the camp.

Jim was really thirsty.

He slid back around, reached carefully over and lifted the cup off the hook. He eased back around out of sight.

A moment passed and there was no sudden onrush of aliens.

Emboldened, Jim moved forward again and held the cup beneath the spout. He had to move his body a bit further in order to open the spigot.

He turned the spigot just a little. The sound of water coming out was louder than he expected. He stiffened at the noise, hurriedly turned the handle back and moved quickly back behind the barrel.

Afraid to move, he stared down into the cup, again listening for an onslaught of All rushing to capture him.

The metal cup was half full. The smell of fresh water rose up and tingled his nose.

When, after several moments, no alarm sounded, Jim brought the cup slowly up to his lips and sipped delicately at the water. He drank slowly, felt the liquid work its way down, soothing his throat and settling coolly into his stomach.

Jim glanced again in the direction of the two humans. He was startled to see the man looking at him, an expression of surprise, and something else, on his face.

The man turned quickly away, looked back out to the camp. He appeared determined to keep his eyes away from the water barrels, away from the boy hiding in their shadow.

The woman looked curiously at her companion. She saw that he was upset. The man said something under his breath.

The woman glanced only once in Jim's direction, then she too looked to the center of the encampment.

The man shook his head slowly from side to side, a signal to Jim.

They don't want me here. They want me to leave.

Jim didn't want to leave without them. He wanted to help them. He really wanted to help them.

As importantly, and he knew this in his heart, now that he knew there were others who had survived the crash, he wanted to be with them.

What am I going to do?

Jim looked to either side, then back up the hillside toward the ridge.

With or without them, it was going to be a lot more difficult getting out than it was getting in.

He felt a sudden stabbing pain in his neck.

I've been stung!

He slapped at his neck. There was something metallic sticking out. He pulled it out and looked at it, only half comprehending. A dart?

I've been shot!

He managed to stand, though there was a numbness spreading throughout his body. He managed to shift to one side, looked to the man and the woman.

They were standing too, looking in his direction. The woman held onto the man's arm with both hands, looking at Jim with sympathy. The man's expression hardened with a stiff resignation.

Jim felt thin, bony, alien fingers grasping his arms. He began to fall forward, was pulled back as hands lifted him up. He knew he should be hearing sounds, but there was nothing.

Jim rolled over onto his back. His head felt thick, as if he had been asleep for days.

Asleep...

He *had* been asleep. For how long, he didn't know. He stared up at the ceiling above him. It was metal.

He could feel a rumbling beneath him. There was a sense of movement.

He sat up then and his head spun dizzily. It took a moment for the world to come back into focus.

The room that he was in was moving. He was inside a vehicle.

The transport vehicle?

Jim was certain. He was in the big, boxy transport vehicle.

The rumbling that he felt he could also hear. It was a grumbling background noise that seemed to come from everywhere and from nowhere.

He looked about the room. It was small, perhaps six feet by eight. The only furniture was the cot that he was sitting on. There were no windows, and only one short, narrow door.

Jim stood. As he reached for the handle on the door, it turned suddenly and Jim stepped quickly back. The door opened and two All stood in the opening, one behind the other.

One chittered sharply and rose quickly up and down on its short, thin legs; once, twice.

It stood silent then, seemingly waiting for a response from Jim.

Jim had no idea what the creature wanted.

The second All chittered to the first. Both stepped back into the hallway beyond the door, stopped and waited.

Jim cautiously approached the door and stepped through. As he did, the two aliens turned about and started down the narrow hallway ahead of him.

Small portholes were set into the right wall every three paces at about the height of the All line of sight. Leaning down at one of these, Jim saw that they were traveling across the desert plain. He was at least forty feet above the ground, which meant that there were one or two floors below the one that they were on.

Doors were set into the left wall. All were closed.

This part of the massive transport was quiet but for the deep rumbling of the engines and the reverberations of the great wheels rolling beneath them.

They passed through an open hatch that separated one section of the vehicle from another. A few steps further and Jim noticed an odor in the air.

He could smell food. Real food... Bread and cheese was all well and good, but the thought of real food made him dizzy all over again. The smell emanating from somewhere up ahead made him salivate.

The doors along this section were set farther apart. The All stopped at the third door; they stood on either side and turned about. The nearer All chittered once, rose up and down once, and waited.

Jim stepped up to the closed door, glanced at the All then again at the door.

There might be food on the other side.

He pushed down on the handle and pushed the door open.

He stepped into a large room—a mess hall. There were half a dozen long tables, all but one of them occupied by All. They turned as he entered and looked at him with open curiosity.

There was a counter on the other side of the room where one of the All was filling a bowl with thick soup that it spooned from a pot. Jim was too hungry to be overly cautious, so he walked bravely through the tables and the All and picked up a bowl for himself. He quickly filled it, took a spoon and sat at the only unoccupied table.

He didn't recognize what was in the soup, and didn't recognize the smell, but it didn't taste bad.

After several uncomfortable moments, most of the All turned away from the human and began talking again amongst themselves. None of it made any sense to Jim. The language was made up of sounds that were impossible for humans to make, and included body gestures; gestures that were apparently different when one was sitting than when one was standing.

Encouraged by his earlier success, Jim rose confidently and served himself a second helping of soup. As he spooned the soup into the bowl, he noticed the large container sitting at the far end of the counter. It was filled with a sweet-smelling liquid. Beside the container was a tray of ceramic cups. Jim poured himself some drink to wash down the thick soup.

The All in the room seemed to grow uneasy at the young human's abrupt boldness. They were very clearly unsettled by something in the manner of the alien in their midst.

Jim finished his meal under wary eyes. As he put down the spoon and slid back from the table, ready to stand up and leave, the room again became very quiet. All eyes watched his every move. Very slowly then, Jim rose the rest of the way to his feet. He felt a rising tension in the room. He took several short, easy, non-threatening steps toward the door.

One of the aliens rose up onto its toes, then down, quickly. Up, down, up, down. Not quite a hop, but close.

It began chittering away sharply in its alien tongue.

Jim stopped. He didn't yet sense actual danger, but felt that at any moment he might do something inappropriate, cross some unseen line, and that these creatures might then turn on him.

The longer he stood there, the more unnerved the aliens became. The chittering grew louder and their movements quickened. Several of them moved nearer, their up and down movements propelling them forward.

Jim found himself being escorted to the door. As he reached it, backed into it, the door opened and he found himself standing out in the hall, the two All guards waiting on either side of him, just as he had left them.

They, at least, seemed calm enough. They turned without comment, one leading the way and the other following behind Jim. They passed several more doors and stepped through another hatchway before the lead All stopped. Jim almost bumped into him.

The All seemed to be waiting for something to happen. A moment later, the floor plate beneath them shimmied and began rising; the ceiling overhead slid aside just in time for them to pass through. The timing was designed for lift passengers the height of the All, so for Jim it had been a close call.

The room above was large and dark, but alive with activity. Aliens were squatting in strange chairs designed for their physique. They were studying light patterns displayed on consoles in front of them, occasionally making adjustments, turning knobs and sliding small levers. As Jim watched, one of the All dimmed one of the lights before him, called to another who then turned on one of his. There was a deep rumble somewhere within the vehicle and Jim felt a change in motion.

Jim's escort led him across the room and down another long, narrow hall. The sounds of the control room quickly faded behind him.

The lead escort pushed aside a door and stepped quickly to one side. The rear guard pushed Jim through and he heard the door close behind him with a solid thump.

Jim stood before the leader of the All.

Leader studied the human from across the sparsely furnished room. There was a small table set against one wall on which were several monitors. There was another of the oddly designed chairs in the middle of the room beside a low table.

Leader began making strange movements with its lips. It didn't make any sounds at first, just moved its lips, as if trying to sort out how it was going to speak.

"Please – forgive – my – talk," said Leader at last. It was a very peculiar sound, but completely recognizable. It was a squeaky sound, almost machine-like.

Leader must have worked long and hard over the years to be able to speak Earth.

It wasn't so much the memorizing of the words that would have been difficult. What was remarkable was for an alien with the All design of mouth and throat to be able to speak the language at all.

"You speak my language very well," said Jim.

"I – speak – fourteen – galactic – languages."

"I speak only Earth language."

"I – assumed." Leader rose quickly up and down, up and down, then stopped. Jim waited until he was sure that it was finished with whatever it was doing.

"What do you want of me?" asked Jim.

Leader showed an expression that Jim found impossible to read. Curiosity? Bewilderment? Amusement? It said nothing.

"Am I a prisoner?"

Several changes of emotion washed over Leader's face.

"Prisoner?"

"Prisoner," said Jim. "You guys shot me with a dart and kidnapped me."

The look on Leader's face was blank.

"If I'm not a prisoner, then I would like some help getting home."

"Human." it stated after thinking on that a long time. "Minds – of – you – of – All – not – same. Think – *different*."

"I can see that."

"You – here – because – you – die – if – you – not – here." Leader chittered once and rose up and down on its toes. "Out – there – alone – you – die."

"Maybe."

"You – here – alive."

"Yes. For now."

"You... – *stay*."

The room grew ominously silent. Leader made small movements with its face and fingers. Jim grew increasingly uncomfortable.

Watching Leader, watching its facial movements, its gestures, Jim began to think that it was reacting to the series of emotions that Jim was feeling. Just as the aliens in the mess hall had seemingly responded to Jim's increasing self-assuredness.

"How long? How long do I have to stay?"

Leader moved its head back slowly, pausing in what looked to be a thinking pose. After several long moments, it made what it assumed to be the appropriate response to the question.

"Human – be – fed – and – cared – for," it stated. "No more – allowed – freedom – of – ship."

Freedom of ship? Had he had the freedom of the transport? Maybe his door had been unlocked, but he hadn't been awake to take advantage of it.

"All – uncomfortable – with – human. – Human – feelings... – loud." Leader's expression changed to something very much like a grimace. " – Loud."

"What are you going to do with me? How long do I have to be here?"

Leader ignored the question, continued with its own line of thought.

"Human – thinking – different – than – All. Human – actions – based – on – emotions. Human – emotions – *feel* – too – strong, – too – disturbing – to All." Leader made a sound that was a combination of a chitter and a grunt. "Bad – for – All."

With that, the door behind Jim opened and he was led away.

Chapter Four

Jim stared dully up at the ceiling. The vibration of the vehicle's wheels rumbling over the plain lulled him into an odd sense of tranquility. Isolated in his small, stark cell, with only the grumbling sound of the engines coming from some distant room and the faint light glowing yellow from a small panel on the wall, Jim felt strangely calm.

Since being returned to his cell, his captors brought his meals to him. At least two days had passed, and the vehicle had only stopped once. He had hoped they were setting up camp and that he would be let out and allowed to visit with the other captives, but after only a few minutes, the vehicle was again on the move.

He wondered about Nebo. Had he been captured as well? Had he freed Hishta? He liked to think that Nebo and his sister were safely back at the peak.

The door opened and an All placed a plate and cup on the floor of his cell, quickly closed the door again and was gone.

Jim swung his legs around and sat up, bent over and picked up his lunch. Or was it dinner? He wasn't sure.

With no window in his cell, he was unable to use the rising and setting of the suns as a guide. He couldn't be sure that his captors were bringing his meals on a set schedule, so he couldn't rely on the number of meals. Every meal consisted of the same soup that he had eaten in the mess hall, so he couldn't even use the content of the meals.

He judged the passing of time by his sleep periods. He couldn't completely rely on this, as he couldn't be sure his captors weren't watching and then bringing him his "breakfast" each time he woke up.

What if he was only sleeping a few hours at a time?

He had taken only two bites of this latest meal when he heard the latch on the door. He glanced up curiously as the door swung open.

This hadn't happened before. They always gave him more than enough time to finish the soup.

It shouldn't be opening now...

A human stood in the doorway; it was the man. He had to lean down quite a bit to put his head into the room.

"Come on, boy," he whispered sharply.

Jim set the plate aside, quickly stood and followed him out the door even as the man hurried down the narrow hall. Just a few doors down, he turned and left the hall.

The cell was larger than Jim's, but not much. There was a three-legged stool, a small table, and two cots.

The woman was sitting patiently on one of the cots. When the man closed the door behind Jim, she moved quickly, standing and pulling the cot away from the wall. Jim could see that they had managed to take up some of the metal floor, folding it back enough that a body could just get through.

The woman knelt beside the hole and began using a short length of pipe to pry at the lower section of floor, what would be the ceiling of the room below.

"Well?" the man asked. He took the two steps and knelt beside her.

"Almost," said the woman. There was a loud pop as a metal rivet pulled free. The man and woman froze, looked at each other anxiously. They listened for any indication that they had been heard. When no one rushed into the room to drag them away, the man reached into the hole with his bare hands. The woman climbed to her feet and watched him work to enlarge the opening.

The man glanced once at Jim as he worked.

"Twice now we thought you were a goner, boy."

"Jim."

"Right. Jim. I'm Robert. That's Ann."

"Hey," said Jim.

"We didn't think you had survived the crash."

"I thought I was alone," said Jim.

"I'm sorry," said Ann. "We did look for you."

Robert grimaced as he pulled up the plating. "We were picked up, rescued we thought—"

"Thought wrong," Ann said sharply.

"—not long after we crashed." Robert nodded brusquely. "I think I've got it, Ann."

Ann knelt beside Robert and the two of them gave the metal plating another pull. It came more freely now and they rolled it back and out of the way.

Robert gave out a loud sigh and looked over at Jim. "There are a lot of ways off this thing, Jim, but this is the only way that we'll make it away alive."

"We're escaping?"

"We certainly are," said Ann.

That's the plan, anyway," said Robert.

Ann grabbed a cloth bag from the cot, handed it to Robert as she climbed down into the opening. Shifting from side to side, she gave Robert a final nod and dropped out of sight.

Robert laid face down on the floor and slid his head and shoulders into the hole. He dropped the bag down to her. A moment later he lifted himself up onto his elbows.

"Okay, Jim. You're next."

Jim took one step closer to the opening, but remained standing. "What's down there?"

"Our way out," said Robert. "Hurry, now."

Jim moved forward and dropped to his knees before the opening. Robert had him swing his legs around and took him by the arms. When Jim slid in, Robert held his hands and lowered him down.

Ann was waiting below. She took hold of him at the hips and eased him down to the floor of the room.

A ground car was parked in the middle of the room, with not much room to spare. Jim had been lowered down into one corner of the small garage. Along the right wall was a narrow door that Jim guessed led to the main passageway on this floor. Opposite, directly in front of the ground car, was a much larger door.

The sound of the engines of the great transport vehicle was much louder here. The engine room had to be nearby.

Ann went to a set of levers on another wall and studied them. As she did, Robert dropped into the room, went immediately to the vehicle and climbed in behind the wheel.

The car looked much like any other that Jim had been in. It had a front seat, a back seat, four wheels, a steering wheel, and a windshield. But the seats were smaller, sat low to the floor, and were shaped peculiarly, as had been the chairs that Jim had seen. The steering wheel was set an odd angle, as was the dash, which had a confusing array of knobs and indicators.

He was surprised that in this environment of two suns and the heat, that it had no roof. But then, he supposed that it wasn't meant for long distance travel. After all, that was what the much larger transport vehicle was for.

"Ah!" Robert gave a satisfying but muted cheer. A moment later the car engine started.

Ann took hold of one of the levers and gave a pull. The outside wall directly in front of the vehicle began to lower, exposing the world outside. As it lowered, the door formed a ramp down to the ground below.

Robert called to Jim. "In you come!"

Jim climbed into the back seat as Ann hurried around the front of the car and climbed into the front seat beside Robert.

Robert put the vehicle into gear and started it forward. As it passed through the opening, Jim could see only sky and plain, both rushing by from left to right.

The nose of the vehicle dropped down as it started down the ramp. Robert tried to steer the car into the direction that the larger vehicle was traveling, but it wasn't nearly enough. When the front wheels rolled off onto the hard surface of the plain, the back end of the vehicle swung violently around. The car almost rolled over before the back wheels came down hard. It fishtailed back and forth several times before Robert got it under control.

As the large transport vehicle went one direction, Robert turned the car around and took them in the opposite direction. He began working with several buttons set into the dash beside the steering wheel, and after several moments Jim was pressed against the back of the seat as the vehicle suddenly picked up speed.

Seen against the vastness of the desert plain, the speeding vehicle was small and insignificant. It was the only feature in the great expanse of an oppressive alien landscape, above which hovered two unforgiving suns.

To Jim, sitting alone in the back seat, none of that mattered. His head resting on the seatback, he had a relaxed, contented look on his face.

Up in front, Robert offered his wife a supportive smile. They allowed themselves a moment to take in their freedom.

After several hours, the terrain began to change. They had been traveling on the hard, flat surface of the open plain faster than Jim had ever traveled before while still on the ground. But by the time the first sun had set, they began to see small trees and brush. The hardpan beneath the wheels began to soften, becoming more of a soil in which plants could grow. Robert finally had to slow the vehicle in order not to hit something.

Before the second sun went down, they stopped and made camp. Brush formed an enclosing circle around the perimeter, and a tall tree grew nearby that offered a bit of shade to the clearing during the day and allowed the ground to cool in the afternoon. This left the site fairly comfortable in the evening.

Jim remembered how cold it got out on the plain at night, so he was more than happy to help gather firewood from the surrounding vegetation as Ann set about getting a fire going.

"What had you on that cruiser all on your own, Jim?" Robert asked as they collected wood and brush for Ann's campfire. "If it's not too personal."

"I was on my way to Port Kimara," said Jim. "My father got a new job. My parent's let be finish school while they went on ahead."

"Kimara?" Robert looked a bit surprised. "Frontier world. Long way from Earth."

"Suppose."

"So you stayed back on Earth to finish up your school year..."

"Stayed with my uncle. It was only a few months," Jim frowned. "Supposed to be..."

"Don't you worry," said Robert. The two of them each had a full armload of twigs and branches.

Ann called out from the struggling fire that she could just barely keep going with what little kindling she had at hand. "You want to bring some of that over here?"

Robert gave Jim a smile and a wink.

"We'll get you on your way again soon enough, Jim. Your parents will hardly have time to start worrying about you."

The night was still and quiet beyond the light of the fire. Robert sat beside it, looking into it. Ann leaned against the parked vehicle, watched the stars overhead as they slowly moved across the sky, clinging to their alien pattern.

Robert continued to tell Jim about the All. "Their minds aren't any better or any worse than ours," he said. "Just different. Alone, in the desert, without them, you would probably die. Therefore, you would choose to stay with them. Logical. For them. But we're not them. We are illogical humans.

"The only reason they locked us up at all and didn't allow us to move about their transport was because our ways made them uncomfortable. We are just too different."

"They never thought we would try to escape?"

"I don't think it would ever have occurred to them." Robert grew thoughtful then. "I don't want you to think badly of them because they think differently than we do, or because they don't happen to be human. Don't ever judge another species along those lines."

Ann spoke up, her words stiff. "Look to their actions."

"Exactly," said Robert. "The actions of the individual."

"Of course," said Jim.

Robert's smile was paternal, that of a parent who is satisfied with his child's answer.

"Good," he said.

"So... what do we do now?"

Robert visibly shifted his thought processes. "We head for Shannyn, the main space port on ShadowWorld. It's just a few days' drive from here."

"It is a city of many faces," said Ann, "from all over the galaxy." In spite of the words, she didn't sound as though she was looking forward to going there.

Robert ignored the veiled anxiety. "We should be able to find a way off-world."

"What about the All?" asked Jim.

"We may cross paths with some of them. They're desert dwellers, but they do go into the city to trade and barter supplies."

"But won't they try to capture us again?"

"No," said Robert.

"Not once we're in the city," agreed Ann.

"Even if we were to run across the same All, once we're safely out of the desert, their reason to hold us no longer exists."

"Not that we'll be safe," said Ann darkly.

"No worries, Ann," said Robert, comfortingly. "It's no worse than any other port in the frontier."

"That's no comfort."

"We'll be safe enough till we get off planet."

Before settling in to sleep, they ate half of a round of bread that Robert and Ann had managed to horde away, washed it down with most of the small amount of water they had.

At the rising of the first sun the next morning, they ate the rest of the food. Ann was even more quiet than usual, spent much of the early morning by herself, with her own thoughts. As they prepared to break camp, she wandered over near the vehicle, began to give it the once-over to make sure it was ready for the harsh travel it was about to make.

Robert looked once in her direction, then squatted before the small fire pit. He used a stick to stir dirt into the dying coals. He spoke calmly to Jim as he worked.

"I saw your Hishta a couple of times, whenever we were allowed outside. Never talked to her, though. The other one... Nebo?" Robert shook his head. "Couldn't say. When they took you, they hauled Ann and me in with you."

"Then he could still be free," said Jim. "Maybe he freed Hishta."

Robert stood and tossed the stick into the ashes. He rubbed his hands clean. "Possible, I suppose. You were a bit of a distraction."

Ann looked ready to be off, so Robert and Jim started toward the vehicle.

"The All are one of the few native races to this world," said Robert. "But your friends are another. They are the Chackee. They know this land. They are at home out here. They are survivors."

Ann climbed in the driver's seat of the vehicle as they reached it. She had overheard the end of the conversation.

"That's why you don't see Chackee in Shannyn. The city is an alien world to them." She indicated their surroundings. "As alien as this is to us."

Robert spoke encouragingly. "I wouldn't put it past this Nebo. He sounds like a sharp character."

They stopped only once during the day, when they came upon a small creek. It was the first open water that Jim had seen on this world.

The terrain continued to change. The longer they traveled, the more vegetation they saw, and the slower they drove in order to avoid hitting something.

Just after the setting of the second sun, they saw a glow on the horizon.

"The lights of the city," said Robert. "Shannyn."

They traveled for another twenty minutes before they stopped for the night.

They entered the city of Shannyn at midday the following day, Ann again behind the wheel. Large, bright buildings, narrow streets filled with thousands of people from a hundred different worlds.

Some had massive heads and flat, smooth faces, with eyes barely visible behind clear skin. Others had bodies that resembled stick-figures. There were aliens that reminded Jim of tall, thin elves, others that looked like wicked witches from fairytale storybooks.

There were also a handful of All.

As they drove slowly through the crowds, there were very few vehicles other than their own. This drew curious looks from some, but most of those on the street ignored them. This, in spite of the fact that they had yet to see anyone else from Earth or its colonies.

"Stop the car," said Robert, calmly.

Ann pulled off to the side of the road and Robert climbed out. Jim and Ann watched him work his way through the crowd and approach a group of tall, thin beings with pale blue skin, small heads, and long, white hair.

"Chantoo," Ann told Jim. "Honorable people. And fortunately for us, Robert speaks their language."

Jim nodded and relaxed. Maybe this whole thing was almost over.

But when Robert returned, he didn't look all that pleased.

"There's nothing leaving the planet," he said. "All ships are grounded because of the pirate attacks."

"What do we do?" asked Ann.

Robert thought a moment, then straightened and tapped the vehicle with the palm of his hand.

"I don't know how long we're going to be stuck here, but while we're here, we're going to need money. I'll sell the car."

"I don't know, Robert. Do you really think—"

"What's the alternative, Ann?"

"I don't like it." Ann looked and sounded very uncomfortable with the idea.

Meanwhile, Jim quietly took in their conversation, curious as to why Ann would be so concerned.

Robert indicated a square, simple building at the far end of the street.

"You two check into the hotel."

Ann glanced over at the three-storey building.

"But—"

"No worries. I'll join you soon."

Ann clearly didn't like the idea of separating, but finally climbed out of the car so that Robert could climb in. "You be careful."

"I promise," said Robert with a smile. He waited for Jim to climb out and then started the car. "I'll be back before you know it."

"You better."

They watched Robert drive away, then crossed the street and went into the hotel.

Inside, they walked across a quiet, cool lobby and up to the check-in counter. The hotel clerk behind the counter was a bulky alien with a large head and a permanent frown.

"We'd like a room, please," said Ann. In spite of the fact that she didn't like the idea of being in Shannyn, interacting with aliens didn't seem to bother her.

The alien responded without changing expression. The words were Earth language, but the way the alien spoke made them sound foreign.

"How long?" he asked.

"Make it one night... for now."

Once in their room, Ann grew ever more fretful. She went into the bathroom, came out a few moments later with a glass of water. She paced back and forth several times before finally settling into a short, narrow chair.

Jim was glad to be off the street. The crowds outside had begun to make him nervous and he liked the solitude of the hotel room.

From their second floor window, he could see much of the busy, bustling city. There were so many different forms of life, all crowded into the narrow streets of one alien city. He could hear strange voices and very alien languages rising up from the street below.

"I see a human," he said. It was the first that he had seen. This one dressed very oddly, in a style he didn't recognize. It made him look as alien as any other being on the street. "I don't think he's from Earth."

"Very few Earthers come out this far," said Ann.

"Aren't you and Robert from Earth?"

A hint of sadness shadowed her expression. "That was a very long time ago."

Hearing the melancholy in Ann's voice, Jim turned from the window to look at her. She was staring into her water glass. From the look on her face, Jim could see that she didn't want to say any more about it.

"I was on my way to Port Kimara."

"So I understand." Ann took a drink, looked at Jim and tried to smile. "That's a long way from home."

"We're moving there. My parents are there." Jim frowned and turned back to the window. "They'll be worried."

"You'll be with them soon."

Jim nodded tiredly. When he spoke again, it sounded distant. "Another human. I don't think he's from Earth, either."

An hour passed. Then a second went by. By the time the first sun had gone down, Ann was again pacing the room. The city began to glow with the yellow lights that sat atop tall poles lining the major streets. Warm light began to push out from hundreds of small windows.

By the time the second sun had set, the City of Shannyn was alive with night life; bizarre sounds of alien laughter, singing, tavern brawls, angry fighting between the drunken crews of space freighters that had been grounded on ShadowWorld.

Ann put on her light jacket.

"I'm going out to look for him," she said. "You wait here."

"No!" said Jim. "I'm coming with you."

"You have to stay here in case he shows up while I'm gone." Ann was out of the room before he could argue.

Jim stood halfway between the door and window. A sudden, ominous silence hung heavy in the room. He finally turned slowly back to the window, looked out across the alien city. Movement directly below caught Jim's attention, and looking down he saw Ann appear in the street. She moved quickly away from the hotel and disappeared into the night crowd.

He was alone again.

Jim woke with a start.

He hadn't meant to fall asleep, but sometime during the night he had dozed off. Realizing that Robert and Ann had still not returned, he got up from the chair and went to the window.

The first sun was rising. The city rooftops shone with the first rays of daylight.

Jim opened the window and leaned out, putting his elbows on the sill. The morning breeze brushed across his face. He could smell food cooking. He couldn't help but wonder how many different kinds of breakfast were being prepared. His stomach grumbled in anticipation.

Footsteps coming from down the street broke the early morning silence. Backing into the window a little, but still allowing enough that he could see, he watched as two figures walked in his direction.

They were human.

The large, muscular man was talking to the thin man. He spoke softly but firmly, in Earth language.

"With the pirate problem taken care of, I want us gone from this forsaken planet."

"Yes, captain," the thin man nodded. "From what I hear, it was quite a firefight up there."

"The Protectorate wasn't about to let a handful of cutthroats shut down business. At least, not for long."

"Yes, sir. They do need their taxes."

They were walking very quickly, and were already under Jim's window and starting to move away.

"I want the ship ready to leave just as soon as you can get it done. Get the crew together and check the cargo to see—" The captain's words were cut off as they rounded the corner.

Humans.

Humans speaking Earth language.

And they were leaving ShadowWorld... Maybe they were going to Port Kimara. Maybe Earth. It didn't matter. Jim could get off this planet and to somewhere safe.

What about Robert and Ann?

First, he had to get to the captain. He had to convince the captain to take them with him. Then he would look for Robert and Ann. Maybe he could get the captain to help him find them.

Jim rushed out of the room and stumbled down the stairs.

As he passed the front desk, the strange looking alien running the hotel called out to him in what Ann had said was the common tongue on ShadowWorld. Jim had no idea what he was saying, but he sounded upset.

Jim ran past without stopping and hurried outside. He jumped from the front stoop of the hotel and out into the street. He turned right and ran.

He reached the first intersection and looked down the cross street. He saw the figures of the captain and his first officer far ahead, continuing to walk away from him.

Some shadow of motion made Jim glance in the other direction.

Three large, hairy creatures were pulling a cart down the center of the narrow roadway, a wooden cage riding atop the cart.

In the cage were Robert and Ann, their hands and feet bound with rope.

Jim looked apprehensively back in the direction of the captain. He and his companion turned right and were lost from Jim's view.

Looking back to Robert and Ann, the aliens were just turning the cart down a side street.

It took Jim only a moment to decide. He followed after Robert and Ann.

He reached the next intersection and turned down the street. The aliens and their cart were just ahead. He trailed cautiously after them, careful not to be seen. The street was quiet but for the sound of the cart's wooden wheels rolling over the rough surface of the street.

Jim wasn't sure what he was going to do. For the moment, he watched and waited and followed. He was close enough that he could see Robert and Ann calmly struggling to free themselves of their bonds. Their captors paid little mind to them.

Robert suddenly leapt to his feet, as best the height of the cage would allow, and began jumping up and down, screaming and throwing himself about within the cage. This startled the three hairy aliens. They recoiled in surprise, then turned and looked into the cage in shock and dismay.

Moments later, Ann started in. The prisoners were apparently going completely berserk. The three hairy aliens looked at each other anxiously, bewildered as to what the heck had happened to the humans and what to do about it. They had never before had to deal with such strange aliens.

They whimpered amongst themselves. They squealed softly at the humans. One alien reached in to take hold and soothe the female human. Ann frantically scampered back out of reach.

The alien turned and whimpered again to its two companions, moved over to the door of the cage. At that, the others moved up quickly, intending to stop their comrade from making a mistake.

Finally, after several more whimpers and the continued unsettling behavior of the humans, they came to an agreement.

The first made ready at the door of the cage as the other two moved into position and guardedly stood by. Once all were ready, the alien unlocked the cage and warily reached in, attempted to grab onto either of the crazed human creatures.

Jim, seeing what Robert and Ann were up to, and without taking the time to analyze what he was about to do, ran down the street toward the cart, screaming and jumping and waving his arms.

All three aliens turned in surprise at the bizarre young human coming out of nowhere, rushing insanely down the street, hurtling toward them on this otherwise quiet morning. It ran past them, circled the cart and rushed past again.

Meanwhile, the two humans in their cart continued with their own fits.

One alien reached out to grab hold of Jim and just missed. Frustrated and growing angry, it started after him.

The second alien looked to the cage, then and at the third alien, which now had hold of Ann but didn't know what to do with her. It looked again at the first, which was chasing the young human around and around the cart.

It looked again at the two crazed humans within the cart. Its lips began to flutter in frustration. As the young human and the first alien rushed past yet again, it joined in the chase.

In that instant, Robert kicked at the alien that was holding Ann, jumped out of the cage and pulled the alien aside, knocking it to the ground. As the two of them tumbled to the ground, Ann climbed out of the cage.

The first alien chasing Jim hadn't noticed the other humans were out of the cage, so intent as it was on catching the young one on the loose.

The second alien stopped, however, uncertain as to which way to turn. Robert took advantage of this and began running around the cart, jumping on the alien still lying on the ground each time it tried to stand up.

The first alien finally saw what was happening. It stopped suddenly and turned to Robert. Robert crashed into the second, frustrated alien. It fell onto its rump, lips quivering and cheeks puffing.

Ann turned and raced down the street, screaming and jumping, arms flailing in all directions.

Jim quickly followed after her, screaming and jumping and arms waving.

Robert jumped over the fallen alien one final time and hurried after Ann and Jim, also screaming and jumping and arms flailing.

One alien chased after the humans. Back at the cart, one hairy alien rested on its backside, lips fluttering, while the third had crawled beneath the cart to avoid being stepped on.

Jim raced down one street, then another, following Ann, who was turning at each intersection. The only sounds were those of their pounding footsteps echoing ahead of them.

Looking back over his shoulder, Jim saw Robert some distance behind, with the alien right at his heels.

Robert gave a quick wave to Jim and then turned off the street. The alien followed Robert. Jim stopped, looked to Ann, and then back to the path the Robert had taken.

When Ann saw Jim stop, she stopped. She waved frantically for him to follow. After several seconds, he started again.

Ahead, Ann turned down another street. Reaching it, Jim turned.

Ann was nowhere in sight.

Jim paused only a few moments and then started slowly ahead. He looked down each side street that he passed, kept going forward.

He almost ran into the captain.

"Hold on there, son," said the captain. He placed a heavy hand on Jim's shoulder.

Jim felt a sudden, desperate elation. Here was the very man that he had been hoping to find. His first officer stood dutifully behind him, and beside the first officer was an alien. It took Jim a few seconds, but it finally came to him that it was the clerk from the hotel.

"What's your rush, boy?" asked the captain, a broadening smile on his face.

Jim's mind raced. He blurted out the first thing that popped into his head.

"We crashed."

"Excuse me?"

"Pirates... we escaped... we crashed... I was... I was out in the desert."

"I see."

The captain doesn't seem at all surprised by this turn of events. He glanced knowingly over his shoulder at the first officer and the hotel clerk. When he turned back to Jim, he stepped up beside him and started them walking forward. They passed between the others, who quietly made way for them.

"Why don't you tell me what happened?"

When the captain stopped, Jim stopped. The first officer and the hotel clerk, patiently keeping pace behind them, stopped two steps back.

The captain looked sympathetically at Jim.

"That's quite a story, Jim," he said.

"Can you help me?"

"Certainly, young sir."

"And my friends?"

"I will if I can." The captain again placed a hand on Jim's shoulder. This time, however, his fingers gripped a bit uncomfortably. He spoke over his shoulder to his first officer.

"Get some help. Find the couple." The tone was different, more firm. It didn't sound right. It didn't fit with the conversation.

It made Jim feel uneasy. "You can get us off the planet?"

"Absolutely. That I can guarantee." The captain looked again at his first officer. "Jahkard may already have them. Check with him first."

"Yes sir." The assistant nodded, turned and left.

The hotel clerk looked on expectantly. The captain reached into his pocket with his free hand, pulled out a handful of coins and dropped several, one at a time, into the waiting hands of the alien. It too, then, turned and left.

The captain looked down at Jim.

"I may pull a decent cargo off this depressing planet after all."

"I don't understand."

"No, I suppose not," said the captain. He began walking, dragging Jim along with him. "You ran out on a debt you owed the hotel, Jim. That was very, very wrong."

"I was going to find you! To help my friends!"

"Friends? Thieves, both of 'em. Stole a vehicle, tried to sell it. That was very wrong, as well. Why do you think they were in that cage? The Benzagi aren't that bright, but they were only trying to do their duty."

"What?"

"Not to worry, lad. All will be made right. I paid your debt." The captain sighed contentedly. "And I shall pay theirs."

"But... what are you..." Jim knew that something was terribly wrong, but couldn't quite sort it out.

"By the laws of Shannyn, boy... you are now my property."

Jim fumbled for words. "You can't do that!"

"Of course I can. The law is most definitely on my side in this matter."

"Then... then the law is wrong."

"I won't argue that," the captain sighed again. "However... right or wrong, it can frequently turn a profit."

"You can't buy people!" Jim struggled to get free, but the captain had a very tight grip on him and kept him off balance as he dragged him along. "Earth won't let you do this! My father won't let you do this!"

"In point of fact, Earth has very little to say in matters concerning the Frontier Worlds; even less about the Outworlds beyond." The captain showed Jim another broad grin. "In any case, very few humans come this far out. You will fetch a very good price indeed."

The captain dragged Jim through a stone gateway guarded by two burly humans. Beyond, in the middle of a large landing field, sat the ship. It was big, squat, almost round, and ugly.

To the left was a fenced enclosure, a thousand feet on a side, containing several hundred aliens of a dozen or more species. The captain handed Jim off to two other guards without another word.

As the captain walked toward a small, wooden building, the guards led Jim to the barbed wire gate and pushed him into the holding pen.

Chapter Five

Jim sat with his back against the wire mesh of the fence that enclosed the large holding yard. The ground beneath him was hard and bare. A cool night breeze blew across his face. He watched as the other captives, hundreds of alien beings of all shapes, sizes and colors, struggled for sleep or milled about dejectedly amongst each other and tiny, makeshift shelters, accepting of their fate as slaves.

He had left his spot by the fence only twice during the day, when the food bins, sitting on benches near the water troughs, were filled and the captives drifted mindlessly over to fill their bowls with the tasteless gruel.

Jim stood slowly now as the bins were filled with the evening meal. Gripping his bowl in hand, he glanced at the gathering crowd and decided that it just wasn't worth it. He stuffed his bowl back into his shirt and turned away, wrapped his fingers into the mesh of the fence and looked out beyond the pen.

Twenty yards from the pen stood a dark, wooden building. Through the open door he could see the tall figure of a man wearing a black cloak. Gathered outside the building was a group of aliens of different species.

As Jim watched, several others came and went, some going inside and doing business with the cloaked figure, others speaking briefly to the aliens and then leaving.

This had been going on through most of the day.

Jim heard the sound of footsteps behind him. He turned in time to see a short figure step up beside him and look through the fence.

Hishta?

"You're from Earth?" she asked, speaking Earth. She continued to gaze half-heartedly at the activity beyond the fence.

She certainly looked like Nebo's sister.

"You're Hishta," said Jim.

The alien looked startled. "How can you know that?"

"I was with Nebo," said Jim. "I was at the peak. We tried to rescue you."

Hishta grumbled low. "Not successful, I would say."

"What about Nebo? Was he captured too?"

"No," Hishta sighed. "He is out there, still."

"That's good."

"Yes. But I fear that he may further endanger himself in another attempt to rescue me."

"He cares very much for you."

"He does." Hishta continued to stare beyond the holding pen. "There is nothing that he can do for me. We are lost."

Jim nodded. He felt empty inside. "What's going to happen to us?" he asked.

"You do not know?"

"I'm kinda new around here."

"I see." Hishta frowned then, grimaced. "We are being sold to one of the Outworlds. I believe we are to be taken to one of the planets along the Outer Rim. The work is hard, made harder by the unpleasant climate."

Hishta looked at Jim as if studying him. "Humans survive the longest. You will bring a good price."

"So I understand," Jim stated flatly. "I'm not staying."

Hishta burst out with a loud laugh. It was sharp and shrill and unexpected. "You will just leave?"

"Yes."

Hishta's expression and tone changed suddenly, to one of empathy. "You sound much like Nebo. You no doubt got along well together."

"Well enough," said Jim, a bit defensively. He rested his hands on the fence, gripped the mesh with his fingers. The cloaked man in the building was alone.

Hishta followed Jim's gaze. "That is Jahkard," she said. "Collector for our owner."

"No one owns me."

Hishta gave a strange, alien shrug. "As you wish." After a few moments, she spoke softly, without looking at Jim. "It looks as though the buying is complete. I would guess that we will depart in the morning."

Jim nodded, his mind running down a dozen different paths. "Then I must leave tonight," he said at last.

"You have yet to tell me how you intend to accomplish this feat."

Jim looked down at the friendly, innocent face. She would not survive long on one of the Outworlds that she had described.

He looked back through the fence. Beyond the small building was a high, stone fence. If this was like other space ports, this field would be surrounded by that enclosing stone barrier.

"What's beyond that wall?" he asked.

"Other landing fields," said Hishta. "Beyond those, the City of Shannyn, of course."

Jim gripped tightly at the fence. Getting over this fence would be easy enough, but reaching the wall, and then finding a way through the gate, unseen, was doubtful; even in the dark.

Getting out of the holding pen unseen... difficult.

And if he could get out of the holding pen, then getting out of the landing field unseen... difficult.

How to get out of the holding pen in such a way that getting out of the landing field was possible?

"Human?" asked Hishta, curious as to Jim's strange lost gaze.

"My name's Jim."

"Jim. You have a way out of our seemingly inescapable predicament?"

Jim had a sudden thought. He wasn't sure where it came from.

"We need to find soft ground."

"In the holding pen?"

"Preferably." Jim tried to hide the sarcasm.

The little alien crinkled her face into a heavy frown, thinking. "I don't know," she said finally.

"Dark soil, not too smooth; out of the way."

"You do not expect to dig your way out of here, do you, Jim?"

"Of course not," said Jim. "Well, not exactly."

"Under the water troughs?" asked Hishta doubtfully.

Jim glanced in the direction of the troughs.

Wet and dark and disturbed from heavy traffic underfoot.

"Maybe."

The troughs were along the side fence. When not in use during meals, the prisoners tended to stay within easy walking distance but not so near as to be bothered by foot traffic. No one would be overly suspicious at seeing fellow captives moving about near the troughs.

Jim stepped away from the fence, began a slow, wandering walk in the direction of the water troughs. Hishta followed beside him.

Around the troughs, as well as beneath, the soil was dark with moisture. Come daylight, the area beneath the troughs would remain in shadow.

Reaching the troughs, Jim walked around to the backside so that he could watch the prisoners. He took his bowl and dipped it into the water, filled it and brought it to his lips. Hishta looked at him curiously, then she took her bowl and did the same.

A prisoner approached. Jim nodded a greeting as the alien filled her bowl with water, warily eyeing Jim.

Jim smiled as the alien walked away.

"What is it you plan to do, Jim?" she asked.

Jim started slowly away from the trough. "Wait for dark," he said.

Most of the prisoners had settled in for the night, though a few continued to wander aimlessly. Kneeling behind one of the troughs, Jim began scraping at the soil beneath with his meal bowl. Hishta watched him uncertainly at first, then knelt beside him and began to help.

The first few inches were easy. After that, it became more difficult. Scraping in the dark, they stopped a number of times, several times to rest, several times to wait for thirsty prisoners to drink and return to their sleeping places.

Jim had Hishta lay in the first of the holes to test for depth three times before he was satisfied. Using hers as a guide, they dug his beneath the second trough.

Finally completed, no more than an hour before dawn, Jim had Hishta return to her hole and lay in it. He covered her over, spreading the excess soil around the base of the troughs. They had found nothing to use to breathe through, so her nostrils were left just poking up through the surface.

He slid back and examined his work. In the darkness, he could see no sign of Hishta buried beneath the trough. In the daylight, he could not be so sure.

He hoped they would come for the prisoners before dawn.

It was more difficult to bury himself. He covered his legs and body, spreading soil as he gradually laid back. Fully within the hole, he pulled soil to himself, covered his head, then laid one arm along his side and covered it with the other. He covered himself fully, then worked his other arm along his side and wriggled his body about to settle the soil.

He had no way to check for telltale signs. Again he hoped they would come for the prisoners in the dark.

As dawn approached, Jim began to hear footsteps around the troughs as fellow captives came to collect water. He was anxious at first, but as more and more came and went he became increasingly confident that the plan might just succeed. All the activity should eliminate any signs of digging.

Jim's body itched from lack of movement. Tiny grains of wet dirt worked their way into his nostrils.

Movement around the troughs lessened. He then heard what sounded like movement en masse as the hundreds of captives were herded in the opposite direction, away from the troughs.

Finally there was silence.

Jim waited.

The ground began to tremble, the trough above him to vibrate. The very air above him rumbled and roared as the nearby cargo ship lifted up from its pad. For a moment Jim was afraid that he and Hishta might be too near the pad, before mentally calculating that the distance from the pad to the nearby buildings wasn't much greater than to the troughs, and noted that the fence, buildings and troughs had probably survived numerous lift-offs and landings prior to this one.

Jim lay unmoving for several minutes more in the absolute silence that followed the departure of the slave ship. He then raised his head just a little, let the dirt fall away from his face, and turned enough to look out across the holding yard.

It was empty.

He rolled himself out of the hole and out from under the trough. In the distance, beyond the fence, he could see that the door of Jahkard's building was closed.

No one was around.

He crawled forward and laid a hand on the dirt mound that was Hishta.

"I think we're safe," he said quietly. Dirt fell away as Hishta lifted herself up. Jim moved back as she rolled over and out from under the trough.

She looked around them, as Jim had done, then looked at Jim.

"We did it," she said, not fully ready to believe it.

Jim grinned, and his teeth and eyes shimmered from within his dirt-covered face.

"Looks that way," he said.

Hishta managed to hold back her own grin. "You did it."

Jim shrugged. Dirt fell away from his shoulders.

Now Hishta did smile, and brushed dirt from Jim's shirt.

"I think we should get cleaned up," she said.

They cleaned up as best they could at the water troughs; hair, face, hands and arms. Jim took off his shirt and rinsed it out, gave his body a splash, taking off the worst of it.

"Do you know how I can get off this planet?" he asked Hishta as he wrung out his shirt.

Hishta pulled her wet hair back from her face. "The Chantoo," she said. "I am certain they will help."

"Yeah... Ann said they were all right."

"I would agree. They are all right."

Jim shook out his shirt and pulled it on. "What about you? What will you do?"

"I will find Nebo," she said matter-of-factly. "He will no doubt be nearby."

Hishta led Jim through a maze of narrow lanes lined with sandstone walls. Occasional archways on either side opened out to landing fields of different sizes; some small, some very large. Ships and shuttles sat on pads at safe distances. Small power carts waited inside some of the archways, ready to take passengers and crew out to the spacecraft.

The primary lanes bustled with aliens rushing about. Now that the problem with the pirates had been resolved, the threat taken care of by the ShadowWorld Protectorate, those who had been stranded were now eager to continue on their way. Freighter crews, losing money each day they were forced to remain planet-side, were eager to deliver their cargo and pick up their next shipments.

They stopped once when Hishta asked directions of a pair of thin, childlike aliens. They nodded kindly and pointed the way.

They turned right onto an even narrower lane...

And came face to face with the tall, dark figure of Jahkard and several of his assistants who were following behind him.

Jahkard stopped in the center of the lane and looked curiously down at the frozen figures of Jim and Hishta. He didn't appear to be angry or concerned. If anything, his expression was one of interest at the unfolding situation.

He smiled pleasantly.

"It is true, then," he said. His voice was smooth and strangely gentle. He exuded calm and confidence. "Just how did you manage this?"

Hishta glanced quickly to Jim without turning her head, then looked sharply up at Jahkard. She held her silence.

Jim shrugged noncommittally.

"Was nothin'," he said.

Jahkard smiled again and nodded.

"I see," he said, pulled absently at one ear. "I'm afraid that my staff have grown overly lax. They didn't realize such a valuable unit in our inventory was missing until they were well off-planet. The discovery caused quite a stir. Some insisted that you had to be somewhere amongst the cargo and were simply hiding; that you would eventually be found."

Jim and Hishta continue to hold their silence.

Jahkard sighed pleasantly. "And so you have... this should ease the ire of my employer."

"The captain is a monster," said Jim. He couldn't help himself.

"Quite," Jahkard chuckled. "So you'll appreciate my relief in having found you."

At some unseen signal, Jahkard's assistants moved into position, one taking Jim by the arm, the other taking Hishta.

At the same time, a third assistant entered the lane and moved quickly up beside Jahkard. He handed his boss a sheet of paper. Jahkard read silently. When finished, he slowly lowered his hand and studied Jim.

"What's your name, boy?"

"Jim."

Jahkard's expression revealed that, while expected, he didn't particularly like Jim's answer. Still, he tried to maintain his air of calm and confidence.

"Where were you headed, Jim?"

"Port Kimara. To join my family."

Jahkard took a moment to absorb this bit of information, then signaled his assistants to release Jim and Hishta. He managed to recover some of his pleasantness.

"There are some important people attempting to locate you, son. They are quite concerned as to your wellbeing."

"S'pose that would be."

"Word of the attack on the cruise liner reached them rather quickly. Their distress apparently reached ShadowWorld's administrative council as swiftly."

Jahkard bowed his head and looked out from under his brow. He put on his most ingenuous smile.

"I shall relay this latest as to your status and standing to my employer," he said. "Please consider his payment of your debts as his gift to you in your time of trouble."

"I'll do that," said Jim.

Jahkard looked side glance at Hishta. There was a moment of apprehension before Jahkard turned smoothly aside and made way for them to pass.

"The young lady is free to go, as well. That is my gift to you both."

Jim and Hishta moved quickly past the tall, dark figure.

Hishta and Jim turned right and started down a long, much quieter lane. Jim could see three archways spaced several hundred yards apart.

"I believe these are the Chantoo landing fields," said Hishta, a bit uncertainly.

"We still need to find Robert and Ann," said Jim. "I can't leave without them."

"Of course." Hishta did not slow her pace. "First let us speak with the Chantoo. Then we will find your friends."

Looking through the first open archway they came upon, they saw only an empty field and landing pad. There was no ship and no Chantoo.

They continued toward the next archway. The further they traveled from the main thoroughfares, the quieter the world around them became.

After a dozen paces more, Jim began to hear a hollow grinding sound: rubber tires rolling across sandstone... He slowed and looked over his shoulder.

A small electric cart was coming towards them.

"Hishta, wait." Jim reached out and took her by the arm.

He recognized the driver as a Chantoo. The being was tall and thin, with pale blue skin, a small head and long white hair.

Sitting next to the alien was Ann. The figure sitting behind Ann must therefore be Robert though he couldn't see his face.

The driver slowed the cart as it approached Jim and Hishta, stopped directly beside them.

"Well, I'll be..." Robert scooted to one side. "We thought we had lost you yet again. This is getting to be a habit. You might want to work on that, kiddo."

Ann smiled at Hishta. "You must be Hishta."

"That's right," said Hishta.

"I know of someone who will be very pleased to see you."

"That would be Nebo."

"It certainly would. He was certain the two of you were on the ship that lifted off this morning."

"Jim showed great ingenuity in gaining us our freedom," said Hishta. "I owe him my life."

From the back seat, Robert indicated the space that he'd made for Jim.

"Climb in, hero. Not much time."

"Where might I find my brother?" Hishta asked Ann.

"We left him just a few minutes ago," said Ann. "Over near the main port office."

"Then I must go." Hishta looked at Jim. "I thank you, Jim."

"All in a night's work," said Jim as he climbed in beside Robert. The Chantoo started the cart forward. Jim called out behind him as they left Hishta behind. "Tell Nebo goodbye for me."

Hishta waved, waited until the cart reached the next archway before she turned about and hurried to find her brother.

The Chantoo driver steered the cart out across a vast landing field toward a small shuttlecraft. Three Chantoo stood at the ramp beneath the craft. When the cart stopped, one of the waiting aliens began waving for the humans to hurry.

As they stepped up on the ramp, Jim looked at Robert with a growing sense of unease.

Something isn't quite right...

"What's going on?" Jim asked Robert.

Robert nudged Jim along, the two of them following Ann up the ramp.

"Let's just say there are certain folks who would disagree with our departure plans."

"You don't make friends easily, do you?"

"Don't get cute."

They walked quickly into the shuttle. The Chantoo followed in after them even as the ramp started to close. Almost immediately, Jim felt the floor beneath him begin to vibrate. They hurried into the forward cabin and sat down in tall, narrow seats obviously designed for the Chantoo physiology. Jim looked out the small round window and watched the space port fall away below them, the shuttle rushing upward toward the larger spaceship waiting in low orbit.

One of the Chantoo said something to Robert before continuing forward and through another doorway. Robert turned to Ann and Jim.

"We'll be docking with the Chantoo cruiser in a couple of hours. They're scheduled to leave orbit soon after."

Ann visibly relaxed. "Thank goodness."

Jim turned and looked again out through the viewport. The planet below appeared to be covered with shadows. He could see the shimmer that was the City of Shannyn.

Robert could see that the boy was lost in troubled thought.

"What's on your mind, Jim?" he asked.

Jim continued looking out the viewport. It took him a moment to find words, and then the words seemed not to be enough.

"It's wrong," he said.   .

"What's that?"

Jim still didn't seem to know how to answer. Nothing was adequate to his feelings.

"I'm not property," he said flatly. "They made me property."

"Ah," said Robert. "That."

"I got away, but... so many didn't."

Ann looked sadly at Jim. "Out here in the Frontier, there is still an awful lot of bad."

That's not an answer...

There was a very long moment of uncomfortable silence.

"I'm going to change that," Jim finally grumbled.

"Is that so?" Robert smiled gently.

"Yes. That is so."

"A noble sentiment, my boy, and I wish you well. But changes like that tend to be painfully slow in coming."

"Not this time."

Robert was about to respond, but Jim's dark tone and darker expression made him stop. He gave the boy a short nod and turned away. He looked at Ann, as if questioning what they might say to the boy. She didn't look as though she had an answer either.

Jim kept his sharp gaze to the view beyond the window.

A few moments later, a Chantoo entered the passenger compartment with an electronic notepad in hand. He handed it to Robert and left without speaking.

"What is it," asked Ann. She didn't want any surprises at this stage in their rescue.

"Don't know... gimme a sec." Robert silently read the message in the display, then lowered the pad and looked in Jim's direction, the slightest smirk on his face.

"Well?" asked Ann, now with growing impatience.

"Well. Ann," Robert continued to look at Jim. "It appears the Chantoo cruiser that we are soon to board will be making a slight detour once en route."

Jim held his silence, held his gaze out the viewport.

"Why?" Ann's impatience had quickly morphed into distress. "What's wrong?"

"Oh, nothing to worry about. Nothing at all. But it seems that we will be making a stop at Port Kimara to drop off a passenger."

Ann looked confused at first, then turned Jim.

"Jim, isn't that where you were going?"

Jim answered without turning from the viewport. "Yes."

When he said nothing further, Ann turned to Robert for answers.

"His father is the new governor of Port Kimara."

"The new—"

Robert looked again directly at Jim. "One of the most powerful positions in the Frontier."

Only now did Jim turn away from the viewport. "My father is not one to flaunt power and position."

"Is that why you were traveling anonymously?" asked Ann.

Jim shrugged in answer.

Robert took a moment to consider this new information. The look of understanding slowly shown on his face.

"Jim, being the son of the governor may open a few doors, particularly after what you've just been through, but make no mistake, the fight you would take on is a very difficult one."

The cabin was silent for a few moments, then Ann spoke softly.

"Robert... Robert, I don't think he has a choice. Do you?"

The cabin was again silent, but for the rumbling of the shuttle's engines. Jim settled back into the alien seat, gazed long through the viewport out at the black of space that surrounded them.

Ann and Robert turned from Jim and looked at each other.

For them, an adventure was ending.

They knew that Jim's was just beginning.

~ End

www.ingramcontent.com/pod-product-compliance
Lightning Source LLC
Chambersburg PA
CBHW021500240626
47154CB00002B/455